Little Black Book
Volume 3
Mr. Oh

STREET LITERATURE

Published by Street Literature. Smashword Edition. All rights reserved. Without limiting the rights under copyright reserved above. No part of this book may be reproduced, stored in or introduced into a retrieval system, or transmitted, in any form, or by any means (electronic, mechanical, photocopying, recording, or otherwise), without prior written consent from both the author, and Street Literature, except brief quotes used in reviews.

CONTENT

Open Up
Scent Of A Wet Patch
Electric Misbehaviour
Becky Becky Two Times - C.L.I.T.S
Hideaway
I Can Convince You
3d (Danielle Discretely Dangerous) - C.L.I.T.S
Lunch Break
One Mouth
Butterfly The Sheet Flipper - C.L.I.T.S
69 Challenges
Strange Moments At Necessary Times
Kwame Sashay And Miss D Destroyer - C.L.I.T.S
Games Beneath The Surface
Banana And Apple Pie
Rhuosia The Kisser - C.L.I.T.S
Intelligent People
Night Shift
Dee Deena The Teaser - C.L.I.T.S
Violence
Marcus And The Favour
Kiki Peachy, Roro The Lady And Charm The Detective - C.L.I.T.S
Power Over The Powerful
Did You Cum?
Nurse Grimy Core - C.L.I.T.S
Money & Mouth
Water
I Will Cut You & Zeah The Ball Crusher - C.L.I.T.S
Keeping It Cool & Christian
Talk To Me

Talk To Me Again
Mystery Of Jill
Chan'glo The Gloved Assassin - C.L.I.T.S
Inside A Masturbator's Mind
Leave A Donation
Fetish Of The Full-Figured
Pandora The Cook - C.L.I.T.S
The Heal Of Heels
Blue Views

ONE UP

"OoOoOoOoooh shit baby... that's it... don't stop moving that pussy... that's my pussy..." Lamar said, grinding on top of Keisha, who was somewhere else in her mind.

Lamar had his hands wrapped around her thighs and was grinding his way to an orgasm.

"Oh shit, I'm cumming... here I cum..."

He took four final hip jerks before exhaling happily then slowing down and rolling off Keisha's body, which was drenched in his sweat.

"Could you pass me a towel please?" Lamar asked.

"Why didn't you get a towel ready if you knew you were gonna sweat the place up?" Keisha replied, reaching for her towel which she stashed under her pillow. She wiped herself down.

"I didn't know I was gonna get so hot... but that's your fault."

Keisha saw the attempt at playful banter but she wasn't in the mood for it. She was bothered. Hot and bothered.

That was the problem.

After sex, that feeling of heat was supposed to be doused and dealt with accordingly. Not still burning like it was right now.

Keisha was all for a bit of hot and sweaty sex but only when both people were benefiting from the motion and dousing their fires together.

And she wasn't benefiting at all.

Keisha watched Lamar rubbing his sweaty body with a t-shirt and throwing it onto his washing pile while sliding the condom off his flaccid penis.

He caught her looking at him and did a double take.
"What?" he said, still breathing heavily.?" We need to talk Lamar."
"What, now?"

"Yes now."

"Come on... I'm feeling a nap coming on after that good loving. Gimme 15 minutes."

"Lamar, if you don't talk to me right now, I guarantee you, someone else will be fucking me. I'm serious!"

Lamar spun to face Keisha with a serious look on his face. "Are you nuts?"

"Oh NOW you wanna pay attention? Okay, good, now I've got your attention... let's talk!"

"What exactly do you wanna talk about that relates to you having sex with someone else?"

Keisha sighed as she sat up, folded her legs underneath and folded her towel neatly.

"Such a man. GOD! Look... you see what we just did just now, the sex, did you enjoy that?"

Lamar smiled. "Hell yes. What's not to enjoy?"

"Well I don't."

"What'd you mean you don't?" Lamar put the filled condom in the bin and wiped his hands with hand wipes.

"I do NOT like it." "Why do you NOT like it?" "Let's be honest and real. It hasn't always been crap, I just..." "Did you just say CRAP?" Lamar tilted his head.?Keisha waved her hands. "No, hold on... what I meant was... yeah

crap. Sorry babe, let's just get it out there." Lamar reached under the duvet and propped pillows behind his back

with a scowl across his face. "Crap!?" "And this is why we need to talk."

Keisha got out of bed and put on her dressing gown and slippers while Lamar watched. He couldn't believe she had just called sex with him crap.

Of all the words she could've used in the English fucking dictionary, she chose the word... crap!

Lamar was sitting with his arms folded across his chest as he watched her open the draw of their dressing table and pull out a A5 notebook.

He frowned.

"I'm sorry the word 'crap' seems to have taken you by surprise but, to be honest babe, it is."

"What the FUCK do you mean its crap? I'm properly shocked by that you know."

"Really babe? Are you honestly shocked that we're having this conversation right now?"

Lamar chuckled. "I really am. You've never once complained or said anything."

"This is my complaint," Keisha said, holding up the notebook decorated in pink and purple hibiscus plants. "Do you wanna get a drink or something?"

"No, no, I'm fine right here. So come on then," Lamar said condescendingly. "Let's hear your complaints."

Keisha folded the duvet neatly before laying down on the covers next to him.

She flipped the cover and sighed as he watched her flick through pages and pages of writing. From top to bottom, even the spaces at the bottom of each page was full of writing.

Each time he tried to catch a sentence, she turned the page, whistling at the same time.

"You've just called our sex life crap and you're whistling Whistle While you Work?"

"I dunno why that came to my mind but it was just in there. And, you know what babe, I'm just glad we're finally having this conversation. I've wanted to talk to you about this for months."

"MONTHS?" Lamar asked with his eyebrows raised.?" Yep, months." "Now THAT'S crap! There's no way it's been months." Keisha showed Lamar the pages as she flicked and he could see

months and dates.?" This is just January. I'm looking for a particular date in February." "You've been writing about our sex lives? What the FUCK FOR?"

Lamar said, feeling anger rise.?" For a moment like this... ah haaa... here it is."

Lamar felt a sense of impending doom wash over him like he knew he was about to hear something he wished he didn't.

He watched Keisha move her hips under her dressing gown, making her backside wiggle and draw his attention.

"So this was the day before Valentine's Day..."

"You have dates of shit we did for the entire year basically, 'cuz it's September now and that book looks mighty full."

"... and on that day, after we had sex, this is what I wrote. I don't want you to interrupt me or jump in, I just want you to listen. I'm reading you this one particularly because it was one of the worse ones."

"Are you serious right now?" Lamar said, resting his arms on his raised knees when he heard the words, 'one of the worse ones'.

"This was when we went to Portugal for Valentine's Day."
"Yeah, I remember," he replied, indignantly.?Keisha inhaled before she ran her finger along the page and started

to read.

"13th February, 23:38pm. Another shit session. Why doesn't he pay attention to me? If I say stay there, that doesn't mean cum quickly for fuck sake! This is getting ridiculous. Does he realise I'm not even having an orgasm? What's there to cum from? I don't get it. How did we go from starting with 20-30 minutes of foreplay to a nipple rub, a clit flick then trying to get in and cumming five minutes later? It's annoying 'cuz Lamar used to fuck me well. Now I'm getting this poor head, creative-less, one position two pumps and done, PlayStation fingers, slap fish kissing shit instead? This is not what I was getting when we first started going out so why am I getting this shit now? We're in sexy ass Portugal, the sun is going down and it's beautiful out here and he's lying next to me snoring already. I wish I wasn't thinking of Marcus right now but I am. Something needs to be done, otherwise I see myself having idle fingers. And you know what your idle fingers are like."

Keisha stopped to look at Lamar who was staring back at her with wide eyes and a heaving chest. She could hear him exhaling heavy breaths with his pupils dilated and his lips pursed.

"So you mean to tell me," he pointed at her book. "And what the fuck do you mean 'thinking about Marcus'?"

"If it's been that bad, yeah, I've written about it. And I did think about him, I'm not gonna lie."

Lamar squinted. "You're being very cool, calm and collected about all of this."

"'Cuz baby, I'm at a stage where I can tell you honestly that I've thought about a lot of my exes. And a few old links as well. I've thought about calling them and just getting myself seen to then coming back to you. I've thought about doing a lot of shit behind your back."

"Keesh, are you fucking MAD? Cheat on me? You're telling me sex between us has gotten so bad that you've thought about cheating on me?"

"I almost did." "What?" Lamar recoiled and his back straightened.?" One of your many many football nights. Marcus randomly knocked

at the door and was asking for you. I told him you were out. But that didn't stop him from offering to eat me out though. He actually got on his knees at the front door but I told him no. I didn't want that. Well I DID. But I didn't want it from him. I wanted it from you."

Lamar found his phone and was scrolling through phone numbers, mumbling to himself.

"Fucking Marcus... how's he gonna try and eat my missus... I'm gonna kill him..."

"Don't worry babe, I heard Marcus has gone into hiding. Apparently some people are looking for him and he doesn't wanna be found. His number has been going to voicemail for ages."

"Oh HAS it? Been trying to call him huh?"

"Don't be like that. And it's not me whose been calling, it's my cousin Maya, she's looking for him... suttin 'bout a favour for a friend in heels."

Lamar put his phone to his ear after finding Marcus' number and waited for a ringing tone.

'The number you have called is not available!'

He ended the call frustrated that he knew one of his oldest friends had tried it with his girlfriend but he couldn't do anything about it.

Right now, he wanted to get dressed, drive to wherever Marcus was and rearrange his insides with a selection of kitchen and garden tools.

"Babe, it's not about Marcus. It's about us. Have you not heard anything I just read to you besides Marcus' name?"

"That's blatant disrespect though. How the fuck is he..."

"What's more important here Lamar is the fact that I wanted to. I wanted to invite him in..."

"Okay, okay, okay, I get it... I don't wanna have to fucking hear about it."

Lamar paused then looked at Keisha and her book. "What?" "Have you written about that?" "About what?"

"About what if you chose to let Marcus in that night?"

Keisha took a long pause. "No, this is only about our sex life, not imaginary shit."

They stared at each other in silence for what seemed like forever and a day. While Keisha was still cool, calm and collected laying on her stomach with her notebook open, Lamar had discarded the duvet and was now naked pacing in front of their bay windows.

"You're lying!"

"Lamar you can take this book and read it yourself. But trust me, you won't like what you read."

"Why the fuck not?"

"'Cuz I can see in your eyes babe, you are happy with the sex we have. To you, there's no problem with anything we do at the moment and all this I'm saying is a big surprise. I can actually see that you're shocked."

"Of course I am. You're lying there basically telling me that my friend tried to eat your pussy on OUR doorstep. And you're doing it calmly. You don't think I'm gonna be a little bit pissed off?"

"When you put it like that, yeah, but this is supposed to be about us. And what we do from here. 'Cuz, seriously, this can't continue."

"So what am I not doing then?" Lamar got back under the duvet with anger emanating through his skin into the space between them.

"You wanna know exactly what you're not doing?" "Yeah, go on then, let's hear it."

Keisha flicked back a few pages and stopped at a 10-point list with her finger on number one.

"Okay. Number one, you seem to have lost track of what it is I like and how I like it. Two: you're foreplay has diminished to under 10% productivity, three: you don't seem to like to kiss me as much as you used to, four: the head you used to do so damn well isn't doing it any more, five: you don't flirt with me anymore, six: you seem to get on top and that's it, seven: why have you forgotten my nipples, eight: you play with my clit like you're playing Grand Theft Auto, nine: why don't you moan anymore and ten, the best of them all, once you pump, you sleep and you slump."

Lamar felt whatever blood was lining the veins of his dick retreat into his body, making his manhood resemble a turtle in hiding. He could

feel his mouth open as his cheeks and tongue dried from a passing breeze. His palms were sweaty and he hadn't blinked since number two on the list.

"You must have lost your FUCKING..."

As Lamar raised his voice and was about to curse Keisha for the way he felt inside, a sound from their open bedroom door caught both of their attention.

They both looked at the darkness of their corridor and watched a dark ball roll along the floor to the foot of their bed.

Keisha recoiled, thinking it was a mouse. She got to her feet and was holding the top of the bed frame, while Lamar followed it with his?eyes.

The ball sounded like distant thunder as it rolled to the other side of the bed and Lamar came face-to-face with it.

That was when Lamar saw it wasn't a mouse.

Suddenly, the bedroom of Keisha and Lamar's Wandsworth flat was covered in a pure white light which caught them both by surprise.

Keisha collapsed on the bed holding her eyes, thinking what the hell was going on while Lamar took the full flash to the face.

He fell back on the bed holding his wrists to his eyes and writhing in pain.

"Fuuuuuuuuck was thaaaaaat?" Lamar screamed.

The first footstep into the room were quiet, making sure to slide rather than walk.

It was followed by 19 other silent sliding steps into the room. Keisha thought she heard someone shushing another but the way her eyes were burning her, she couldn't see a thing.

She did hear her bedroom window open and felt a rising breeze whistle through the net curtains.

She turned to the window, still rubbing her watering eyes.?That was when she heard a countdown from another female voice. "Three, two, one... GO!" Keisha squinted through her blurred vision and saw something

disappear through the open window.?The more she tried to open her eyes, the less she could see and the

more her eyes watered.?" And we're out," another female voice said.?" WHO'S THERE?" Keisha asked the room. "LAMAR? THERE'S

SOMEONE IN THE ROOM!"

Keisha suddenly felt a presence approach her quickly and brush her natural curls away from her face.

"Shhh... you sleep now!"

A fresh scent of cinnamon and nutmeg rushed up her nose as the presence blew in her face. The sudden scent explosion made Keisha cringe as she took a full inhale before coughing.

That was the last thing Keisha remembered doing.

The memory of the white light was what woke Keisha from her sleep.

She rubbed her eyes vigorously and sat up in her dressing gown and slippers quickly.

Her eyes scanned the room and everything was the way it should've been. The only thing missing was...

"LAMAR? BAAABE?" Silence replied.

Keisha got up from the bed and walked to the window, remembering the dream and that moment in her slumber she thought she saw something go flying out of the window.

It was still dark outside, though birds began to chirp amongst a haze of early morning fog.

"What kinda messed up dream was that? BABE... I JUST HAD ONE HELLUVA..."

As Keisha began to walk out of the bedroom, she saw something on the neatly made bed.

Walking to Lamar's side of the king-sized bed, Keisha picked up a piece of paper and read a very beautifully hand-written note.

Dear Keisha,

We here at C.L.I.T.S heard about your situation and we're here to help.

We've taken Lamar for 'reprogramming' and will return him to you in 24 hours.

You could call the police or you could wait and see if Lamar returns delivering orgasms.

Your choice. Yours sincerely,

The Ladies of C.L.I.T.S?Clever Ladies Investigating Terrible Situations

SCENT OF A WET PATCH

"One..." "Two..."

By the count of three Jessy, a five foot five, bright caramel office manager from Croydon knocked back an extra large shot of Wray and Nephews white rum.

The shot went down her throat in four stages: shock, disgust, warmth and finally fire.

Her floor length dress, with an image of Rosa Parks covering the front, was wrapped comfortably around her body and she shuddered as if she fought off an evil spirit.

Her drinking partner for the night, Katrina, a five foot seven chocolate school teacher from Wood Green, could only watch as she held her shot in her hand, scared of going through the same foursome of stages.

Coming straight from a terrible day at work, in a pinstripe trouser suit, Katrina was not even half way to her desired level of inebriated.

Sitting at the bar of East Ham's freshly refurbished Playa's Club, Jessy and Katrina were in the middle of a competition; who could drink the most.

It had been a long month for both of them and, having booked the drinking date with their respective others, they were both glad to be out of their homes and partner-free.

Jessy was excited at being away from her seven month old son who was staying home with daddy for the first time.

Katrina's husband was having a boys night in which comprised of football on TV, then Fifa 14 on PS4, followed by football conversations, mixed with weed and alcohol.

"Boys and their toys," she always said when his grown in age but child at heart friends would come round.

With a 'Ladies Night' event going on around them and the DJ playing a particularly reminiscent set of ragga, Jessy and Katrina hugged the bar.

"So, what, you gonna leave me hanging like some chicken in the butchers?" Jessy said, shaking her head at the residual effects of the rum.

"That looked like it HURT sistrin... yu mus tink say mi mad!" Katrina replied, turning her Patois on.

"It fucking did," Jessy said, clearing her throat. "But you still gotta do it, otherwise I've already won this competition."

Buju Banton's Batty Rider played behind them and Jessy flashed her lighter to the ceiling while Katrina inspected her shot.

"Yeah but..."

"Buts are for gay people. I thought you were some bad gyal drinker." Jessy said, trying to get the barman's attention.

"Fuck it, count me down."

Jessy bounced in her stool. "That's what I'm talking about. Okay, ready?"

Katrina lifted the shot and held it in front of her face, with the rum wafting past her nose.

"One..." Jessy counted slowly.

Katrina shook her head, trying to shake away the doubt that was already telling her this was a bad idea.

"Two..."

She palmed the shot in her hand as she felt her wrist began to shake.

"Thr..."

Katrina knocked the shot back before Jessy could finish her three count and slammed the glass down on the bar repeatedly, drawing looks from thirsty ravers around her.

She looked at Jessy with strong eyes and held an angry gaze as the four stages of Wray and Nephews started in her throat and ended in the pit of her stomach.

"You better hold it bredrin, hooooold it..." Jessy said teasingly. "Ain't no pussy shit round here... you best hold it."

Katrina licked her lips, "Only pussy is between your legs. I told you I'm no rookie when it comes to this drinking thing."

The barman finished serving and came to Jessy with a smile. "What can I get you ladies?" "Excuse me Mr sexy barman..." Jessy said leaning closer. "We're

having a drinking competition and my friend here thinks she can hang. We just had Wray and Nephew shots so it's time to raise the bar, what would you suggest?"

Katrina was swaying as Buju went into Shabba which mixed into Ninjaman.

"Well, if you've already done the Wray shots, how about JaegerBombs?"

"Done 'em." Katrina replied.?" B-52?" "Puhleeeze, we want a challenge tuh rass," Jessy replied.?The barman smiled. "Okay, I'm gonna run through some shots and

you tell me if you've had it yet." Both women were now leaning towards the barman with the

pronounced dimples.?" Okay, have you had a Mind eraser, 3 fires, 3rd nipple, an Irish

Catholic, a Barbara Streisand, a Bear Fucker, Cock Sucking Cowboy, Dirty Traffic Lights, Electric Sex, Fuck Me Blue, Golden Shower, Harry Potter, Incredible Hulk..."

The ladies nodded with every name, waiting for something they were yet to sample in the three hours, two bars and one club they'd been in.

"...a Jack Off, Kick in the balls, Leprachaun Orgasm, Mexican Priest, No Thanks, One shot one kill, Papa Smurf..."

"Wait," Katrina said. "Did you say One shot one kill?" "Yeah." "We had that already, at that first place, but it was called One Kill

one shot." Jessy added.?" Oh yeaaaaaaah, sorry, carry on pretty boy." "Erm, how 'bout a Reach Around, Salty Cum Shot..." "Is that an offer?" Jessy said with a sultry, tipsy smile.?" Behave you tramp, go on sir..." "Have you had a Titty Fuck, Uppercut, Vaginal Opening, Witches Tit, a Youporn or a Zipperhead?" Both women continued to stare at him. "Told you, we don't play," Jessy smiled. "Bloooood cleet," the barman said. "I dunno what to say to you ladies. After two of those drinks, I'd need a nap and a bucket by my bed."

Katrina put her pinky in his right dimple, "You LOOK young."

They giggled and attempted a hi-five, missed, then giggled some more.

"A'ight bad gyals, have you had Fine Wine?"

Katrina's eyebrows raised first and Jessy's followed. They looked at each other for confirmation that they hadn't had a drink with such a name.

"Ah wha dat?" Jessy said, swallowing a burp. "Do you want one?" "BRING IT COME!" Jessy shouted as Shabba Ranks ting a linged through the speakers.

30 seconds later, two flaming shots slammed in front of the ladies. "Down it in one," the barman said. Katrina picked one and Jessy the other. They looked at each other, raised their eyebrows and knocked them back. Unlike the Wray shots, there were six stages to this drink. A shot of sweet followed by the shock, disgust, warmth, fire then the final burn. Katrina frowned while Jessy slapped the bar continuously with her hand and the barman laughed. "What the FUCK is that?" Katrina said in a deep voice, fanning her mouth. "Fine Wine." "That is NOT wine," Jessy managed, puffing out her cheeks. "That one is on the house. Want another one?" "Fuck no." "Fuck yes," Katrina said quickly with a stinging burp.

An hour later, the friends stumbled out with their coats and handbags into the brisk night air.

Oxygen slapped them first then the scent of barbecue chicken followed. A dreadlocked elder had his barrel set up in the club car park and was brushing chicken with a delicious smelling marinade that filled the air and had a throng of ravers surrounding him.

Jessy held Katrina's arm as they pigeon-walked past the barrel, looking left and right.

"That smells wicked but I won't keep it down." "Me neither, come we go."

Stumbling and giggling to Jessy's car, the ladies both took off their shoes and walked barefoot through the gravel car park.

Katrina felt the rumblings of vomit in her stomach.

"I think I'm gonna have to call Freddie to come and get us 'cuz I can't drive. I can't even see properly."

Jessy burst out laughing. "Call someone 'cuz I'm colder than an icicle's testicle and I need to pee."

She then pulled up her dress to her waist, exposing her French knickers, while staggering to a dark corner.

"Oh, ya not gonna..." "I already am," Jessy said, as she crouched next to a huge tree. Katrina could hear the trickle of urine as she drunkenly searched

through her handbag "Where's my phone?" She drunkenly swiped through her phone.?" Hello?" Freddie said, answering the phone on the fourth ring. "BABY... can you come..." Katrina said then laughed. "Not come...

well maybe later... I mean pick us up please? I'm in no fit drunk to drive."

"Oh God, did you at least win?" Katrina's husband asked. "We drawed... come and get us plase..." He sighed heavily. "Where are you?" "Meet you at the dark... I mean the park..."

"Which park babe, I dunno where you are."

Katrina watched Jessy pull up her panties then drop her dress down to her ankles. "Oh... silly billy Trina... we went to Playa's Club."

"In East Ham? That's a sweat box." "You're a sweat box!" "What? You know what, don't worry about it, I'll meet you at Central Park in 15 minutes." "Love you... very so much..." She hung up.

"IS he on his coming?" Jessy said. "On his coming?"

They both laughed a raucously then linked arms, trying to hold each other up enough to complete four steps.

The concrete of the high road was ice cold on their bear feet but did nothing to sober them up as they laughed and talked with no regard for their sound levels.

Katrina dropped twice while Jessy fell flat on her face catching her foot in an empty McDonalds bag.

Crossing Barking road sobered them up quickly and they both put their shoes back on.

"Hold my hand Trina." Jessy said, standing still but nodding. "Are we dating?" "Huh?" "Oh,you mean 'cuz of the road..."

Jessy pulled Katrina across the road and they both tripped on the pavement, sprawling next to each other.

A group of boys who were perched on the corner of St Bartholomews road laughed loudly until Katrina helped Jessy to her feet and approached them with a drunken swagger.

"Do I look like a joke to you? Am I a funny?"

Jessy was right behind her. "Come we go before they decide to take turns with us."

"Take turns with who? And live where? I'll kill all of 'em... dutty necked monkey looking boys..."

Jessy took Katrina by the hand again and they made off down the road towards the park, looking back at the boys who were still laughing.

Pulling her phone from her handbag, Jessy faked a loud phone call. "YEAH BABE, WE'RE THERE...SEE YOU SOON..."

"Who you talking to?" Katrina asked.?" A fake call phone will stop us from being raped, trust ...me..." "OoOoOoOoOoOoOoh, I get what you did there. Good thinking

Batman."

The first taste of a hangover hit Katrina as she slowed down and rested against a car. Letting her body flop onto the parked BMW X5, she didn't react as the car's alarm went off.

Jessy did and pulled her by the wrist. "Let's keep this moving shall we?" Then patted her friend on the backside.

"Get your own batty."

"THERE'S THE PARK..." Jessy said to no one in particular with her arm around Katrina's slumped shoulders.

"I know, that's where we're going." "Where's Jimmy meeting us?" "Who's Jimmy?" "Your husband innit?"

"FREDDIE."

Jessy's voice was loudly drunk. "Jimmy, Freddie, Russell, muscle, same sin ting... Ooooooh, let's go to the park..."

"Let's not."

Before she could grab hold of her, Katrina watched Jessy shake her off and run towards the locked gate. She forced the locked gates apart as far as they would go, hiked her dress up to her thigh and squeezed through.

"I wanna go on the swings," Jessy said, running into the darkness of the park.

Katrina sighed, taking in the fresh air, feeling drunk all over again.

She wobbled in her work heels as she leaned against the gate before sliding through.

Before her was pitch black. The outline of trees showed her the path her drunk friend ran. She could hear her in the darkness screaming 'WEEEEEEEE'.

"So you found the swings?" Katrina said into the darkness.

After a few misplaced steps, one lone light shone above a set of swings, a roundabout and slide, followed by the sound of Jessy's voice.

"Come swing with me." "Oh I bet that's what you want." Katrina said with a laugh.?Sitting on a tyre swing with her dress still hiked at her waist, Jessy

was working the legs back, legs forward technique.?" I haven't been on a swing in ages." "You're a big ol' woman... We gotta go, Freddie is gonna be here

soon." "WEEEEEEEEEE..." Jessy said with her legs wide open.?Katrina walked to the side of her but caught the flash of her grey panties. She didn't make anything of it, but she saw what she saw. Jessy swung back then forward, slightly higher with her legs wider. So close was Katrina to Jessy's spread legs, she could she the imprint of her lips as she swung past.?" We've gotta go."

Katrina grabbed for Jessy's ankle as it swung past her. She tried to grab it and immediately knew that was a bad idea. With alcohol having her way passed woozy, she missed the ankle and her body toppled forward uncontrollably.

"Oh shit," Jessy said as she slid forward on the tire and felt it slip out from under her.

One foot hit the ground before she saw Katrina tumbling towards her.

"You dozy tart," Katrina said, with her arms splayed.

They knocked the air out of each other as they slammed chest to chest before falling backwards.

Jessy hit the ground first and Katrina landed on top of her. The pain they both felt was masked by their drunk levels and they both broke into rowdy laughter.

Katrina rolled and lay next to Jessy who was doubled over in pain and hysterics.

"A video camera and that would've been £250 on You've Been Framed." Jessy managed through the laughter.

"I dunno what's wrong with you gyal but let's go."

Checking her watch, Katrina saw that they had about ten minutes until her husband was meant to meet them.

Just then, her phone rang.?Reaching into her trousers, she pulled her phone out and screamed. "Oh for FUCK SAKE!" The screen of her Samsung S3 had cracked from the top all the way to the bottom, with spider web cracks splitting across in different directions.

"OoOoOoOoOoooo," Jessy said, sitting up straight and covering her mouth. "How did you do that?"

"When I fell over, trying to get your drunk ass home!" "Oh baby, I'm sooooo sorry... I didn't mean it..." "This is the THIRD time since I got it and I only got it 'bout a month and a half ago."

Katrina's broken phone was still ringing as she tried to answer the call across her broken screen.

"Come on, come on... for fuck sake... HELLO?" The phone answered.?Laying back on the ground, Katrina rubbed her forehead.?" Hello, babe? What's wrong?" her husband asked.?" What'd you mean what's wrong? I broke my phone again." "How was I supposed to know that?" Freddie shouted back while

driving. "Anyway, where are you lot, I'm almost... OH, what the FUCK is this?"

"What?" Katrina replied

"There's some stupid traffic on the road... it looks like an accident. I'm gonna be a 'bout ten minutes."

"Come ON babe, I'm cold." Katrina said, swinging the swing above her head.

"It's not my fault, it's an accident. For fuck sake." "Where?" Jessy asked, looking around the park.?" Nah, I'm talking to Freddie. There was an accident on the road." Jessy recoiled in horror. "OH NO, IS HE OKAY?" Covering the mouth piece with her hand, Katrina whispered, "Keep

ya voice down! God knows what kinda weirdo winos live in the park at night... huh, what babe?"

"I said how's Jess?" "Fucked up. My girl pissed on the..." Jessy sat up immediately. "OI, STOP TELLING PEOPLE MY

BUSINESS."

She raised her knees and rested her arms, showing the inside of her thighs. Katrina tried not to notice but, in trying not to notice, she was doing exactly that.

"What?" Katrina shrugged. "You're drunk, so it's okay, right babe?" "Tell Jessy the rule babe," Freddie said on the phone.?" The rule is," Katrina said, enjoying the thigh on display. "It's all

good when your drunk." "Gotcha." Jessy said, giving a drunken wink and the gun.

While Katrina was laying down on the ground, Jessy stood up with the help of the swing, her legs like jelly. She made it to her feet and stretched her back. The back of her dress was hitched over her panties, giving Katrina something to pretend she didn't see. And admire.

"What'd you say babe?" Katrina mumbled, remembering she was still on the phone to her husband.

"I was telling you about the accident. Looks like some boy racer fucked up his car."

"Sorry, I fell asleep for a second," she lied.

Jessy reached her arms to the sky and gave Katrina a look at her shape. She couldn't explain the way she was looking at Katrina because she couldn't understand it herself. It was as if she never really noticed how beautiful her friend was. She'd noticed her lips before and admired her behind but never really seen how attractive she was in the way she looked right now.

Jessy watched Katrina laying down on the phone and made a drunken decision with a pivot of her feet, a stumble, then falling to her knees at Katrina's waist while reaching for her belt buckle.

Gazing up at the stars, listening to her husband, Katrina took a few seconds of feeling her hips shake before she looked down at Jessy, who had her belt open and was about to unzip her.

"WHOA... JESS... HOLD ON BABE..."

Katrina covered her broken phone and looked down at Jessy, who'd hiked her skirt up to her waist and was swaying as she tried to slide her friend's trousers down.

"Shhhh..." Jessy held a finger to her lips. "I'm drunk, so it's all good."

Katrina held a second of thought between what was going on between her thighs and her husband on the phone. She knew he couldn't see her, but, being under the influence, her thinking wasn't exactly straight.

"Are you out of your tree? Get off me, wha' do you gyal??" Talk to ya man... don't worry about me," Jessy whispered. "Yeah, talk to me," Freddie said, still on the phone.?Katrina felt confused. "Sorry babe... so... is the... driver alright?"

Jessy had Katrina's trousers open and was struggling to get them below her waist and hips. Holding such equilibrium, Jessy started to growl as the trousers failed to scoot the way she wanted them to.

Katrina smiled, raised her hips and stuck her tongue out. Jessy pulled and her trousers slid down to her knees.

"So how long 'till you get to here?" Katrina said, dropping her head and feeling drunk all over again.

"It's moving slowly so maybe about five to ten minutes?"
"So you'll be here in five to ten minutes?" Katrina repeated.?Jessy looked up at her friend, having pulled her trousers down over

her heels and followed with her panties.?She separated her friend's legs, got between them and dropped her

head without hesitation, while looking at Katrina with five fingers up. "Where shall I meet you lot?" "Meet us ATTTTTTT..." Katrina didn't want to look down at what her friend was doing

between her thighs because what she was feeling was more than enough.

Her free hand reached up for her face as she turned away from the phone. Her heart was picking up speed, her skin was heating up, the stars were clear above and Jessy found out that she was already wet.

In general, Katrina was always at a moderate level of moistness throughout a normal day. That's just how she was. But Jessy had her past that. Her fingers were stroking her inner thigh while lightly brushing over a low trim of hair.

Katrina still refused to look, even though she was writhing on the cold ground under the swings.

"The traffic is moving now babe, you two ready?"

"Where... erm... wheeere... yes... whereee are you gonnna meet us?"

In her head, Katrina was speaking fluently but her inability to talk was covered by the drink. Or at least she hoped that's how her husband heard it.

"GOD babe, how much did you lot have to drink?" "OOOOh we had a LOT!"

Jessy looked up with a finger rubbing Katrina's clitoris, dabbing her tongue and watching the results.

Katrina parted her thighs as wide as she could while locked in the prison of her knickers and trousers around her ankles.

Then she looked down for the first time.?Just as Jessy was looking up at her.?Katrina's entire body shuddered when their eyes met and the thing

she was trying to ignore by not looking washed over her.?She wanted this.?" So where are you lot?" Freddie asked on the phone.?Katrina heard a voice from her phone but realised she dropped it.

"Sorry babe, what?" "Where ARE you?" "Player's Club." Katrina lied.?" Didn't you leave already?" "Yeahhh.... yeah we did... WEEEEE did... but Jessy forgot her...

herrrr purse." Their eyes were arrested by each other as Jessy looked up at Katrina

with the phone next to her face and her features contorting in silent ecstasy. Her friend looked down at her, trying to stop from saying some of the filthy words that were running through her mind on a wave of rum and tequila.

The sound of absolute silence in such an open space felt amazing. Traffic in the distance reminded them they were in London but the air of nothing except the noises they made was deafening.

Jessy responded by swirling her head from side to side, making Katrina's waist rise.

"Alright I'm here, where are you?"

Katrina was locked in a staring match with Jessy and it was getting serious. She couldn't see what she was doing with her mouth but she could feel it.

Jessy was soft with her lips and her tongue, making sure not to bite. She had two wet fingers together and were making soft slow circles on her opening.

"KATRINA? HELLO?!?!"

In her mind, Katrina heard and answered Freddie. But the words never made it to her mouth. All that escaped was a long drawn out sigh as her thighs began to shake.

"FOR FUCK SAKE, HELLO?!" Then the phone went dead.

Jessy's eyes read like 'tut tut tut'.

Her lips, fingers and tongue were triple-teaming Katrina's clit in one smooth motion. She leaned into her friend's hand as she reached down and stroked Jessy's face.

Katrina closed her eyes. She had to.

There was no way she was going to watch the look on Jessy's face when she came.

Then her phone rang.?" HelloOoOoOoooo yellow..." "Are you lot near the park?" Freddie said.?With her eyes still closed, her thighs shaking, a handful of Jessy's

hair in her grip and her back arched, Katrina struggled for any form of balance. In her mind, she was dealing with a lot. Her friend, bona fide bredrin was eating her pussy, WELL, and her husband had seemingly found out where they were.

"Yeaaaaahhh... Weee walked to the park... Jessy wanted to go on the swiiiiiiiiiiings..."

Katrina gave the swing above her head a tap and watched it sway as her hips began to move on Jessy's face.

"I found you on the GPS. I'm parked outside the gates, where are you?"

Katrina's hips moved faster as Jessy's eyes smiled back.

With each grind of her hips, she clenched her cheeks, helping to grind it out.

Jessy moaned between her thighs and slurped between her lips. Katrina opened her mouth but words weren't her friend.
"KATRINA? FUCKING HELL, WHERE ARE YOU LOT?"
"CoOoOoOoOooooming... one minuteeee, we're runnnning..." "Hurry up, it's late, I'm tired, I've still gotta drop Jessy home..."
"Okaaaaaaaaay... we're almooooooost there..."

Jessy worked her fingers until Katrina's mid-section rose off the ground and she balanced on her head, electricity and a wicked feeling running through her.

Katrina came. Hard.

The intensity of it held her in the air for a moment as it slowly washed away and she dropped back to the ground, her hips throbbing like a pulse.

Her last memory was of the feeling of her trousers and panties untangling from her heels.

Katrina couldn't remember how she made it into the car but she was suddenly aware of being on a back seat with her face on the seat. A car door slammed shut next to her feet as she slowly unfolded from the foetal position she was bunched in.

Freddie turned from the front seat and looked back at his wife, who looked like she drunk a River Thames amount of alcohol.

"You know you lot are on a long ting?!" he asked, rhetorically.

Jessy slid in next to Katrina's head and closed the door behind her as Freddie pulled off with annoyed wheel spin.

Coasting through roads, making it back onto the A406, Freddie was off and speeding while listening to soul tunes on Solar Radio.

In the back, Katrina struggled to an upright position and slumped against the door. Across the back seat, she watched Jessy, who was watching her back.

"So how was ladies drunk night out?" Freddie asked, looking at them in his rear-view mirror.

Jessy leaned forward, burped, tasting a mix of drinks then laughed. "I'm drunk, so it's all good!"

Katrina didn't know whether to laugh, moan a little bit more, relive exactly what just happened or fall back to sleep. Looking at Jessy's

back, remembering how that same dress was hiked up as she ate her pussy, was the start of a flashback.

Just as she started to drift away, she looked down at Jessy's hands, which were behind her back.

Katrina could see something in her hands but she couldn't make out what it was.

Jessy unclenched her hands and Katrina watched the ball unfold into a pair of panties.

Quick as a flash, Jessy snatched them and put them in her purse.

"Babe, you okay?" Freddie asked his drunk wife who was watching the scenery blur past.

"Yeah sugar honey iced tea," Katrina said with a giggle, while running her fingers down the inside of her trousers and feeling nothing. "I too am drunk, so it's all good."

"I don't know this area that well..." Terae said, driving while looking left and right over his shoulders, trying to pay attention to the road. "If you know anywhere, let me know."

"For fuck sake." Francine said in the passenger seat, closing her legs and taking her fingers out of her mouth. "Okay, don't have a cow. You won't get lost. Mama knows where she's going. Turn right here."

Terae turned the wheel of his Renault Clio and came off Mare street trying to open his zip while controlling the car.

"So how was work?" Terae asked, turning to Francine.

"If I wanted to talk about work, I would've gone straight home to my husband. As long as I'm with you, don't ask me about work!"

"Fine... take your breasts out then and open your legs."

Francine lifted her pinstripe skirt to her waist, unveiling her thighs to Terae's peripheral vision. She hooked her panties to the side and slid down in the front seat and put her heeled feet on the dashboard.

At a set of traffic lights, Terae waited until the car was at a complete stop before turning to watch her single out her middle finger and run it up and down her lips.

"Are you gonna fuck me before you take me home?" she asked, pulling a creamy finger from between her thighs.

"You asking stupid questions again? Of course I'm fucking you. I don't know where but I'm getting my dick in you one way or another." "Turn left then take the sharp right at the end there and, as soon as

you hit that right, turn your lights off." "Alright." Terae followed the instructions given, trying to remember the way he came just in case he had to pull out and speed off. Worst thing in his mind was being lost in the maze of Hackney streets trying to find his way to a familiar road.

The car park with no lights was completely empty as Terae turned off the engine while the car was still rolling. He dry turned the car into a space and had the handbrake up as Francine was climbing into the back seat with her skirt around her hips.

By the time he had his seatbelt off, Francine was bent over on the back seat holding her cheeks open.

"Oh that's what you want?" Terae asked, undoing his belt and pulling his legs through the space between the two front seats.

"I just want my dick!"

Terae didn't respond, instead he got into position behind her and rubbed his semi-erection against her lips, trying to get the blood flowing.

"Come on either give it to me or I take it. I need that dick. Do you know how much I've been thinking about you?"

"Obviously not enough," he sniggered as he spat on his erection. With an index finger inside her, Terae twirled his digit, enjoying the feeling of her pussy getting wetter around him.

He lined himself up and pushed hard into Francine, who lifted her head quickly.

"Thereeeeeeeee's my dick!" she screamed, arching her back and drawing him all the way in. With her cheeks open, she bit into the back seat and didn't let go as Terae's first stroke made her thighs shake. His hands wrapping her hair around his wrist in a ponytail made her walls contract.

"Fuck your dick then!" Terae said, leaning against the car door and letting Francine's rump do the work.

Holding her knickers to the side, Terae was at full standing inside her and was loving the view of her pussy sliding back and forwards on his dick, with her asshole pouting at him.

"Oh... that's my dick... that is my DIICK!"

Francine grabbed her shirt and ripped at the buttons as they flew off in different directions, bouncing off windows, the gear stick, the CD player and falling under the seats.

In his head, Terae was counting how many buttons he heard so he could make sure he found and disposed of them appropriately.

"Come on young buck COME ON... FUCK ME FOR FUCK SAKE!"

"SHUT UP AND JUST TAKE THE DICK!" Terae said while spanking Francine's chocolate.

She started pounding her hips on him with nowhere to go. He absorbed the pressure she was throwing back and could feel the build- up on his thighs and knees while the windows were beginning to steam up.

"Where did you tell him you are?" Terae asked, poising his finger to play with her ass.

"Drinks with friends from work, you?" she replied, rolling her hips. "Football with the boys." "Tut tut tut, naughty naughty..."

Terae could feel his car rocking as Francine put an arm on the roof of the car to balance herself and was throwing her body back on him so hard that their bodies were slapping. The windows were fogged up completely and Francine was holding her orgasms back and stopping Terae's goodness when it got too good in order to save for one big massive juicy orgasm.

"You ready to cum on your dick?!" Terae asked.?" Yes daddy!" "Go on then," he added with a spank on both cheeks.?He rested an arm on the small of her back so that every time he

gave her a thrust, her ass bounced forward and back to him. Concentrating on the good wet feeling around his penis, Terae was

rocking the back seat. She pushed back and he pushed forward in a rhythm and their moans matched.

"FUCKING CUM!!!" Terae shouted, wrapping an arm under her neck.

Francine's body shook and her body collapsed under her as she came. She hit her head on the arm rest and let out an almighty scream.

"SHIIIIT FUUUUUUCK... OOOOOOH I LOVE THIS DICK!" "I'M GONNA..." Terae massaged the head of his dick until he began to spray his

seed, which painted her bum, lower back and her suit jacket and shirt which she'd pulled up to her shoulders. The rest of his shots sprayed on the back seat and the foggy window streaked with her fingernails.

With his dick dripping between her cheeks, Terae flicked the rest of his sperm on her back.

"Whooooooo... and that feeling right there is exactly why I can't stop fucking you!" she said, reaching back and playing with the white streaks on her cheeks.

"Good dick is good dick!" Terae laughed as Francine pulled her clothes back on without cleaning herself.

They looked at each other, enjoying the fact that they were both doing wrong and both felt good about it.

Terae's phone rang and he answered it, while telling Francine to shush.

"Hello?"

"Hey babe, you on your way home? I need the car to go and pick up my parents."

"Where you going?"

"My dad's sister died so we have to go down there. I'll tell you about it when you come home."

"Alright, I'll see you soon." "Love you baby." "Love you too." He hung up and stared at his phone.?" Was that my lovely daughter?" Francine asked.?" Yeah, she said she's coming to yours to pick you guys up." "In this car?"

"Yep." Francine giggled and sucked her finger.

BECKY BECKY TWO TIMES – C.L.I.T.S

Lamar was woken out of a strange sleep by Norman Conners singing You Are My Starship. His eyes started to focus and he immediately woke up when he realised he was looking down at the ground instead of in his bed where he last remembered being.

"Whooooa... what the..." "Wakey wakey eggs and bakey bakey..." Lamar locked eyes with the voice below him and he saw a thick
chocolate of a woman laying down on a single bed directly underneath him. He wanted to ask who she was but then he caught sight of his arm extended to the left and right. He was secured in a Jesus-like pose on a cross.

"Morning morning... Lamar. Now we don't have a lot of time so let's get straight to it it. I've heard that you don't know how to play with the pussy pussy."

"Who the fuck are you? Where am I?"

"There's two techniques I'm gonna show you. Frank Spencer and Ike Turner."

"Where's Keisha? Where the fuck am I?"

"Now now, the Ike Turner – my personal favourite – is the more strong, demanding style of..."

"HELP!!!" Lamar shouted.

"Shhh... Be cool cool La La... you're gonna be here for a while. Now, the Ike Turner..."

"Who are you?"

The woman who called herself Becky Becky Two Times was laying down with a white sheet between her legs and over her breasts and she appeared to be wearing nothing but a black bra and a smile while her hand was somewhere beneath the sheet.

Her hand moved roughly under the sheet and Lamar stop worrying about where he was and began to watch.

"Got your attention now haven't I?" Becky Becky said.

"The Ike Turner is more of a niche movement and not everyone likes rough pussy play. Me personally, I love it. But to each their own. It's not about me, it's about what Keisha wants."

Becky Becky's hand was flicking hard from the left to the right under the sheet and she had Lamar's attention.

"PAY ATTENTION LAMAR! Good boy!" "Why don't you move that sheet?" "Geeez... you men! I haven't even showed you the Frank Spencer

and you're ready to cheat on your girlfriend. What's wrong with you men? Huh? Why are you always ready to do the wrong fucking thing? Huh? I'm here trying to show you something that could save your relationship."

"Bitch, you tied me to a cross and you wanna teach me about how to touch my girl? You must be out of your fucking mind!"

Becky Becky's cool and calm demeanour switched and she sat up from the single bed and started to put her panties on.

"See, this is why we exist because fuckers like you don't know how to appreciate what you've got."

She discarded the sheet on the floor and stood on the bed, inches from his face. She looked at his naked body, except for his groin cup, and stroked his face.

"Who are you?" Lamar asked again, sweat beginning to trickle down his temple.

"I already told you who I am but all you seem to be interested in is my breasts and watching me play with my pussy."

Lamar looked back at her face.

"This is why we provide this service Lamar. Because of shaky eyed bitches like you who would rather move on to the next than learn something. When was the last time you made Keisha come more than once? Huh? Tell me."

Becky Becky slapped him across the face then stared at his angry eyes, enjoying the fire in his face.

"Who the fuck are you bitch?" "Oh no no..." Becky Becky reached into her hair, which was pulled up in a bun and

removed a small blade.?" Oh shiiiiiiit," Lamar said.
"HELLLLP!" "That's the thing Lamar. We ARE the help. We're here to help you be

a better man but nooooo... you have to start calling people bitches. So now I have to cut you."

"Whoa whoa... I'm sorry..."

"Oh NOW you're sorry. When the blade comes out and shit gets real, now you're sorry? Well I've put my panties back on so it's too late. I was gonna show you how to touch your woman. Make her have orgasms on her orgasms but you.... YOU and your fucking mouth..."

Becky Becky ran the blade on the side of his face as he turned his head away from her, trying to avoid the blade.

"I'm sorry, okay? I'm sorry." "You don't have to say everything twice. That's what I do do." "I'm sorry okay? Show me the Frank Spencer again." "Too too late Lamar... now I have to see you bleed... just like the

last one." "Whoa, what last one?" "You men and your bullshit! I wish you guys would learn a lot

quicker quicker." As Becky Becky put the blade to his neck, watching his jugular vein

throb in anticipation, a loud voice filled the room through a speaker in the corner of the room.

"Becky Becky? Drop the blade. We're not going through this again."

She looked up. "Really? But this one isn't gonna learn anything." "Sleep him and move on," the voice said.?Becky Becky sighed heavily then looked at him with a frown then

pressed a button on his neck. Lamar fell asleep instantly.

HIDEAWAY

"Fuck honey, fuck strawberries, its all about the banana ladies. The best food to freak a man with is a banana. That nigga can put the thing in my mouth and watch me do that thing then he can put it inside me then he can eat it out!"

The room erupted with laughter from the group of pyjama and onesie wearing women as they agreed and shared high fives.

Snacks on a centre table were nibbled and devoured while empty alcohol bottles rolled around on the floor.

The group of 11 university women were having a ladies night in; take away, PJs, nonsense TV, alcohol and weed for those who liked the herbal chill out.

The conversation, as always, started with course drama, which lecturer was the 'wanker of the week' and how the sandwiches from the Revay Café had gotten a lot better recently.

But now the conversation was on sex and Elise began to squirm. It had been far too long since she had seen a man naked, let alone been anywhere near getting some so these girly sex conversations were always a moment she wanted to hide.

Her life was so uniform that her girls knew where she would be, when she arrived and which route she took to get there.

Though she was living away from home, she felt like she was elbow deep in the academic side of uni and not tasting enough of the life experience side. Further made worse by the many many stories her girls regularly told about their dick-taking exploits in bars, corridors and behind the administration building.

The coffee table before her was a mixture of wine, brandy, a big bottle of Malibu, weed, roll up paper and tobacco with black hair magazines at the base.

As a high grade spliff was passed in front of her, Elise took it and listened to a story.

"I'm telling you, I met this guy last week and I was feeling kinda 'right now' about it so we went back to his place and as I took my clothes off, I swear he wanted to drool all over me..."

Elise was sitting on the edge of the sofa with her feet underneath her. She was still sipping her wine and taking a few puffs of the weed and she was listening intently as sometimes, when she listened to other people's sexual exploits, she went to bed masturbating with those images in mind.

"...And we got going and he came in, I tell you girls, his mum should've named him Mack, 'cuz his dick was built like a fucking truck."

The room erupted with laughter again as the storyteller took a long sip of her beverage and waved her hands around for extra emphasis.

Prince's Sign O' The Times was playing in the background and his high voice popped up in between the breaks of conversation.

"...So he's on his back and, you know me, so I'm on top and I'm killing him with it. I swear, I'm trying to kill him with the tun' tun'."

The storyteller got onto her knees and flexed her body, imitating the exploits of her story. Elise watched the way her body flexed from her head down to her waist and remembered the last time she ever tried something like that. It was two years ago when she met that guy Marcus at Harmony in Tottenham Court Road and, impulsively, opened a can of whup ass on him that made her squirt for the first time. But since then, Elise hadn't been around a man for long enough for him to put that work in. Although, the times she did want a man, there were none that appealed to her.

"...Then out of the blue, he closed his eyes and, oh my God, I swear I thought he was dying, he just began like...throwing his arms around like he was doing a bootleg Azonto. His arms were in the air and shit, he nearly knocked me out then he let out one scream and then he died. I thought I was with D'Angelo by the sound he made."

"When men come, they make the ugliest faces... proper Shrek looking faces..."

"...I know, it's funny 'cuz some of the faces I've seen look so funny, they remind me of monkeys..."

"...But that just means we women know how to work it..."

"...Oh that's for damn sure..." The girls gave each other hi-fives while Elise feigned a smile

amongst their raucous chuckles.?" Elise, when was the last time you had sex?" The question came out of the blue from Esther, one of Elise's

roommates, and everyone looked at the chocolate beauty in the onesie with her arms tucked between her thighs. She wasn't expecting anything from anyone so she looked up wide-eyed and wondering where the hell that came from.

"What?!" she replied.?" When was the last time you had sex?!" "Why?" "I just wanna know, 'cuz I know I haven't seen you with a guy ever

since we moved in here and we've been here for, what, two years now!?"

Elise tightened up in her ball and began to get defensive as her drunken roommate spoke loud enough for the room to concentrate all their attention on her.

"Look, its not that I'm not interested in sex, it's just that I haven't seen anyone who I wanna give myself too."

"Maybe that's your problem. Sex these days isn't about holding out for the right person, it's just about getting yours." The drunk Esther pointed and raised her voice at Elise who was not looking to get into her shit today.

Some of the room agreed, others kept quiet and paid attention to see how the conversation went. But Elise knew what she was going to

do. Go to her bed. As she unfolded her legs and put them down, she looked at the room of women, especially Esther, and downed her remaining wine.

"Look, don't worry bout me okay, I'll be fine. I don't need you to tell me what I need."

With that, Elise turned around and made her way to her bedroom. Her girls tried to call her back to the discussion but Elise was already closing her bedroom door.

"Don't worry 'bout her, she's probably gonna knock one out. That's all she does!"

Elise unzipped her onesie and stepped out of it, climbing straight under her duvet. She shuffled her feet and wiggled her waist, warming her body under the cold sheets as raucous laughter exploded from the living room. She closed her eyes and pictured the strong hands of a stranger on her face, running hands from her cheeks down to her chest. Her clit was hot and she flinched as her finger graced it for the first time. As her mind worked with thoughts of a random stranger's strong back and ass working on top of her, she followed her pinkness all the way down until she slipped inside herself. Her back arched and she dared to dip her fingers deeper. The mystery man was lying on top of her using his hands to follow each curve of her body. Each finger tickled an individual part of her body and she shivered slightly as his invisible dick rubbed itself against her clit. Elise wanted him to come inside her but she wanted him to wait.

"Come inside me," she whispered to the empty room as her imagination took control.

The stranger slid inside her slowly and she winced with every inch she took. She wrapped an arm around his imaginary back and could feel the muscles in his back working with his stroke.

"HOLY FUCK FINGERS..." she shouted as he put himself all the way inside her. By now Elise' finger was working in small semi-circles as her waist rose off the bed and she balanced on the tips of her toes. As her orgasm jumped out of her, she pushed her fingers out and squirted a cascade of liquid onto the floor. She rolled around her bed while trying not to make too much noise.

"OHHH...DAMN...thank you baby." Elise murmured to the stranger, opening her eyes to her empty room.

The noise from the living room died down and by the time she fell asleep, the last thing she remembered was the beat from Bilal's Soul Sista thumping against her wall. Her body was still throbbing from the orgasm that had mini ripples coursing through her being as she drifted off with the stranger in mind.

As the weekend came, Elise spent most of Saturday in bed. Checking her Instagram, updating her Facebook, reposting funny and erotic images on Tumblr and watching anything her travel aerial could pick up on her TV.

By late afternoon, Elise climbed out of bed and threw a few tops, leggings, panties, socks and toiletries into a bag and tossed it by the door, ready for her weekend away. She and Esther decided since they'd done every piece of revision in anticipation of their upcoming exams, they deserved a pre-exam spa getaway in Wales. Face masks, mud baths, strong hands rubbing their troubles away, beautiful scents designed to make you chill out. Elise was excited, even though her body moved lethargically.

"Good evening, this is your pilot Prince speaking. You are flying aboard the Seduction 747. This plane is fully equipped with anything your body desires..."

As Prince's International Lover crawled through the speakers and Esther rolled onto her other side, squashing her face against the cold window, trying to get comfortable, Elise sang along. She listened to the lyrics and wished her stranger with no face would appear and apply some pressure on her. The Sunday morning roads were clear except for a rising mist of fog on the the horizon. Elise, with her hooded jumper draped over her head, was focussed on the road, but she had her stranger playing at the corners of her mind. She thought she saw someone who looked like him more than twenty minutes ago when she drove past a man standing on the side of the motorway with his thumb sticking out. He was tall, dark and sort of resembled her stranger but the car was travelling so fast that he went by in a flash.

"Good morning Sleepy Sleeperson."

"Hmmm..." Esther replied, wiping drool from her cheek as she sat up and looked out the window.

"We're nearly there. You missed the bus full of naked black men that flashed me. It was like a coach full of big dicks. I was thinking of making a little stop, getting on the bus and getting me some."

"Bitch please," Esther said with a yawn. "If a dick jumped in front of you, you'd probably use it as a doorstop. I know nun's who've seen more dick than you." Esther sunk into the seat and coughed as her cold showed signs of returning.

"Yeah, you can go back to sleep now if you want!" Elise retorted.

"You're just mad 'cuz the only sex you see is on the Discovery channel."

Esther began to laugh and coughed hard as she turned the heater on full blast, clapping her lips together.

Cars became a blur to Elise as she frowned at Esther's comments. Comedy they were but she knew that the truth was hidden within and that bothered her more than anything. Her pussy had serious withdrawal symptoms and had become more used to her fingers than anything else. And that was a fact she wanted to change.

"Bitch," Elise murmured under her breath.

After driving for two more hours, they reached the hotel where they were going to be receiving relaxation and complete tranquillity. Massages, mud baths, facials, feet rubs, relaxing baths and everything the girls needed to exhale and prepare themselves for the stress of exams.

The hotel, which looked like a medieval castle, stood in the middle of nowhere. A gravel drive led to the hotel entrance and the girls parked up, stretched out and dragged their bags to the reception.

Elise confirmed their reservation while Esther kept yawning without covering her mouth, drawing the ire of anyone in her vicinity. The receptionist quoted their order of a double room with two single beds, en suite bathroom, television, and the complete package when it came to activities. Every sort of rub, massage, kneed, work, press, manipulation of their bodies, they wanted it. They wanted their bodies loose and free and ready to kick some exam ass when they got back to university.

They excitedly skipped down the hall and smiled as the room looked just like it did online. The beds were made, small sofa in the corner, television and DVD wide-screen connected to the wall, mini fridge filled with water and health snacks and an en suite bathroom that made their bathroom at home look like a wishing well.

"Do we really have to go home El? I mean we could bring some men up here, well I could, sneak some ice cream in and have a party." "You're funny, almost as funny as when your man came in your

mouth and it came out your nose." Elise knew she owed Esther some sort of hot return and this was perfect.

"Go fuck yourself you lonely bitch! And it didn't come out my nose, it just looked like it did."

Elise flopped onto her bed in hysterics as Esther's painful memories came flooding back.

The room was warm and had a slight hint of cinnamon in the air, like someone had been cooking in the bathroom. Elise was bouncing around the room in excitement as she looked at the menu for what type of activities they could take up.

"So what first?"

"Sleep!" Esther threw her bag next to her bed, unravelled the covers on her bed and got under the sheets.

"You can't go to bed, we gotta get out there and get limber." Elise was ready to go out and get into some sort of massage. She wanted to survey the grounds, take a walk, see what kind of people frequented this type of grand establishment.

"Oh forget you, I'm gone. I'm taking the key okay? Your one is on the desk over there." Elise said, taking her purse and a towel.

Esther wrapped herself in the pillow and exhaled.

Walking down corridors that all looked alike, Elise charted her way via an app on her phone. She walked to the massage quarters, sharing smiles with random folk that passed, enjoying the air of positive

energy that was pulsating around her. There was no queue system at the massage quarters, all you had to do was find out what you wanted and take a number. She ran her hands through her twists and felt her head tip back as scents and oils filled her nose. She cleared her throat and moved quickly to a cubicle where she could get changed. Drawing the curtain, she took her clothes off and folded them neatly before sliding into a white hooded dressing gown and flip flops.

With her locker secured, she moved through a door of beads and saw the names of each type of massage she could receive. The first was a Mud Massage, second was Cucumber Massage and the third was Deep Body Massage.

She folded her arms in front of her, keeping her dressing gown closed, then took a ticket for a Deep Body massage. She was intrigued as to how deep they could get and sat down on a stone slab outside the room.

She crossed her legs and fiddled with her ticket, scowling at her chipped toe nail polish. Her thoughts began to drift to her stranger but a woman sat so close to her, she couldn't help but take notice. As Elise was bout to look at the woman and give her the worst 'what-the-fuck- can't-you-see-all-that-space-over-there' look, the door to the Deep Body Massage room opened and steam filled the room.

"Number 10 please."

Elise looked down at her ticket and saw she the same number printed on her black ticket. She scrunched the ticket into her pocket as she got up, still confused about the woman who damn near sat on her lap. As she turned around, the woman looked up, opened her dressing gown to reveal her naked body and winked while clicking her teeth. Elise wasn't sure she was seeing what her eyes were telling her she was seeing. The woman was a lovely shade of chocolate that shone through the haze. Her eyes were reading Elise's reaction, which was one of shock, surprise, bewilderment, excitement, horniness and wonder.

The woman's thighs opened and Elise couldn't help but grin at the bald V between her thighs.

"You ready?" said a voice from behind.?" Yeah, yeah, erm... yeah." She walked backwards into the room, not taking her eyes off the woman who was sucking one of her fingers. Elise watched her intently as she slipped the finger out of her mouth with a pop and began to slide it down her stomach.

The door closed before Elise saw where the finger ended up. She even tried to look around the door as it closed.

The room was nothing but a table, a tray of oils and creams and a shelf of candles that surrounded the room. Before Elise could admire the room, two hands came from behind her and reached for her shoulders. She tried to turn around but the hands were already drawing her dressing gown down her arms.

"I can do that," Elise said, drawing it back over her shoulders.

"Sure, no problem. My name is Riley. Just lie down on the table and cover yourself and let me know when you're ready."

The masseur turned around and faced the wall while rubbing his hands together. She couldn't get a look at his face, just a bald caramel head and a wide back.

Watching him from behind, making sure he didn't turn around, she slid one side of her dressing gown off her shoulder, waiting for him to respond. He adjusted one of the candles on the shelf and went back to rubbing his hands. Quickly, she dropped the dressing gown and climbed onto the table, throwing the sheet over her back, adjusting to make sure none of her nakedness was on show.

"I'm ready!"

Elise listened as trumpets sounded from nowhere and mixed with the candlelight and the light strawberry incense that filled the room. Miles Davis' Blue in Green played as the masseur opened a bottle of oil and began to pour it into his hand.

She watched him with her face turned to the side. His hips came into her view and she began to imagine where in his tight white trousers his dick could be hiding. Was it straight down, was it up, to the left, or tucked under?

"Okay, I'm gonna touch you now," he said softly, pulling the sheet down to her waist.

Elise sighed and nodded as she tucked her arms into her sides and closed her eyes.

She could hear him rubbing his hands together while catching a scent of eucalyptus from his fingers. He spread his fingers and walked around to the other side of the table.

The first time his fingers made contact with her skin, a beautiful piano poured through the room and Elise felt her muscles relax instantly. His palms flattened and he ran his hands from her shoulders to the base of spine.

As he rubbed her back, Elise dissolved into liquid as she felt her stress of no sex, school work and an annoying family leave her body. She wanted to exhale but she felt like she'd moan inappropriately.

"Is this okay for you?" Riley asked.

"Yeah, that's fine." she lied. It was more than fine. He'd only just started and Elise could feel her nipples getting hard against the mattress. A smile crept across her face as strong hands kneaded her hips, rubbing in circles to the sound of the music.

Riley moved around to where her head was turned with her eyes closed and he leaned over to reach down her back when something bounced off the top of her head. In her calm, serene state she thought it was a figment of her imagination. Maybe her mind was imagining the meaty length that was reaching over her head and down to her

ear. She opened her eyes and didn't need to turn her head to know that there was a dick resting on her head.

Before she could register a sound or reaction, the foreskin-less dick moved from her head and dropped in front of her face.

She frowned first. She wrinkled her cheeks as it graced the button of her nose, smelling freshly cleaned. Then her eyes opened wide.

"What the fuuu..."

She fully focussed and realised that Riley had his dick out on the table next to her face. Her body was still relaxed and becoming more and more chilled even though she could see the veins on the underside of his dick.

The fact she didn't scream out in disgust while cursing him and running out of the room spoke volumes to her. She stared at it, confused as to why it looked so brand new. No hair around the shaft or testicles, fluff-free and smelling like nutmeg and mint.

Elise blinked once, then twice.

Is he expecting me to do something to it, Elise thought as the dick got closer and closer to her face. She wanted to just grab it, spit on it and suck him until he came but it had been too long and she had lost the self-confidence to do so with conviction.

"Could you turn over please?" Riley asked calmly, like his penis wasn't on the table ready for her to take advantage of.

She didn't know what to say. She didn't know whether to do what he said or run out of the room while lodging a complaint.

Lying completely still, Elise made her choice, lifted the sheet over her back and spun onto her back. Looking up at him, she let out a strained grin while his penis rested next to her ear.

He'd gone from trouser-less to completely naked and Elise was looking up at his toned mid-section, wondering if this was really happening. She'd heard stories of her lucky girlfriends getting rubbed up and dicked down by students who were training to be qualified masseurs. But those were just stories. She'd never seen or encountered any of these men but she knew they existed.

Their eyes met and Elise stared at Riley for the first time. He was cute, not handsome. A touch of youthful exuberance about him with a large dash of maturity around his eyes.

He smiled with a cheeky glint while rolling the sheet from her shoulders down to her arms. They both turned their eyes to the sheet and watched it roll down her chest.

Elise wasn't as nervous as she was when his dick flopped out and slapped her on the head but now, with his smile and his dick in her face, she felt braver with what was put on the table.

"Is this a part of the full body massage package?" Elise asked.?" Yes ma'am it is. With extras of course." The sheet rolled down past her chest and the warm air washed over

her nipples. She shivered beyond her control while fighting to keep her

arms by her side and not cover her nakedness. She could feel her cheeks flushing over and goose bumps rising over her skin. Her stomach sucked in as the sheet continued rolling and stopped below her navel.

She let out a tiny whimper, hoping the sheet would keep rolling beyond her waist. Her skin was tingling in anticipation, waiting for his slippery hands to electrify her soul and make her thighs open uncontrollably.

The music faded to silence as Riley rubbed his hands together. Elise watched him slip his fingers between each other, enjoying the squelching sounds. He stole a quick look at her nipples and smirked.

"Tell me the truth. Do you do this a lot?" Elise asked, looking at the ceiling.

"Today? Not a lot. I've had a few."

With those words, Riley opens his palms and brought them down over her head. Watching his hands move closer and closer, Elise started to breathe heavily.

"Don't worry; you'll be taken care of. Just relax."

Elise tried to close her eyes but they opened as soon as his hands touched her neck.

With a strong sigh, Elise watched his hands slide from her neck to her breasts and she took in a large breath of air when his finger graced her nipple.

The feeling of another man's hands on her breasts was more delicious than ice cream with strawberry sauce. And Elise loved ice cream and strawberry sauce. His remaining fingers ran over her nipples and her back arched slightly. The look in his eyes was something between concentrated and amorous and she licked her lips.

"Hmmm..." she moaned from her throat and let her eyes drift closed.

Riley moved from the head of table to the foot while humming to himself. His soft footsteps matched the throb of her heartbeat as he began to roll the bottom of the sheet up her legs. She began to sweat and her legs twitched while his hands began to massage her calves. Strong fingers rolled across her skin up to the back of her knees and she hummed. In her mind, Riley was slowly morphing into her perfect stranger. Not talking or making any noise except for the heavy sound of her breathing, Riley was soft with his touch as her rounded thighs came into his view.

"Jeeeeeeeeesus..." Elise let out. "Sorry, it's been..." "Don't worry. Just relax." The way he said the word 'relax' made Elise do exactly what she was

told. Her shoulders slouched, she let go of the breath she was holding and she tensed her stomach muscles as the sheet rolled over her thighs and stopped at her waist.

Elise felt too exposed and unrolled the sheet back to her ankles with her hands over her nipples.

"I'm sorry, I'm trying to relax but I just..."

"It's okay. We can keep the sheet where it is."

Still looking at the ceiling, Elise felt overly embarrassed. Here she was about to get a wonderful massage with a guaranteed happy ending and fear had her too scared to have her body on show. She slapped a hand over her face and shook her head to herself, thinking she'd wanted to be touched by a man for so long and the first one to do so made her have a panic attack.

"Let's try this," Riley said.

He rolled the sheet all the way down past her feet while rubbing her ankles. With an ankle in each hand, Riley began to part her legs. She fought the urge to resist him with her hands still over her breasts.

Elise felt her thighs become unstuck as the sheet drooped between her thighs. She suddenly felt a shape under the sheet between her legs and she covered her mouth to stop from screaming in surprise. Lifting her head, she looked down to see Riley was no longer standing and had his bald dome under the sheet.

"Erm, I don't think... oooh..." Elise said as Riley's hands snaked between her thighs and over the hood of her clitoris.

All he did was run two fingers over it and Elise was moaning like she was on her third orgasm. She wanted to open her legs wide to the world and give him all the space he needed but she was still feeling embarrassment at what was going on. Her hands wanted to wrap around his head so she could ride his face into the sunset and really have a story to tell when the next girl's night came around. But for now, she just watched.

Because she couldn't see him, her mind began to play with the image of her perfect stranger. Never seeing his face but knowing that he could make her cum just the way she liked. Not having any idea of his name yet calling him 'God' every time he made her feel good. Never seeing his dick, yet imagining his girth as her fingers mimicked his movement.

Riley had her clit hood pulled back and one finger rubbing it while another finger played with the moist opening of her lips while his breath spread across her inner thighs.

The shuffling sound of the sheet and her inner screams made the room sound like the volume was turned up even though there was no sound in the room. She removed a hand from her breast and slowly reached for the white covered ball that was protruding from between her thighs. Fighting nerves, she touched his head and, when he didn't recoil in horror as she expected, she cupped the back of his skull and pulled him into her.

The positive growl from beneath the sheet dissipated any fears she was having and his lips on her lips made her stop watching and drop her head back.

The last time Elise got any fellatio-like activity was... a long time ago. So long ago that she wasn't even able to recall the guy's name or

what he looked like. In her mind she was thinking it might've been Mike or Jamal in her first year at uni but, since then, no mouth had visited her down below. And now, here she was, about to face fuck a masseur who showed her that he was more than willing to do what she needed done.

With her hand on the top of his head, Elise made a slow and deliberate rhythm to warm up to, even though she could already hear her juices being lapped and combined with his saliva beneath the sheet.

"Well... if your gonna give a full body..." Elise said, feeling brave in herself. Her other hand reached down and wrapped around his head and the contact made him stick his tongue out, trail from her clit to her opening and slowly slide between her lips.

"Wois... thigvs... okway?" Riley mumbled with a mouth full of her pussy.

"Yeah, yeah, yeeah..." Elise said, forcing his mouth back to work.

Her fingers interlocked around his head and her legs dropped off the side of the mattress giving him the space to take full advantage, which he did.

His free hand appeared from beneath the sheet, ran up her stomach, between her breasts and massaged her neck and Elise could feel herself ready to come.

"Don't... oh my God, how are you... don't stop... oh God don't stop."

Riley did as he was told and didn't stop. Even as she came, he held her thighs down and didn't stop fucking her with his tongue while his fingers were playing with her liquid coated clitoris.

Elise covered her mouth and pressed down like she was trying to weld it shut. The sound from her mouth muffled against her hand and she thought of the beautiful flasher outside the room.

If she was still there, she definitely heard me, Elise thought to herself.

Riley's hand around her neck disappeared beneath the sheet and Elise could hear what he was doing. He sucked a finger or two and slowly slid them down her trail until they met with his tongue which was still inside her.

"OH... MY... FUCKING... GOD!" Elise screamed through her fingers. "You don't play do you?"

Riley mumbled something but Elise wasn't listening because her eyes had rolled in the back of her head and his voice sounded like waa waa waaaaaa waa.

Her stomach muscles were tense and her arms were trying to pull him into her heart the way he was reaching inside her.

A loud bang on the door made Elise cover her breasts again. "Riley," a man's voice said. "We've gotta go. This ting is done." Elise didn't know who the voice belonged to but all she cared about

was the fact that Riley did not move from his position. She watched

the sheet continue to bob and weave between her thighs as the door kept knocking.

"Onphe minoute..." Riley mumbled.?" You think you can do that again in one minute?" "Waptich..."

Elise felt his fingers sliding in one rhythm and his tongue sliding on another rhythm while his finger was running back and forth over her clit. Her inner thighs were wet from a mix of cum, saliva and sweat but it all felt beautiful to her.

"Yes...do not... stop... THAT!"

Riley continued to do as he was told, keeping the three-peat rhythm going as her nipples stood tall in anticipation of the deliciousness that was starting to boil in her midsection.

Elise humped his face, making his fingers and tongue wiggle inside her, touching parts of her walls he hadn't touched before. Her mind went blank, she began to develop a headache and the muscles in her arms were aching from the way she was forcing him into her pussy.

"Gwan bredrin'," Elise yelled. "Get it!"

Riley withdrew his fingers and his tongue while still playing with her clit. Her body was dancing across the mattress, rising and falling with each shock that rippled through her and Elise knew she was about to be written off.

"OOO... OoO... ooo..." Elise trailed off.

Her feet planted back on the thin mattress and she arched her back as her orgasm began. Her hips and her waist stayed airborne under the sheet as she felt her pussy walls contracting. Her cheeks clenched together and liquid began to drip between them and onto the surface beneath.

She could hear Riley lapping at the rain that poured down on him while she continued clenching and unclenching her pussy. The rain that poured under the sheet didn't stop as Elise touched her clit and started another stream.

Her ear-piercing scream filled the room, bounced off the walls and returned to her mind but she couldn't stop. Her body was still arched and one of her hands were still wrapped around his head. The moment her body began to drop, she heard and felt Riley playing with the liquid dripping from his face and between her thighs. She let her body drop but arched again when her cheeks touched the large wet patch under her.

Slowly dropping again, Elise put her hand on her forehead, trying to subdue the headache that was pounding her temple. Her eyes were clamped shut and her skin was tingling as Riley withdrew his head from the sheet.

Breathing as fast as her heart was beating, Elise kept her eyes closed, unable to look at the man who was responsible for making her squirt for the second time in her life. She wanted to look him in the

eye and speak volumes without saying a word but her eyes refused to cooperate.

"Uno momento, I'll be right back." Riley said, wiping his face with a hand towel.

"Sure... take all the time you need," Elise replied, still breathing like she was at the finish line of a marathon.

Riley left the room and Elise looked through her fingers to make sure he had gone before she threw the sheet off to look at the mess she'd made.

"Fuck me forwards," she said to herself, parting her thighs.

She touched the sheet and the cold made her pull her hand back while laughing to herself.

"What a massage!"

Her chuckle turned into loud, raucous laughter as the door began to open. She grabbed the sheet and threw it over her body as another masseur in the same uniform walked in, closing the door behind him.

"Hello, my name is..."

"Where's Riley? I'm already being seen to." Elise asked, hoping he'd keep the deep massage going, deep inside her.

"Who? There's no Riley who works here!?"

"WHAT?! But he was just here?" Elise said angrily while sitting in a patch of her own juice.

I CAN CONVINCE YOU

"I'll tell Nelson!" "I don't give a fuck who you tell, he's not my dad is he?!" Yvette couldn't speak. She knew Nelson wasn't Isaac's natural father

but he had a lot of respect for him and that was all she had to throw at him.

"Son, please..." Yvette's chest was heaving up and down for a few reasons. Standing outside of Lewisham police station, arguing with her son in

a house coat and pyjamas was dripping embarrassment all over her. Many times during shopping trips in Lewisham, she'd watched parents collecting their children from the police station and waiting until they were outside the building before cursing them to within an inch of their lives. She didn't think she would become one of those parents. But here she was, looking at him, trying to find an ounce of remorse in his face for being arrested for GBH and robbery of a mobile phone. But her 15-year-old son wasn't even looking in her direction as she spoke to him.

"Mum, I didn't do it."

"You muss tink seh I'm stupid boy! They got you on CCTV. We just watched it."

"Fuck CCTV, that's pagan business right there."

Yvette watched her son swear and had no control over her hand as it crossed his face and turned the direction he was looking in.

"Who are you talking to BOY? I'm not one of your little friends, you hear me? I'm not one of your little friends."

"How you gonna slap man's face on road?" Isaac said, staring at his mum with disgust. In his head he was thinking, 'if you weren't my mum, I'd write off your face'.

"I'm your mother! You don't talk to me like one of your little bredrins from school. Do you know how angry and disappointed I am right now?"

"I don't give a fuck. You slapped man on road!?!"

Yvette could feel tears growing under her eyes as she looked at her son. Though she tried to hold on to the picture of the baby she held in her arms, she could see that he was not the same baby.

"Yeah I slapped you. Because you're behaving like these silly boys on this road who go around robbing and stabbing people. Look at you. Pick up your clothes. Your trousers are dragging on the floor and..."

"FUCK YOU MUM!" "WHO THE FUCK ARE YOU TALKING TO?!"

The voice full of bass made Yvette and Isaac both jump as they watched the broad, milk chocolate man with salt and pepper in his hair and beard walk towards them, swinging a large bunch of keys on his finger.

Even though he wasn't Isaac's father, or even Yvette's partner, he was well respected in the local area, opening a number of corner shops and always there with free plantain or a bag full of shopping they would never have to pay for.

"Thank God you're here Nelson," Yvette said, exhaling heavily.

"Nah, it's okay Yvey." Nelson said, putting a hand on her arm then he turned to Isaac with a frown. "So you think you can be one of those man who talks to his mum any sort of way?"

"Allow it Nelson," Isaac said, his demeanour softening in front of the hulking shape of a man. "It's nothing."

"Nothing?! You put the guy in hospital?" "How did you know that?" Isaac cut his eyes at his mum.?" BOY! Who do you think you're looking at like that?" Yvette charged at her son with her finger pushing the middle of his

forehead. His head shot back as Nelson got in the space between them.

Isaac backed away and had his attention stolen by a car that beeped and stopped in the middle of a bus stop, holding three approaching buses behind it.

The occupants of the car whooped and bellowed at Isaac and he took off towards them, holding the front of his tracksuit bottoms as he ran.

"ISAAC? Don't you dare get into that car? ISAAC?!" Yvette shouted, drawing attention from everyone in earshot.

"I'll be back later innit?" "Isaac, why are you treating your mum like this?" "FAM, you're not my dad innit! Fuck off from around my mum."

Nelson and Yvette stood there dumbstruck by what they'd just heard and the emotions attached to it.

Yvette wasn't trying to replace Isaac's father – wherever he'd run to – but she liked the mutual male respect her son had for the local 'knows everyone' shopkeeper and to hear her son speak in such a way brought tears to her eyes.

She rubbed the salty streaks with the back of her hand as the car pulled away from the bus lane, jumped a red light and disappeared through the market, which was shutting down for the day.

"ISAAC!?!" she shouted after the car.

"Don't watch that boy Yvey, he'll be back," Nelson said behind her, watching the car zoom into the distance.

"But he's gonna hurt himself doing something stupid."

"But what can you do? You can't lock him up, you can't keep him hostage in the house, all you can do is wait and pray he comes home in one piece."

"You know what I can do?" Yvette said, reaching into her handbag. "I bet you I have a better answer." "What?" "Rum?" Nelson replied.

"YES please! A large one too."

Yvette could feel tears welling in her eyes, thinking about her son and the path he was walking before her eyes. As a social worker, she'd seen many children wear the same Air Forces in the same path to nothing and disappointment. It was hurting her more that she was watching her own son go the way she fought so hard against for so many years as a single mum.

"You're doing your best Yvey, that's all you can do." "Yeah but my best isn't good enough." "Putting too much pressure on yaself is what ya good at." "I have to! Otherwise I'll be watching my son as another victim on

the news and I won't have that."

Nelson drove Yvette to his flat, over his double front corner shop based deep in the heart of Thamesmead. She'd been there many times before where they'd talk over the world's ills while puffing shisha and listening to Dennis Brown. Today, Nelson brought out the bong and a mix CD of Lee 'Scratch' Perry, Toots and the Maytals, Wailing Souls, Burning Spear, Junior Reid, Lucky Dube and The Ethopians

By the time Yvette poured her fourth glass of straight Wray and Nephews, while on the topic of social care children and street gangs, she could feel herself getting more and more inebriated.

"See the youths out here?" she shouted towards an open window. "They don't know what's going on. They think they're too bad these days and they know it all. They don't know FUCK ALL!"

With her hand flailing behind her, Yvette's drink danced in the glass, spilling on Nelson's carpet.

"SORRY NEL... I'LL WASH YOUR CARPET WHOLE... I MEAN ALL..." "Don't worry about it Yvey, its a'ight." "No it's not alright Nelson... My son is out there somewhere doing

God knows what with God knows who. Running around like he's Don Juan Scarface... who the fuck does he think he is?"

Yvette went to lean on the window frame and felt her hand slip instantly. It all happened so quickly, she didn't even realise she was on her way down after she watched her drink jump out of her glass.

"Shiiiiiiiiiiiit," she said as her elbow knocked on a radiator.

She landed on her side and Nelson was quickly at her side. His curtains were covered in rum and the glass landed upside down but didn't break.

"Come on lady; get your drunk self off my floor."

"What for? This is where I'm gonna end up so why not stay here?" She said making it to her feet with Nelson helping her.

"Just because the boy wants to run around with the youts dem, doesn't mean you haven't been raising your son well..."

"Yes it does. I'm supposed to be his mother and father and..."

"Just shut up ya mouth woman! You have a well-mannered, respectful child there. Yeah so he has some hood friends, they won't last, they never do."

"So what do I do in the meantime while he's running with these fucking delinquents, huh? Wait for him to come home in a box?"

"Don't think like that..."

Yvette got to her feet and stumbled with Nelson holding her arm. She shook him off, reaching that stage of her inebriation where she didn't want to be touched. As well as fuming that her drink dropped on the floor, she made her way back to the kitchen, feeling sweat grow on her brow.

"Nelson... look... I can only do so much, but it's just me by myself. His father doesn't care otherwise he'd put the Tennents Super down and come find us. But noooooo... he wants to sit around and drink all fucking day, let him."

"I know Isaac needs him..." "I need him! What about me? What about me?" "Fuck him!" Nelson said, taking the last sip of his drink. "Fuck me Nelson!"

The darkness creeping over the horizon. The Jah Cure song coming out of the speakers. The high grade scent and the sound of Nelson's boiler all seemed to stop as he frowned, looking at his friend as she fiddled with her fingers and looked at the floor.

"Wha' you seh?" Nelson asked.?" You heard me. I want you to fuck me!" "You muss be drunk." "I'm tipsy, not drunk." Yvette said. "And I'm sober enough to know

what I want. I don't want you Nel. You're not my type. I just need to feel good. I want YOU to make me feel good."

He looked at her sitting across from him with her sweatshirt leaning off one side of her shoulder, breathing heavily

58

and frowning. The look in her eye was not friendly and Nelson could feel heat emanating from her direction as she looked through him.

"Come on Yvey. You know that's not what we're about. You're just feeling angry and upset and..."

"Horny! Yeah we never talk about that. I'm fucking horny as fucking horny can be."

"Nah your drunk..."

"What's got to do with me getting some? Don't act like you've never thought about it."

Yvette stumbled to an upright base and waddled towards Nelson, who was now up on his feet with his eyes wide. He'd never seen Yvette in this state before and, as much as he'd thought about having sex with her in his mind, he never thought about actually doing it. He saw

her as a good friend and didn't even think she would be into him like that.

She was standing in front of him as he looked up at her from his chair, daring himself not to move.

"Whether I've thought about it or not, it's not the point. We just can't..."

"I CAN'T control my son. But I CAN get some. If you don't do it, I'll get it from somewhere else."

"You know what you're asking for?"

"Yes I know," Yvette said, reaching for his groin. "A sex favour that's all. Geez, why you making it seem like I'm asking you for a million pounds? I'm asking for a favour."

Nelson put his hands on the armrests, and recoiled in shock as Yvette took and held a handful of his groin, staring at him as she felt that he was already hard.

He looked in her eyes and could see sadness mixed with arousal and drunken swaying. What she needed right now was to be soothed internally and Nelson was going to be the man to do it.

"Nelson, I need to be fucked!" "But wait..." "Wait for what?! I said I need to be FUCKED! My life is shit, my son is out on road, and I've got no money. I need to be fucked Nelson!" "It just feels weird." "It doesn't feel weird at all," she replied, taking a stronger grip in his

groin. "You might fuck me quite good." "Yvey, please..." "Please WHAT?"

Yvette didn't mean to slap Nelson in his face and she wasn't sure she did until his face looked back at her with shock and disgust. Her hand was stinging and the muscles in her arm were flexing.

Nelson stood up in front of her and held his anger. He knew whatever was going on inside Yvette, this was not the answer. He knew they'd wake up in the morning, guilty as hell, confused and agree to never do it again. Maybe even never talk again.

She slapped him again. "Are you gonna fuck me or what?"

"Bwoooi... you're lucky 'cuz if it weren't for you being upset, me and you would fight. Ain't no woman ever put her hands on me."

She punched him in his nose. "Fuck me Nelson!" "No." She kicked him in his shin and stumbled. "Fuck me NOW!" "I'm not gonna do it!" "Oh yes you will!" Nelson stood in front of her, holding his ground through her drunken

violence as he watched her arm swing back. He knew this was just an alcohol-sponsored lash out and since he was the only one within arm's reach, he was to be the punching bag.

"You don't want this Yvey! You'll regret it afterwards and its only because of what Isaac is doing at the..."

"Ya know who I'm thinking about? ME! Right now, I'm thinking about myself and the fact that I haven't had sex in fifteen years. I can't even get a vibrator in there."

The mental picture struck Nelson and he winced, hoping her hands would stay where they were instead of trying to connect with his face. He now knew the real reason behind her frustrating blows but he also knew she had to let it out.

Yvette had been chasing behind her road-running son for a number of years; midday calls to her work place to come and pick him up from school for misbehaviour, police calls and final warnings at random police stations, constant denials of incidents involving his name. She worked hard and always made time for Isaac, yet Nelson, with an ear to the community's anti-social network, knew that her son aka Yung HandSlap was working hard on his street reputation. And he was slowly gaining a name, which was drawing attention from the boys in blue. As well as some unsavoury others.

"Nelson!"

Yvette had tears streaming down her face as she slung her jacket over his shoulder and pulled her bra from the arm of her t-shirt.

"Yvette," he said with his hands up in surrender. "We can't do this. I don't wanna do anything that might affect..."

"AM I A FUCKING TEENAGER?" she yelled, stepping out of her trainers. "I'm not planning to fall in love with you old man. I just need a fuck."

"Old which part, we're the same age. Look, I know you're upset about Isaac..."

"Lemme tell you suttin'. I'm pissed off about that boy. No I'm fucking livid actually. But that's nothing to do with you fucking me, okay? I've had a drink or three, I'm fucking pissed off and I want sex. Now!"

He didn't have anything else to say. His friend had literally put everything on the table and left him to make a choice. Not that there was any.

Yvette becoming his friend was a gift and curse. The bow of happiness was wrapped around the fact that they got on so well with no awkwardly intimate moments. The bubbling curse was the fact that he had a wealth of feelings for the 50 plus half Jamaican, half Nigerian woman with the extension braids with salt and pepper flavour at the roots. He didn't want anything to make their friendship weird in any way and with his feelings for Isaac becoming quite father-like, he accepted less rather than reaching for more.

His feelings weren't helped by the fact that Yvette didn't look her age, had a pair of the fullest, roundest breasts he'd ever seen and had

a backside that always managed to show through whatever she was wearing.

Looking up from her hips, Nelson watched Yvette pull her t-shirt over her head and drop it on the floor while wiping tears from her face.

"Yvey, we..." he said. " FUCK me!" she replied. Her eyes were steel, boring into him. He felt like he was being hypnotised the way her light brown eyes were locked on his. Nelson felt like he couldn't move as he stared at Yvette's breasts and stomach which both hung low. Yvette stared at him without blinking. There was pain and arousal etched across her face, making her appear vulnerable and yet in control. The first time she blinked was when she reached down for her belt buckle.

Nelson was fighting anticipation. But he was also thinking in the back of his mind that he had to stop this at some point before it went too far.

He knew allowing her to get to such a state of nakedness was already past a point of no return, but he believed he had the strength to put a stop to the strip tease, even though she was about to complete it.

"Just the fact you've let me get this naked Nelson... come on. I know you've wanted to. Just do it and let's go back to being friends, okay? I could really do with some dick right now."

"Listen to you!? You don't sound like a 50-year-old woman with a 15-year-old son."

"Age has nothing to do with sex Nelson," she said, blinking for the second time and unbuckling her belt. He watched her jeans and knickers come down together as she drew them down to her ankles and stepped out of them.

Nelson caught himself staring at her behind as she bent over and wiggled with each step out of her crumpled jeans and panties.

She stood up straight and walked towards him so quickly, he stumbled backwards and had to catch himself. She put two hands in the middle of his chest and walked him out of his living room with her eyes still locked on his.

"For all your protests, you're moving quite willingly Nelson."

He shrugged as he walked backwards towards his bedroom. "Maybe I've just said fuck it."

"Took long enough old man."

"Been waiting for this old woman," he said, draining his glass and leaving it on a cabinet he past in his corridor while walking backwards.

They made it through his corridor and into his bedroom without breaking eye contact. His peripheral vision was catching the sight of her nipples which were rising. He backed into his bedroom door and stumbled but kept his eyes on her, enjoying the fact that he was now able to look at her with eyes of desire instead of friendship.

Yvette opened the door into his dark bedroom which was illuminated by a series of CCTV cameras by the side of his bed.

"Clothes off, now!" Yvette said, pushing him onto his bed and closing the door without looking away.

"Can I just..." "No, now. Hurry up about it as well." The vulnerability he saw in her previously was gone and replaced

with a strong talking, let's get it on, stern voice of a woman who was staring at him with 'why aren't you taking your clothes off' eyes.

Undoing the buttons of his shirt and kicking off his shoes, Nelson took a quick look at the four screens showing live shots of the front door of the shop, the back door, the till and one over the aisles.

Everything looked silent and peaceful.

Yvette cleared her throat as he got to his last button and reached for his zipper.

"Good. Now, it's been a while so I might be a little rusty." Yvette said, walking towards him.

"Rusty at what?"

She looked down at him and slowly tilted her head before dropping to her knees as he wrestled his arms out of his shirt.

Taking his erection in her hand, Yvette looked at his penis, tilting it to the left, inspecting it to the right. Nelson looked down at her, finally getting free of his shirt and throwing it somewhere.

He looked down in time to see Yvette – his friend, his therapist, his surrogate partner in secret, his desire – take the head of his erection into her mouth with her eyes closed.

A moment of 'we shouldn't be doing this' washed over him as she took curious strokes with her mouth, finding her way around a rhythm.

With his eyes locked on her face, hoping she would open her eyes and look back at him, Nelson watched Yvette search her forgotten talents as she worked his dick in her mouth, wrapping her lips lower with every second stroke.

He wished he turned on the light before he hit the bed so he could watch everything in live, bright reality HD, though the cameras by his bed gave enough light that he could see the sheen left by her mouth.

She had him three quarters of the way in her mouth and she didn't seem to be satisfied as she dipped for more.

He couldn't believe what he was seeing in the darkness of his bedroom. Yvette squeezed the base of his erection and continued working her way down, taking him deeper and deeper into her throat with each stroke. She was a small flex of her lips away from taking him all the way as she came up and returned to the head, giving soft kisses and letting him go with frown lines across her brow.

Nelson couldn't watch any more. Not only was his dream coming true, but his expectations were being fulfilled, surpassed and rewritten

as Yvette, the rusty head giver, happened to be Yvette, the deeepthroat veteran.

"Rusty you said?"

"I used to be good at this," she said, taking laps of his dick with her tongue. "I think I can do it. Let's see."

Yvette put him back in her mouth and got deeper and deeper with each stroke, starting from the top. Nelson forced himself to watch. If this was going to be a one time, not going to happen again moment then he was going to watch and mentally download everything that happened.

She moaned as she got him half way into her mouth and got deeper, sliding quickly to three quarters. Her stroke slowed down as she adjusted her throat and opened her mouth. Her lips moved further down his dick with the sound of the seconds ticking on Nelson's grandfather clock in the corner of his room.

He watched her reach the same depth as before until she slowly took him all the way into her throat and stayed there for a moment.

Nelson's eyes crossed. He felt her throat tense on his erection as she slowly moved up and down, keeping him not far from the back of her throat. His hands were gripping the duvet beneath him and he started to breathe like he was jogging.

"Rusty yuh rass!"

"Hmmm..." Yvette replied with his dick going from glistening to slippery in her mouth.

She slowly came up until her lips kissed the head of his penis. Then she stood up and climbed on top of him without stopping to get comfortable or talk about how they were going to do this.

Her thighs slid either side of him and his wet dick slid between her thighs, across a low stubble of hair atop a thick pair of lips.

Yvette looked down at him as she moved her hips slowly on top of him.

"OoOoOoOoOoOoOoookay..." Nelson said as Yvette's smooth hip and waist grinding made his slick dick slide inside her before either of them realised.

"Siiiiiiiiiiiiiiii..." Yvette sucked air through her teeth and her hip movement stopped and she kept perfectly still.

Nelson put his hands on her hips and tried to get a movement moving when she quickly moved his hands from her waist and put a finger on his lips.

"Juuuust... just shhhh... for a minute okay?"

She put a hand on his chest, closed her eyes and began to nod to herself in agreement. Her chest began to heave and she began to slowly rock back and forth on top of him, with his dick reaching deeper with every rock and roll of her lower half.

Her body jerked five times and she moaned.

"I'll shush..." Nelson said, watching Yvette have an orgasm.

"You shush," she whispered, turning her face away from him and mouthing something he couldn't hear. With each stop came another orgasm and Yvette was taking them silently but the ripple down the back of her spine and the electricity that made her body shake was evident.

Looking up at her, being able to watch his beautiful friend have an orgasm was definitely crossing a line and a moment he reminded himself to put in the upper echelons of his mentally video files.

"Okay, let's try something," Nelson said, wrapping his arms around her waist and pulling her down on top of him.

"Try what? You better not do... look... just be easy with me ya hear? It's been a while and..."

"Yeah, I know... a little rusty. But your 'rusty' is brilliant." "Awwww, thank you Nelson. Nice to know I still got it." "Okay, let ME try something..."

Nelson lay Yvette flat down on top of him and put one hand on her lower back, while starting a slow stroke that slid nicely in and out of her.

Holding the speed, he listened to Yvette mumble to herself in his neck as her body continued to vibrate on top of him. Though he wasn't counting, he knew she was somewhere around eight or nine orgasms so far and he barely moved for most of them.

He took his stroke up a notch and listened to the sound of their sex slopping in the darkness as her he moved a hand to her cheek and opened her up. Deeper inside her he reached and her back hunched.

Nelson felt her stomach tense and release then tense and hold as she held onto his shoulders. He heard and felt between his thighs what made her tense up like that as she exhaled and lay completely flat on top of him.

Yvette dripped liquid down his dick, through his closed thighs, onto the duvet and a coolness began to spread under him.

"I haven't done that in ten years," Yvette said, regulating her breathing.

"So not only are you a deepthroat vet, you squirt as well?" "I used to." "Rusty yeah?" "I AM rus..."

Yvette stopped, mid-word, and began to breath quicker and quicker as if she was running and gaining speed. She held onto his shoulders and gripped tightly as her stomach tensed before another pulse of liquid dripped between his thighs.

Everything from her molecules to her atoms to the earrings in her ears were vibrating nicely and each wave of pleasure brought another wave of liquid.

"OHMIGOD! This is too much..." Yvette said. "It really HAS been a while!"

"We're only doing this once right? You sure just once?" "Look, all I know is I hav..." She stopped again and a stronger wave hit her and she rolled off his

body and onto her stomach, moaning heavily into his sheets.?He watched her, enjoying the fact that, though he hadn't done

much, she'd become a quivering wreck.?The vibrations from her moans tickled his shoulders, which began to

sting. Realising, he'd been cut by her finger nails, he turned onto his stomach and reached for the side lamp, stealing a look at Yvette, who was still face first in the duvet rolling her hips with a finger underneath her.

As the side lamp came on, Nelson saw something out of the corner of his eye and drew his attention to the screens. His eyes scanned the four screens, looking for what it was that he saw.

When it came to the security of his establishment, he learned to ignore little things like cats, stray dogs and foxes, but people, he paid attention to. He had to develop a wicked eye owning a shop where he did, which was why he slept with the screens next to his bed. He also had a silent alarm that linked to a police line that would have them there in three minutes.

His eyes stayed on each screen, scanning every inch of the scene then moving on and that's when he saw the movement.

Back door.

"You'll get an orgasm in a minute, yeah Nelson? Just gimm..." A figure walking to the back door of the shop.?" You take all the time you need over there," he replied, watching the

figure hulk over the lock.?His heart was beating for a different reason as he swung himself off

the bed and got on his knees in front of the screens, reaching for his phone.

If this was someone coming in to try and rob him, as soon as they open the door, the silent alarm goes off and Nelson will receive a phone call asking if he's okay. If they managed to find him and get past the baseball bat by his bed and the selection of knives he kept hidden, then good luck to them.

"Hoodie, black and grey, five foot eight or nine, black tracksuit bottoms..."

Nelson watched the figure casually open his back door and close it behind him. Then the door opened again and the figure reached for the keys left in the lock. He watched the figure walk into the shop and jump the counter, straight to the spirits, which went into a rucksack.

"He's got keys... how the fuck did he... oh SHIT!"

"What's wrong over there?" Yvette asked, fighting to turn her head towards him.

"Isaac is downstairs stealing drink from my shop."

"Where? When?" Yvette said, still struggling, but throwing more effort into moving.

"He's down there right now, look."

Yvette made it to her elbows and crawled across Nelson's bed, with her body still tensing in rhythm.

"Where?" she said, looking at the screens.

"He's gonna pop up over there. I can tell its him 'cuz he has a key to the backdoor on his house keys. I could see his keys. "

"Where did he get a key for your back door?" "I don't know Yvey, I dunno but... there he is!" A figure skulked in the shadows, making his way through the shop from one screen to another until it was jumping the counter and checking the till for change before turning to the spirit bottles behind.

Yvette's eyes widened as she saw the shape of someone in front of his spirit bottles display, picking random bottles and stuffing them into a rucksack.

Then the figure turned around to a noise behind them and Yvette saw Isaac's face caught in the light of Nelson's lottery scratch card display.

"Oh my GOD, it's him!" "And the police are gonna call any..."

Nelson's bed side table draw vibrated. He opened the draw and pulled out a phone.

"Hello..." he said, covering the mouthpiece. "It's the police. They wanna know..."

"So tell them then," Yvette said, watching her son stuffing cigarettes and bottles of beer into his backpack. "His name is Isaac Christian, he's wearing a black hoodie, black tracksuit bottoms..."

"YVETTE! Are you sure you wanna..."

"The likkle bwoiii wants to go on as a big man... and rob YOU? So yeah, he's five foot nine, short hair, fade on the side, grey rucksack..." Nelson went back to the phone. "Yeah, I'm being robbed... yeah he's

still here... yeah I know him. His name is Isaac Christian... he's wearing a black hoodie..."

3D (DANIELLE DISCRETELY DANGEROUS) – C.L.I.T.S

"Do you love me Mary Janeeeeeeeee..." "Who is that? Who are you?" Lamar woke up quicker than he had before and his eyes focussed
immediately. He recognised an empty basement with low lighting and three figures sitting around him. Two either side and one in front.?His arms were tied behind his back and his legs were tied to the
chair legs of a wooden chair.?He blinked repeatedly and focussed on the face closest to his left and
he saw a beautiful woman exhaling smoke from her mouth. His nostrils recognised the smell of marijuana as he looked at the person on the other side of him who looked exactly like the woman on his left. He did a double take between both of them and realised they must be twins. He slowly looked at the shape in front of him and he spoke up.

"Triplets huh?" "Nope," all three women replied.?" I'm Danielle," said the woman on his left.?" Discretely," said the woman in front raising her hand.?" And I'm Dangerous," said the woman to his right.?He frowned and looked down at a dusty, graffiti-covered table with
an ashtray in the middle.?" So... Lamar is it?" asked Discretely as she was handed the spliff. "Fuck off about your not triplets!" "OoOoOoo... he is angry. I bet he hasn't had a blowjob in a long
time. When did you last get some head?" Dangerous mocked.?Lamar turned to his right. "Look, I don't care about you or your bitch
sisters here. Just..." "Did he just call us bitch sisters?" "I think he did Dangerous. I think you need to show him just how

dangerous you are." "Finally," Dangerous said standing up. She pulled Lamar's chair back
until he tipped backwards and fell to the floor. His head banged on concrete and the one known as Dangerous stepped over him and sat on his knees looking down at him.

"Be easy on him D," Danielle said.?" Yeah, remember what happened to the last one." "The last one?" Lamar shrieked.?" Thanks babe," Dangerous said as she was handed the spliff. She
tapped it over his face and watched the black and white ashes sprinkle over his eyes and nose. "Now... I can tell you have anger issues. Why can I tell that? Because I have anger issues. I've got lots of 'em. Mainly with men like you. Men who seem happy to just be secretly and silently angry all the time."

"I haven't got anger issues. I've got hate being tied up by a bunch of fucking women I don't know issues."

"See? Anger!" Discretely mumbled, sprinkling weed in another roll up.

"Are you this angry with Keisha?"

"No. We don't argue or fight or... anyway, that's none of your fucking business."

"Do you smoke Lamar?" Danielle asked looking down at him. "Yes." "Weed?" Dangerous added, putting her bare feet on his chest. "Yeah, why?"

"Want some?"

She offered the spliff to his lips and he pouted his lips as far out as he could. Just as the end reached him, Dangerous pulled it away.

"SIKE!"

The three women laughed and high fived each other while Lamar closed his eyes, trying to hold the anger in.

Danielle slid off her chair and sat on the floor next to his head.

"Listen Lamar, we don't really have anger issues and we're not sisters. But we are here to help you, like all the C.L.I.T.S are."

"Exactly!" Discretely added, sitting on the other side of his head. "We aren't monsters or animals. We're educated women who are here to help you be a better you. Our lesson is anger. You gotta keep it cool, calm and collected at all times."

Dangerous cut in, "especially with Keisha. We've seen the tapes of you getting angry with her and lashing out at her when Arsenal lose. And that is not on. She isn't a whipping post for your anger."

"What the fuck do you mean you've seen the tapes? What tapes?" "Give him some Dangerous," mumbled Danielle.?" You always want me to give him some, why not give him some

when you got the spliff?" "It's not an argument girls," Discretely jumped in. "It's just to calm

his nerves. God knows he's gonna go through some shit by the end of the night."

Looking straight up, Lamar watched the three women argue over him while a thick haze of smoke bounced around their heads.

"Love your woman Lamar, treat her like a queen and make sure her orgasms are strong enough that she has to tell her friends about 'em."

"Is that your advice to him?" Dangerous asked as she passed the spliff. "Okay, my turn. I'm gonna say... if I find out you've been anything other than a gentleman and a scholar to Keisha, I'm gonna come down and I'm gonna use you as my human ashtray, okay?"

Lamar's eyes widened at the thought of having cigarettes and other roll ups put out on his body.

"Just be happy Lamar," Discretely added as she stood over his head so she appeared upside down. "Otherwise you'll end up right back here again and you don't want that. And you're only meeting some of us now. Trust me, you DON'T wanna meet the rest."

"Whatever bitches," Lamar mumbled.?" Give me that spliff Discrete, I'm gonna put it out in his eye." Danielle and Discretely rushed to hold Dangerous back as she

reached down with the spliff over Lamar's face.?" Put him out Dis," said Danielle as she wrestled with her angry alter ego while Discretely pressed the button on his neck and he fell asleep.

LUNCH BREAK

STUART

The office seemed to be sweltering in the summer and it didn't matter how many times he fanned himself, the heat still fought its way through. Stuart spent the last two summers in this same building, doing the same thing. As the computer hummed and Jill Scott made love about being free, he typed away on his keyboard and sent work- related emails.

Publishing companies these days had so many worries that they couldn't worry about the little people who helped build the company but Stuart allowed these thoughts to slip in and out of his mind. The air from a desk fan flew past him and he let his thoughts fly with the breeze. When he had all his emails sent, work related and personal, he leaned over the wall of his cubicle and looked at his neighbour, who he hadn't noticed before, probably because he was deep in the thought of how he'd tell his supervisor when he was quitting this hell hole.

THAT'S WHEN IT HAPPENED!

Like a movie when the big explosion happens, or the culmination of fireworks erupting in the sky, Stuart stopped what he was doing and stared at the chocolate dairy queen who seemed to be setting her keyboard on fire. Her fingers zipped from letter to letter and across the space bar like nothing he had ever seen before. From the chair, Stuart could only see half her body but that was enough. Deep chocolate skin, smooth features, at least a C, maybe D cup, lips that folded over and screamed beauty, natural hair that was cornrowed half way and then plaited the rest of the way down her neck.

If he ever had a reason to quit, it was lost in the thoughts of making love to this woman in various ways. Her face was bright and her lips would move as if she was speaking the words she was typing. Stuart moved back to his desk and fixed his tie in preparation of approaching the woman with the mad typing skills. Breath, check, shirt and tie, check, face feeling good, check.

As Stuart leaned over the wall again, he met her staring back at him. He looked at her deep in her eyes and she returned the stare with a glint of misbehaviour in her eyes.

Shit, now what, Stuart thought. The heat made him uncomfortable as she continued to stare, as her fingers were poised to place another word on the screen.

"Hello," Stuart said, digging deep for a great opening line.

She smiled, looked him up and down and then giggled as she went back to her work. Never one to shy away from a challenge, Stuart laughed and wheeled his chair next to her. Before he even asked a question, the lady quieted him, raised a finger and spoke.

"Well hello to you too!"

ASIA

Asia was new to the world of publishing having previously been a Paralegal for a solicitor in the area. She'd been soured by the corruptness of the legal world after learning that it wasn't evidence that slammed the steel bars or granted righteous freedom, it was the deals that were made before the case ever made it to court. After three years of harbouring contempt for the system and her superiors, she finally left the firm deciding to find a career that would allow her to sleep in peace at night.

Answering the advert for Assistant Editor at Creative Minds Unite Consultancy proved to be a smart move on her part. She'd strolled her sexy self in the office and sold the GM with her savvy appearance and smooth way with big words. Asia left the interview thinking that with her big, round eyes, thick, luscious lips and the way her skirt had struggled to keep her legs hidden, she could have walked out of there with the position of Vice President if she wanted it.

The layout of her floor was open, as there were no huge walls between the employees in each section, only short, desk-height sectors between the various areas. The editing department was adjacent to the cubicle of the brother who'd been staring off into space for the past few days occasionally swaying his head in response to the lyrics spilling out of the small speakers on his desk. At times, he appeared to have rather been anywhere but here at his desk and try as she might, Asia hadn't been able to catch his attention and convert his tormented thoughts to ones of pure pleasure and ecstasy.

He must have either been really preoccupied or he had to be happily married not to have noticed her, because they weren't far from each other and she'd done her best to make him notice. Finally, after three weeks of him not paying her any attention, Asia decided she'd focus her attention his way and let his subconscious intuition tell him she was looking. Her mesh, fuchsia blouse had been filling with air as her desk fan that she'd intentionally angled toward her chest, sent the breeze of the outdoors onto her ample breasts. Asia watched as the feeling hit him. She saw his big-brown eyes look up then cut almost as though he'd heard something. His demeanour went from 'why am I here' to that of a person who'd been in solitary confinement and was looking at the sky for the first time in years.

"Damn." As she looked him up and down, she determined that he was nicer looking than she'd originally thought.

She smiled in response to his "Hello." As she concentrated on editing chapter five of the 17-chapter book, she caught his movement out of the corner of her eye. Her ears were filled with the sound of rolling wheels as he scooted his chair over to her 'private' corner of the office. As he began to speak again, she put her hand up.

"Well hello to you too." "How's life on your side of the world?"

She smiled and batted her lashes at him.

The last thing Asia wanted to do was let him think she was uninterested after having waited three weeks for the caramel-skinned six foot three man she'd fantasised about having in the shower, in her bed, and in her downstairs laundry room on top the washer.

"Have you had lunch yet?" she asked.

STUART

"Not yet, no...erm...no!"

He didn't know what to say, her voice sounded like angelic harmonies used to soothe the mind. Her lips wrapped themselves each word and made him pay attention as she spoke. Looking at her as she continued to type, stopping only once to look at him, smile and then continue her typing, Stuart felt a little overwhelmed by the question. He was used to approaching women and getting a response but this time, she put the ball in his court, which threw him off.

Stuart looked at his watch and moved back to his desk, not letting her get the best of him and also not to let her know that he was as thirsty for her as he was. He actually wanted to let her know that he wanted to take her to the stock room downstairs, bend her over a box of envelopes and have his way with her.

Wonder what her name is, Stuart asked himself. She looks like a India.Arie type with her beautiful skin and all-white smile which lit up the space between them.

His desk was cluttered with reports, figures, numbers, graphs, letters, but his personal items stood out. He owned a paperweight with an ankh symbol carved in silver and floating lifelessly in the clear liquid.

"That's a nice paperweight," Asia said, leaning over into Stuart's personal space. Her perfume invaded his nostrils making the hair on his neck stand up.

"Thank you, my friend made it for me. It's not really this small, I've got the bigger version at home."

"Have you? I'd love to see that one day!"

Now what, Stuart thought? That was as good as asking him out on a date but Stuart had never been put in this predicament before so he didn't know how to react being on the receiving end.

She leaned across his desk and picked up his paperweight, admiring the way the ankh swirled in the liquid. All the while, Stuart admired her neck and dreamed about using his tongue to run up and down while she threw her head back and praised him with moans.

"I love this symbol, it's so beautiful and means so much. I mean, the male and female genitalia meeting at one point to bring new life. Just beautiful."

Two things registered to Stuart:?1. She was educated.?2. She was beautiful and intelligent.

She was sending messages of electricity down his back and shaking his spine like a Michael Jackson dance spin. As he continued to stare at her neck, she looked down at him and made direct eye contact. He returned the stare and they both held the silence as the office continued around them.

She put the ankh paperweight down, got up and sat on the edge of his desk and made herself comfortable. In doing this, her skirt raised a few inches, showing Stuart that the stairs to heaven were thick and looked good enough to eat.

As they continued to stare, Stuart tilted his head to the left and then to the right, in a distracting manner. It didn't work but she did smile and then licked her lips, leaving a film of saliva on her lipstick, which made them shine.

"So what about lunch then?" Stuart asked, trying to distract her again.

"I'm looking at it!" she replied.?" I'm... excuse me?" Stuart blinked and stared back at the woman who had raised her

hand in an introductory manner.?" Asia...pleased to meet you..." "Oh... erm... Stuart, my name's Stuart..." "Nice to finally meet you Stuart." "You too Asia, you too!" Stuart held her hand softly and rubbed his

thumb over the back of her hand. He didn't want to let it go.?As he released his hand, Asia held onto it and began rubbing it with her thumb.?" So, lunch?" she asked.

ASIA

Asia could tell by his responses that he wasn't used to being on the receiving end of the flirting game. The way he answered when she said she was "looking at lunch" made her laugh inwardly and heat radiated from her cheeks as she watched his eyes undressing her. Licking her lips made men watch her mouth and apparently, this brother was no different. Asia had lips that seemed like they'd offer a home-away- from home for Stuart's however many inches. She knew she was a woman who had it going on. Smart, educated, handled her own, and she was an accomplished, professional woman. In addition, at 28, she had no children and one incredible sex drive. There was no end to her assets.

Ten slow, time forsaking minutes later, Asia locked her computer and signed out for lunch. As she walked past Stuart's desk, her fingernails traced a curvy line across his shoulders. He instantly relaxed into the motion of her nails which left his shoulders and were travelling down his ever-flexing arm.

"Ready for lunch?" She asked in her most intriguingly, seductive voice. "I feel like I haven't chowed down in weeks."

Her play on words had an unspoken truth within. She hadn't 'eaten out' in weeks and couldn't wait to see what Stuart was serving. He nervously adjusted his tie and stood up, adjusting his erection.

As they stepped into the lift, both checking each other out when the other wasn't looking, Stuart attempted to make conversation. The 'ground floor' button glowed as Stuart chose the destination and took a look at Asia full on. He stood next to her and couldn't believe what was happening as Asia unbuttoned her fuschia blouse and her ample breasts spilled out of her canary yellow brassier. The elevator slowed to a stop at the third floor. She grabbed Stuart at his waist and pulled him in front of her to face the elevator's opening door. A heavy woman got on and took no notice of them as they tried to hold straight faces. The lift chimed at the second floor and the woman stepped off.

As the doors closed, she reached her hands around Stuart's body and grasped his dick through his trousers and found that he was as ready for lunch as she was.

As he turned to ravish her, the elevator chimed sending notice that they'd reached their destination. Asia buttoned four buttons quickly.

"You'd better be hungry." Stuart strangled the words between clenched teeth and moved her in front of him in an effort to hide the very obvious desire on his part. She giggled and ground her plump ass against his need. "Starving."

STUART

As the doors opened, Stuart felt like he was holding a leash straight out in front of him with no dog. His dick was leading him out of the building, and he could do nothing except fold his suit jacket over his front. When the beautifully, teasing Asia stepped from around him and into the lobby, she looked down and saw his protruding surprise. She licked her lips and turned back around. This did nothing to help his dick go down as they walked out of the building and into the afternoon air, which was humid and stifling. Stuart watched, as Asia put her arms into the air, and stretched her body as far up as it would go. She turned around, as if trying to entice Stuart into her heaving bosom, which was screaming under her blouse.

I know when someone is flirting with me dammit, Stuart thought to himself but now it's my turn.

"So where shall we go for...lunch?" Stuart caught up with Asia, who was skipping ahead in front of him.

She turned around and smiled at him and the fact that the sun was out in London for once.

"Well, we could go to The Soso room or maybe a quick Burger King. To be honest though, I'm hungry for some real meat and I don't mean that processed crap they be selling."

Stuart couldn't move his feet as Asia walked up to him as she spoke and threw her finger behind her, gesturing to the restaurants behind her. The closer she got, the more Stuart could smell her perfume and, mixed with the afternoon sun, felt dangerously intoxicating. He looked her in the eyes, which seemed a blend of mahogany and sunlight cinnamon and stood still as she stared directly at him.

"I...want...you...right..."

The remaining word didn't make it out as Stuart grabbed Asia close to him and gave her a full, pressing kiss. She seemed to be ready for it but shock still registered on her face. Her eyes closed slowly and she ran a hand behind him and onto his left cheek.

Stay down, Stuart barked at his dick, which was now getting that feeling all over again.

When Asia opened her eyes and rubbed her index finger over his lips, her face became very serious and that worried him. Was the kiss too much? Did he over step the mark?

After what felt like an eternity, Stuart decided it was time to find out why she was looking at him like he was the devil incarnate.

"Are you okay? I'm sorry if I offended you when I..."
"Shhh..." She closed her eyes again and then opened them abruptly, looking

as if she wanted to say something but lost it in the abyss of her thoughts.

Finally, she wrapped her fingers softly around his neck and pulled him closer but at an angle and put her lips to his ear.

As he moved in closer, he felt Asia's other hand tracing it's way down his shirt and past his stomach.

"What do you want to eat?" "What do YOU want to eat?" he fired back.?" That kiss made me wet." Stuart looked down at her legs. "How about lunch at my place?" "Sounds like we're not gonna make it back to work."

ONE MOUTH

"That dude CANNOT sing," hollered Wayne at his TV, while spitting out Doritos.

"What? Are you deaf, he has a beautiful voice!" Nazaria replied, draining a Desperado. "Listen..."

Both friends leaned towards the TV.

"You must be hearing something I'm missing 'cuz he sounds like he's quivering his voice. And that's not singing."

Dual heritage Wayne was lying on his sofa with his hand picking at the scraps of cheese-flavoured tortillas while his Asian good friend and neighbour Nazaria was sitting with her feet up in a matching solo chair.

This night in the middle of winter was too crisp for a journey into London's bar life so they vegged out in front of Saturday night TV.

The sarcastic friends spent every other Saturday night in front of You've Been Framed, Take Me Out, X Factor and Strictly Come Dancing while drinking a mix of beers, wines and spirits.

At the start of the night, they played rock, paper, scissors to decide who would have to go to the Waitrose downstairs and get the snacks. Wayne lost.

He came back with biscuits, crisps, oven nibbles, cheesecakes, eclairs, profiteroles, bottles of wine, Desperados and Hennessey.

They'd made it through half the nibbles and were giggling through their second bottle of wine, in an advert break of You've Been Framed.

"WHAT? FUCK NO!!!" Nazaria said out loud, reading something on her phone.

"What?" Wayne said, looking in her direction.?" My friend just sent me a link to a blog and this guy says that men give better head that women." Wayne flashed gun fingers in the air, "BLAAAP

BLAAAP BLAAAP, he's right. Whoever he is, he's a fucking... wait. He means on women right? Men give better head to women?"

"Yeah." "Oh hell yeah... he knows what he's talking about." "Or he's a Jhadhino! That means dickhead in

Gujarati. There's no way men give better head than women."

"How you mean?" Wayne said, sitting up with Doritos crumbs trickling to the floor. "D'you know how much time men spend eating pussy?"

1

"And you sali's never get it right, do you? We end up having to show you this and teach you that then we end up faking it until you lot go home then we rub one out."

"You gotta some cursing me in your language, it's not fair. You could be calling me a goat fucker for all I know."

Nazaria laughed. "Tutelli nirodh no aulad." "What the fuck is that?" "I just called you the son of a broken condom!" "See, that's what I'm talking about. Who would think

to call someone that?" "Someone who's experienced a lot of bad head over

the course of her sexual career." "It's not my fault you've met those chompers out

there. I know for sure you've met a lot of dudes who say that don't give head but still try to push your head down, right?"

"Jhadhinos... all of 'em." "Well at least I represented." "Is that what you think?" Wayne gave her a long stare. "I know." Nazaria looked at him with evil eyes as she got up

and walked to the kitchen. "But I'm not lying though am I? Might as well get a woman to do it 'cuz she'll know how to do it, the way to do and she won't need any instructions."

"Fuck off. I've never been instructed in my life!"

"If you want something done, get a good woman to do it! And yes you have. You ain't no bhadvo."

Nazaria walked back into the living room with two bottles of Desperado lime and mint and a quarter bottle of Hennessey.

She handed him one of the bottles and put the brandy on the table in front of the TV.

"The day a woman eats pussy better than a man, I'll put a picture of my dick as my Twitter avi."

"That sounds like a bet bredrin," Nazaria grinned.

@waynes_world

Just made a bet with @nazine_tasty – if I lose, I'll put my dick as my avi #Nothappenin

Wayne sent his tweet then looked back at Nazaria with challenging eyes.

"Sounds like you want a challenge. What, you want me to eat your pussy Naz? I didn't know we were still..."

"Oi oi... before you start getting hard, kutari, slow ya roll. Besides, you never ate my pussy that well ANYWAY."

Wayne sat up straight and offended. He opened his bottle of beer with his teeth and stared at Nazaria while tossing the cap on the table.

"FUCK YOU BOLLYWOOD! How you gonna try say that I never ate you well? You came didn't you? Many times."

"First of all, babhuchuk, I had to damn near force you to eat me out and second, who says I didn't fake it? "

@Nazine_tasty

Men hate it when u tell dem the truth. I faked it once or twice&now he's pissed. #TruthHurts #Chodu

Taking a large swig from his bottle, Wayne peeked at his timeline and sneered.

Thinking back over his past head performances, never had his head game been challenged in such a way.

His tongue wasn't reaching the ground but he knew what to do with it and no woman he'd gone down on ever complained before.

Wayne pointed his finger. "So lemme get this straight: do you think YOU give better head than me?"

"Well, bwoiii..." Nazaria said, turning to the TV. "NAAAAH, you could never be better than me." "That's a matter of opinion chutiya. All I know is that

I've never had any complaints, just orgasms on my face."

"Me too," Wayne said, standing and talking with his hands.

"Why you getting so hype for? Just 'cuz I eat pussy better than you..."

"But you don't though! OH MY DAYS..." "Alright Wayne, whatever you say."

@waynes_world

My bredrin is a dickhead. A proper dick out of her forehead dickhead. Do women give head better than men? #NoFuckingWay

3

"Let's do it. You and your fucking curry mouth have gone and got into some shit now. Let's do it."

"Do what?" Nazaria asked innocently, pouring a healthy does of Hennessey into her beer.

"You really think..." Wayne trailed off in laughter then took a long swig of his beer before topping it up with Henny. "You know what, fuck this!"

"Woooooow, hit a nerve? Didn't know you were so sensitive about your head game Wayneage."

@Nazine_tasty

Bun them sensitive ass men who cant take the truth&competition. Nex time I wont fake it,str8 tel em ur head game is shit. #Buckwass

Wayne stormed off to the toilet as Nazaria waited to hear him slam the bathroom door before jumping into his space on the sofa. Her elbow-length hair draped around her shoulders and liquid jumped out of her bottle and splashed on the floor as The X Factor started.

She looked out the window as raindrops continued to fall on Wayne's glass balcony.

Grey skies filled her view of of London as the memory of her last woman drifted into her mind.

The feel of her skin, the softness of her curves, her hair thrashing as pleasure took over, the desire in her eyes as she came on Nazaria's face.

Her nipples rose under her wife beater and she stared at them before rubbing them out and taking a handful of M&Ms.

In the distance, the toilet flushed, followed by water running in the sink.

Wayne walked back in the room with his beer and an idea stretched across his forehead.

"What?" Nazaria asked.

"What'd you mean what?" Wayne shot back, walking towards his phone.

"I've known you for a long time, I know that look." Wayne laughed. "First of all, come out my seat." "You move it, you lose it," she replied, slapping her

ass.?" Secondly, I've got an idea." "What?" "You'll see."
@Waynes_world

Who gives better head, men or women? @Nazine_tasty thinks she's better than me. We need a judge. RT

Kevin Hart screamed 'PINEAPPLES' from Nazaria's phone and she picked it up, while looking at Wayne with a raised eyebrow.

"You are SUCH an idiot," she said laughing at her phone. So powerful was her laughter that she dropped her Galaxy Note 3 and watched it bounce on Wayne's hardwood floor. "Alright, cool, I'm in."
@Nazine_tasty

RT Who gives better head, men or women @Nazine_tasty thinks she's better than me. We need a judge. RT

Wayne took the solo chair as his Twitter notification buzzed, while pushing Nazaria's feet as he past her. They grunted at each other and shared a smile .

Nazaria was thinking of the most undesirable, ugliest, most unattractive woman sitting at home alone replying to the tweet.

Wayne was picturing some of the sexiest, faceless, most delicious woman on his timeline replying to his tweet.

One, two, three hours past. Not one reply.

By the fourth hour, on their seventh bottle of wine, nibbles were running low, TV options were becoming more and more limited, Wayne stood up and stretched.

Nazaria was playing with her phone.

"Guess no one on your timeline wants their pussy eaten on a Saturday night."

"I know," Wayne said. "And I was really looking forward to just showing you right up."

"There is nothing you could've shown me that I couldn't have shown you, improved on it and thrown in five or six variations. Madachod!"

"What the fuck ever... all I know is..."

Wayne's phone alert broke his speech and drew both of their eyes. He smiled at his friend, who sat up from her horizontal position and was very interested in what his phone had to reveal.

Unlocking his phone swiftly, he had a direct message from one of his new followers.

@some_more_ah

You need a judge, I've got pussy that hasn't been eaten for ages. I'm involved.

The smile forming on Wayne's face was sneaky, sprinkled with conniving and troublesome and Nazaria caught it as he passed his phone to her.

She smiled the same smile.

Clicking on her profile and enlarging her picture, Nazaria nodded approvingly to herself.

In the picture, a short dark caramel woman sat on the illuminated stairs outside Stratford station in a pair of Timberland boots, leggings and a waist-length bomber jacket with a fur hood and a smile.

"Who's that?"

"Her name's Samara. She's someone I started following recently. I haven't spoken to her really, but she retweets my nasty shit."

"She looks alright STILL!" "Lemme see." Wayne took his phone back and tilted his head at the picture, nodding accordingly.?Nazaria felt her nipples rise as she sipped a Disaranno and ginger beer, no longer interested in what was on TV.

"Where is she?" "Let's find out."

@Waynes_world

Im in Chelsea. A judge has to take an eating and say who has the better technique. If ur up, we're down!

"OoOoOoOoOoOoOoOoOo... you gon' learn today!" Nazaria said, bouncing on the sofa.

"Bitch please... if this chick comes round, watch what happens."

His phone alerted again, this time quicker than before and he jumped.

@some_more_ah

I can be there in 10 mins, I live off Fulham road. Got health test results too.

"Look!"

Wayne threw his phone to Nazaria with a huge smile on his face. She caught it and read the message.

"Oh shit, so you're really gonna lose tonight?" she said.

"Look, I know it's been a while since I went down on you..."

"You are such a Pikina! If we're gonna talk about it, let's be real. Your head was alright but that's about it. Nothing special or exciting, just alright head."

"You weren't 'alright' when I making you cum..."

"You never got multiples out of me," Nazaria said, bouncing her leg on the sofa. "It WAS good... but you ain't got shit on me. I'm a woman for fuck sake. You could learn all you want from whoever you want, you still won't..."

Wayne gestured for his phone. "I see your mouth moving but all I hear is blah blah blaaaaaah. IF she comes, then we'll see innit?!"

@Waynes_world?18 Brown apartments, Kings road. See you soon.

As Nazaria tied her hair with a hair-band, Wayne sent the message and started flicking through TV channels, anticipation making him fidgety.

He jumped out of his seat and rushed to the kitchen and appeared in the doorway with a bottle of Ciroc blueberry, taking a sip straight from the bottle.

He didn't need the dutch courage but it was slowly dawning on him what he was about to get himself into. It wasn't the challenge that was worrying him or the idea of eating the pussy of someone he didn't know. It was the thought of losing to Nazaria that was warming his stomach.

That and the Ciroc shot.

@some_more_ah See you soon.

"She's on her way."

"Sweeeeeeet," Nazaria said, stretching her arms and legs. "Lemme see her picture again."

7

"No. You've seen her once, you'll see her when she gets here."

"Why you being a Pikina for? If I'm gonna be eating her out, I'd like to see what she looks like."

"But you saw her though," Wayne giggled looking at her picture again. "I saw from the way you looked at her picture, you wanna do it. So, just get ya game ready, yeah?"

Nazaria yawned. "I'm always ready."

Continually flicking through Saturday night TV, stopping on The Blues Brothers, Wayne was getting more and more anxious. Besides the fact that he was in competition with his good friend in the pussy eating stakes, he had also given out his address to a complete stranger.

Initially he got caught up in the challenge of having his head game questioned but now, with his address out there and a mystery follower about to descend upon his private space, he did not feel so comfortable as he did when the idea came to him in the toilet.

Fiddling with the Ciroc bottle, reading the ingredients and spiel on the side, Wayne sighed and felt his breath quiver.

Nazaria caught his shaky sigh. "You sound nervous there Waynage."

"Whatever Asian Rapunzel."

She chuckled. "Tut tut tut. That sounds like definite fear in your voice."

That was when his buzzer made him jump in his seat, spilling Ciroc on the floor.

He knew Nazaria was watching him and met her eyes while giving her the finger as he got up.

"Hello?" he said skipping to his intercom, nerves ripping through him.

"Ya judge is here."

He turned to Nazaria, who was sitting up, wiping crumbs from her vest, downing her drink while sliding in her socks to the kitchen for a top up.

He pressed the entry button and opened his front door a crack.

"Last chance to back out and save yaself the..."

"Let ya mouth do the talking" she shouted from the kitchen.

Standing in front of the TV, changing the channel to something random on BET, Wayne scanned his flat, picking empty alcohol bottles and straightening cushions as he went.

He scooped his Ciroc and poured a double in a glass with two cubes of ice while Nazaria fell into his sofa with one leg folded under her and a fresh drink.

They looked at each other, then at the door.

There was a lot of brave talk between them during the set-up of the contest but now their judge was making her way up the stairs of his apartment block, nerves were setting in on both sides.

Nazaria adjusted her position, trying to achieve the sexiest first impression while Wayne was swirling the ice in his glass sitting back in his comfy chair.

He recognised the creaking sound of the door from the stairs opening, which means someone was on his floor, walking in heels.

"If she doesn't look like her profile picture, the challenge is off, deal?"

"Deal!" Nazaria agreed.

The sound of heels got closer to his door and his heart beat faster while his thoughts ran wilder.

Each step closer got slower and slower to the open door and the two friends, who were buzzing, sat forward in their seats.

Nazaria wanted to see what her shoes looked like, how sexy her legs were, how pretty her lips were while Wayne wanted to see if her breasts were as shapely in person as they were in her picture.

Samara knocked on the door and it creaked open, still giving Wayne and Nazaria nothing to look at.

"Come in," Wayne shouted to the door.

White-tipped fingernails appeared on the door and pushed it open.

The pair of them watched as Samara filled the door with her slender frame. Covered in an ankle-length faux fur coat over a Rihanna t-shirt, stretch jeans and heels, Samara locked eyes with Nazaria first before looking to Wayne with a smile. She dropped her hood and revealed a bald fade with sharp edges and Nazaria sucked in a deep breath.

"Samara?" Wayne said, standing up to greet her.

"If I'm not then you should be worried," she said, closing the door behind her. "Wayne's world right?"

9

"That's me. Well just Wayne and the heap on the sofa is Nazaria."

Jumping up from the sofa, Nazaria stood up, while breathing in and moved towards Samara with her hand outstretched.

They shook hands with both off their fingers stroking the other and their eyes smiling.

"Ignore him, he's just... nervous." "Shut ya face Naz. Do I look nervous?" "You don't look ready." "I bet I'm more ready than you are." "ANYWAY," Nazaria said, turning back to Samara, who was still holding her hand. "Come in, lemme take your coat."

"Thank you," Samara said, laughing at the bickering pair.

She shook out of her jacket, turning as she went, giving the pair a full look at her slim yet shapely figure.

Wayne squinted with a smirk while Nazaria kept her eyes locked. She took Samara's jacket and handed it to Wayne who tried to act offended.

"Go on Geoffrey, fuck off... would you like a drink babe?"

"Yes PUHLEEZE, I'm definitely gonna need one of those."

Wayne walked off to his bedroom while Nazaria took Samara to the kitchen, with her heels clopping on floor in a perfect sound.

"Okay, I can offer you Ciroc... actually, no, Wayne had his mouth on that. There's Alize, wine, red wine, beer, Hennessey..."

"Hennessey all day." "Good choice." Wayne came back from the bedroom, swirling his drink in his glass, trying to look as cool as possible as the girls walked back into the living room. Nazaria walked behind Samara, looking her up and down and biting her fist.

"So, you only live up the road?" Wayne asked, taking a long sip of his drink.

Samara turned to him. "Yeah, didn't take me long to get here. I actually go shopping up the road from where you live. There's a brilliant shoe shop down the road that sells amazing shoes."

While her attention was on Wayne, Nazaria was still drinking in Samara's shape. She looked her up and down from the smoothness of her hair, down the back of her neck, over her petite backside, descending her long legs and finishing at her cute peep-toe heels.

The more she looked, the more excited she felt about the competition.

She handed Samara her drink with a smile.

"Thank you." Samara said, running a free hand over her head. "So... how'd you two wanna do this?"

Nazaria was mid-sip when she choked and Wayne was swallowing a finishing sip when he felt alcohol burning the back of his nose as he coughed.

"Erm..." he managed. "We... can... erm..."

"Okay, YOU figure out how to talk, and I'll talk to Naz 'cuz she seems like she's more ready than you are. So how we doing this Naz?"

Continually clearing her throat, Naz took another sip while laughing hysterically.

"Okay, seems like its up to the women to handle this. Let's go."

"Alrighty, here's how this is gonna go. Wayne, your spare room is the venue."

Draping her arm on the sofa behind Samara's head, Nazaria looked at both of them as the alcohol in her system helped her find some clarity for the competition.

Wayne felt his dick filling up as he watched the two women sitting so close to each other. His mind removed their clothes and had them naked, on his sofa, in between each other's thighs rubbing their clits together in a hard grinding session.

He wasn't sure how long he was lost in the fantasy before Nazaria started talking again.

"We both get 10 minutes each to do our... thing, we get judged on four categories. Final score out of ten and the judge's ruling is final."

The more she spoke, the more Samara smiled and the more nervous Wayne felt.

"What four categories?" Wayne enquired, feeling his original idea being taken away from him.

"Yeah, what four?" Samara asked.

"First category is skill. Your head game skills. Second is visuals. How GOOD you make the head look. Thirdly, handiwork. How much you can make Samara's hands

11

move, grip, grab and caress. You know like the back of your head. Or a gripping of the sheets, etc."

Samara sighed heavily as she sipped her drink while seductively looking at Wayne, who had goosebumps rising on the back of his neck.

"And four and the tastiest category is orgasms. How many times can you make her cum in ten minutes, if you can make her cum at all!"

Wayne frowned. "Oh whatever..."

"Well I'm FULLY involved." Samara said, downing her wine. She stood up and circled her neck. "Can I have a top up please?"

"Sure, drinks are in..."

Samara was gone before Wayne could finish speaking, leaving the two challenging friends looking at each other with wide eyes and O-shaped mouths which said they were both involved in the challenge ahead.

They both watched her leave the room, working her heels and her walk accordingly with a swish and a swash of her hips.

"Okay, so four categories, judged out of ten? Ten minutes per head..." Samara said from the kitchen.

"Yep," Nazaria replied, feeling her nipples rise.

Below his waistline, Wayne could feel his dick getting harder in anticipation.

Samara walked into the doorway of the kitchen with a short glass of liquid in her hand and her t-shirt slung over he shoulder.

"Okay, two questions then."

Nazaria and Wayne looked at each other with their eyebrows up. He reacted first.

"Shoot."

"Okay," Samara said, taking a sip. "Firstly, which way to the spare room and secondly, which one of you is first?"

Nazaria looked to Wayne who looked back at her and they both looked at Samara.

"It's down the hall, second door on your right."

"Okay, gimme five minutes to take these jeans off. I've gotta literally peel em off. Then I'll take the first contestant."

Samara took a long sip of her drink and walked out of his lounge, leaving both of them watching her walk away.

"Dayuuuuum... I am gonna have fun making HER cum." Wayne said, feeling his entire body warm up.

"Yeah, I don't see that happening benchod. Your tongue's not long enough. Now mine on the contrary..."

Nazaria stuck her tongue out before finishing her drink and sliding to the kitchen for another.

Wayne reached into his pocket. "Fuck it, flip a coin." "Wait, wait, wait, wait... I don't trust you." She slid back into the room with a short glass of

Hennessey and cranberry.?" Ready for the first contestant." Samara said from

his spare room.?" Call it in the air." He flipped the coin into the air. "Tails never fails."

Wayne

Walking away from Nazaria, who was huffing and puffing as she fell into the sofa, reaching for his Sky Plus remote, Wayne pimp walked out of the lounge and made his way to his spare room.

Turning the corner, he slow walked to the door as nerves made his hands shake. He had the big talk in front of Nazaria, but now he was on his own, things were different.

There was a woman lying in his spare bed, naked and waiting for him to eat her pussy for ten minutes. A woman he didn't know, a woman he never met before. A woman who he had no time to chat up and learn about what she liked and didn't like.

All these thoughts were running through his head with each step he took towards the door.

"Man up bro!" he said to himself.

He knocked on the door, looking at his feet, sipping a looooong sip of his drink.

"Enter!"

He opened the door slowly and carefully, not sure what he would see when the bed came into view.

Samara was under the covers with the duvet pulled up to her neck with not an inch of skin showing. He laughed in his mind because she looked like just a head.

He smiled, closed the door and stood there with his drink in his hand, staring at the head in his bed.

"And your time starts... NOW!"

He heard a muffled beep from under the covers and imagined a clock counting down.

"Oh, you're REALLY timing me?"

"Yessur. I'm taking my judging seriously. I've helped you a lil' bit by playing with my clit, but the rest is up to you."

She removed the covers with one swoop of her hand and it fell aside, revealing her chocolate naked body.

However Wayne thought she would look in his mind's eye was nothing compared to how she actually looked. Her skin was a creamier flavour of chocolate than his mind could create, her nipples were more erect and her groin was draped in a low bald fade of hair.

With on leg bent and one straight, she spread her thighs to him and smiled as she sipped her drink and

returned it to the night-stand next to the bed where her health results were laid out on display.

She looked at her phone next to her drink then back to him.

"Have you never seen a naked woman before? You're going on like it's your first time. All this looky looky and you've wasted a good 30 seconds. Better get to work."

Wayne pushed himself off the door and moved towards the bed.

She giggled a tipsy giggle while Wayne nervously laughed, put his drink down and took his t-shirt off.

"I'm kool and the gang, just working on a mental plan of attack."

"Less planning, more doing." Samara said, pointing between her thighs.

Through the walls, he could hear the Match of the Day theme music playing on his TV, but he wasn't distracted.

He had a job to do and, according to her phone, he had just under eight minutes to do it.

"Let's see what you got Wayne's world."

Sliding onto his stomach, trying to appear smooth and sensual while looking into her eyes, Wayne's first contact with her thighs made his dick jump in his boxers.

She looked down at him as he got into position between her thighs and she grinned nervously at him.

"Ready?"

"You've taken over a minute to get from the door to my pussy."

"Oh fuck..."

He watched her pussy lips move in front of him as he licked his lips and swallowed saliva that was building in his mouth. A warm scent of pussy and aloe vera wafted in front of him and he touched her pussy for the first time by parting her lips.

Wayne saw that she wasn't lying when she said she had pre-moistened for his arrival as strings of liquid stretched between her lips. He ran two fingers between her lips, clearing an unobstructed path for his mouth.

Samara checked her phone again before looking down at Wayne.

He puckered his lips and gave her clit a single kiss, looking for a reaction from her. He was hoping for a sigh, a sound, a movement from her pussy, something.

He got nothing.

Moving in for a second kiss, he stuck his tongue out and poked her clit, followed by a slow lick up and an even slower one down. With his eyes still locked on her, he waited for a reaction and she sucked in a tiny bit of air through her teeth, followed by a melodic hum.

Bringing his lips directly onto her clit, Wayne closed his eyes and gave her clit a full-on kiss, which she enjoyed by arching wining her waist.

Confidence was rising from a trickle to a full flow inside as he took a strong grip of her thighs, forced them further apart and licked from her clit down to her vaginal opening.

Samara whistled once, took a deep breath then whistled again.

Up and down he licked swiftly with her thighs in his hands, watching for secretions.

"You got six minutes left down there," Samara said, with a degree of complete normality in her voice.

Wayne felt the pressure of time on his shoulders. He suddenly realised that he spent way too much time trying to be slick instead of putting his skills to good use. And now he had just over five minutes to show what he could do.

In his head he was screaming 'fuck fuck fuck fuck'.

He took a deep breath in, held it then exhaled as he stuck his tongue out and slid it inside her slowly, keeping his eyes on her.

Samara didn't react to his tongue, but her eyes widened.

She reached down to her nipples and give her left one a strong squeeze, while massaging her right one.

Wayne's eyes smiled as he watched her turn her head to the side, moving her hips closer to his open mouth.

Feeling a wave of moisture on his tongue, Wayne extended his tongue and swirled it inside her, using a wet finger to circle on her clit at the same time.

Her arms began to move from her breasts to her head, with her fingers massaging her scalp. Her stomach tensed and Wayne could feel her pussy walls tensing on his tongue.

She reached for her phone to check the time before showing Wayne two fingers.

He nodded, still with his tongue inside her and could feel his jaw starting to ache. Just as he was about to take a break and switch up his style, Samara reached down and grabbed the back of his head with both hands.

Tallying points in his head, Wayne figured that although he had a slow start, he could rack up his best points in the last few minutes.

With jaw ache pushed to the back of his mind, Wayne extended his tongue as far as it would go and jerked his head forward and backwards, stabbing the tip against her walls.

Samara moaned for the first time, holding onto the back of Wayne's head. His nose was squashed against her clit and he was inhaling liquid that squeezed out onto his lips.

She looked at him with evil eyes while locking her fingers behind his head, keeping an eye on her phone, which was down to one minute.

"Oh shit... come on Wayne, you can do it, make me cum...

Her breathless encouragement fought off another bout of pain in his jaw and he withdrew his tongue, taking with him a full dose of her flavour into his mouth.

From what she just said, he knew he was in the home stretch of his ten minutes and had to put in a minute of amazing work if he was going to win this competition.

He watched and listened to his tongue slide between her walls, hoping the wetness would make her speed her orgasm along.

Her fingers began to dig into his scalp, a stinging pain rising in the back of his mind but he didn't care. Wayne could see the finish line in front of him as Samara began to ride his face like an ocean wave.

"Oh shi... there... thereeeee... thereeeeeeee... fucking there..."

Wayne watched her thrash from side-to-side, slapping his mattress like she was tapping out of a submission manoeuvre. Keeping his tongue as rigid as possible, Wayne let her ride his face for as long as his jaw could stand. The back of his neck had past the

stage of aching and he began to see stars as her thighs clamped around his head.

"Ten seconds... go, go... goooooo... GOOOO... FUCKING GOOOOOO..."

Wayne couldn't hear her cum but he could feel it in his mouth. The change in flavour and consistency of liquid that coated his tongue told him he managed to pull off an orgasm in the dying seconds.

Samara's thighs slowly released their grip from his head and clear sound returned. He retracted his tongue slowly.

With her chest heaving and his mouth aching beyond belief, he sat up, waiting for her to open her eyes.

"How did I do?" Wayne asked, wiping his mouth with the back of his hand for effect.

Samara opened her eyes, looking for the ceiling to find her equilibrium. She made eye contact with him, smiled then picked up her phone and started pressing buttons and sliding her fingers across.

"Gimme five minutes then could you send in the next contestant please?! Thank you."

Nazaria

Laying on the sofa, with her fingers circling the rim of her umpteenth glass of wine watching a repeat of Friends on Comedy Central, Nazaria was trying to ignore the sounds she was hearing from the corridor and through the walls. With each moan she cringed, each scream she took another sip, each slap of the bed she closed her eyes and shook her head.

Keeping her own time, she counted a silent four minutes before any type of sound action came through the walls.

"Slick Rick spent too much time being slick," she said to herself, wishing she brought her weed from home. That would've mellowed her out and balanced the nerves that were starting to course through her body.

Attempting to mask them with alcohol wasn't working and the distraction of the TV was only making her listen harder for the type of noises Samara was making behind closed doors.

She fought the urge to put her ear to the door and instead filled a large glass with wine and stared at the ceiling waiting her turn.

The sound of the bedroom door opening made her sit up quick, fast and in a hurry. She swung her feet to the floor and watched the lounge door, waiting for it to open.

By the sound of the approaching footsteps, she wasn't sure who would open the door but she knocked back the rest of her wine in anticipation.

The handle creaked, the door slid slowly open and Wayne poked his head around the door with a 'I've- just-handled-my-business' smile.

"Bet you was listening innit?" Wayne asked proudly. "If I was, I didn't hear shit!" she chuckled.?" Oh whatever, you know you heard them points

racking up. I was like Mario in a room full of coins in there."

Nazaria sighed and rolled her eyes. "And THEN you woke up right?"

Walking into the kitchen and pouring himself a drink, Wayne stood in the doorway with cocky dripping off his stance.

"You really think you did something in there don't you?" Nazaria said, joining him in the kitchen.

19

"You heard her, what'd you think?"

"I think this is gonna be an easy win for me. When it comes to head, there is no way a man can beat a woman, I'm TELLING you! You can do any trick you want, use your mouth in any way you want to, but, at the end of the day, a woman gets a woman in a way a man never will!"

Wayne took a deep sip of a double shot of Hennessey, looked Nazaria in the eyes and winked.

"Fuck all that, I ate that pussy like a champ!"

Breaking the tension was Nazaria's phone which told her she had a message. She took her phone from her bra and saw she had a tweet waiting.

@some_more_ah?@Nazine_tasty I'm ready when you are...

"ANYWAY... I've got business to take care of. Make sure you pay attention, 'cuz school is about to be in session."

Nazaria walked towards the lounge door, before succumbing to a drunken stumble.

"If you make it. Don't throw up." Wayne laughed.

"What the fuck ever bhosad pappu... just trying to throw me off my game..." she said followed by a hiccup.

In her stomach, a long croak groaned. She rubbed her midsection before opening the door.

"Good luck." Wayne offered full of sarcasm.

She gave him the finger then made her way to the corridor, lit by a closed door with light surrounding the frame.

With two fresh drinks, and her steps more than tipsy, Nazaria walked with her nipples hard and her nerves on high alert.

The door handle to the bedroom creaked as she wasted no time and walked into the room and stood for a moment.

Samara lay on the bed, with the duvet still on the floor, her knees up and leaning to the right, playing with her phone. She looked up and they smiled at the same time.

"Heeeeeeeeeeey," Samara said. "Welcome."

"Why thank you. So..." Nazaria took a sip from one glass and gave her the other. "You ready?"

Samara took the drink "OoOoOoOoOo... a ready and willing contestant? I like I like..."

"I'm looking to win the car and the holiday right now!"

"That's what I'm talking about. Alright... let's do this."

Taking a strong sip from her new drink, Samara put it down and played with her phone while Nazaria took her vest off and was in the process of taking her leggings off.

"Whoa... wait... why are you?" "If I'm gonna be eating pussy, I'm gonna be comfy." Stripped down to her bra, panties and socks, Nazaria

approached the bed confidently, never taking her eyes off the naked woman laying down.

"Up you get," she said, offering her hand.

Samara looked confused as she grabbed the outstretched hand and was pulled to her feet. Standing naked in front of the Asian woman in her underwear, she inhaled heavily.

"Excuse me," Nazaria said, brushing past her before laying down on the bed.

She got comfortable real quick, adjusting pillows under her head and making sure her body was where she wanted it. Then she looked at Samara again.

"Clock doesn't start until your seated."

The naked woman stood on the bed, with her feet either side of Nazaria's head, looking down at a smiling face.

"You really ARE a willing contestant aren't you?" she said, slowly dropping to her knees.

"I REALLY wanna win!"

Samara reached for her phone and set her timer while walking on her knees until her clit touched Nazaria's bottom lip.

"You ready down there?" "I've BEEN ready!" "And your time starts... NOW!" As she started the timer, she moved her pussy onto

Nazaria's mouth.?Their eyes met and they held the glare as Samara's

clit moved over her mouth and Nazaria's mouth accommodated her.

Before she could move her lips or her tongue, something in Samara's eyes smiled. A tiny squint and a sneer gave her face a delighted tint. Running her

21

hands over her head and stretching her back, she looked to the ceiling as the tongue below began to flick slowly over her clit. With their eyes still beaming at each other, they shared the feeling in their stare.

Instinctively, Samara began to move her hips on the mouth below before any good feeling started.

Reaching for Samara's lower lips, Nazaria parted them, giving her nothing but clit to lick. She started with slow circles, letting her lips rub against her pussy. Before she could start a rhythm and keep it going, Samara's hips started to grind back and forth. She couldn't control the urge to feel herself, as if her skin was on fire and her hands were the cool water to douse the flames.

Staying conscious of the time, Nazaria switched her flow. From slow flicks back and forth to pursed lips and hard quick flicks. During the change, Samara inhaled and shakily exhaled then wolf whistled.

"Okay, okay..." the hip grinding woman said.

"Yompgh likphom thaopgh yegmph?" Nazaria mumbled from below, watching her work take effect.

Samara nodded quickly. Her arms were resting on her head and she closed her eyes tightly, hoping whatever she was feeling would pass quickly. Slowing her movement, she stayed still letting the contestant doing all the work but that was a mistake.

Nazaria hummed, sending vibrations through her tongue. She closed her eyes as a taste of warm juice passed her lips and down her throat.

The pleasure opened one of her eyes, making her watch Samara, who was silent and gritting her teeth. The muscles in her arms flexed, her stomach muscles contracted and her lips began to quiver.

Watching and tasting, Nazaria poked the tip of her tongue and held it there, waiting for Samara to start moving her hips.

She opened both her eyes and looked up as the judge above looked down, knowing what she was expected to do. For a moment of silence they just stared at each other.

"I'm not gonna do it..." Samara said.

Nazaria's response was a strong flick of her tongue, followed by a throaty moan.

"You can't MAKE me do it..."

Another strong flick followed by a feather soft nibble and two more moans.

"Please don't make me do it! Pleaseeeee..."

Making her tongue as rigid as possible, Nazaria squinted up. She could taste new warmth in her mouth, trickling down the inside of her lips, down her throat. Her hands spanked Samara's cheeks and she yelped in between breathless pleas. With each request, asking the mouth to stop doing what it was doing, she thrust her hips forward.

"No no no no... don't... do... that...FUCKKKKK..."

She leaned forward on the headboard, resting her head on her arms, circling her hips in quick circles that felt like necessities to go with the good feeling that was pouring down her body.

Samara yelped again. Then a second time. The third yelp made her slap the wall, which reverberated through the bed frame.

Nazaria knew that Wayne would hear the sound and she smiled as a fresh batch of liquid coated her lips.

Samara looked down and shook her head in disagreement.

With a free arm, Nazaria reached for the phone on the bedside table and saw she had over five minutes left as she looked up and nodded in response, making her rigid tongue slide hard over the clit in her mouth. One stroke too many as sudden jerks and pulses grabbed Samara's body.

She looked down with wide, apologetic eyes as a demonic sound erupted in her throat.

Starting at a low sound, Samara gripped the headboard tight so her fingernails marked the wood. Her stomach tensed and the sound got louder and more evil. Her eyes never left Nazaria who was smiling below.

She watched the thighs either side of her head grip her ears and muffle the sound the lady on her face was continually making.

"DON'T... DON'T... OHHHH... FOR... THE... LOVE... OF... FUCK..."

With her throat open, Nazaria was ready for the crescendo of Samara's orgasm but was still surprised when the first squirt of liquid shot past her lips down her throat. The next stream was longer and more powerful than the first, following her tongue like a yellow brick road to the back of her teeth, with a series of flows exiting her mouth and spraying her face.

23

Swallowing quickly and expecting more, Nazaria felt the headboard rocking above her head thinking it might come flying off. Such was the power of the orgasm taking place in her mouth.

The thighs she was wearing like earmuffs were muffling just how loud Samara was screaming and they also muffled the sound of Wayne opening the bedroom door to watch.

The last squirt made Samara roll off Nazaria's face, fall off the bed and into the foetal position on the floor, where she was trying to breathe, mumbling under her breath.

"Shiiiiit... damnnn... fuuuuuuck..." Samara quivered as her second contestant sat up with liquid dripping off her face. Nazaria grinned at Wayne while rubbing her mouth with the back of her hand.

She smiled at him before wiping her face with his sheets then scooting off the bed to check on the living heap on the floor.

"You alright down there?" "Shhhh... hhh... hhhh..." A puddle formed around her inner thighs on the

hardwood floor as Nazaria got her back on the bed. Wayne kissed his teeth and walked back to the lounge, cursing as he went.

"...some bullshit lesbian business..."

"SoOoOoOoOooorry Wayne..." Samara said, her voice rising and falling with a feeling that showed no signs of stopping inside her.

"Told you, chodhru!" Nazaria shouted after him.

BUTTERFLY THE SHEET FLIPPER – C.L.I.T.S

Contrary to what they thought, Lamar was awake as he was dragged into another room. His nose was set on fire with the smell of delicious food. He wasn't sure what the food was or if any was for him but he was suddenly hungry.

He was plopped in a chair and he could hear chains dragging across the ground towards him

Soft hands attached chains to his wrists and he let his head fall back as if he was still knocked out. Squinting out of one eye, he watched the women walk off to open a metal cabinet and that's when Lamar tried to take off running. Remembering where the door was, he moved in the dark and tried to push the door open but he ran into a wall and fell back as a table of food and cutlery broke his fall.

"Tut tut tut," said a voice in the dark. "Get him up ladies in fact leave him down there."

Lamar's head was pounding and the darkness didn't help his equilibrium. Female voices mumbled around him but he couldn't see anyone talking. He could just hear high heels clopping around him.

"Lights on please ladies." "Do you want us to..." "Nah, he'll be alright."

Tube lights buzzed to life above his head and brought the small room to life. Looking down at his feet, he saw a broken table and what looked like a meal on the floor.

"All you had to do was sit down and you would've gotten fed. I made chicken parmigiana with garlic royal potatoes, salad and there was soufflé. WAS being the operative word."

Lamar stood up, realising for the first time, there were no chains, handcuffs or anything holding him down.

He looked up. "So who are you then?" "Butterfly the Sheet Flipper." Lamar looked himself up and down. "What kind of name is that? "You'll find out.?" What are you here for?" "Same thing as you. To learn." "Learn what?" He was walking around her as she walked around him, never taking

their eyes off each other. He was clocking her clothes, enjoying how much she filled out her spandex catsuit. They circled the mess on the floor, waiting for the other person to do something.

"What IT is," she replied, sneering at the food on the floor.?" What IT is? What is IT?" "I'm sorry. I can't get over what the hell you did to my food. I had a

whole thing planned for you and now you've fucked it all up!" "Oh well, unlike the other bitches I've met tonight, you haven't tied

me up, so I'm gonna get the fuck out of here."

Butterfly looked at him then her food. "Trust me, you aren't going anywhere. God, so unappreciative."

"Excuse me?" Lamar said, looking at the door.?" I said SO UNAPPRECIATIVE!" "Of what?" "Are you gonna try and leave? 'Cuz you're looking at the door like

you wanna make a run for it. Go 'head, give it a try." Butterfly moved out of the way of the door and led an arm out. Lamar wasted no time and hopped over the food on the floor and

began to run to the door. As he got level with Butterfly, he didn't see her feet move towards his. One foot slipped on something and he started to fall.

He hit the floor hard and didn't have time to complain about the pain as Butterfly latched something cold onto his arm. He looked at his wrist but his arm was being pulled behind his back and attached to his other arm.

"There you go! Now lemme see you go somewhere." "For fuck sake... YOU BUNCH OF CUNTS... LET ME GO!!!" "Not with that mouth. You know what I was supposed to be teaching

you Lamar? Appreciation. Appreciation for the little things in your life. Appreciation for the woman in your life. Appreciation in general. What do you appreciate in your life Lamar?"

"I appreciate my boys who are gonna come through here and fuck all of you women up!"

Butterfly frowned. "I really wish you didn't say that." "What the fuck are you gonna do? Huh? Fuck you." She turned him onto his back and started to kneel next to his head. "Right now, do you appreciate your life?" "You can't do shiiiiiiiii..." Butterfly slapped the rest of the word out of his mouth.?" While we have you Lamar, we can do what we want. You can't call

anybody, you can't complain to anybody... you are now our bitch. So you better start learning what we're trying to teach you otherwise this process is gonna take a turn for the worst for you."

"SLAP ME AGAIN BITCH AND I SWEAR I'LL KILL YOU!" "You'll what?" Butterfly stood up. Her eyes were wide and stoic and she now had a

steak knife in her hand.?" What're you gonna do Lamar?" Suddenly, a voice erupted from a speaker system.?" Erm... could I have six C.L.I.T.S to Butterfly's room. Another one

has threatened to kill her again. Quickly please ladies!" Lamar heard the tannoy announcement and he began to feel fear

course through him. Staring up at her with the knife in her hand and a confused look on her face, Lamar could see her twitching.

"Kill who Lamar, huh?" she whispered.

Suddenly, six women barged into the room and surrounded Butterfly while getting in between her and Lamar.

"Nah, don't worry ladies, I just wanna talk to him." Butterfly said as she fought against the women trying to get to Lamar. "Lemme just talk to him. I swear, it'll be the last conversation he ever has!"

One of the women pressed his neck and he fell asleep instantly.

"Are you sure you're sure?" Germain asked, sitting on the bed next to the love of his life.

"Don't look now but your starting to sound a bit pussy-ish." "Well I am what I eat!" "Not yet your not." Adele said, taking her work shirt and trousers off. "So, what are the stakes? What are we playing for? We playing for

pinks?" "Easy Kenickie," she said unclasping her bra. "It's not that serious.

IF you win I'll cook dinner for our parents tomorrow night. And when I say dinner, I mean one of my 'throw down' dinners. But when I win, you'll be cooking dinner for them and you best believe I want all the trimmings. I want full roast veg, roast potatoes in duck fat, one big ol' piece of meat, mac and cheese, stuffing, salad, coleslaw... yeah the whole shebang!"

"And you won't be bitter when you lose right?"

Germain was flexing his wrists and stretching the muscles in his neck while pouting his lips.

"Erm, what are you doing?" Adele asked, standing up to take her knickers off.

"Lip exercises. See, if you weren't blessed with John Major lips, you'd know why you need to do these exercises."

Adele punched him in the arm and grabbed his groin. "A'ight, lets see what John Major can do on this LONG DICK!"

Germain frowned as his mind took him to a place where John Major was on his knees in front of him. Before he could see anything else...

"Ewwwww... why the fuck would you wanna make me see that?! Good luck getting an erection outta that!"

Germain and Adele both looked at his dick. "We'll see," she said.

They both stood in front of each other naked, looking the other up and down with screwed faces and arched eyebrows. She had her hands on top of very curved hips while he folded his arms across his chest.

"Classic rules?" she said.

"Always," he replied, jumping up and down on the spot like he was about to go for a run.

"You sure baby? I mean, we can play COD or Guitar Hero and sort it out that way?

Germain got loud. "FIRST OF ALL, I'm not playing you in COD until I get more time on that game. You've played it a lot more than me and I've barely touched it that's why you keep on beating me. Same with Guitar Hero. Second of all, not sure if it's just me but you sound pretty scared right about now."

"Of who?" Adele laughed, balancing her weight on her thick right leg and flicking her hair with extra diva. "Of YOU? Bitch please!"

"Bitch huh?" Germain began shadow boxing in front of her, bouncing up and down again as if he could hear the Eye Of The Tiger in his head.

"How'd you want it?"

"Botttom all day!" He smacked her on the rear and the sound caught both of them off guard.

"Well then sir. I wish you all the luck in the world and... good eating I guess."

Adele offered a handshake to Germain, who slapped her hand away theatrically. "See you at the finish line chump!"

"You'll see me there alright!"

She held her hand out in the direction of the bed and he climbed on, laying on his back, while keeping his eyes firmly locked on her. He let his head fall back and he was flat and ready.

Adele nodded and climbed on the bed, keeping her own sultry eyes on him. She crawled to his head head and sat back on her knees.

"Last chance baby. FIFA, Pro, Dead or Alive, Marvel vs Capcom..." "I can beat you here. Then I'll can beat you there."
"Alright, your funeral everywhere," Adele mumbled sarcastically.

Her thigh swung over his face and nestled comfortably next to his ear. Thigh meat arched over his face like a bridge of chocolate and Germain got hard instantly.

"Oh, well hello to you to you," Adele said to his dick. "Ready to lose?"

"You must tink say your name is Lethal Lipps..."

Germain wasted no time in slapping both her cheeks, pulled her down onto his face and was engulfed by a delicious mix of sweat, ass and her vagina scent. She held her cheeks open as she sat down on his face.

She looked back as she slowly began to grind on his mouth, making the skin on his forehead push back while he mumble moaned underneath her. He used his hands to keep the weight of her cheeks off his face so he could concentrate on his head game, especially as there were such high stakes.

He wasted no time in extending his tongue fully and sliding it as far as he could inside her. He could feel an ache at the back of his mouth where his tongue was overstretched but it didn't stop him reaching.

Leaning forward, balancing herself on the bed, Adele looked at his erection that was pulsing below her. A single stream of liquid began to leak down his shaft as Adele wrapped a hand around it and jerked it once. His moan from behind told her that he was ready for the competition.

Her mouth lowered while a glob of saliva missed his dick and landed on his stomach. She extended his erection and rubbed it in the mess she made.

"Winner takes all!" she said before plunging her mouth over his dick, making sure the insides of her cheeks didn't touch him.

Germain's hips instantly moved in a circle as he pushed down on Adele's backside, giving him more to eat.

"Shiiiiiiiiiiiiiit... you ain't playing are ya?" Adele moaned with his dick in her mouth.

"Fphtuck no..." he mumbled with his tongue tickling her labia.

Germain had two hands holding her cheeks open, licking from her vaginal opening to her clit and back along the same pink road. He could feel her hips grinding under his grip and enjoyed the ocean wave her body was riding on.

On top, Adele was taking his tongue well and throwing her own mouth moves at him, taking him deep, spitting, gagging and hot-dogging, which he loved more than anything.

"Any woman who can get your dick and your balls in her mouth at the same time is a woman I need to marry," Germain would always say.

She had two hands either side of his legs and was bobbing and weaving like a boxing champion. She heard him slurping beneath her so made her own slurping sounds, which drown him out completely. Both their hips were responding to the good feeling, grinding of their own accord as Germain and Adele moaned in-sync.

His arm wrapped around her waist and tried to push her down further but only succeeded in making her lips slide further down his shaft until his dick disappeared completely.

"Wow, look at me!" Adele said to herself.?In his mind, great head was great head. Nothing in the world wrong

with that at all. Ever. But the curse came through what the good head made him think and feel, which was 'where did she learn these skills?' which was an answer he just didn't want to know.

Adele popped his dick out of her mouth and looked back. He turned and looked up at her.

"You have NO idea how hard it is to hold this back," she said with a heavy sexy sigh.

"Oh, so your ready to buss? Which means I've already won!" "Until you get the orgasm, it doesn't count rookie." "Rookie?"

Germain got his face back into position before sticking his tongue out and up, sliding it between her soaking wet lips. He went further by sucking his index finger and sliding it above where his tongue was raiding, rubbing her asshole in circles. He knew how much such a simple move turned her on as she lifted her mouth off his dick.

"So you wanna cheat now?"

Germain didn't reply, he just kept his finger moving the way it was and his tongue circling. Adele moaned on his testicles as she tried to kiss them seductively but whatever he was doing was messing up her concentration.

"Don't start nothing, won't be nothing. You think I didn't feel the hot dog?"

Germain was in trouble. He knew the truth about what was going to happen but he couldn't let her talk him down. Any challenge between him and Adele had to be met with trash talk and bravado and a 'I'm gonna whup your ass' attitude. Anything less than that wasn't fun and, as a couple, they were all about fun in its many shapes and sizes.

"Oh, very tasty..." Adele said, tasting Germain's pre-cum as he felt it drift up to the head of his dick.

His jaw was getting tired, his tongue ached from being outstretched for so long and his neck hurt from the angle he was staying in. Any concentration he had was seeping away as he tried to keep his mouth game as focussed as it was when he started but he was finding it hard, with Adele's dripping wet mouth making a mockery of his dick.

In his mind, he was thanking God he couldn't see what she was doing or he would've come already.

With each dip of her mouth, Adele's moans got louder and louder which stopped Germain from being able to drift away to his happy place where thoughts of Boris Johnson's knees stopped any orgasmic feelings.

Germain's head dropped back, with his mouth covered in Adele's throbbing pussy. With everything feeling so good, he knew this would be one of those times when Adele would not let him live down the fact that he lost.

"Oh shiiiiiiiiiit," he moaned.

Adele was a shark smelling blood in the ocean and she went in for the kill. He could no longer play with her in any way shape or form.

She opened her mouth and let him fuck her with the helmet of his dick pushing against her soft muscles in her throat.

"Yeah? I knew it..." Adele mumbled, while dipping and rising in front of the growing puddle of saliva at the base of his dick.

"Oh fuck baby," he griped as he slapped her ass, tossing his head from left to right. "Alright, you win, you win... you win!!!"

"Baby, I know I win! I've been winning, I just wanted to make you suffer!"

"You bit..."

Adele shut him up by stroking the underside of his dick with the tip of her tongue which made him squeal like a stuck pig. His hips shot straight into the air, forcing his dick as far into her throat as possible with his hands reaching for her head. With his last thrust, he felt his orgasm rush out of him, which inspired more hip thrusting, more squealing and covering his face while calling for God to help.

"Now what?" Adele said, swallowing and jumping off his face to see the weary shell of Germain with his hands covering his face.

"Seems like you ain't got shit to say now!"

"Look, yeah," he started with a shaky voice. "Just 'cuz you can get a nut, don't make you a squirrel."

"Is that loser talk for you win? 'Cuz you just could've said that instead."

Germain exhaled. "How was I expected to win with those skills?"

"You know what I expect?" Adele said, looking at Germain and smiling while wiping her mouth with the back of her hand. "I expect BBQ chicken, mac and cheese – with two cheeses – I want pasta salad, Jollof rice, Yorkshires, rum punch...

"For fuck sake..." Germain mumbled with Adele still dripping from his lips.

STRANGE MOMENTS AT NECESSARY TIMES

"Fucking wanker... wasting my damn time and all the while he's there with his coughing bitch!"

As you can hear, Bernadine is not in a good mood.

Standing in a lift, watching the numbers count down to the ground floor, in her good heels, she was pissed off.

She was smelling sexy in Coco Chanel and she was feeling sultry in a mesh teddy and seamed stockings under a full-length Burberry mac.

But frown lines in her forehead showed that she was not in a good mood.

By this point in her evening, Bernadine hoped to be bent over and twisted in a position that allowed Byron's dick to reach her the way it did.

But that wasn't going to happen.

Because his wife had been taken to hospital for an "asthma attack", or so he said on the phone when he called.

Bernadine was laying on the queen-sized bed of an executive suite in a Royal London hotel waiting for her lover man when he called with the good news.

She tried to stay calm when she sat up and said "WHAT?!" extremely loud.

She didn't care that she could hear what sounded like an ambulance radio in Byron's background, all she cared about was the fact that she was now dickless for the evening.

For the lengths and the lies Bernadine went to in her own life to make the night happen, disappointment washed over her uncontrollably.

"Of ALL the nights for your wife chooses to have an asthma attack, tonight? REALLY? Look, if you don't wanna..."

"YEAH, WE'RE READY... I have to go. Sorry." Then he hung up. Left Bernadine staring at her phone with her leg folded under her looking and smelling good with no one to see it. She went from staring at her phone to breaking the seals on mini bottles of vodka, brandy and whiskey from the minibar. The thought of going home and getting into bed next to her own husband wasn't one she entertained with pleasurable hope. He was the reason she was here in the first place. Him and his slick ways. Problem was, he didn't realise his wife was slicker and was out with 'friend'" and 'work colleagues' more than he was out with the 'boys'.

With the lift reaching the ground floor, Bernadine ran her hands through her bush of curly natural hair, stole a look at herself in the mirror and greeted herself with anger.

After a long sigh, she raised her head and let the spotlights above bathe her chocolate skin.

"Let's find a real fucking drink shall we?" she said to herself as the doors opened and she moved with a touch of tipsy in her walk.

Straight into the hotel lobby, she followed signs for the bar, while following the sound of a piano playing random jazz favourites she recognised.

Even though her night had been ruined by Byron's asthmatic bed warmer, the music she could hear made her walk work.

The concoction of minature bottles from the mini bar – which were going to cost her – warmed but weren't the burning fire she needed to feel for the evening.

Her ruined evening. She was planning to let Byron go anal as well.

Bernadine pushed through a pair of glass doors and she found the bar.

117

A wide open space of opulent dining tables surrounded by a thick mahogany bar pointing to a stage with a white baby grand piano tinkling love songs.

She wasted no time walking to the virtually empty bar and parking herself on a stool, covering her legs as her mac fell open.

Behind her, the piano player switched to a slow and sexy version of Bess, You Is My Woman Now and Bernadine needed a drink now more than ever.

Her rule with such a beautiful piece of jazz music was: any time that song was playing, she either needed to be fucking or drinking. Right now she was doing neither.

Scanning the long bar for a member of staff, she leaned over looking left and right. That was when her eyes caught a red book sitting under the bar.

It was plain red, A5 with thick letters spelling WORDS on the front.

Her head twisted to get a better look then she reached for it and had it in her lap before anyone could see her.

She took a look around her at the sparsely filled bar then back at the book in her lap.

Bernadine folded her hair behind her ears and cracked the cover and was greeted with a beautifully hand written script that said:

Sometimes words just help express the little things

That was when two barmen and a taller man in a shirt who looked like a manager appeared from either side of the bar.

They walked behind the bar laughing until they saw Bernadine and stopped.

Instantly, the manager pointed for them to stock drinks and collect glasses as he approached with a grin.

"Evening madam, what can I get you?" In her head, she was thinking, 'you don't look like a words man'

She dressed him down with her eyes; slender, caramel shade, early stages of working out.

But he didn't look like someone who would write a book of words with such an interesting first page.

"I need a drink sir. A strong one." "Are we talking strong cocktail or straight to the shots?" "I'm talking strong cocktail AND a straight shot!" Bernadine said, slamming her hand on the bar." It's THAT kinda evening huh?" "It's a strong cocktail and a strong shot kinda evening my man. I don't know what I want, just make them both strong." With a chuckle, he was off getting a glass and mixing drinks and juices.?Her eyes followed the other two barmen; a young mixed race looking guy was collecting glasses from tables with a slouch in his work trousers nodding his head. The other was chocolate, slightly chubby with a cute face who was bent over stocking drinks behind the bar.

"Hmmm... so who's the one with the words?" Bernadine asked herself.

Flipping over the next page, she saw two pages fully covered in random words. Some large, some medium, some small, but they all fit around each other end to end.

Twisting her head to read every word, they were random and strangely connected at the same time.

Whoever wrote this page of random words was doing something without realising it. Maybe they did but she was intrigued.

She flicked to the next page, hoping for more.

A poem stared back at her and she smiled as the manager-looking guy came back with her two drinks.

One of them looked like paradise in blue, red and green with a cherry, a little umbrella and a straw. The other was a shot glass of gold.

"Are you staying at the hotel?" he asked.?" Yeah... why?" Bernadine replied curiously.?" Drinks are on the house then... you look like you could do with a free drink... shhh..." Bernadine winked and gave him a thumbs up as she took three long

sips of each colour in the drink.?She didn't know what they were but she loved each taste individually
and the way they combined together.?The shot could wait, her priority was to find out what was next in the
book of words in her lap.?Keeping eyes on the three barmen, she couldn't notice if any of them
were looking for a missing book.?That just made the book more interesting.

Sometimes I just like to do things

For the sake of doing things?To feel like I'm doing

something?For the life experience of doing

something Real things?Sweet things?Enjoyable

things?Things that come with smiles type things

Sunset things?Beautiful music things?Stolen moment

things?Pretty flowers and things?You and me

things?Forever things?Holding hand things?Cook for

you things?You know, just little things...

Bernadine sighed at the end.
"Hmmm... which one of you could've written that I wonder?" she said to herself.
A second and third read just to be sure the good feeling it rumbled in her stomach wasn't just a glitch in the the matrix. Each time the words hit the same.
Right in the warm part of her stomach.
With her paradise in a glass in her hand, she flicked through page after page of words, some brilliant expressions of life's

little moments, others random rants of sexual frustration and a deeply romantic soul.

By the time she sipped three-quarters of the way through her drink, she'd read every page of words written.

Whoever owned the book, hadn't finished his work. Bernadine was actually disappointed. She was enjoying reading what this creative mind had to offer. It made it more interesting to not know who that mind was. Her fingers ran over the front of the book and she caught herself grinning. With her back straight, she reached for her shot and knocked it back without thinking about it. It tasted like tequila but she wasn't sure because it burnt the shit out of her chest. She held the bar for a few seconds and grimaced as it travelled down to her stomach. Shaking her head wildly, Bernadine let out a long "Wooooooooo..." She caught the eyes of the manager guy and she called him over. "Excuse me sir, what time does the bar close?" He looked at his watch. "About 20 minutes." "Thanks... Oh, and do you have a pen please?" she asked. "Sure."

He handed her a pen and gave her a grin before moving off to serve a customer.

A low groan growled in her stomach as the shot hit home and she frowned then burped.

"Eassssy lady..." Bernadine said to herself.

Gaining some decorum, she sat back in her chair and flicked to the page after the last page of words about the best way to hold a flower.

That one made her back straighten.

On a blank page, she wrote...

Simply believe, I'm a woman in need of a reprieve, come to room 609, see me, then leave...

She looked at it once. Then twice, then a third time. Then she closed the book, took a quick look down the bar and put it back exactly where she found it and was back in her seat sipping her drink like nothing happened.

With her paradise in a glass down to its last drop, she reached for the cherry and chewed it slowly, thinking about what she had just written.

Really she was hoping she would be able to save her evening but the words in that book... the passion behind them... if those words could translate into actions, she could end up with that orgasm she needed.

But the who was bugging her. And sweetly intriguing her at the same time.

What if it didn't belong to any of the staff and was left there by a random drinker?

"Oh shit..." Bernadine said to herself.

Just then, the manager came over. "We're closing now madam. How was the drink?"

"Very nice, thank you... erm..." "Was there something else I could help you with madam?" She stuttered. "No... it's okay. Thanks for the drinks. I needed

them." "No problem... you have a good night." "Thanks... nite."

Bernadine hopped off her seat and held her mac close to her body as she walked past tables and back into the lobby, thinking about nothing but that book.

For the way she wanted her evening to go, she didn't see this coming but the words had her hooked. The way that words can make you physically feel something, that's where Bernadine was.

On the way up to her room, Bernadine looked at herself in the mirror and her smile was definitely tipsy with a touch of slutty.

But that was where she was at that moment. It was 'fuck Byron, I'm gonna get mine!'

The lift opened at her floor and she flowed on her heels to her door, excitement coursing through her veins.

She took one last look at the corridor, thinking whoever wrote those words would be coming up this hallway.

Her keycard gained her access to her room and she opened the door to darkness.

As the door closed behind her, she walked to the bed, making her way to the bedside lamp.

The small lamp gave the room a soft glow, but not enough... just warm.

Taking off her mac, Bernadine stretched her arms to the ceiling and sighed a hopeful sigh.

That was when two arms wrapped around her from behind and not only made her jump but forced her to bend over at the same time.

"OooooOooooh my GOD!" Bernadine screamed.?" Shhhh..." a voice said from behind.?A strong hand held the middle of her back and made her arch her

waist.?She heard a zip come down and a sweet feeling made her roll her

neck in anticipation.?The next sound she heard was a rip and tear of a condom packet. A

few seconds past before she felt the warmth of his thighs press behind her.

"Are you gonna..." Was the last words Bernadine said with any sort of coherency.?The stranger behind her slid through her already wet lips and was all

the way inside her before she could finish her question.?A strong sharp breath sucked into her body and she looked at the

ceiling with her eyes crossed.?Whoever he was slid out slowly and made her feel every inch of him

before he slowly returned.?Her mouth curved to say words but nothing came out as he grabbed

her hips and controlled her movement.?Her first orgasm was quick and over before she knew it.?Her second one that followed instantly after took her by surprise as

he grabbed her hair and pulled it in a ponytail.?That was when her third and fourth hit, shaking into her fifth and

sixth.?Bernadine was barking like a dog and slapping the bed in front of her.?He slowed down to a grounding stroke flow and pulled her to meet

him. Then she heard a SHUUUCK sound behind her.?That was when she felt her mesh teddy rip open down to her hips

and down to the back of her tights.

She wanted to scream as she felt the blade of the knife slowly slide down her skin but only cut the material of her sexy underwear.

Her back was exposed to him and he stabbed his knife into the bed side table before rubbing his hands up and down her back,

Bernadine purred like a cat as he continued stroking inside her while she stared at the knife sticking out of the table.

Feeling the tatters of her underwear sliding down her skin while this complete stranger was fucking her WELL made Bernadine's seventh and eighth orgasms real sweet.

She reached for a pillow and buried her face in it, letting out random sounds, mumbling to herself incoherently.

Her hands reached round and opened her cheeks for him to drive deeper and he did. Then he stayed there.

Bernadine yelped.

She shook silently as her ninth and tenth hit her from her head to her toes.

That was when he put a hand on the back of her neck and pressed her into the bed and whispered in her ear.

"Don't move!"

From the strength he was putting in to the point where she was already ten orgasms in made Bernadine do as she was told.

She felt his fingers massage her neck as his other hand tickled her back from her left shoulder to her right shoulder then down her back.

An interesting feeling of being tickled across her back while dick was so deep inside her at the same time.

It was as if the stranger was writing on her back. She looked back and watched him throw a Sharpie on the bed.

He caught her looking back and made her face forward as she turned his hips in circles. She looked back to her scream pillow and felt him dig deeper inside her, squeezing her cheeks together.

She could hear him grunting behind her and it made her nipples hard as her knees started to buckle for a stomach shaking eleventh orgasm.

The stranger behind her didn't stop for her to enjoy it and kept digging deep inside her as she wanted to tell him to stop just for a second so she could enjoy the orgasm but before she could talk, another one crept up on her and number twelve and thirteen hit her and made her black out just as she felt him slide out then splash on her back, sighing pleasurably.

With her face turned to the side, Bernadine could see through slanted eyes as the stranger walked past the bed, pulled up his trousers and walked to the front door of her suite.

He walked out without looking back, closing the door quietly behind him.

Bernadine heard the door close before she fully blacked out.

Waking up the next morning, Bernadine was face down on a pillow bent over her hotel bed, with her sexy underwear ripped up the middle

and sliding down her shoulders as she stood up, rubbing her hair in confusion.

The book of words flashed in her mind and the night came back to her.

The stranger with the book of words.

Taking off the tatters of her underwear, Bernadine walked to the bathroom, with her thighs contracting in memory of the solid gold pounding she took last night.

She leaned over to run the shower and caught the sight of her back and frowned,

"What the fuck is that? He REALLY did write on me?!"

Turning her back to the mirror, Bernadine read the message backwards, covered in a thick stream of dried semen

Hope you got the release you needed... keep ya pretty fingers out of my shit or next time I won't be so nice!

KWAMÈ SASHAY & MISS D DESTROYER – C.L.I.T.S

"Morning La La... sleep well?" "Why the fuck..." "We don't have much time for that so shhh and let's keep it movnig.

My name is Kwamè Sashay and I'm you're host for the moment..." A woman's hands stretched across his face and left a large strap of

grey duct tape across his mouth. He looked around his surroundings and realised he was sitting in a motorised wheelchair on the welcome mat of Marks and Spencers. His arms were strapped to the arm rests, his legs too and he was suddenly moving.

"Come on, let's go, we haven't got a lot of time," said a woman in a ra-ra skirt and grey wife beater.

The fact most of the lights were out in the numerous aisles scared him that little bit more as he rolled behind a beautiful shape that had his attention.

"Do you go shopping with Keisha?" she asked looking over her shoulder. "I bet you're one of those stand behind her while she shops and just says 'yeah that's nice' so you can get out quick, right?"

Lamar mumbled.

"Yeah, you look like that kind of guy. Me? I like my man to pay attention to me when I'm shopping, especially when it could benefit him later on."

The woman with the amazing walk was pressing a remote control that was making Lamar's wheelchair move behind her.

Out of the corner of his eye, he thought he saw a figure walking down a different aisle. By the time he turned his head, he saw no one.

"OoOoOooo... these are nice," Kwamè said, stopping in the underwear aisle and looking at a matching pink polka dot bra and panties set. "Anyway, what kind of underwear does Keisha like? Frenchies, thongs, boy cut, boxers?"

Lamar mumbled and shrugged.?" Oh Lamar, tut tut tut." Something moved in his peripheral vision and he turned his head with his heart beating ridiculously fast. Again nothing.?" Focus Lamar." Kwamè said.?Lamar turned back to watch her stepping into a pair of polka dots panties and lifting her skirt up her thigh. "What'd you think?" He nodded as she took the tape off his mouth and he flexed his lips. "Yeah, those are niiiice." "I like 'em. I might keep these actually." "Excuse me, when can I go home?" "When we're done with you!?" "The fuck do you mean 'when you're done with me'?" "HEY SASHAY, what'd think about this bra?" said another voice from somewhere behind him.?She looked over his head. "Damn... your titties have never looked more tasty...if only you could turn your head."

Lamar tried to flex his muscles and strong his way out of the wheelchair. His neck muscles flexed and veins popped up from his shoulders, arms and his chest but he didn't move.

"YOU FUCKING BITCHES LET ME THE FUCK OUT OF HERE!"

As his voice fell silent, he could hear and feel footsteps running up behind him. Kwamè looked over his shoulder and was watching as Miss D Destroyer slid around Lamar's shoulder and knelt in front of him.

"I don't like you Lamar. You remind me of my ex-boyfriend and he was a real prick. I mean a real deal Holyfield prick. Like, I wanted to kill him with a thousand cuts. And you look like him too. He never wanted to do anything with me. Shopping, walks in the park, taking me out for drinks, dinner, flowers, none of that. He just wanted to fuck! That used to make me feel like a piece of meat, like he didn't love me, he just loved my pussy. Do you make Keisha feel like that?"

Lamar was staring at her chest that was jiggling in front of him.

"See?" Kwamè said. "The lesson you're supposed to be learning is focus Lamar. When you go shopping with your girl, do you look at other women? No, does she CATCH you looking at other women?"

"I'm not saying shit... if you like your life then you best let me go or help me get out of here or its night night bitches!"

Miss D frowned and stood up. Kwamè screwed up her lips and they stood next to each other looking Lamar up and down.

"He looks your ex a lot," Kwamè mumbled with a hand over her mouth. "Oh shit... whoa, hold on, did he just call us bitches?"

"Yes he did," Miss D said putting on a tight t-shirt from a rail close to her.

"Flip a coin?" "That's how we always do it." Kwamè pulled a £2 coin from beneath her ra-ra skirt." Heads I win, tails you lose?" "You fool. Tails never fails." "If you're flipping coins to see which one of you is gonna suck my

dick, no flip needed. I got nuts for both of you." The women looked at him with disgust.?" Or how 'bout I cum on YOUR face and you share it with her?" he

added.?The look of disgust turned into revolt.?" Fuck the coin?" Kwamè said with anger across her brow.?" Oh definitely fuck the coin!" Miss D replied. "Fuck the button too." "Huh? Lamar added.?Kwamè grinned at her counterpart. "Well, I tried with this one, you

tried with this one. I'm done. You done?" "Yep." Miss D replied happily.?" Ready to pass him on?" "Yep."

Miss D Destroyer walked around behind him where he couldn't see her while Kwamè knelt in front of him.

"It doesn't pay to be a prick. You best learn suttin' and FAST!"

Suddenly an arm slid around his neck, applying pressure to his throat. He tried to fight by turning his head but, with his hands tied down, he had nowhere to go except sleep.

GAMES BENEATH THE SURFACE

"What do you want from me?"

"I want you to be a man for me. I want you to get pissed off when you see another man talking to me, well not pissed off but it'd be nice to know you feel something."

Standing on the underground platform of London Bridge's Jubilee Line, Joshua and Carmen walked the length of the platform having a very loud conversation. In his black tuxedo with bow tie and suspenders, he was trying to keep his voice down and avoid the random stares he was getting from people they passed on the platform. Carmen, in a floor length Alessandra Rich Leopard lace gown with silk shawl draped across her shoulders, had champagne bubbles in her head and was thinking her outside voice was actually her inside voice.

"There's nothing wrong with who I am, and keep your voice down!" he whispered.

"My voice IS down," Carmen said, with a diva sway and a swing of her arm, just missing his face.

The sound of her voice was beginning to annoy him just as much as the subject matter that sprung up randomly.

"If you saw me rubbing up against another man, what would you do?"

"What would you want me to do?"

"Wouldn't it make you feel a little jealous? Like a little smidgen of a teeny tiny bit? What if I grabbed this guy and..."

Carmen put her arm around a man on the platform on her right and pulled him along with her as she continued.

"...told him that I wanted him to fuck me and I wanted you to watch, what would you say to that?"

Joshua frowned. First at Carmen, then at the man, who was smiling in the conversation. A strong squint from Joshua and Carmen let the man go, who was smiling to himself as they kept on walking to the top of the platform.

"I don't care how much you've had to drink tonight, that was uncalled for. Just because I don't get all sensitive and insecure about myself if you feel you wanna flirt with other men, doesn't mean I'm not a man."

Carmen mumbled, "Marcus used to get jeal..."

"You HAD to mention his fucking name didn't you?" Joshua exploded, drawing eyes from everyone on the platform, which was filling with late night travellers.

"I'm just saying..."

"Fuck you Carmen," was the last thing Joshua said as he looked forward and walked at a slower pace.

"First of all, you can fuck me any time you like, we're married. Second of all, I didn't mean to piss you off, I'm just saying... he used to get really upset when other men even got near me and that used to

make me feel wanted. Made me feel protected. Yeah, it's kinda caveman-ish but I liked it."

"Well then maybe you should've married Marcus then!"
"Maybe I should've." Silence hung between them after those last words until the train

pulled into the platform, rousing everyone to gather around the doors, ready to pile in. Joshua stood to one side of a set of double doors and Carmen stood on the other, stealing evil looks at each other between the heave of people who got off the train.

With the last person off, Joshua and Carmen walked on first and went in different directions of the carriage. Joshua tried to scoot and pass through a packed train to make it to the window at the end of the carriage. He needed the air after hearing his wife say what she just said. Carmen didn't look back as she found a space for her slender shape next to a pole, in between two guys who were off in separate conversations. At that moment, she didn't care where her husband was, she was frustrated. She couldn't understand why he didn't get what she was trying to say, which was making perfect sense in her head. She wanted him to make more of an effort to be with her, not just become lazy at the fact that he already had her. Flowers every once in a while, breakfast in bed or dinner after work, dates and random nights out, the little things. According to her aunts, she was still in the honeymoon phase, yet she felt like she was verging towards resentment and separation.

On the other side of the carriage, Joshua got the window down and enjoyed the air on the back of his neck as the train left the platform and gathered speed. With his eyes closed and a heavy sigh leaving his body, he put his hands in his pocket and rocked with the rhythm of the train. Carmen's last words were rolling around his brain, stopping at the lanes of thought he already had about the fact that he could feel his wife pining for something she didn't have. He didn't think it was Marcus, the last love of her life, but he always had his feelings about the guy and that just confirmed it.

Joshua did love his wife and he was glad to wake up everyday knowing he was married to her but he wasn't going to be forced to be something he wasn't and that's what he felt Carmen was trying to do to. Build a carbon copy of her ex using the shell of her present. And that pissed him off because Carmen was doing it without even realising. Buying Joshua a bottle of David Beckham aftershave for his birthday, not remembering she told him that it was Marcus' favourite, suggesting trips she had taken with Marcus, Marcus, Marcus, Marcus.

The name clattered in his mind like the sound of the tracks beneath him and Joshua opened his eyes, cutting through the crowd and catching Carmen starring at him. Her face was stone cold, eyes baring down on him like a weight on his shoulders. He returned the stare with no emotion on his face.

This was not the way he saw his evening ending.

He thought a night out at a casino, followed by dinner and dancing would be a nice change and, hopefully end in some sex.

Apparently not tonight.

The train rocked from side-to-side and made Carmen lean her weight onto the chest of the man in front of her. From his view, Joshua could see the tall man's eyes twinkle as he put his arm around Carmen to keep her balance. He watched Carmen laugh at herself and engage the man in conversation that continued past the point of embarrassed small talk. Every now and then, Carmen would look at Joshua, just to make sure he was looking.

She was looking for a response. A squint of anger, a grimace of being uncomfortable, some kind of sign but all she got was the same dead eyes she gave to him when not talking to the thick chested man with the overpowering stench of alcohol emanating from his skin.

Joshua thrust his hands into his pockets and huffed, more annoyed at the blatant attempt by Carmen to irritate him. The most she got out of him was the need to jingle the change in his pockets.

After a few rolls with the coins sliding in and out of his fingers, something brushed past his finger in his left pocket and he frowned.

"What the hell is... OH YEAH!!!" Joshua said to himself, laughing at the black plastic he held in the palm of his hand. "How could I forget about this?"

He looked up at Carmen, who'd managed to engage the man in front and behind her. With her arm holding the rail above her head, she rocked with the train, pushing and pulling her body into the space in front and behind her.

"Alright then," Joshua said. "You wanna play games tonight do you? Alright let's play."

Wrapping his hand around the little black plastic box, Joshua dropped his hand by his side, out of the view of anyone around him. Just then, the train slowed to a halt and the driver's voice came through the PA system.

"Sorry about the delay folks, we've got a train at the station ahead of us so as soon as it's gone, we'll be on the move again. Shouldn't be a few minutes."

Still grinning to himself, Joshua watched his wife openly flirting with two men in front of him through a carriage full of people pressed against each other.

Carmen was continually looking back at him, making sure her flirt level was fully turned up.

He smirked at her, nodding slowly and raising his lips while rubbing the little black box between his fingers, waiting for the right moment. And then it came.

Carmen let out a raucous laugh that caught everyone's attention as she slapped one of the men on the chest. Joshua turned the box in his fingers and then pressed the one red button.

From where he was standing, he watched Carmen's eyes cut through the carriage directly at him. Their eyes spoke to each other.

'You forgot about the balls didn't you?' 'Don't!'?'I forgot about them too until just now.' 'J, dont!'

'Don't what? This?'

Joshua pressed the button again and watched Carmen bring a hand across her chest, trying to hold an air of demure about the fact that she had two vibrating balls in her vagina.

She looked at him again with a more serious look on her face.

'Joshua... I'm TELLING you, don't!' her eyes screamed.?'This is what you wanted. You wanted me to react so I'm reacting.' 'Joshua!'

He pressed the button again and Carmen closed her eyes and inhaled a deep breath, throwing a laugh into the conversation that was happening around her. Joshua leaned off the door so he cold get a better view to watch Carmen suffer.

He pressed the button again for longer and Carmen leaned forward with her eyes closed, resting on the back of the man behind her. In front of her, the man with the brick wall of a chest asked if she was okay but she waved her hand and he watched her lips.

"Period pains." Joshua grinned harder, letting out a little chuckle.?Carmen had her eyes shut tight as the vibrations seemed to ripple

throughout her whole body. She forgot she put them in and gave Joshua the control and, with the argument they were having, the jiggle balls went right out of her mind.

Joshua pressed the button again and Carmen tensed up and cringed while moaning, making it appear like cramps were getting the better of her. The man in front turned and got someone to stand up and offer her a seat, which she took and fell into her seat, making sure she could still lock eyes on Joshua.

'Don't do this. Not here!'?'Why not here? Why not now?'?'Please... don't!'?'You wanted me to react. This is my reaction.'

He pressed the button three times in quick succession, watching his wife curl up in her seat, making those around her give her space. The
men she was talking to were watching with the other people in the packed carriage. Women who recognised the symptoms tried to offer comfort to Carmen, offering her water but she turned them all down, wiggling in her seat.

Another four pulses and Carmen had her first orgasm, which she let out in a long moan which trailed out into "OH FOR FUCK SAKE!"

Carmen's voice travelled over the different conversations of the carriage and drew all eyes in her direction. Joshua was already watching and felt his dick start to rise as Carmen took a long breath, leaning her head to look at him and the smile on his face.

She shook her head but the evil that spread across his lips told her to prepare for the worst as he pressed the button for five seconds, stopped for two, then went on for another ten.

Carmen rocked back and forth, holding her stomach when really, she wanted to put two fingers on her clitoris and grind her orgasm out the right way. But she'd now created a wide berth around her, with a free seat next to her because the old man next to her felt so uncomfortable, he got up and moved.

In his mind, Joshua was jumping up and down, throwing his arms all over the place and shouting at the top of his lungs. In reality, he was rubbing the black box against his dick, waiting for Carmen to reach a level of calm before hitting her again.

She caught a breath before he hit the button for 20 seconds, while making his way through the ogling crowd towards her. He could hear her sucking air through her teeth, snapping her fingers and nervously tapping her heels on the floor.

By 50 yards, he hit her with three short bursts and she screamed out again.

She squinted and reached out for him as he slid into the seat next to her. She hid her face in his neck while he put his free arm around her shoulders.

"Baby... you made me cum on the Jubilee Line," Carmen whispered. "Made? Made means I'm done. I'm not done." "Baby don't..."

The train began to move and Joshua took his jacket off and draped it over the front of Carmen's thighs then pressed the button in his pocket, holding her shoulders strongly. He could hear her moaning in his neck as her body heaved as if she was in a deep sleep. Her thighs clamped together and she put a hand on his neck and gripped on, knowing another orgasm was closer than the next station.

"Baby... stop... please..." Carmen whispered, her body moving more than a little bit.

"Not until... well you know..." "HERE?" "And now!"

Carmen closing her thighs only made the vibrations rumble deeper between her walls. Her nipples were pressing against her strapless bra and she wanted to scream out a bowlful of obscenities and blasphemies. Joshua began to stroke her hair, feeling the vibrations travel between her leg to his. He wasn't sure if anyone else could hear it but, to him, it sounded and felt pretty loud.

Carmen didn't stop grinding her hips against the seat as Joshua kept his finger on the button. Her breathing quickened and her fingers began to dig into his neck. The pain registered quickly but he didn't take his finger off the button. He knew the more pain he endured, the closer she was to squirting. And that's what he wanted.

"The next stop is Bermondsey."

A deep sting ran up the back of his neck and Carmen tensed up and hunched her shoulders while holding onto Joshua for dear life. She was breathing like she was about to give birth and people were giving her side stares.

Enjoying the look on peoples faces, Joshua kept his finger on the button while stroking Carmen's neck and she groaned in his neck. He watched a couple sitting across from him look up at Carmen's growl then look away instantly.

"No... no... no..." Carmen said angrily. She raised one of her legs and rested it on Joshua's thigh but that didn't help as she lifted her hips off the seat and stayed there as the train pulled into Bermondsey station. She sat down but raised her hips again as the orgasm began and the first squirt squeezed through her thighs. The second dripped down between her cheeks. The third began to create a wet patch under her and she exhaled loudly.

Joshua didn't feel the fourth, fifth, sixth and seventh. He was too interested in the droplets of liquid he could see running down the back of her calves and making dark streaks down her dress.

Her nails dug fully into his neck but he politely grimaced through it as the doors opened and people started to get off.

"We need to get off this train babe," Carmen said dreamily. "We're not home yet." "We NEED to get off this train, NOW!"

Catching everyone by surprise, Carmen sprung up from her seat, grabbing Joshua by the hand and pulled him off the train, leaving a leaky trail behind her. As the doors closed, Joshua turned to see the couple sitting across from him pointing at the trail that led to the couple that just got off the train. As more people began to turn to face them, the train began to pull off.

Carmen was hunched over, breathing heavily and flushed. With the train on the move, she exhaled.

"Whoever sits on that seat is gonna be pissed." Carmen said, laughing. "I soaked that thing, look."

She turned around and Joshua felt a wet patch that started between her shoulders and ended below her knees.

"You ruined your dress!"

"Yeah, we'll get to that in a minute. In fact YOU ruined that dress! What the FUCK was that?!" Carmen said, slapping Joshua around the head.

"Says you the flirt?" "Touché. Look babe, I..." "Just don't babe. Let's just forget it and go home." "I'm not going anywhere yet," Carmen said, shuffling to a bench with

Joshua's jacket wrapped around her waist. "I knew I shouldn't have given you that button."

"You know what the worst thing is, we have to get back on a train in two minutes."

"Baby, don't!" Carmen pleaded. Joshua pressed the button again.

BANANA AND APPLE PIE

Monday 19th May 2014?
From: nubianeverstops@gmail.com
To: missinginaction@gmail.com

I really miss you this morning!
I had a dream last night that you were still here and you were holding me in your sleep. With your arms wrapped around me. I never tell you how much I miss that. But I really do.
You know what I really miss? Monday morning malarkey.

Your arm across my chest, a hand being mischievous between my thighs. The feel of your breath on the back of my neck. Then I start humming Erykah Badu and you kiss me on my neck and – yet again – I'm late for work.

I'm not late on Monday mornings any more. I fucking hate that. One of many things I hate about you not being here.

I woke up this morning and got to work early. And I've been sitting here, watching these miserable people walk in and all I can think about is the smile I used to have when I'd walk in, knowing you just gave me an absolute wrestling match of a dick down.

It feels like my skin doesn't have the same glow when your not here to illuminate on me.
And, on top of all that, you know what it's the countdown to, don't ya? Another miserable birthday without you.

Right, gotta go, manager is calling for a staff meeting. I'm gonna go in the meeting and play with your toy under the desk. Something to think about...

Love ya... Nubs...

Monday 19th May 2014?

From: nubianeverstops@gmail.com

To: missinginaction@gmail.com

That meeting was a waste of fucking time!? The whole time, I was thinking of you? Writing random shit to make it look like I was paying attention when my other hand was focussed on some good shit. I swear I left a little wet patch on the chair as I got up. I know that turns you on you little pervert.

Reminded me of that time we went to Frankie and Bennys and we saw that woman eating by herself and you dared me to play with myself while staring at her. Remember that? That was the first time I squirted in public... I STILL can't believe you made me do that.

I haven't been able to do it since you've been gone. Orgasms haven't been the same since... well you know. Even when you were here, but you were at work or out, playing with my pussy used to feel a lot different. It's like I knew you were eventually coming back from wherever you were and you'd check to make sure my pussy was ready for you.

Knowing your not here or on your way... it's like my pussy is depressed.

Me and my pussy are depressed. I HATE THIS!!!

Monday 19th May 2014?
From: nubianeverstops@gmail.com
To: missinginaction@gmail.com

You know I'm not looking forward to Friday so why ask? Anything I do won't feel the same as doing it with you. Remember Amsterdam 2012? Or Scotland 2010? Or what about the chick with the goldfish heels in Vegas? The one that did the splits on my face... she sent me a FaceBook message the other day actually.

Just a hi and bye but... hmm hmmm hmmmm... that was a good night.
So with the memories of all those birthdays we spent together, why would I be looking forward to another birthday without you here to enjoy it with me? You and my mum say the same thing but, I'm just not in the mood. I wasn't in the mood last year, or the other four years you've been away from me.
I know you hate when I say this but missing you just makes me guilty because it's my fault that your there in the first

place. I can hear you telling me to shut up and not to think like that but what else can I think? If nothing happened then... I'm gonna go before I burst into tears... Too late...

Love you Enabooboo

Monday 19th May 2014?
From: nubianeverstops@gmail.com
To: missinginaction@gmail.com

I just spoke to your solicitor... says he should have some good news in the next few days. Whoooo hooooo...

Monday 19th May 2014
From: nubianeverstops@gmail.com
To: missinginaction@gmail.com

You know what I had for dinner tonight? Absolute bullshit. I went to Dixy and got a chicken sandwich with cheese AND chips AND I finished that with a Sainsburys Apple Pie with spray cream and I ate the whole thing. Not forgetting the bottle of Gallo Family wine which I'm drinking from the bottle.
The laptop is sitting on a small mountain which is my stomach and I'm laid out on the sofa with serious niggeritis hitting me.

Yes I know... I can already hear you cussing me. You know I have random days where good eating and healthy living goes out the window and I just wanna have something greasy and not good for me.
If I'm honest, I've been having more days like that. My thighs are getting bigger, my stomach is a bit more pudgy and... it's like I don't see the point in keeping fit.

I don't see the point in doing a lot right now. Not 'cuz of the food but in general. Mum said I should stop living like I've lost an arm and a leg but I can't help it. I wish I could stop pissing you off and live my life with a smile and every email you get from me is a bright and happy message telling you everything is great and I'm living like a white woman in a Bodyform advert but I'm not babe.

I'm miserable, lonely, I feel immensely guilty, I miss you, I can't take this distance thing any more and, on top of all that, you want me to have a great birthday?
You and my mum can get fucked.

I'm gonna take a nap...

Nite boo...

Tuesday 20th May
From: nubianeverstops@gmail.com
To: missinginaction@gmail.com

NIGGERITIS is real!
I woke up 20 minutes after I was supposed to be at work this morning. You know that wake up... that 'oh fuck oh fuck oh shiiiiiiit' and jumped straight in the shower. Told my manger it was lady problems and he was like 'yeah yeah whatever'. And just as I was about to say something really grimy and sexy and all the things you wanna hear, someone behind me said HIS name and now I don't wanna do anything.
I'm not gonna cry... I swear I'm not gonna cry...
Aww babe... why the fuck did this have to happen to us?
Me and my big fucking mouth! Just couldn't keep quiet, had to give it the big talk. I know you see it differently and, that's why I like emails 'cuz there's nothing you can do to stop me saying this.
I'm sorry baby. I'm sorry my big fucking mouth caused this rift in our relationship. More than a rift even. A fucking Red Sea parting in our relationship. I wouldn't be surprised if one

day I get a message from you saying you've come to your senses and don't wanna be with me any more.
In my head I can hear you saying over and over again...
'No one touches my queen...'
I've never felt so scared and so protected at the same time.

Tuesday 20th May 2014
From: nubianeverstops@gmail.com
To: missinginaction@gmail.com

Fine... I won't mention that night again... promise.
Now, can we just talk about what the FUCK you said in your last message and may I reply with HAVE YOU LOST YOUR FUCKING MIND?
Me and some of the girls from the office are going out to some bar in Camden... I
've never heard of it but it's supposed to be the place where all the cool kids go. I really hope it's not a place full of youts 'cuz you know I don't like those places. Haven't got time for all that crap. I just wanna sit at home with a bottle of wine, maybe smoke a spliff... and yes, I've started smoking again. If you have to ask why then you don't love me at all, lol.

I miss you, I hate how lonely this house is without you and I'm turning 30 in three days time so I decided to hook up with the herb. I'm sitting on a bench, staring at the Thames and I just wanna get away. Stage a daring break-in, pick you up, straight to the airport and on the first flight onto another continent. I don't care where we go or how much it costs.

Hmmm... I might just do that. When you hear a wolf whistle, get ready, lol...
(You'd be really shocked if I actually did that.) 2014 Bonnie and Clyde, Nubia and E... HOLLA...

Wednesday 21st May 2014
From: nubianeverstops@gmail.com
To: missinginaction@gmail.com

Hey sugar...

Why would I ever think about doing that with someone else? Your mind is something else. For me, it could be a dude I know or it could be an escort, but it's still cheating in my eyes baby. I know you want me to be happy and, I'm not gonna lie, some dick would be fucking marvellous , but if its not yours, its not the same.

It's like you and my mum are planning something... she left a flyer in my room the other day for this escort agency called Desserts for Ladies and she said I should get suttin' sweet in my belly. You know how my mum is... doesn't mince her words.?And you saying what you said... I just couldn't do it babe.
I know in the past we've done what we've done with other couples and other dudes but, if you're not there, it'd be weird.

Why can't you be here to put that Tyrese dick down on me on my birthday?
I know why you can't, but, why can't you though?

If you can't tell... I'm sulking.?And I'm horny as fuck.?I think I'm gonna watch our Vegas video... you know
I like watching you fuck her.?And this is when I miss you the most...

Wednesday 21st May 2014
From: nubianeverstops@gmail.com
To: missinginaction@gmail.com

I can't sleep baby. I watched the video and had a fiddle but, as always, it wasn't the same.
You weren't there. Opening me up with those fingers of yours, doing that thing you do that no one has been able to do before. You know that way you play with my whole pussy and my thighs... not just trying to fuck me. That tease.

And then looking at me while you do it. I had that picture of you on my night-stand and I put it on a pillow next to me while I watched the video 'cuz I just wanted to feel you looking at me. With those awesome fucking eyes of yours. It's like everything feels ten times better when I know your looking at me. I know I'm a mover but you like that don't you? You like watching me suffer whatever you do to me. I can always tell by that dirty grin you get when I open my eyes. Some Loki looking face.

Right now, I miss your hands. I try not to think about the next time I'll be able to have them all over me but I can't help it.

I don't think I can do this any more. I can't live with missing you and being the reason why we're not together.
I wanna fuck.

As you can tell, I'm all over the place right now, I'm tipsy on that Wrays, I've got work in the morning, people are dropping out of this bar ting in Camden and I haven't heard from your solicitor yet...
And, oh yeah, I wanna fuck... Nite... xxx

Thursday 22nd May 2014

From: nubianeverstops@gmail.com

To: missinginaction@gmail.com

Morning you
.

And this is why I don't like planning things!
What day is it today, Thursday, and guess what... damn near all of the chicks from the office who said they were coming to this drinks ting on Friday have dropped out. Only me and the receptionist from upstairs are going...
What's the fucking point?!

So now, its back to staying at home with a bottle or four of wine and doing fuck all! I knew this thing would flop and I'd be back to doing nothing. I even bought the wine 'cuz I knew this night wouldn't happen.
I miss you sugar... I need sweetness in my diet again.

Thursday 22nd May 2014
From: nubianeverstops@gmail.com
To: missinginaction@gmail.com

Now that's not fair!
You can't make me do this and tell me I have to do it for you.
You know someone is really not being fair when they add 'if you love me you'll do it'.
In any normal relationship, a man wouldn't ask his girlfriend to go out and fuck someone else whatever the situation.

No you equals no sex. I've got an itch – a BIG itch – and only you can scratch it.
On a whole different thing, my mum asked for your email address, God knows why but I gave it to her. She said she wants to talk to you. Why does my mum wanna talk to you? Why aren't you here sending me dirty messages with dirty pictures, making me wanna leave work in the middle of the day?

Remember the time you came to my office and we fucked in the meeting room?
Every meeting I have in that room is a memory adventure for me.

Thursday 22nd May 2014
From: nubianeverstops@gmail.com
To: missinginaction@gmail.com

My mum just said she emailed you... what did she say? And, again, why is my mum emailing you?!

You guys are up to something. I don't know what or how but you're up to something.
Oh and the last woman from my work place who was supposed to be going to that bar ting has dropped out. I'm telling you babe, I work with some shady, absolute slag, miserable ass women. All like to talk talk and love to drink drink but when it comes to my birthday, everyone flops.

I didn't even wanna go in the first place but then I was TOLD I was going so I got myself in the mood for it and now I don't even wanna wake up tomorrow. In fact, you know what, I'm gonna take tomorrow off and just be miserable at home without you.

I've got a feeling this is gonna be one birthday I spend in tears. My birthdays have never been fun since that night but I thought I'd try and have a good one this year but that's a flop. This isn't what you want from me, I know. You hate to hear me blame myself but honestly babe, who else is there to blame? Can't blame you 'cuz if it wasn't for me... I'm not gonna...

Look, I told you I'm never gonna about that night, I've never been able to talk about it, not even to mum but... you being locked up for ten years is my fault.
All mine. And I'm never gonna forgive myself...
I think a long bath with some tears is in order...
I love you baby... I love you so much and I just want you back inside me where you belong.
Love?

The queen that misses her king.

Friday 23rd May 2014
From: nubianeverstops@gmail.com
To: missinginaction@gmail.com

Morning baby... hope you dreamt about me.

Hey baby, you are an amazing hunk of man, you know that?! I love the fuck out of you, you sexy Nigerian beast of a man. Thank you for the card and the flowers and the bottle of champagne. It came in the post this morning and was the only piece of mail that came as well. I wasn't expecting anything so I was ready to hibernate in my duvet, roll up a high grade spliff (don't judge me) and watch crap TV all day.

I don't know how you pulled this off but I love it. Such a handsome picture of you on the card... I atually kissed it. Oh, is that why my mum wanted your email address?

It doesn't matter how you did it baby but thank you. I'm gonna take your advice and stay in all damn day. I've opened the champagne and I'm drinking it from a Liverpool mug with a full English breakfast watching Jeremy Kyle. This is a good birthday if you ask me. But you know what's wrong with it, don't you?! I'm not even gonna say it and give myself something else to think about today... like I ever stop thinking about it.

And just like that... guilt.

I just wanted to say thank you for the flowers and the champagne...

I'll email you again when I've stopped feeling sorry for myself. I don't have the right to feel like that when you are where you are.

PS. I'll see if I can send you some boring birthday pics of me and my fingers later on.

Friday 23rd May 2014?From: nubianeverstops@gmail.com
To: missinginaction@gmail.com

An hour and a half later, that bottle of champagne is done and my head is spinning all over the place. Mixing with niggeritis and it's nap time for me baby.

I didn't make a proper English, just the basics: sausages, well frankfuters but the extra large ones, six streaks of bacon, scrambled eggs with spring onions, cheesy beans, hash brown, plantain, fried bami, toast and that bottle of champagne.

Even as I'm typing, I'm falling asleep.

Friday 23rd May 2014
From: nubianeverstops@gmail.com
To: missinginaction@gmail.com

Waking up and reaching out for you is one of the worst things about your absence.

Friday 23rd May 2014
From: nubianeverstops@gmail.com
To: missinginaction@gmail.com

That nap was ridiculously necessary.
It's dark outside and I feel bloated as fuck right now. I really wish I didn't eat all that food but you know me, if there's food on the plate, I've gotta finish it.

Been watching the news and they say more and more people are getting caught up in this 'point 'em out, knock 'em out' game. I saw it on the news and in the Metro yesterday. That's gotta be good news for us right? The more people that talk about it, the more attention it gets and there'll be more hope of you coming home, right?
I know not to get my hopes up but, I can't help it. Have you heard from your solicitor yet?

Friday 23rd May 2014
From: nubianeverstops@gmail.com
To: missinginaction@gmail.com

You know a nap is powerful when an aftershock comes through and makes you sleep for another 45 minutes. I feel like I don't know what time it is or what day it is. That sleep came like a coma.

Well my birthday so far has been... full of sleep. After that munch, and that drink, I haven't done fuck all. Hardly watched any Jeremy, been curled up on the sofa and I'm high as fuck. Now I'm having a long ass soak with Solar radio playing, incense burning and the bath oils you got me making it all steamy and yummy.

I dunno what I did different but I was in the bath and, well you know my hands like to wander, and I came but I came, ya know, like I used to. I haven't had a cum like that in a good four years babe.

I just wish you were here to clean me up (she says from the bath, lol) but you know what I mean.
I've said it before and I'll say it again...
I'm lonely without you!
Love?Naked and in your bed.

PS. Did you get the pictures I sent?

Friday 23rd May 2014
From: nubianeverstops@gmail.com
To: missinginaction@gmail.com

Babe... something weird just happened.
I got a call from Desserts for Ladies asking if I'm home.
Please tell me you didn't!?

Saturday 24th May 2014?From: nubianeverstops@gmail.com
To: missinginaction@gmail.com Good morning YOU!
Yes I'm calling you YOU and you know why!?YOU did this didn't you you pervert??How did you even do it??Bet your gonna act like you had nothing to do with
what happened last night??It's like I can see you grinning that devious grin of
yours.
Well you know what thank you!
Thank you for the best birthday I've had since the last one I had with you.
It was fucking amazing. I got so many pictures to send you, we made videos, I haven't even watched them yet.

I'm still laid out on the bed, tangled up in sheets and rope and... there's a pair of handcuffs around my ankle. I didn't even feel those... why the fuck are there handcuffs on my ankle?

So... guess you wanna know what you paid for huh?

Hold on, is that what my mum wanted your email address for? As you can tell, I'm tryna figure shit out but my mum isn't answering her phone, probably on purpose.

I swear if I find out my mum is responsible for paying for this in anyway shape or form, I'm gonna be a lil' freaked out so... you've been warned.

Either way, it was a birthday to remember. Would've been the best birthday ever if you were here.

Lemme not fill this email with my guilt and my miserableness, lemme tell you about the night I had.

So...

After I got out of the bath, I got a phone call from Desserts for Ladies asking me if I was at home. I was

like, 'of course I'm at home, where else would I be?' And that's when I emailed you.

I had no idea what the fuck was going on. It's just me at home, I wasn't expecting to see or hear from anyone so, you can imagine, it was a weird phone call to hear someone say 'you're banana and apple pie is on the way'.

So I got dressed and I was just waiting. I didn't know what I was waiting for but I wasn't about to open the door naked or nothing like that. Only you get that privilege.

I waited for about 20-25 minutes and then the door knocked. I was so scared babe, you have no idea. I put the big knife by the door just in case, 'cuz I didn't know who the hell was coming. Could've been a mad man for all I knew. You know me and my nerves.

Opened the door and these two women were standing there in long white jackets, looking like two doctors at my door. Before I even opened my mouth to ask who they were, one of them hands me a card that says 'Banana from Desserts for Ladies'. Then the other one gave me her card and it said, 'Apple Pie from Desserts from Ladies'. Then they smiled at me like, 'you know what it is'.

I didn't know what to say babe. I swear I just giggled 'cuz it was like "erm, what do I do now?"

From what I remembered from the menu, I thought a banana was a dude with a big dick and an apple pie was another dude with a good head game. So I didn't understand why these two women were standing at my door.

Of course I didn't ask, 'cuz by the time I even read the cards, both of 'em walked in, took me by the hand and walked me to my room like they knew the layout of the house. They didn't talk, they didn't say anything to each other, they walked straight to the bedroom .

Babe, when I tell you I was so scared...

It's only me in the house, there's these two women pulling me through the house like I'm some human sacrifice.

Took me into the bedroom, closed the door. Went to the CD player... oh yeah, how much did you tell them? 'Cuz they knew where the music was, the candles, they even knew where my toys were.

Then the banana said she had another name. It was erm... what was her name... that's it, she said her name was Stay Still See. What a name.

So, while the other one was putting on OUR playlist, Stay Still said that they're were here to help me celebrate a good birthday, one I'll never forget.

That's when I knew it was you.

Then the pair of them stood in front of me and, babe, I have never laughed so hard in my life. I didn't mean to but they took of their jackets and I couldn't help it. Stay Still was wearing a thong and a strap-on and the other one called Disha The Creeper was wearing boy shorts and knee pads.

What was I supposed to say to that?! The way my mouth was wide open.

They were wearing these t-shirts that had some letters on them that made me laugh. The letters were C.L.I.T.S and they stood for Clever Ladies Investigating Terrible Situations, loooooool.

After I composed myself, the one with the knee pads said "it's been a long time since you had a great orgasm on my birthday since he's been gone so we're here to change that."

Trust me sugar, the way they were looking at me, I knew what time it was. Disha was adjusting her knee pads and putting Vaseline on her lips and baby oil on her fingers and Stay Still was taking off her t-shirt and rubbing baby oil all over. Joke was, they were looking at me like 'so, are you gonna take your clothes off or what?'

I was stuck. Like, two random women walk up inna mi yard, put me in my room and basically asked me to get naked.

Well they didn't ask me, they made me stand up and took my clothes off me. One took my t-shirt off, one took my leggings off and they told me how this was gonna go.

When I tell you, these girls were on some military precision shit. They were like 'right we're gonna put you in this position' and 'this is the best position because it allows us both to work you at the same time' and 'we're not responsible for how many orgasms you have'.

LMAO!!!!

I was bussing up babe... these girls from Desserts for Ladies came to PLAY! Real pretty women; one looked like a creamy chocolate version of Sanaa Lathan and the other one with the knee pads looked like a MILF. That's all I can say. Pure sexy mouthed MILF. And with those breasts, I was not about to complain sweetie.

So Stay Still laid on the bed, on your side and started playing with the eight-inch strap on. As you know it's been a hot minute since I'd been with a woman so I wasn't feeling good about any form of dick. I was nervous. I didn't know these women nor did I know they were coming, so I didn't have time to get my head around it.

By the time I was fully getting my head around it, I was looking down at Disha, and I know why they call her the Creeper. I dunno how and when she managed to get her head in between my legs but I looked down and she had her mouth all up in my crease. I couldn't believe it.

Yeah, they'd introduced themselves and told me what was going down but I expected a little bit more of an intro into the ting, ya know? Anyway, so Disha with the knee pads is on her knees eating me out and the other one with the strap-on is looking me in my eye, playing with this big black thing in front of her. It was one of those strap-ons that have an attachment that goes inside her so she gets hers too.

Few seconds later, I came. Right on her face. It was a quick one like pheeeeeeeeeeew...

Then she looked up at me and she goes, 'She's ready!'

My girl then pushes me onto the bed, makes me climb on the woman with the strap-on, who was rubbing it like it was actually attached to her, lol...

She put her arms around me and they whispered in my both my ears. One of them said, 'We've got you now!' and the other one said 'Let's have a great birthday!'

So while one of them is laying under me and holding me down, the other one went and slipped the strap-on into me and, babe, I don't know how – maybe because it's the first piece of dick I've felt since you left – but it felt like you were fucking me. I mean, the size of the

it, the depth, all of it felt like I had you back in my pussy where you belong.

Whatever nerves I was feeling before went out the window when that dick slipped in. That felt instantly good then other went down and started licking me again while I was riding the strap-on. I'm telling you babe, it felt so fucking good, you have no idea. In all the crazy shit we've done, I don't think I've ever felt anything like that. It's not like that threesome we had with that guy and we did the double penetration. She was licking my pussy lips while the other one was fucking me.

The way I came on that thing babe, you would've been proud of me. You would've been there cheering me on, telling me to make sure I get it all over her face, which I did. To be honest, the more I came, the more it seemed to sweet her. She was growling like some hungry animal back there.

Then they flipped me into doggy with my clit being licked by Disha who lay underneath me. I didn't last long in that position 'cuz they had one demon stroke that just killed my life.

While Stay Still pulled out quickly, Disha ate my pussy really fast. Then when Stay Still came back in slowly, Disha ate me slowly. They did that for about ten straight minutes. I started coming after two. But they didn't stop. They just kept me there while I was coming all over the place and did the same thing; quick, quick, slow, slow.

I could HEAR myself squirting on both of them, on the pillows, the duvet, the sheets were soaked, I even hit the picture on the wall behind the bed tuh rahtid.

By the time I had my last orgasm – or the last orgasm I remember – I was laying flat on one of them with my face resting on her pussy trying to catch my breath. I swear to you babe, that's the last thing I remember. Then I woke up and here I am, with a pair of handcuffs around both ankles and there's rope on the bed, my toys are everywhere. It looks like the mattress was moved, there's new pictures and videos in my phone and I've got a migraine from coming so much. What the hell did you do you freak you?!

Saturday 24th May 2014

From: missinginaction@gmail.com

To: nubianeverstops@gmail.com

Hey my sugar honey iced tea...
Glad you had a great birthday, glad you enjoyed the treat I got you. I think it's best for all parties concerned if I don't talk about your mother's involvement... it'll save us money on therapy later on down the line, loool...
Couple things...

You said that two women turned up? I ordered two guys for you. I'm looking at a copy of the receipt from the order your mu.. I mean the order I gave and I asked for one chocolate banana, which is one big black dick basically and a caramel apple pie, which is self- explanatory.
Unless they sent replacements, but then I haven't heard anything about that so I'm gonna have to find out what's going on?

And what did these women look like? The way you described 'em, they sound like... nah, that'd be too weird. We had two new nurses giving us medicals this week but they were too sexy to be working in a prison. Remember when I told you I woke up in my cell with little white bits stuck to my pubes? Looool...

I don't know nothing 'bout no C.L.I.T.S either. Only clit I know of is yours, lol.

But I'm glad you had a good time and even more glad that you had a happy birthday even though I'm not there to share it with you.

I've told you time and time again, you and your bloody guilt. We've talked about this hundreds of times haven't we? You didn't do a thing to anyone so no one and I mean no one had the right to put there hands on you. And in front of me? You know I couldn't have that! Putting their hands on my queen? Should've I have hit him so many times? No, I should've listened to you and stopped hitting him but, I've said it before

and I'll say it again, no one touches my queen like that.

You are the love of my life and you have nothing to feel guilty about.

I love you, I'll be home 1,825 days and counting. Get some rest... sounds like you need it.

Love you my Queen...

Love Enakhe

RHUOSIA THE KISSER - CLITS

"Wake up handsome!"

The sound of Keisha's voice made Lamar stir. His head wobbled from side-to-side then his eyes opened automatically and all he could see was a pair of eyes.

"What the fuck?"

All around him was darkness except for the eyes. He focussed and could see a nose, lips and a face.

"Hi!" the face before him said. "Where the fuck am I? Where's Keisha?" Suddenly a rip-roaring electric shock coursed through him and made

him scream. The face moved back and let him suffer until the shock stopped.

"I hate foul language Lamar so every time I hear some, that's what you're gonna get, okay?"

"Fuu..."

Electricity coursed through him again and he struggled against the chair he was tied to. His fingers flexed and a flash of white covered his vision.

"Are you done? You through? Good... now... my name is Rhuosia the kisser and I'm here because you do not know how to kiss. According to Keisha, you used to but now you're slacking on your macking. And as someone who's been there, I can't have that. Keisha seems like a nice girl and she deserves better. And I'm gonna teach it to ya."

"Could you at least tell me where I am?" "C.L.I.T.S HQ." "Where's that?" "You'll never need to know, you'll never find out and you won't even

believe you were here. That's all you need to know." "Let me go please. My girlfriend doesn't know where I am." "So... let's talk about why you don't like kissing." "That's none of your fucking business now, let me... SHIIIIIIIIIT!" The electricity caught him by surprise and made his head look up at

the ceiling. The veins in his neck throbbed and he gritted his teeth. "Can we talk now?" Lamar was breathless. "Yes, yes, let's talk. Just please don't do that

again." "Good boy. Everyone seems to become very agreeable when the

electricity hits 'em." "Okay, okay... erm... I don't like kissing anymore. Well not that I

don't like it. I just..." "Just what?" "Kissing is too much like foreplay. It's like passing the ball around in

football instead of going for the goal." "Is it because you can't kiss? You don't look you have the lips for it?" Lamar frowned. "Who the fuuu... hold on... erm... I just don' like

kissing, that's all."

"Yeah but you're girlfriend does. And that's who you do it for. Women likes things that men don't like but they do them anyway."

Lamar was looking around at the darkness that surrounded them. He tried to trace the source of the light that was shining on Rhuosia's face but he couldn't follow it.

"Kissing is the ultimate foreplay. A kiss can take you from standing in front of someone to laying down under someone. Believe me, a good kiss can do that!"

"I just... I dunno... I don't really want all that foreplay shit, I just wanna... erm... have sex."

"Exactly! You are school on a sunday, no class. I don't understand how you got her with that attitude. Kissing is one of the major aspects of foreplay. Of sex itself. Haven't you ever had one of those kisses like the movies? Clothes flying all over the place, furniture being moved, not quite making it to the bedroom? You never had that?"

"NO, never." Lamar mumbled.

"Figures. Okay. I'm gonna talk you through some techniques to utilise the next time you get to kiss Keisha, okay?"

"How do you know Keisha? Where is she? Where am I?"

"Listen and learn. I've got the lips for it so I know what I'm talking about. Now, where you put your hands on a woman is important when kissing. Don't just hold her hands or put them on her arms. You need to let her know the kiss is as sensual for you as it is for her. Good places to put hands are on the neck, her back, shoulders, oh oh back of the head, base of her spine..."

"And these are places to put my hands right? Not to kiss?" "Exactly." "What's the point of learning that? How the fuck is that..." "SHIIIIIIIIIIIIIIIIIIIIIIIIT!" Lamar swore again as the electricity rumbled through him in his chair.?After 15 seconds of electric shock, Lamar exhaled strongly and looked at Rhuosia with manic eyes that said he wanted to kill. "Becky Becky was right, you are a prick. It's like you don't wanna learn anything." "Learn from who? That fat bitch Beck..." Electricity passed through him, making his fingers and toes stretch out. He wanted to scream but he grit his teeth and rode the pain. "Lemme give you some advice Lamar. You are gonna be here for a while and you are gonna meet me a lot of us so the best thing you can do is calm down, watch your mouth and do what they tell you to do. But listen as well. Because there's a lot of clever women who are about to give you some information that could save your relationship."

"What makes you think my relationship is in trouble?" Lamar asked.

"You're here aren't you? Then, your relationship is in trouble. Remember soft lips and a soft skin stroke wins every time. Night night."

Rhuoia pressed the button on his neck and watched Lamar close his eyes in slumber.

INTELLIGENT PEOPLE

"Could I have the same again please?" Tabrin said to the barman, pointing at her empty glass.

Her glass was whisked away and her fourth Long Island Ice Tea with cranberry was on it's way as she brushed her curly hair away from her face with a sigh. She looked down at her phone, no texts, no What's App messages, no direct messages on Twitter, no Tumblr messages, no emails... nothing.

All dressed up with no where to go, she thought to herself looking over her shoulder. Groups of people who appeared to be exhaling the stresses of their week were laughing and conversing extra loud while she held her seat at the bar, trying not to be noticed. And she did well not to be seen, although the odd straggler from the toilet would spot her and attempt some sort of approach, which was instantly shut down.

She brought her phone to life with her thumb and turned her mobile data off then back on to be sure she was getting full service.

Focused on the top of her phone for any updates, Tabrin didn't notice her drink arrive in front of her with two cherries and a straw.

"Come on," she grumbled to herself.

The groove of Bootsy Collins' I'd Rather Be With You poured through the speakers and Tabrin couldn't control the way her head snapped back and forth with her eyes closed. She was a fan of the funk and this was the equivalent of a hit to a crack addict. Her lips folded up and she let her neck and stank face grind on the beat.

A mix of her drink with a stirrer and a long sip and Tabrin was beginning to feel nice. Not hazy enough that she couldn't focus, but a nice adrenaline on her alertness.

Wearing a sleek green thigh-length dress from New Look and River Island shoes, Tabrin was dressed simply, but she was aroused at how yummy she looked in her reflection behind the bar.

Snaking her head from side to side, waiting for her phone to tell her something, Tabrin dropped her head inches away from her drink and just stared, thinking about all the other things or people she could doing at this exact moment. She had a list a mile long and, though nights out were good fun on the company's ticket, she wasn't going to move forward wasting time like this.

Two toilet trips and three other cocktails later, Tabrin was sitting in the same spot but now verging on tipsy. The crowd around her had changed but the vibe was still the same as she crossed and uncrossed her legs, dangling her feet to the beats.

And then HE walked in.

She spotted him through the crowd out of the corner of her eye and turned to watch him. He caught her eye because he seemed to be the only person in the bar who seemed to be alone, besides her.

Cutting between different people, Tabrin could see different angles of his face. The thick-rimmed glasses, smooth cheeks with maybe two

days stubble, fluffy scarf wrapped around his neck and a long black jacket down to his knees draped over him perfectly.

Her hands vibrated, or so she thought, and she checked her phone but no new messages came through. She refreshed her apps but nothing new appeared. By the time she looked up, she realised she'd lost the face that was starting to brightening up her evening.

Flashing her eyes through the crowd, trying to find his lovely chocolate face, she turned in her seat ad spun right into him as he walked past her.

"Oh shiiiit, I'm sorry," he said, adjusting his stance to absorb her shoulder which turned into him.

"There you are!" Tabrin said.?" Who, me?" "Yes, you... come and talk to me, I'm bored. All these people up in

here and no one to talk to." He smiled and took a second as if he was contemplating his answer.

"Well, alright then, I've got some time to kill." "Thank you..." "Timson, my name is Timson." "Nice to meet you Timson, I'm Tabrin and it's a pleasure to make

your acquaintance.?" Yeah you too," he said, unwrapping his scarf from his neck. "So, the

first question has to be why are you sitting in a pretty lively bar with no one to talk to?"

"I've got a late meeting but I'm waiting for the address as it's so top secret, they can't tell you the address beforehand." Tabrin said, looking him straight in the eye. She searched his face for any recognition that he didn't believe her.

"Wow, sounds really serious. That kind of organisation means it's an important meeting, right? And after business hours too?"

She frowned then giggled. "Erm, before you even think it, I'm not a lady of the night, okay?"

"That's okay if you were, I wouldn't judge. I mean, it'd make sense. Not that you look dressed like a..."

"I was about to say! Do I look like a prostitute?" Tabrin turned her body towards him and felt her body tingle as she took him all in.

"No, not a prostitute. Then again, high class escorts don't exactly wear cheap clothes anyway so..."

"So NOW I look like a high class escort?" "NO!" Tabrin was enjoying watching him squirm and Timson was hating the

fact that he was digging himself into a larger hole with each response. He knew what he was trying to say but what came out seemed to be the wrong thing.

"I was just trying to say you look...

"... like my milkshake brings all the boys to the yard, is that what your saying?"

"Erm..."

Just as he stuttered and stammered again, the bar man came over and he ordered a Jamaican Sunrise with extra rum, while using the silent moments to think about what he was trying to say.

"So, what kind of prostitute do I look like then? Julia Roberts in Pretty Woman, Divine Brown on Sunset Boulevard or Jennifer Hills in I Spit On Your Grave?"

"Yeah but Jennifer wasn't a prostitute." Timson added, taking his jacket off and draping it over the chair.

Tabrin couldn't help but watch.?" True, but they treated her like a prostitute though." Timson's drink arrived while Tabrin ordered another one.?" SO... back to the original question. Why are you here sitting by

yourself and this bar is popping off around you? Are you related to Casper?"

Tabrin caught herself mentally undressing this man before her. She lost interest in trying to wish a message into her phone and inhaled his scent while imagining his chest pressed against her face.

"What?!" she said, staring at his shoulders, imagining her arms wrapped around them and holding on for dear life. "Oh, erm... I've got a meeting remember?"

"Yeah, I remember that," Timson said, taking a strong first sip. "But that doesn't answer why your here in a bar by yourself? Where's the man in your life?"

Tabrin sighed exasperatedly. "There's no man in my life Mr Timson. There was but then he tried to fuck my cousin, my best friend and my aunty during a family reunion so he's not my man anymore."

He recoiled back with an uncomfortable smirk. "Whoa... erm... that's a way to become an ex."

"Yep, you ain't lying pretty man."

Tabrin knocked back her drink and closed her eyes, hating the fact that the words she was thinking came out of her mouth instead of staying internal.

"Pretty man huh? Least we know where your mind's at then," Timson said, checking his phone for any messages.

"Nah, I was talking about..." Tabrin scanned the bar, looking for someone worthy to point at. "Fuck it, I meant you. But look at those eyes and those cheekbones. You probably one of those men who knows he's pretty as well."

He turned to Tabrin, taking in the shape of her face, her lips, her form and the way her glass balanced lightly between her fingers. In his mind, he couldn't believe it was so easy to engage in a conversation with someone so beautiful.

"I'm not pretty. Men aren't called pretty. We can have pretty elements but you can't call us pretty, it's the equivalent of putting a dildo in a man's ass."

She wasn't ready for the comment as she took a sip of her drink and coughed in the middle. She slapped her chest, put her drink down and planted her hands on the bar in laughter.

"How is that even the same?!" she said with tears in her eyes.

"Call a guy pretty and you might as well call him gay. Not in the homosexual way but in the way that women will now look at him. They won't see him as a normal man, they'll see him as something special who is used to having his own way due to the fact that he's so pretty. You know like those pretty men who get dumped and freak the fuck out 'cuz they're usually the ones doing the dumping? Yeah, I'm not that guy. Hate that guy actually!"

He patted Tabrin on the back as A Tribe Called Quest mix played around the bar. From a soft tap to a circular rub against her bra strap and Timson was taking her in as she arched her back and cleared her throat. Staring at her neck, trailing his eyes down to the spot where her top met the top of her trousers, Timson could see the line of a thong reaching around her hips.

Clearing her throat, Tabrin sat back and smiled with a hand on her chest. "You must be trying to kill me! That's funny, but I see what you're trying to say though."

"Thank you. Excuse me, can I have another Jamaican Sunrise with an extra shot of rum and..."

"Can I have a double grape Martini please?"

They both watched the barman walk away before catching each other trying to steal a glance before looking away.

"So," Timson said first. "Can I ask you a question? And you can totally say no if you want."

"Well technically you already asked me a question so now it's my turn."

He laughed. "Ahhh, someone went to uni I see."

"For a degree I'm not bloody using, yeah. Anyway, what did you wanna ask?"

Watching his face and groin for a reaction, Tabrin swivelled to face him with one arm resting on the back of the chair and the other resting on the bar.

She crossed her legs and made sure to do so in a way that her dress rose high on her leg, uncovering her inner thigh. Watching him watching her, she leaned forward.

"Do you masturbate Timson?"

He frowned. "I don't know anyone who doesn't and I know a priest for crying out loud so yes I do, why?"

"Because I wanna watch!" "Pardon me?" Timson said with fresh frown lines across his brow. "I wanna watch you masturbate!" Their drinks arrived and Timson sucked half through his straw as soon as it hit the bar.?" Seee, I thought that's what you said but I wasn't sure." Tabrin took a slow, seductive sip of her drink. "Well, now you know what you thought you heard was what you heard so, what'd you think?"

"Of what?" Timson said, feeling flushed with heat. "Masturbating and letting me watch!"

"Sure why not," he replied sarcastically. "What, right now in the toilets? Let's go."

"Okay then, cool."

Tabrin tilted her head back and took long gulp after long gulp of her drink before slamming her empty glass on the bar and looking at Timson with a smile.

"Erm... okay, now I don't think your joking," Timson said taking another long sip of his drink.

"What made you think I was joking?!" she said hopping off her chair. "I'm on my way to the toilet, cubicle three, four or five. See you in a minute."

Picking up her phone and her handbag, Tabrin adjusted her dress, and walked towards the toilet, knowing she'd left Timson with no choice but to follow her. She knew he was watching as she could feel his eyes on her sashay that worked like a part time job.

Cutting through the crowd and reaching the toilets, she pushed the door and looked back at him at the same time and caught him in full stare.

She grinned and disappeared into the toilets, waiting for him to arrive.

Her eyes and ears scanned the toilets for signs of life. No flushing, no toilet roll pulling, no high heeled scuffling on the floor. Nothing but the beat and bass of the music from the bar and the hum of the air conditioner. She walked into the first stall and closed the door behind her, listening with her ear to the door.

Swinging her handbag on the hook on the back of the toilet door, Tabrin inhaled deeply, feeling nerves coursing through her. When she asked Timson if she could ask him a question, she wanted to ask if she could kiss him. No repercussions or one night about it, just a kiss. The way his lips moved when he spoke had her lost in thoughts of all the things he could do with those tools. Instead, the question she had in her mind came out of her lips and she couldn't take it back.

And now she was standing in a toilet cubicle with her ear to a cold door, waiting for a strange guy to come in and masturbate in front of her. She didn't care about any messages coming through on her phone or any updates, all she wanted was to see how delectable Timson looked when he came.

Work can wait, she thought.

Her work thinking stopped as she heard footsteps approaching the toilet and the door to the women's toilet creaked open. Keeping her feet away from the door, she shakily balanced against the door and listened. The footsteps that entered weren't heeled, steps were heavy as well as the breathing that followed.

Suddenly, someone knocked on her door and made her jump out of her skin as the reverberations bounced off her head.

"Yes, how may I help you?" she said.

"I was told to meet someone here," Timson replied. "Though they're not where they said they would be."

She unlocked the door and pulled him in quickly before anyone caught the man in the women's toilets. With the door closed and locked, they were forced to stand closer than they had been before.

Tabrin looked up at his lips and he looked down at her cleavage that was pressed up between the neckline of her dress.

"So... let's see it then," Tabrin said, dropping the toilet lid so she could sit.

Timson, with erection pressing against the front of his trousers, watched her sit back and fold then unfold her legs. She leaned back against the wall and stared at him with her heels slowly sliding apart on the tiled floor.

"I'm not scared of getting my dick out..." Timson said, reaching for his belt buckle.

Tabrin couldn't believe what she was seeing as she watched his fingers unhook, unclip and unzip. He opened his shirt but didn't take it off and pulled his trousers down but didn't take them off.

Not his first time in a toilet doing this kind of thing, Tabrin thought.

Her mouth snarled.

She looked at him in sections. From his torso to his groin and from his groin to his feet.

"How you wanna do this Tabrin?" he asked.

She shook her shoulders with a smile. "Oh wow, how do we do this? Hmm... decisions decisions. How 'bout you take your dick out and work it until I say otherwise?"

"Okay, no problem." "Well, okay then." Timson didn't waste any time in pulling his boxer shorts down,

making his dick flop out and bounce against his thighs. Tabrin couldn't hide the excitement in her face as he wrapped his right hand around his dick and began to stroke it slowly at the tip.

He sucked in a deep breath and looked up from his dick to see Tabrin staring with enlarged eyes. He tilted his dick up and rubbed down, showing her his entire length.

"Come here," she said with a come hither finger.

He shuffled towards her with his dick in his hand and a hopeful grin on his face. She watched him get closer, feeling her mouth get wetter. He was now close enough that she could reach out and touch him if she wanted to.

She called him forward with her finger until his head halted in front of her face.

"Stop," she said, then leaned forward.

Timson's eyes widened as Tabrin looked up at him, letting his dick brush her chin. He stopped rubbing his dick and enjoyed the connection with her face. She giggled then spat a strain of liquid through her teeth that hit him at the base of his dick and stretched up to his head.

"Now you can get busy!"

Washing the look of disappointment from his face, Timson shuffled back but was stopped by Tabrin, who wrapped her legs around his ankles. He paused, looking deeply in her eyes and she grinned in response.

"Well alright then," he said quietly as the door to the toilets opened and a group of women walked in laughing.

Shuffling back to his former footing, Timson pointed his erection at her chin, wrapped his fingers around it – enjoying the cool feeling of liquid on his length – and began rubbing it for her pleasure.

He could see she the excitement in her eyes, sitting back against the toilet wall, trying to balance on the pipe connected to the cistern above her head. She was staring at him as if she was mesmerised and she was. She honestly didn't think she would be able to put such an offer forward and have such a response, especially considering what she was meant to be doing in the bar in the first place.

Watching the veins of his dick coursing under his chocolate skin, Tabrin licked her lips every time he grunted. Every five or six strokes, he'd spit into his palm to keep his dick moving fluidly then look at the amazement in her eyes.

The group of loud, laughing women were flushed toilets and washing hands while talking about the dick they were going to be taking home from the bar, with a pair of women planning to share a guy, as they left the bathroom.

Timson used the imagery of two women on their knees in front of him to inspire his erection to stay strong in his grip. Looking to the ceiling and starting to sweat, he met Tabrin's eyes latched on his. A sudden flow of blood rushed to his dick and he straightened instantly.

He tried not to moan or look away from her, feeling the sticky residue of pre-cum gliding around his head. She was flicking between keeping the eye competition going and the now furious flow he was working on his dick. His back was arching in spasms and sweat droplets were popping up on his temples.

"You have no idea how delicious this looks," Tabrin said, not feeling as tipsy as she was before. The dick before her sobered her up.

Timson's blur of a hand had her attention and she could see the gleam of pre-cum shine in the dingy toilet light as Barry White sang Can't Get Enough Of Your Love.

"You not gonna... you know..." Timson said, staring at Tabrin's lips and tilting his head from side to side.

"Not this time... maybe next time..." Tabrin said then pursed her lips and spat on his working hand. "Come on then, I've had enough of the previews, gimme the show."

Tabrin scooted forward on the toilet seat with her heeled feet still wrapped around his ankles. She was smiling foolishly as she brought a hand up to cup his testicles which reacted to her touch.

Running a hand up and down the curve of his sack, Tabrin leaned forward and opened her mouth wide, while looking at Timson with a vivacious smile. His face acknowledged the message she'd just given him and he put all his attention into jerking his dick. He aimed so he was pointed right at her open mouth and kept working, waiting for the familiar creep of his seed along the base of his dick.

"Cum, cum cum, cum, cum cum..." Tabrin chanted.

His face was contorting and changing, the muscles in his stomach started to crunch together and he was at maximum extension and wasn't getting any harder.

His breathing changed. "Oh shiiiiiiiiiiiiiii..." "Shhhh..." Tabrin said, grabbing his balls and squeezing them softly. "Come on baby... yeah... almost there... oh fuck yeah..." At her feet, Tabrin felt her handbag vibrate and everything around

her froze as she remembered where she was and what she was doing there. She wanted to wait until Timson was finished before checking the message but she had to find out the vital information contained within otherwise someone else would get the job and she'd be pissed off for not getting it.

"Don't stop handsome... but you gotta be quick though," she said reaching into her handbag and checking her phone. Looking at the top of her screen for message icons, she saw the one she had been waiting for all night.

"YES!" Tabrin shouted to her phone, catching the huffing, puffing Timson off his stroke. He slowed down as she wiped her finger across her screen numerous times, tapping and swiping as she went.

With her attention stolen by her phone, Tabrin was lost in opening an intricately locked message that needed passwords sent to her Tumblr messages, Twitter direct message and Yahoo email.

Timson was watching her with his dick in his hand and as he could feel his dick drooping, he could also feel his annoyance rising. He wasn't planning to go into the women's toilets, whip his dick out and masturbate, but since he was, he'd at least get an orgasm out of it.

His thoughts began to wander about the possibility of another man sending her a message and he felt anger rise. He wasn't sure where the anger was coming from considering he just met this woman but he knows what he felt.

He was jealous.

With Tabrin's face illuminated by her phone, Timson could see the pleasure he was previously receiving now concentrated on her phone. He spat in his hand which was still wrapped around his dick and focussed his rubbing on the underside of his dick, just under his head. The section of his penis that, when stroked quickly and with the right amount of pressure, could bring on an orgasm in under 30 seconds.

Timson wanted his attention back.

While he was masturbating inches away from her face, Tabrin was three quarters of the way through her maze of passwords and swipes taking no notice of him. He was only meant to pass the time and now the time had passed.

"Soon as I open this bloody thing, I'm out and off to work," Tabrin mumbled to herself.

Taking her mumbles as a sign of annoyance and boredom, Timson rubbed faster, hoping he'd come unexpectedly and hit her right in the mouth. So placed was the anger that he was feeling. Then, his phone rang.

He pressed the hands free attachment on his ear and the call answered, while he looked at Tabrin and gave her the shush signal.

Timson was told to hold on while random pop music played in his ear, mixing with his confusion and the music being played from the bar. With his dick rock hard and feeling good, Timson knew he wasn't far away from an orgasm. His only worry was his aim. He wanted to make sure he caught her right in her face for the disrespect she was currently showing him.

Silently working, Timson was full on sweating, wiping his brow with the back of his hand. He was close and getting closer.

The hold music stopped and caught him by surprise.?" Yeah?" he said.?" We've got your target. Her name is Tabrin, last known location was

Birds of Paradise bar, we have her on CCTV wearing a green dress and heels, chocolate skin, curly hair... please know she is extremely dangerous and armed to the teeth. Whatever you do, do not engage her. She WILL kill you! She's trained in mixed martial..."

Timson slowed his dick rubbing as the list of his latest target went on and on, proving that Tabrin was in fact, the most dangerous target he'd ever chased and here he was masturbating only inches away from her face.

"Finally," Tabrin said to herself. She looked up at Timson, who had a strange look on his face and was no longer rubbing his dick, which was leaking misty pre-cum. "Why'd you stop? Carry on!"

For a moment, Timson reached for his dick then stopped, remembering what he had just been told by the voice in his ear.

She looked back at her phone and the look on her face said she wasn't happy with what looked back at her. She pulled the phone away from her face and slowly looked up at Timson, who was looking back at her.

Subject name: Timson (picture below)

Musiq's Previous Cats played in the bar as Timson and Tabrin stared at each other with strange eyes. He was sizing her up, feeling open to attack, especially with his dick out in front of him. She was looking up at him, watching his hands for any quick movement, thinking of reaching for the weapon she tucked comfortably in her bra.

With the pair of them not moving, they moved at the same time, mirroring the same movement.

She thrust her hand into her bra and had her weapon trained on him just as he reached into the back of his waistband and pointed his weapon at her.

"Timson!" she said with her gun pointed at his chest.

"Hiya Tabrin!" he replied with his own weapon pointed at her neck. "So... now what?"

"Of all the people for me to have to kill... it had to be the sexy one. Oh well... business is business."

"I don't see you killing me to be honest," he said, trying to fold his erection into his trousers.

"Whoa whoa whoa... hold on... how about this? Why don't you finish what you were doing then we sort out this murdering each other business after?"

Timson frowned. "Sure, why not. But you have to join me."

"I was going to," Tabrin said, leaning back against the wall while hiking her dress up to her waist.

She stood up suddenly, making Timson take a step back but keeping his gun pointed at her neck. He watched her nervously as she used one hand to slide her panties to her ankles and stepping out of one side before sitting down on the cold toilet seat.

"I'm pretty close so you best be quick, because if I come before you, I'm gonna shoot you in the face."

"Oooooh, a game? Alrighty then... I'll play," Tabrin said with a sadistic smile while parting her thighs.

Timson couldn't help but look at the triangle of chocolate that appeared from between her thighs. His eyes widened as he tried to focus in the darkness, while trying to keep Tabrin in his sights.

"Hey, eyes up here. If you know who I am, then you know not to get distracted around me."

He adjusted his interest in her vagina and was back to focussing on his orgasm. His dick shrunk instantly as soon as Tabrin pointed her very big gun with sound suppressor at his chest but he held onto it. Pre-cum dribbled down his hand and dangled off his wrist in the space between them. As it broke off, Tabrin leaned forward suddenly and caught in her mouth and was back against the wall before Timson could adjust his gun hand.

She licked her lips as she leaned back against the wall, lifting one leg and resting it on the toilet roll holder.

"Alright, last one to come dies, deal?" Tabrin said, humming approvingly at the taste in her mouth.

"Deal... COME ONNNNNN premature ejaculation," Timson called out and they both laughed but neither gun hand wavered.

Tabrin moved first, using three fingers to spread her lips. Timson replied her movement by spitting a huge glob of bubble-filled liquid onto the hood of his dick.

She moved again, sliding a finger over her exposed clitoris and using another finger to play with her opening. He let the spit mash between his fingers and cover his dick as he gave one full stroke.

Res' Golden Boys thumped in the bar but Tabrin and Timson were eye-locked in a masturbation battle that held both of their lives in the balance. She worked her middle finger inside then added her second middle finger and arched her back.

Watching her enjoy herself made Timson feel nervous and he picked up the pace, thrusting his waist forward to get full erection benefits. His dick gleamed in his hand, which was working at a furious pace.

As a lover, Timson was used to using every trick in the book to prolong an orgasm but now he wished it felt good too quickly.

Tabrin was stroking her fingers in and out at a steady pace, watching Timson struggle to gain and hold a good feeling and hold his gun straight at the same time. She let out a long moan as the doors to the toilet opened and a woman walked in and went into the stall right next to them.

Both their eyes trailed to the partition between them and the woman who unbuckled a belt and sat down on the toilet with a heavy sigh. Then their eyes returned to each other, wondering if the other would try something sneaky.

The sound of the woman next door passing gas threw Timson out of his groove and made him shrink in his hand. He gripped tighter and worked harder to get his erection back to former glory and, with a few concentrated strokes and a daydream of Tabrin sucking his dick, he returned to a strong eight and a quarter inches.

Tabrin's walls began to secrete with liquid that began to coat her fingers, making her strokes smoother.

The woman next door strained before Tabrin and Timson heard a splash and that was when Timson knew he was going to die.

He could feel the blood drawing away from the tip of his penis and was forced to watch his proud hammer of meat shrink into what looked like a smoked and discarded cigar. And all of this before the smell hit him.

The stench hit his eyes first and they started to water then his nose twitched violently and he shook his head as if he was being force fed caster oil.

He spat again, hoping the feeling of warm liquid would force his erection back into action but the more he forced it, the smaller he got.

'This is the smallest my dick has ever been', he thought to himself.

Meanwhile, Tabrin had liquid crawling down the crack of her ass, with her eyes stoically staring at him. There was no emotion on her face that said that the smell affected her or her fingers. With her leg still up, she gave Timson a full view of her fingers sliding in and out.

He stared, hoping the view of pussy would bring him back from the dead but he wasn't rising, despite his best efforts. In her closed mouth, she was using her tongue to push against her 12th molar, which had been replaced by a button, which she pressed.

She heard the click from Timson's gun but kept her face still and calm, keeping her fingers moving in the same rhythm.

Fear began to paint Timson's face as the woman next door continued straining and making the toilet water splash multiple times. He couldn't control the way his face screwed and his lips turned up. And for the first time since his teens, Timson wasn't in control of his dick.

Tabrin's forehead frowned and she let out a light groan that Timson wished he didn't hear. That type of sound was indicative of a ride to orgasm land while he was lounging in the hills of erectile dysfunction. Her fingers stroked faster and faster while her back arched but her face stayed the same and her gun hand was steady as a spirit level.

Timson knew he was losing this race and, of all the nights to not be wearing his bulletproof vest. He looked back at his dick, hoping for a sudden riser erection. But all he had in his hand was a sticky stump that refused to follow instructions.

He looked up and could see that Tabrin was close. With the smell from next door becoming more potent, Timson began to think about his survival. His erection was nowhere near ready to give him the finish he needed to win while his opponent was galloping to the red tape at the finish line.

"Fuck it," he said before aiming his gun at the right side of her chest and pulling the trigger.

The look of absolute surprise on his face when nothing happened was priceless and Tabrin wished she recorded it.

He pulled the trigger again and the same thing happened. Nothing. He pulled the slide back and could see the bullet in the chamber and tried to fire a third time but nothing happened.

Completely freaked out, he ejected the magazine and could see a full clip. He stole a quick glance at Tabrin, who had her gun hand pointed at him wherever he moved and her other hand arched over so she could get quick full finger strokes.

"Tut tut tut," she said shaking her head. "That wasn't the agreement was it?"

Tabrin's leg which was balanced on the toilet roll holder swung towards him before he saw it. Her heel planted firmly in the middle of his chest and forced him back against the locked door. With his feet bunched in his trousers and boxer shorts, he stumbled back and fell to his bare naked ass.

Instantly horrified, he tried to jump up but Tabrin's heel kept him on the floor. "You deserve to stay there for now!"

The toilet next door flushed and the woman left to wash her hands. Tabrin followed her with her eyes until she left the toilet then she stared at Timson.

"We had a deal didn't we Timson? We made... an... agreement didn't we?" Tabrin asked, with her chest heaving up and down and her finger movements becoming more erratic.

"The rule was whoever... comes – geeeez that feels good – last dies, right, that's what weeeeeee... agreed, right?"

Tabrin's fingers were digging deep into her pussy, hooking and holding against her walls.

"Silence time now." Tabrin said then closed her eyes with her heel still holding Timson on the floor holding onto his gun which was now useless.

Her fingers dug deep and stayed there for a few seconds. Then her eyes opened wide and she removed her fingers as a long stream of liquid followed.

Timson watched the stream of liquid fly straight into the air then arch down in his direction in slow motion.

'This is gonna hit me right in the...' Timson thought as the stream hit the door behind him and cascaded down his face and the front of his clothes.

The following streams hit him more directly, making him cower behind his hands to protect himself.

He could hear Tabrin laughing behind his shield and could see her continually rubbing her lips which sloshed between her fingers.

"MARRRRY, SWEET MOTHER JESUS! Now that is how you have an orgasm. And I'm not a squirter either, look at that. Did I get you?"

Timson dropped his arms and showed Tabrin the liquid that covered his face, neck and clothes. "Just a little bit."

"Whew, I haven't come like that in a long time," she said, sitting upright and drawing her panties up her thighs with her gun hand still focussed on Timson who was trying to get up.

"So now what?" "Now? Hmmm... what do we do?" She pulled the slide back on her gun." We DID have rules," he said, pointing his chin to the ceiling.?" Yeah we did... but rules can be broken sometimes." "Really? Well I'm all for breaking rules," Timson said excitedly. "You

wanna break the rule?" "Nah, not really," she said.

Then shot him three times in the face.

NIGHT SHIFT

Ellis couldn't believe he fell asleep.?AGAIN!?He sat up and looked at the other side of the bed and he saw

Tammy's chocolate back rising and dropping as she slept.?" Tammy?" he whispered to himself. What the hell was he doing with

Tammy? And in a hospital bed as well.?Ellis held his head and tried his best to recollect what happened the

night before and why the hell he was in bed with the sexiest nurse on the night watch. As he got up from the bed, he got silently dressed but not before looking at Tammy's ass and how beautiful it looked as she slept. He wanted to bite it but that would've woken her up ad he hadn't figured out how he ended up there. When he was dressed, he sat in the chair opposite the bed and found a can of ginger ale on the side table. He took a big sip in his dry mouth and his tongue unstuck from the roof of his mouth.

What happened here? Ellis thought. He held his head up with his right hand and looked at the sleeping beauty, whose breasts were now resting on top of the cream sheets that covered her. He took another sip as he watched the moonlight shine through the window over her shoulder.

"Oh yeah!!" Ellis spoke to himself and began to think back to one of the best days he'd ever had at work.

Ellis arrived at work for his final night shift in the God forsaken hellhole he called work. He inhaled as the hospital smell filled his nose, for the last time. He strolled past a busy waiting room but he didn't care because in eight hours, he was gone. He picked up his time sheet and clocked in, ready for the night's work.

"Hey Ellis, how you feeling tonight?" Ellis turned around as he saw Atanya, the head nurse and with her was Tammy, the focus of his dreams for the past two years, his work wife, the face on his masturbation fantasies, his dream woman.

"I'm ok. Excited that it's one more shift and I'm out this bitch! Wassup Tammy?"

Tammy looked up as if she just noticed him.?" Hey El, how you doing baby?" If there was one thing Ellis couldn't take, it was when Tammy called

him 'baby'. The possible connotations and benefits that come with being called 'baby' ran through his dirty mind. That voice filled his head as he masturbated to the thought of what her mouth felt like.

"Ready to get gone." "Lucky bastard. Leaving us all here." Just then, Atanya nudged Tammy and they made eye contact,

holding their own conversation with their eyes. Ellis shuffled to the staff room.

"Ellie?" Tammy called out to him.

"Yes ma'am?" Ellis hoped that she was calling him over so she could run into his arms like in all the movies. That wasn't the case!

"Ermm...remind me to ask you something later okay?"

She walked straight into his erection as he was coming out and she was walking into the staff room. Tammy smiled a little and then fixed her face as she saw the embarrassment in his eyes.

"Ellis...you've got the old people ward with me tonight!"

Her smile that felt his dick press against her made him more embarrassed but by this point he didn't care, the erection was for her anyway.

"Yeah that's fine Tammy, I'll see you in a minute."

After a while, Ellis realised that his dick wouldn't go down until he used the only tactic he knew of. He opened his locker again and stood facing it as he used his thumb and his forefinger under his helmet and squeezed until his raging erection became a limp bump in his scrubs.

He walked out of the staff room and Tammy was waiting for him at the reception desk. Her hair in two braided ponytails, skin the colour of pine wood and, though technically obese, she carried her weight attractively well.

"Erm, Ellis, are we going to start this night shift or are you just gonna stare at my backside all day?"

"You giving me a choice?!"

"You so nasty! I told you, we work together so we can't do anything."

"Sure, you always say that. Say something different."
"Different." Tammy looked at Ellis and he smiled back as they both understood

that if they weren't working together, they would be somewhere right now fucking up head boards. There was an obvious attraction between the two, and there was that kiss at the Christmas party, but they understood that nothing could happen. But Tammy felt that if her plans went right, then something WOULD happen.

"Ha!" Tammy's laugh escaped from her lips and into the hospital air. "What's funny?" Ellis asked.?" Nothing El, nothing at all!"

The night dragged on as Tammy and Ellis visited all the patients on their ward. They administered drugs, checked the conditions of the more serious patients and conversed with the bored ones. All the while brushing by each other with their clipboards and passing each other tightly, when there was more than enough space.

Many times, Tammy brushed Ellis' dick, causing him to rise, but his clipboard came in handy as it covered the rising obstruction.

By 2.00am, the pair took their first break together. They sat in the partially deserted café drinking coffee from plastic cups.

Tammy sipped her coffee and looked at Ellis as she licked a drip of liquid from her lips.

Ellis knew what she was doing, so he knew they had to talk about something or they'd go missing in a stockroom somewhere with her legs in the air.

"So what are you gonna do without me?" Ellis asked.

"Well, after my shift, I'm gonna go home and slit my wrists. Don't think for once second that you got it like that." Tammy looked at Ellis as he smiled at her, winking and looking at her plunging cleavage that was screaming his name.

"I'm sorry El, is there something for you down here?" As Tammy asked Ellis, she unbuttoned her nurse's blouse and showed him her full cleavage.

Ellis opened his mouth in a wide O, as if he was trying to receive her breasts into his mouth. His eyes stayed on her wood brown skin as she buttoned her top back up. He slid into the chair next to her trying to get a better view.

"You'll be lucky if you ever see these babies. Ever!"

Ellis' heart was pounding as he contemplated taking his hand from his thigh and putting it between hers. He looked into her eyes and saw the want, the desire in her eyes for him to do something. She sipped her coffee and tilted her head back as she finished her drink. Ellis saw this as the perfect opportunity. If he was going to do it, it had to be now.

Ellis, in one swift movement, ran his hand across her thigh and slid up until he could feel her pussy through her scrubs. He looked at Tammy, waiting for the eyes of disapproval but she was still sipping from her cup.

He ran his fingers up and down, imagining where her clit was. Her thighs parted slightly and he began to grind his fingers harder against her groin. He watched the surrounding café to make sure no one was coming. Trying to manoeuvre his hand for a better angle, he watched Tammy's hand reach under the table for his erection.

The feeling of a new hand on his dick made him close his eyes for a moment so he could enjoy it. His mind took him to a bedroom where he had Tammy on all fours rubbing his dick with two hands and all the spit he could handle.

She massaged it softly, wrapping her hand around it with slow jerks. He felt himself beginning to drift away with the good feeling as he heard voices coming from behind them. The doors to the café flew open and he quickly removed his hand while Tammy continued to jerk his dick.

"Tammy, what are you doing? We're gonna get caught. Oh shit..."

As the voices reached their backs, Tammy quickly snatched her hand, moved forward and then kissed her hand. As the orderlies walked straight past them, Ellis let out a sigh of relief as Tammy sprung up from her seat and walked towards the wards. She turned around, rubbing anti-bacterial liquid on her hands and looked back at Ellis who was struggling to fix himself.

"Ellis, come on, we've got work to do!" Tammy's demanding voice shook Ellis down to his bones. He adjusted himself again, holding his clipboard to his groin as he caught up with Tammy.

The remainder of the shift was as sexually charged as the start. Tammy would bend over to check statistics on the patients and Ellis would bump into her ass with his groin, followed by an 'oooppsie'. He'd drop his pen, pick it up then brush his dick up against her thigh while patients slept in front of them.

But Tammy would get her own back and on one occasion, she took it to an extreme. While Ellis was talking to a patient, Tammy went under the bed to look for her clipboard, which she dropped 'accidentally', reached into Ellis' scrubs and began to suck him softly. Ellis tried his best to listen to the patient's problems and how come his family hadn't been to see him since he'd been admitted, but he found it impossible as Tammy's lips moved softly around his dick, with her tongue ring tickling him.

"DID YOU FIND YOUR CLIPBOARD TAMMY?"

"Yes I did, thank you very much," she said wiping her mouth with the back of her hand.

"You okay down there?" the patient asked.?" Yes sir, I'm fine, dropped my clipboard. It was HARD but I found it!"

Ellis got up and walked out of the room almost laughing at Tammy's antics. She came out of the room, closed the door and looked at Ellis' dick to see if it was still standing.

"That was wrong Tammy. Shit, what if someone came in?"

"Yeah, well no one did, did they? You have to admit, that was fun though?"

"You ramp too much Tammy!" "Like you wouldn't ramp with me though!?"

4:30am came around. Patients were sleeping, the waiting room was dead quiet and Tammy and Ellis were in the middle of their rounds, moaning about how tired they were.

Tammy ran ahead and saw Atanya, who was about to leave. Ellis could see it was girlie talk because Atanya kept on looking back at him and smiling. The ladies shared a high five then Tammy came back towards Ellis.

"What was that about?" "Girl talk." "Yeah right, you were probably bragging about this LONG dick!" "You wish! Could you come with me to the kids ward, I need to get

something?" "What do you need to get from there, it's not even open yet?"

"I know, I was helping out there yesterday ready for the opening and I left it there." Tammy began to pull Ellis towards the elevators.

"So why do you want me to come with you?" Ellis gave the classic man answer.

"Well, it's cold and the thing is really heavy." "Ahhh haaa!" Ellis said with his eyebrows raised.?When they reached the ward, the silence was deafening.?" This way..." Tammy walked ahead of Ellis and looked at each door

she passed.?" What did you leave up here?" Ellis asked as he watched Tammy's

behind before him.?" Oh, erm...I left my... it's a..." Her words were evasive as she

continued to look at each door.?" What thing?" "Here!" Tammy stopped dead in her tracks and Ellis nearly bumped

into her ass, unprepared for the sudden stop. She grabbed Ellis by his waistband and dragged him into the room.

"What are you..."

The darkness of the room made Ellis uneasy until he began to hear the sound of clothes coming off.

"Tammy? You there?"

"Yeah, I'm here!" Ellis felt Tammy's hand as she walked into his space. "Take your clothes off NOW!"

Ellis was speechless as he felt himself being led towards what looked like a bed. The moonlight from the window shone through showing a silhouette of Tammy's naked body as she moved through the room.

"Come here."

"Where is here?" Ellis felt like a blind man. The room was partially lit but the ground was pitch black.

"By the window." Tammy's voice became seductive as she called out to him.

Ellis followed instructions and walked to the window. Following the light, he walked into what he thought was a chair. As he tried to move it, he felt Tammy's hair at waist height. Before he knew it, Tammy had his dick in her hands.

"Oh shit..."

He put his hands on the back of her head and with, no one around, began fucking her mouth, controlling the movement. Tammy used her tongue, mouth and throat to please every part of Ellis' dick. The moonlight glistened off him as it moved in and out Tammy's working mouth. She held his thighs as she poked her head into his dick. Hard as it was, Ellis knew that level of throat taking would end him prematurely and he wanted to more of what she had to offer. He picked her up from her knees and kissed her full on the lips. He felt his mini – me standing at full attention against Tammy's naked body and he throbbed. He broke the kiss by pushing her onto the bed. He lifted

his scrubs over his head, kicked off his trainers and dropped his bottoms and stepped out of them quick, fast and in a hurry.

Ellis walked up to the bed and looked at Tammy, as she lay on the bed with a hand between her thighs. He grabbed her arms and swung her onto her stomach. She made a sound as he slid an arm under her waist and lifted her onto all fours.

"So what are you gonna do back there?!"

Ellis grabbed her hips, getting a good look as his dick moved in and out of her pussy, squelching as he entered. And with the sight of her asshole contracting, Ellis was turned on.

Placing both hands on her shoulders, Ellis massaged Tammy's neck while pushing his dick deeper. As a nurse, Ellis knew that the key to a good massage wasn't big hands, but touching the right places with enough pressure to unlock those stress doors. And he was opening all of Tammy's doors.

Combined with the dick that she was enjoying, she was laying flat on her stomach humming with appreciation.

"OHHHHH, ELLLIIIISSSSSSSSS!!!!!"

Tammy exhaled loudly as she relaxed her body into a heap under him. Ellis felt his stroke become smoother with each thrust while she tried catching her breath. His hands moved further down her back, massaging the base of her spine.

"YES...YES...HARDER...YES..." "Hands or dick?" he asked back.?Tammy screamed as he suddenly picked her up by her waist and

spun the naked Tammy around so she was facing him. They kissed noisily, running their hands on every piece of skin available to them. Ellis backed into the window and felt the coolness of the windowsill and the shine of the moonlight on his back.

Tammy was ready to be bent, stretched, strained, lengthened, elongated and all that sweet, that nasty, that gushy stuff. During the kiss, he picked up one of Tammy's legs and placed it on his shoulder, putting her in a standing split position.

"What...how...ohhh..."

"Oh Tammy..." Ellis echoed into her ear as he pumped her pussy hard and kissed her ankle.

Tammy began to grind herself hard, grabbing his back and holding on for dear life.

The shock of pain forced Ellis to speed up his grind. His hips pumped faster and faster.

"YES...YES...YES...THAT'S...IT...FUCK...ME..." Tammy managed as her walls became slick.

"OHHH TAMMY...OH THAT'S IT! SHIT...I'M GONNA COME!" "NO!" In the blink of an eye, Tammy dropped her leg and dropped to her knees in front of Ellis. As she came face to face with his dick, she took

her thumb and forefinger and squeezed softly until he shrunk with a dribble of pre-cum leaking from the tip.

"How did you do that?" Ellis wondered. "Female secret!" Tammy winked.

She jumped up and Ellis watched everything jiggle. She pushed him back on the bed, woke his dick up with a wet palm wrapped around it and jumped on before he could fully get comfortable.

Tammy leaned forward causing her back to arch and her ass to jiggle independently from the rest of her body. It banged against Ellis' groin as she picked up speed with a deep clap.

"YES...YES...YES...THAT'S IT...OH SHIT...OHHH SHIT...I'M GONNA..." "GET IT..." he growled.?" SHIT, COME...COME...WITH...COME...WITH ME!?Tammy bounced her ass at top speed as Ellis raised his hips so his

dick poked further into her. Faster...faster...louder...?" THAT'S IT...KEEP IT THERE EL! I'M GONNA COME...I'M GONNA..." "YES TAMMY..." "- COME!" Tammy's body shuddered as her orgasm drained from out of her. "I'M COMING...HOLD ON...I'M...COMING!" At that moment, Ellis shot his streams into Tammy's pussy, holding

her onto hips. He felt his hot seed surround his dick while still inside her as she laid on his chest.

"Thank you Tammy." "Oh no, thank you baby!"

Sitting in the chair with his can of ginger ale, wearing creased scrubs and feeling woozy as hell, Ellis smiled to himself. At the same time, Tammy stirred in her sleep before dozing off again.

After writing down his new address and phone number, Ellis crept out of the room and closed the door softly.

The sun started to rise as he rubbed his eyes, looking at the time and taking the stairs to the ground floor. Turning to the staff room, Ellis walked straight into Atanya who made him jump.

"So how was the rest of your night shift?" She smiled.?" Fine thank you." Ellis answered, trying not to smile too much. "Wanna

clock out before you go?" "Sure!?" he said as Tammy took him by the hand and led him to a
>disabled toilet. "Follow me!"
>Ellis followed willingly.

DEE DEENA THE TEASER - CLITS

"Who the fuck are you now?! How many of you bitches are there? And when the fuck are you letting me go?"

His eyes focussed instantly. He was in an empty room with a full wall mirror in front of him and he was looking back at himself wearing a black onsie.

"First of all," said a female voice with an accent that he didn't recognise. "My name is Dee Deena The Teaser but you can call me Dee."

"Hi Dee."

"Hello Lamar." The voice from behind him came around his front and his eyes zoned in on a colourful pair of leggings wrapped around tight thighs and toned buttocks.

"So what are you supposed to be teaching me then?"

"Well, I'm not gonna be shocking you if that's what you're worried about. I've got some work to do and I'm gonna be asking you a few questions. That's it."

"What'd you wanna know?" "I'm here to find out about your flirting. Are you good at it?" "What?" He looked at his arms which were tied down with plastic.?" Flirting," Dee said as she stretched her arms and moved to a yoga

mat on the floor in front of him. "Are you a flirtatious person? Do you even know how to flirt?"

"I must do 'cuz I got a girlfriend so I be pretty good at it." "Hmmm... I disagree." Dee sat on the mat and laid flat while stretching her limbs.?" Well thank God I don't give a fuck about what you think. How are

you gonna ask me if I know how to flirt? Who are you?" "Not everyone is good at it. And I'm Dee Deena The Teaser, I

already told you that. And not everyone flirts with the right person at the right time. Are you one of those people Lamar?"

Dee turned onto her stomach and walked her hands back until she was on her feet in an arch in a downward dog position. Lamar watched her backside arch upwards and tilted his head to the side.

"Erm... no... I erm... I'm not a super duper flirt. I know the difference between innocent flirting and stupid flirting."

"Do you now?" Dee said, lifting one leg into the air and holding it there. "So that time you were out at Tiger Tiger for your work party and you went into the women's toilets with your work friend's girlfriend, that was just flirting right? Or the time you went to that swinger's party with your 'friend' but forgot to tell Keisha, that was a night full of innocent flirting right?"

Dee changed her position and was now sitting with her legs in her lap and her back straight looking right at Lamar, who was dumbstruck.

"So, you lot are watching me as well?"

"Let's just say if I know then Keisha knows. And she is not happy about it."

Lamar sighed heavily. "Okay, I think you need to let me go. NOW!" "Or what?" "Or I'm gonna get myself out and then I'm gonna come back here

with some real road dudes and..." "Really Lamar? We're here trying to help you be better and you want

to come and bring some road youts here? Really Lamar? I'll give you some free advice.. don't say that shit around the Nurse. She will REALLY fuck you up."

"GET ME THE FUUUUUUCK OUT OF HERE..."

Dee got up , walked behind him and came back with a chair which she placed in front of him then stood behind it.

"When was the last time you flirted with Keisha?" "What?" She put her hands on the back of the chair and lifted her feet off the

floor and hovered before lifting her legs higher and higher. Her feet were level with her face as she lifted them straight to the ceiling. Lamar watched her entire shape, looking like an upside Coca-Cola bottle.

"What'd you know about the art of the tease?" "The what?" "Have you ever flirted Keisha into bed? Like said things and done little things that have excited her?" "No, but I've fucked her into bed." Dee jumped down to her feet and looked at him. "And that's the same crass attitude that got you here in the first place." "Look, I don't know what you are trying to teach me but just give up and let me go." "But then you'll go home, you'll be the same shit boyfriend you've been who can't fuck, can't flirt or kiss. And I don't know about you, but that sounds like someone who's gonna be single real soon."

She moved the chair, sat back on the mat with her legs together and leaned her head towards her knees.

"Flirting is important. It let's someone know you are interested without being too obvious or too sexual. It can start a new relationship out of a look or it could let someone in a long term relationship know that their partner is still interested in them."

"Yeah I know that." Lamar mumbled.

"Do you remember the list Keisha gave you of all the things you aren't doing?"

Lamar looked up. "Yeah, I remember." He didn't.?" Remember point five... you don't flirt with her any more." "Oh yeah." Dee made it to her feet with a long stretch of her body.?" Lamar, I don't know what you think about us but we're here to keep you and Keisha happy."

"How, by kidnapping me?" "No, by educating you." "I already went to school and passed with flying fucking colours thanks very much." "You DID go to school but you didn't pass. You didn't even make it out of college with good grades so you keep lying to yourself about your flying fucking colours."

"Yeah well..." he mumbled.

Dee Deena The Teaser stood up in front of him and lifted her knee to her chest and extended her foot until it was at the same level as the button next to his head. "Pay attention to us Lamar."

VIOLENCE

"Fuck each and every single one of those no imagination, no vision having, pretentious, fuck mouth, wank faces."

Zephane was livid.

His chocolate bald head was dripping sweat down his neck, making the collar of his shirt cold and he wasn't driving with due care and attention. All he could see was red.

He checked his phone, still waiting for the reception to kick back in. "Absolute and total bunch of animal fuckers." Curse words were lining up in his mind as he took off from a set of

traffic lights with the wheels of his Audi TT RS screeching underneath him. He was listening to an early Dipset mixtape because he was in such an angry mood.

He didn't start out being so pissed off.

When Zephane was putting on his three-piece black suit and bow-tie at the start of the evening, he was in the bathroom of his creation, singing off-key to Jazz FM classics on the radio.

He was electric-sliding across his heated bathroom floor in his socks and boxers because he was excited. Today was supposed to be the day he would receive the validation he deserved for all the effort he put into his work. His living, breathing, amazing piece of work.

Not a brick, wood plank or pane of glass out of place. Everything where it was supposed to be.

Neat, tidy, minimalist.

That's what Kevin McCloud said to him when the cameras of Channel 4's Grand Design came into his house, which he designed and built himself.

Stepping out of his en-suite, he walked into his bedroom and caught his reflection in the glass of the balcony doors. He suddenly got hard.

Sliding his balcony open, he watched the sun go down with a Wray and Nephews and ginger beer.

Looking at the London skyline, with a hell of an evening to come, Zephane felt like he had the world in the palm of his hands.

And now here he was.

Driving like he was on the Top Gear race track, his bow-tie untied and dangling.

"What a bunch of utter bitch whores," he said to himself, anticipating a large drink when he got home.

Zephane's anger was based on the decision that took place earlier while he was sitting in Earls Court Exhibition Centre, with the who's who of architecture around him, fighting it out for some of the most coveted awards in the home design community.

Zephane was sitting up straight, slow sipping a glass of champagne constantly checking his watch and his phone. He took no notice of the people sitting on his table, he didn't know them and, honestly, he wasn't interested in chit chat. He wanted his work to speak for him.

His creation was a three-floor detatched modern structure, using a mix of concrete, wood and glass to make it look more like a museum than a house. Ground floor was a spacious kitchen and dining area behind floor-to-ceiling glass in the front and the back. First floor was a massive living area and bathroom with a beautiful Greek roll-top bath.

Top floor was the master bedroom, which was the size of most community halls. The en-suite was connected to the side of the bedroom in a glass case that caught Kevin McCloud with his mouth open.

Throw in an underground garage for his car and Zephane was being touted as the 'next big thing' in architect circles. Considering it was what he did for a living, he knew this day would come and the world would recognise him as the genius he knew he was.

There were no nerves running through him as he watched the stage, waiting for his category to come up. He checked his phone, unhappy that his reception was so sketchy.

Zephane had set up the CCTV cameras in his home to his phone so no reception meant he couldn't see his creation from all angles. Not like he didn't set every alarm before he left, but he always liked to be able to see it.

He kept that annoying thought in the back of his mind as he stared at the stage, imagining what it would be like to stand there and look out toward the crowd.

It was the biggest award of the night and he knew he had to win.

Looking at the event programme, scanning the other homes in his category, he knew he was a shoe in.

They were good attempts but their vision was lost in things that came before.

"Carbon copy," Zephane mumbled to himself.

A male presenter came on stage and announced his category and Zephane sat up.

Each nominee was read out and a 30 second montage of their home was shown.

Zephane tisked and tutted his way through each montage until his vision of beauty came up. He flexed the muscles in his neck, listening for sounds of wonder and amazement from the seated crowd around him. Confidence was forcing him to smile and he took another slow sip from his flute, swirling the glass like a cocky sunnuvabitch.

"And the winner is..."

Zephane was flooded with adrenaline. He couldn't hear anything as he watched the presenter open the envelope.

He flicked between the presenter and the screen, waiting to find out if he won.

Zephane didn't hear the name called but the house that flashed largely on the screen wasn't his.

The crowd were applauding in the direction of a balding hump of a man who shuffled to the stage in a poorly fitted suit and boat shoes.

"Fucking cuntbag, shit stuffing, tit kickers..." Zephane said, under the round of applause with the flakiest of grins.

His whole body was willing him out of the room before the speech started but he didn't want to look like a poor loser. Even though he was.

In his mind, there was no home nominated that was better than his. The risks he took, the vision he put into it, the hard work he lost sleep over.

He knew it. And he knew that the judges would see that too. But they didn't.

Courteously, he sat through the winner's speech, all sorts of curse word combinations flying through his mind.

Soon as the chunky butt of a man left the stage, Zephane got up and was in his car, playing ignorant rap full blast within five minutes of leaving his seat.

Turning onto Birkbeck Place, looking down the road for the outline of light created by his path, Zephane began to relax.

"They don't know what good architecture is. They just like that same old, carbon copy, throwback to old shit design."

He turned down the Phonte mixtape that was providing his mind with the clever wordplay he wanted to hear. Cursing extra hard, Zephane took a deep breath as he turned into his drive. A button on his dash opened his underground garage and he turned off the engine and rolled in.

Braking softly, Zephane got out, gave the car the over the shoulder lock, watched the doors close then made his way up to his kitchen.

Up one flight of steps, he reached a door with a keypad with a solid red light above it. He entered the code.

The door clicked then clacked and the red light turned green. At the same time, he pulled his phone out and saw that his home Wi-Fi kicked in on his phone.

Logging on to his CCTV camera app and pushing the door at the same time, Zephane immediately knew something was wrong.

When he pushed the door, he felt something bang against the other side. Sticking his head around the door, he saw a broken jar scattered on his marble floor.

He turned the lights on with his phone and realised the jar was the least of his problems.

Every cupboard in his kitchen was open, every draw pulled out, his tap was running, his expensive cereal was scattered over everything and his fridge and freezer were wide open.

Zephane stood mouth open in absolute shock.

To see his beautiful kitchen so utterly disrespected was filling him with new rage. Looking through, he could see his glass dining table had a solid metal chair directly in the middle of it and graffitti was flowing over his furniture.

Being on the ground floor, he knew that if he'd just been robbed, then there'd be more annoyance the higher up he went.

He wanted to move but he couldn't stop surveying the carnage. On top of the night he had, Zephane could feel his blood boiling.

Taking slow careful steps over his broken things, he made it to his umbrella cupboard and reached in without looking, keeping his eyes on his surroundings.

His fingers latched onto the firm lumber of his Louisville Slugger baseball bat he brought back from a business trip to New York.

Sliding it out slowly, he rested it on his shoulder and looked at the cameras of his house on his phone. Instead of loading each camera together, Zephane only got one screen at a time. The middle floor bathroom loaded in black light and showed the thief had gone crazy in there too. The screen switched to his living room in black light and he could feel himself getting more and more angry.

"How the fuck did they get in without the alarm going off?" Zephane was asking himself a thousand and one questions. Where was the malfunction in his perfect system?

Sliding his feet up each step to his second floor living room with the bat over his shoulder, Zephane turned on the light before he entered. His thinking was if anyone was in there, they'd scuttle like roaches and he can swing free in self-defence.

There was no movement as he looked around. His expensive surround sound system was gone. His Mac was gone, his new PS4 was gone. His iPad that was charging was gone. TV, Blu-Ray and DVDs gone. His sofa was turned over, his pictures were smashed and, he could see remnants of his cereal on the floor.

"So you brought shit up just to fuck up my carpet? I sweaaaaaaar, if I ever find who did this.... ooooooo..." Zephane said to himself.

He wasn't so pissed about losing the gadgets, they were insured. He would get them back within the week. It was the absolute mindless bullshit they had done which was making him want to kill.

The way he lived, Zephane had everything in a place. There were no odd things here or things out of place there; everything had a place. And it stayed there.

Shoes were taken off at the door and guests were given slippers to wear throughout the house. There were hidden stashes of glass cleaner on each floor, in case of a random smudge.

To see his perfection massacred this way was grinding on his last nerve.

"Fucking thick glob devil sperm..." Zephane mumbled.

He checked his phone and the camera in his top floor en-suite came on. But for some reason the light in the bathroom was on and showed the room had been untouched.

Sliding his finger across his iPhone, a feed of his bedroom came up. Again, the lights were on as the camera panned from side-to-side. When the camera came into view of his bed, he did a double take,

then squinted and shook his head all at the same time.?Whatever or whoever was going on, they were in his bed, under his

sheets.?Zephane looked up at the ceiling, picturing exactly where they were

above him. He stopped the camera panning and watched as a man came up from the depths of a woman's thighs. His back muscles suddenly contracted and Zephane knew the bastard in his bed had just slipped it in.

In HIS bed. Messing up HIS expensive mattress. Getting their sweat and juices in HIS sheets. Rubbing their grimy heads on HIS pillows.

Zooming in slowly, he couldn't make out their faces but he could see it was definitely a man and a woman.

Stepping back out into the corridor, shuffling his feet rather than taking steps, Zephane moved towards the stairs.

With the bat resting comfortably on his shoulder in one hand and his phone in the other, he took each step carefully. He knew his stairs wouldn't creak but he would hate to be wrong.

With each step he climbed, he could hear random moments of human pleasure. A female yelp, a male groan, a hand slapping against skin, a call for God.

On his phone, he could see the bastard was on top and was pounding away, with her arms out to the sides.

"In MY bed for fuck sake."

Reaching the top step, he froze and listened to the couple fucking in his bed. With his door open, he could see five huge duffel bags that bulged in the shape of his stolen belongings.

If he wasn't so angry, he'd find this funny. Maybe even be slightly flattered. Robbers came to rob him then felt like fucking in such beautiful surroundings.

Such a funny thought made some of the anger retreat but then he had a flashback to the can of Spam with legs that beat him to his prestigious award earlier on and the anger returned.

With his back against the door, he leaned his ear and watched the couple fuck in his bed. Considering all that was going on, Zephane didn't know why he suddenly started to critique the man in his bed and his technique. He was quick fingered, no finesse, no style to what he was doing.

He had to shake that thinking off. He had to do something.

They broke into his house. His beautiful creation of a house. They fucked up his beautiful creation.

"So I have to fuck someone up!" Zephane muttered.

Sliding his phone into his pocket, he took a strong grip of his bat and pushed the door open. The woman was yelping like a Chihuahua and Zephane saw an opportunity to slide it further.

Her voice covered the sound of the door moving and Zephane crouched into the room. The door closed behind him silently and he looked around, wondering if they were alone.

His white blinds were down over his windows and single spot lights on the floor gave the room a beautiful light.

Standing up and stretching his neck, Zephane grabbed the bat at each end and walked up on the bed with quick steps. He moved so quickly, the man didn't realise what happened until he lifted backwards out of the bed.

Zephane slid the bat around the man's neck and locked his elbows around either end while dragging him out of the bed. The woman opened her eyes in shock and started to scream.

"Shut up... shut your fucking mouth... if you..." Zephane said, before applying more pressure on his elbows.

The naked man's arms were flailing and his legs were kicking as Zephane fell back to the floor, pulling the man with him. He kept the pressure on as the man elbowed him in the ribs, which he took with ease in his penguin tuxedo.

A few seconds and the man's arms were slowing down, his legs were down to a twitch and then he stopped moving all together.

Listening to the man breathing told Zephane he didn't kill him, just put him to sleep.

"Thanks Jack Bauer," he thought to himself.

With a swift push, the naked man rolled onto his front with his ass in the air.

Zephane made it to his feet, with his adrenaline pumping.

He instantly locked eyes with the woman, who was still laying down on the bed.

"Oh my God, is he dead? Did you just kill my..." "Shhhh..." Zephane said. "He's asleep." He picked up the bat and walked towards the bed where the woman had been tied by her arms to his headboard with handcuffs. He couldn't help looking her over once and she noticed by turning her head to the side. From the floor, he picked his sheets and covered her nakedness before sitting on the end of the bed. Tearful mumbles started behind him. " Look, we're sorry okay? Your stuff is over there, just..." "Just WHAT?" Zephane shouted. "What should I JUST DO, HUH? Do you really think for one funk fucking moment that you can..."

He raised his hand to calm himself down. " What's your name?" he asked. " What?" she replied. He asked again, but quieter. "What is your name?" "Mallory."

"And what's sleepy's name over there?" "MuuMuuuuuu... Mustufa." "Mallory and Mustufa? Really?" Zephane asked, feeling genuinely tickled. "That's funny." Attitude grew in Mallory. "So what the fuck then? You just choked my boyfriend..." "He's asleep." "What the fuck ever, just..." "For someone who just got caught robbing from and fucking in the bed of a complete stranger, you got a lot to say." "I told him we should've just gone but he had to... Zephane laughed to himself. "You REALLY think I'm not calling the police? Don't think I won't get off for self-defence for putting him to sleep."

"Just take your shit back and we'll just..." "Shhh..." Zephane looked at her with an angry side eye as he took his phone from his pocket and began to dial the police. Holding the phone to his ear, he watched Mallory start to cry.

"Please... don't..."

"I'm sorry, you've just robbed me, fucked up my place, spilt my cereal all over the gaff and you DON'T want me to call the police?"

"We'll just leave and that'll be..." "You know what your right," Zephane said and hung up the phone. Surprise washed over Mallory's face, which was buried in her bush of auburn curls as Zephane stared at her. She frowned. "What?" "Where did you go to school Mallory?" "What?"

"Come on, you're not fucking deaf, what SCHOOL did you go to?" His voice made her jump. "I went to Holy Family in..." "...Walthamstow." Zephane finished.?It was her turn to give him the side eye as she looked at him, trying to recognise him as someone she may have known in her past. "Yeah, how did you know?" "I went there too. I was in the same year as you. Oh I remember you. Mallory Francois." She was squinting. "Erm... I don't..." "You wouldn't remember me. I was into my books while you and your people would sneak off-site and do whatever you wanted. You never spoke to me. But I remember you."

"Well here's a story to leave out of the class reunion." Mallory joked. "So now what?"

"It's simple. You fuck me and I'll let you both go."

Zephane spoke so honestly and his voice had such a melody to it, Mallory felt like she had no choice but to say yes.

Looking at her properly, he remembered her all too well. She was the pinnacle of the playground girls walking during his school days and was the fantasy of every boy in their year and the year above. Any time she would walk past him, he'd have to stop and watch her walk away, such was her allure.

"I don't know what to say to that to be honest," Mallory said with a scoff.

"It's pretty simple. This is MY house. This is MY bat. Your dude is asleep. You ROBBED me. You had sex in MY bed. Really I wanna kill someone but it'd be tougher to claim self-defence if I..."

The way he talked about ending life like it was throwing something in the bin made Mallory physically nervous.

"So, here's the deal... you gimme some, I let you both go. And you don't have long to decide either 'cuz sleeping beauty is gonna wake up soon."

Turning her head from side-to-side, Mallory felt like she was stuck between a rock and a hard place. She knew full well that Mustufa was on his third strike, while she was on her second. She could get off with some community service, maybe even classes, but he'd be sent away for a very long time.

"What'd you wanna..." Mallory started.

"This is not a negotiation or a questionnaire, it's very fucking simple. And, by the way, your thinking time is up!"

Freshly flustered, Mallory looked to the glass ceiling and tried to make a tough decision in an even tougher situation.

She closed her eyes and nodded." I can't hear you," Zephane said, holding the bat to his ear." Yes, alright?" "Alright what?" She sighed. "Alright... we can do it. But you'll let us go afterwards

right?" "Right."

Zephane stood up, dropped the bat and took off his jacket and his waistcoat. The more he thought about what he just proposed, the more aroused he became. He unbuttoned his shirt and, if the situation wasn't so strange, she would've been impressed by his physique.

The more naked he became, the more he wanted to fuck while she just watched Mustufa sleeping on the floor.

Down to his boxers, he was already hard.

Whipping the covers off the bed and throwing them on the sleeping heap on the floor, Zephane crawled on his knees until he was level with her knees, which were up.

She looked at him, still trying to remember his face but nothing came to her.

"You ready?" Zephane asked." Where's the condom?" "Don't have one." "Well then you ain't fucking me then..." "Cool," Zephane said then reached down for his phone and started

dialling." Hold on, hold on, hold on..." "Fuck that!" Mallory sighed. "You haven't got anything have you?" "Look at how clean my place was. You think I'd live nice like this and

have some community dick?" "Just don't cum inside me." Zephane parted her thighs with minimal resistance. She let her feet slide down until she was flat again. He parting her thighs with his knees looking at her body.

Mallory was fidgeting with her hands, trying to cover herself with her thighs open. Zephane looked down and spat on his dick and rubbed it with his fingers before rubbing his head up and down, searching for her opening.

Still wet from her previous encounter, Mallory knew he'd find his way in and he did with a deep thrust that took her by surprise.

Her eyes opened and she looked down to see that he only had half his dick inside her.

Zephane grinned and dipped himself deeper, watching her eyes widen and her hands grip the air. He fell forward on top of her and moved his hips until he was all the way in. He absorbed her whimper in his shoulder and took a handful of her hair and just squeezed. His hips moved slow enough that she could feel it. Slow enough that they could hear the movement. Slow enough that she couldn't help but move her hips to it.

Withdrawing up to his head, then sliding all the way back in quickly made her scream a big dog sound.

Zephane was holding onto her body as he rammed his hips against her, giving her no option but to take it.

Mallory felt her legs rising in order to give him more clearance to keep doing what he was doing.

She instantly felt wrong for beginning to enjoy it felt good and that was what made it all such a mind fuck for her.

He was grunting in her hair, with his other hand supporting her ass to help him get deeper.

Slamming inside her, Mallory didn't want to enjoy it but it was getting better with each stroke.

Zephane's grunts turned into growls which turned into mumbling in her ear.

"You tried to rob me... didn't you bitch?"

He prodded so deep inside her, the words came before she had a chance to filter. "Yeeeeeeesss..."

"But I got you... now your mine... yeaaaahhh... I'm gonna make you pay... takeeee... it out on this pussy..."

His breathy words were warming her ear and continuing to make her wet.

"I'm sorry... sooo... soo ooo... soorrrrry..." Mallory said in a shaky voice.

Zephane slid all the way inside and moved his hips to push deeper. Mallory hoped she hid her four orgasms well.

Slowly withdrawing, they both felt every moment and Zephane knew it was over.

Her walls felt too smooth, too silky and he felt his dick begin to charge while he growled.

He took a few more long deep strokes before he pulled out and began to pump his dick between her thighs.

Nothing happened for two seconds, then he came.

The strength and anger in his shot went over her head and landed in her hair. The following eruptions landed on her face, neck, breasts and stomach.

Zephane was still pumping his dick and trying to catch his breath as Mallory lay there, silently enjoying an orgasm that began as soon as his semen began shooting.

"PHEEEEEWWW..." Zephane said, cool as a cat. It was as if he came and all his previous anger had dissipated.

He walked to his bathroom and came back out with a towel.

Breathing heavily, Mallory watched him wipe her down with a warm hand towel that smelled like aloe vera.

Now she had cum, the guilt of what she just did began to kick in and then she remembered Mustufa, who was still lying on the floor.

"Is he okay down there?" Mallory asked.?Zephane crouched to the end of the bed and checked his pulse. "Yeah. Out cold." "So..." she started.?" Oh yeah, hold on..." Zephane said with an air of levity in his voice

then he bent down and picked up his phone again. Mallory frowned. "Who you calling?" "The police." "What, why?"

"Yeah, hello, could I be put through to the police please?" "I thought we had a deal." "We do." "So why are you still calling the police?!"

"Yeah hi, erm, I live at 23 Birkbeck place, and I've come home and I've been burgled. I think I can hear someone in my bedroom."

Then he hung up.

"What the FUCK?" she screamed, making Mustufa twitch in his slumber.

"It's simple. You can either be here when they arrive or not. But SOMEONE is getting arrested."

"You can't..." "I did... stay or go, stay or go, stay or go?" Mallory felt like she was back between that rock and hard place

where she had to make a tough decision in a tough situation.?Her face was confused and torn in so many ways, she didn't know

what to do. Either way someone loses out. There was no way she and Mustufa could both get out of this unscathed. And that was the thinking that helped her decide.

She unwrapped a hair band from her wrist and tied her hair down before jumping off the bed and reaching for her tracksuit bottoms and hooded jumper.

"I'd be quick if I were you, police station is only round the corner."

MARCUS AND THE FAVOUR

Sitting on the edge of his bed with his hand rubbing his dick through his shorts, Marcus was a man on a mission.

His iPhone was heating up in his hand as he hung up and called another random name from his phone book. So far, the response had been the same. No answer, voice mail or the sound of someone uninterested.

After spending what the news called the 'hottest day of the year' in his office, on a Saturday, Marcus reached home as streaks of darkness crept across London's skyline from south of the river. He'd opened YouTube on his PlayStation 4 and was listening to another neo soul mix by DJ Raphael. His first port of call was getting rid of his uniform, opening a Desperado and finding someone to do before night time fell.

Marcus was used to having a full stable of names in his phone that would answer on the first or second ring. Legs would open for him as he'd send text messages announcing his arousal and nipples would rise and poke through shirts as he stood at front doors with a bottle of something in one hand and two condoms in his back pocket. But with the summer season sprinkled with rainy days and windy nights, Marcus was sitting on his bed, trying to find someone who was at the same loose end as him. Maybe someone who was in between plans; quarter of the way through finding an outfit for a night out they don't really want to endure or bored enough that an offer of a drink and DVD would entice them out of their home.

Marcus' frustration was rising as he scrolled through his phone book, looking at names, trying to remember faces and shapes.

Alexia – no answer.?Bobbie – she sent the call to voicemail after two rings.?Carina – voicemail.?Diane – sounded like she answered then hung up.?Emily – disconnected tone.?Fiona – found God judging from the 'God bless you' on her voicemail. Gillian – a guy with a serious cockney tone answered.?Helga – voicemail.?Indiana – international ringing tone.?Jacqueline – dead tone.?Katisha – continuous ringing.?Leigh – no answer.?Mada – a man with an Asian accent asked, "Cab service?" Neve – voicemail.?Olivia – sounds like she answered in her handbag.?Paulina – sent to voicemail after one ring.?Quinn – no answer.?Rabia – answered and said "DON'T CALL MY PHONE AGAIN!" Sariya – answered then hung up before he spoke.

Taryn – no answer.?Uma – answered but no one spoke.?Vicky – voicemail.?Wendi – voicemail.?Xiesha – no answer.?Yasmin – one ring before going to voicemail. Zoey – disconnected number.

"What the actual fuck?" Marcus said to himself, adjusting his erection which was slipping through the button hole of his boxers. "This is STRICTLY ridiculous. Not one woman answering her phone?"

Flicking through more names, hoping one of them would answer, Marcus laid back against his headboard and was getting to the stage where he was about to give up. The strength in his erection was diminishing slowly and he could feel blood rushing away from his groin and into other parts of his body.

"Come on Anthea... she ALWAYS answers," Marcus said, hoping his number one back up fuck would answer the phone and make herself available to him.

Her phone rang for so long, it automatically hung up.

That was the moment Marcus hung up the phone and gave up on any chance of getting some. His erection wilted as he went online through his phone to check the football scores with a massive sigh of frustration. Marcus was resolved to the fact that he was spending this Saturday night alone.

He switched off his PlayStation and turned his Sky Plus on, switching straight to the news. A line of models walked on a catwalk in ridiculously high heels and, for the first time in a long time, Marcus thought about someone he thought he'd forgotten. It'd been a good few years since she walked in her high heels through his mind, with her baby dreadlocks growing nicely over a seriously nice body and a crazy obsession with shoes.

His train of thought ended as he remembered his angry response to the disrespect she showed him by sending pictures to another man. She tried to deny it, but Marcus knew what he saw that day.

"Fuck her... I still would though... that Blue pussy was the silk shit."

With his phone charging, Marcus skipped to the kitchen in his boxer shorts. He was in the cupboard for a glass, next into the fridge for the Captain Morgan's and fruit juice and back up the stairs before his bed space got cold.

Frustrated at how boring his night was going to be, he turned his PlayStation3 back on, planning a quick self-pleasure session with a Lethal Lipps clip. His irritation over spending a Saturday night with himself, literally, told him that he probably wouldn't make it past Lethal's vicious, chin-coating blowjob. Follow that with some Call of Duty and his juice and that was his night.

He logged on to the internet with his controller and found the Lethal Lipps video he had in mind when his phone rang next to his thigh.

"I was gonna SAY... someone has to be sucking my dick tonight," Marcus said to himself as he answered his phone without looking at the display.

"Marcus? Are you home? Buzz me in please." "Hello? Oh, Stephen, wassup? Yeah, I'm at home, what's wrong?" "Buzz me in, I need a massive favour." "Yeah, yeah..." Marcus waited for Stephen to buzz his door before letting him in. He

unlocked the front door and went back to his room, making sure to close the open porn scene that was ready to go.

Stephen crashed into the flat, breathing heavily and making the front door bang off the wall.

"Oi oii oiiiii... fix up yaself," Marcus shouted from his bedroom.

"Sorry, sorry..." Stephen yelled back, closing the front door behind him.

The six-foot seven chocolate Adonis that was Stephen walked into Marcus' bedroom in a grey sweatsuit and fresh Jordans. Muscular in all the right places, finely groomed and carrying a large duffle bag, he sat on the edge of the bed and exhaled heavily.

Marcus, sitting at the head of the bed, looked at his friend's back and could see heat waves rising from his neck.

"Don't put your sweaty ass on my bed," Marcus said, playing Camp Lo's 80 Blocks From Tiffany's mixtape.

"Oh shut up... It's hot out there and I ran up the stairs so allow me." "Yeah, but your sweating on my bed though." "Do you want me to sweat on you?" Stephen said, turning to face

Marcus with liquid dripping down his temple.?" Look, Black Fabio, if you wanna fuck me, just ask me innit?" Marcus

laughed.?" And that's why your gay. Where's the drink at?" "Are you a visitor? You know where the kitchen is." "If I was a chick, I bet you would've got me a drink." "And some dick too. So what's this favour?" "Hold on, lemme get a drink first."

With Stephen off in the kitchen, Marcus looked at his phone, checking to make sure he had enough reception to receive any messages or phone calls that might've come through at the last minute. He had full bars.

"Okay, so... here's the thing..." Stephen said, walking back into the room with a pint glass of gold liquid. "The modelling work has been slow for me at the moment, yeah? So I've been... erm..."

"What?" Marcus said, suddenly interested. "You been selling dick to lonely baby mothers in south London?"

"What? No... you fool. I'm not that broke... yet." Stephen laughed after a large sip. "Okay. I've been... dancing."

"Dancing how Stephen?" Marcus was leaning so far forward, waiting to let out a howl of laughter, he spilt his drink on his duvet.

"Oh NOW you wanna know? Alright, I've been doing stripper work for hen parties and..."

The sound Marcus released reverberated around the room and felt good in his soul.

"Ohhhh my God... no waaaay? YOU Stephen?" "What? You don't think I could..." "Oh wait... hold on? Do you dance to Jodeci?" "Okay... get the jokes out now and we can get back to business." "Let's see... do you have any shares in baby oil?" Marcus laughed. "Yeah... of COURSE Marcus," Stephen said, dismissively.

"When they throw £1 coins at you, do you catch them between your cheeks?"

"Yes Marcus, I get extra tips if they hit my brown eye." "Ewww... you had to go and ruin it for me."

Marcus gathered himself and cleared his throat, followed by a sip of his drink. His eyes drew to Stephen's large bag sitting on the floor by the door.

"What's in the bag?" "That's actually why I'm here." "Uh oh... here it comes." "I was supposed to be doing a small intimate 'show' tonight with this

other guy but he's dropped out at the last minute 'cuz of some issues he's got at home."

"No, no fuck no!" "I haven't asked you anything yet," Stephen said.?" Okay, so lemme finish your story for you shall I? So the guy's

cancelled on ya and left you stuck as the booking was for two strippers. If I had to think like you, I bet the money is too good for you to cancel and lose a booking so you thought you'd come here and see if I'd help you out by being a STRIPPER? A male stripper? Sound about right?"

"For an hour's work, they'll pay us £10,000."

"You really want me to... hold on... wait... you mean £5,000 each for 60 minutes? Are you sure?"

"No. I mean £10,000 EACH!"

Marcus stopped laughing when he saw the serious look on Stephen's face. From the start of the story, it had been an absolute laugh-fest in his mind for him to imagine his friend dancing for a group of women, dripping in oil, getting his grind on to a 90's slow jam. That was until the idea of an hour dancing for women and walking away with £10,000 started to sound better than the evening he had planned.

"Ten G... for an hour..." Marcus stuttered on himself in disbelief.

"Bet you wanna do me that favour now!?" Stephen said, finishing his drink.

Marcus looked at the floor, a thousand thoughts running through his mind. With his phone strangely silent, with not even a What's App message to play with, he had a wank and some random TV planned for the night.

"Yeah, yeah..." Marcus' mouth was still thinking thousands. "I think I can buss two moves for ten grand."

In exactly 30 minutes, Marcus was showered, shaved and holding a bag of his own as he stood with Stephen outside his flat.

"How we getting there?" Marcus asked, hunching his shoulders. "We're being picked up." "How did you know to tell the driver to come and pick you up from

here?" Stephen laughed. "Because I knew as soon as you heard how much

you could earn, you'd say yes." "I'm the king of the hard wine. Trust me, you saved me night." "Thank me after we're... WHAT?!" Stephen said, looking off into the

distance.?Marcus turned to see what had him so stuck as a stretch limo pulled

up in front of them. The back doors opened and drew both of their attention as they stood and watched the door for a moment. Marcus gave Stephen a shove towards the door.

With the front window blacked out, they couldn't see the driver except for the outline of a driver's hat.

"After you," Marcus said to Stephen, holding his arm out.

They both got in and sat down cautiously, as if they expected the back seats to become chairs of torture that would cut their dicks off. A crackle above their heads drew their attention to a speaker on the roof.

"Evening gentlemen," a female voice said. "I'm the driver with no name and I'll be making sure you get to the party on time. I can tell you now, the girls are gonna LOVE you two."

Marcus mouthed, "She's talking about me." "It'll take about 25 minutes to get to where we're going..." "Which is?" Marcus replied.?Her voice changed. "Follow the third star on the left and straight on

until £10,000 for an hour's work and don't ask me no damn questions, you hear me?"

Stephen looked at Marcus with his eyebrows raised. "Yeah, no problem."

"Good. Now sit back, have a drink, there's rum in the little cabinet there and if you look in the centre console, there's some weed; kush, thai and I think I put a bit of high grade in there as well. Go nuts boys."

Marcus turned to the arm rest next to him and lifted it to see small clingfilm wraps of different types of weed.

"Oh we will," Marcus said excitedly while pulling out RAW rolling papers and rolling tobacco. "We'll be fine back here."

"Let's go then," the voice said and disappeared as the limo pulled away with a sudden jolt and jumped a changing light.

Marcus and Stephen held onto the leather underneath and gave each other the 'let's put on our seatbelts' frown.

Three cocktail spliffs between them and double shots of rum for Dutch courage had Marcus and Stephen folded like pieces of paper. Stephen was slouched low in his seat, almost horizontal while Marcus gave up on trying to see where they were going and closed his eyes to the 90's music that was playing.

"Hold on, wait, what are we gonna do?" Marcus said, as if he just had a eureka moment.

"About what" Stephen said sleepily.

"An hour's worth of dancing! Don't we need to plan a set or learn some moves?"

"Not at all Marcus my boy. That's the beauty of it. I'm finding out that this job is like being a magician. You gotta give them a show, but you also have to be an illusionist when it comes to time keeping. So, think about. An hour show. Break it down into a five to ten minute slow intro. A few minutes of standing while music is playing then individual dance moments while I back you up. Then I do my thing. All dramatic and shit. Then we do the Kid and Play bit then individual lap dances, which is where the tips come in..."

"Whoa whoa..." Marcus said, opening his eyes. "Jump back a bit. Did you say the 'Kid and Play'?"

"YEAH! You have no idea how well that routine goes down. The women start screaming, money starts raining... cha CHING!"

"So that's extra on TOP of the £10,000?" Stephen groaned as he sat up straight. "Any tips you get, you keep." Marcus thought he commanded his eyes to open wide in shock but

he only felt his eyebrows spasm a little.?He looked out of the window as the limo slowed down and nudged

Stephen in his thigh.?" Oi oi oiiiiii... is this how they're going on?" Stephen looked out of the black windows and his mouth fell open.

"Fuuuuuuck me!"

They looked out in time to see the limo pass through a pair of large gold gates along a gravel path that crunched beneath the limousine's tyres. Marcus looked up and saw a beautifully lit building that looked like a mini castle or stately home owned by some rich white old guy. He counted 16 windows across and five windows down and each one was lit up. Security cameras watched the limo from all angles leading up to the house and added to the awe that had Marcus' mouth wide open. The kind of house that looked like it had different wings and required travel carts to get to the different rooms. Large stone work walls and the sheer size made it look like a recently renovated Grand Designs experiment.

The speaker on the roof crackled again as the car slowed down to a stop. "We're here boys. Get ya shit and let's get it!"

Marcus looked at Stephen through slanted eyes and they both sighed heavily, taking the last swigs of their drinks. Stephen stumbled out of

the limo with his bag and Marcus clattered into him, almost losing his balance.

The driver's side door opened and their driver walked around the back of the limo. Marcus could see that the driver's suit she was wearing wasn't hers as it hung off her to the point where the arms of the jacket covered her hands. The beauty of her chocolate face came through as she took off the hat and ran a hand over her bald head.

"You guys ready?" she asked them as Marcus bent over and stretched the muscles in the back of his legs while Stephen stretched to the sky.

"What kind of building is this?" Marcus asked, his eyes scanning the entire grounds.

"It used to be a repository. But now its a hired hall. Nice innit?"

"Imagine how much the mortgage is on a place like this?" Stephen said.

"How much did it cost to rent this place out for the evening?" Marcus directed at the driver.

"I dunno. I'm just a driver. I was told to drive you here and escort you to that door." She pointed to a doorway that was illuminated by a single light and security camera at the side of the main building.

Marcus turned to Stephen, leading him to go first. "Well let's go then."

"Why you keep making me go first? It's like your scared or something. You scared Marcus?"

"Of what? Dancing for a bunch of women? Oh whatever. I've done more for less so this will be a walk in the park."

"I hope so, for your sakes," The driver said walking behind them to the side entrance. "I've seen these women. If you're not careful, they'll literally eat you up. They will properly divide and conquer you lot."

"Don't worry," Stephen said, hoisting his bag onto his shoulder. "We've done this before so we know how to handle rowdy women." "Yeah, we're pros!" Marcus added to the lie. "Remember the time

in..." "Okay Marcus... it's game face time," Stephen said, cutting Marcus

off. He knew his friend was about to launch into a story that would verify their status as a stripping double team that had ground their hips to hundreds of pounds in tips. Marcus caught the hint and trailed off while still gobsmacked at being in the grounds of such a regal building.

"They're here!" the driver said into her phone as she tapped the wrought-iron knocker on the door. She hung up the phone and stopped walking. "Okay fellas. This is where we part ways."

"You not coming in with us?" Marcus asked, giving the driver an extra interested stare.

"I can't. I gotta go for another drop off. Plus, and I mean this in the best way, I can't watch."

Stephen recoiled. "You don't like strippers?"

"I do but... let's just say you're the wrong sex."

"Oh really REALLY?" Marcus said with his eyebrows up, enjoying the threesome images that were creeping across his thoughts.

"That's a shame," Stephen added. "You look..." "Good enough for a woman to eat? I am, believe me." Marcus and Stephen turned to the sound of footsteps behind the

door. A succession of locks and traps began to open from the other side of the door.

They held their breath in anticipation. The first thing they saw was a high-heeled foot as the large door creaked open and music, laughter and female voices could be heard.

"Good evening gentlemen," a raspy voice said from behind the door. "My name is Cleo."

The door opened fully and the men were face-to-face with a solid woman, six foot three, long auburn hair, chocolate skin and a floor length sparkly dress with slits on both sides running up to her hips. She brushed hair away from her face and looked them up and down while swinging a full champagne flute in her hand.

"I'm the maid of honour and... yes yes yes... we've been expecting you."

"Evening Cleo, I'm Stephen and this is Marcus, nice to meet you."

From behind his friend, Marcus was undressing Cleo, imagining running his hands up the slits of her dress and running fingers over her lips, which he judged from her size, to be thick and tasty looking.

"Come on in fellas. Let's get you guys sorted, there's a show to get going. Umm hmm hmm..." Cleo said as Stephen and Marcus walked past her. She made sure to leave her hand out as Marcus walked past and brushed past his thigh. They shared a knowing look as the driver tipped her hat and turned back to the limo.

Closing the door, Cleo tilted her head and sized up the entertainment standing in front of her. Standing in a corridor of marble stoned walls with fire lanterns swirling paraffin scents into the air, Stephen and Marcus were lost in the décor around them.

"So, which way to the..."

Before Marcus could finish his sentence, Cleo grabbed the back of his head and pulled him to her lips. Stronger than she looked, Marcus wasn't sure what happened until he saw a pair of closed eyes in front of him and lips pressed against his. Her tongue pressed against his lips and he slowly got over the shock and accepted by flicking his tongue.

After separating and taking a long breath, Marcus stared in shock while rubbing his bottom lip with a sneaky smile on his face.

"Sorry, I had to... just as I thought..." Cleo said.

"That's okay," Marcus said, staring at Stephen with eyes that said 'so is this how it's gonna run tonight?'

Stephen winked a reply.

"Well let's show you to your changing room so you can get ready. There's some real hungry bitches out there and its a free bar so it's gonna be a good tips night for you guys. Let's go, you too cutie." With

her last comment, she grabbed Marcus on the rear and ushered them up a stone staircase and into a lamp-lit corridor.

"This is such a nice place, house, castle... I think," Stephen said as they passed large oil paintings and what looked like cashmere rugs on the floor.

"Bet the mortgage on this place is ridiculous."

"No mortgage, this is owned outright," Cleo added, swaying her hips in front of them up the stairs.

"Owned by who?" Marcus asked his with his eyebrows raised.

"Federica, that's the bride-to-be got it from a dead uncle who left it to her in his will. Thank God she's my cousin 'cuz I got the east wing to myself. It's like a house in a house."

Marcus was mouth open as he walked behind Cleo, stealing looks at the paintings on the wall in between glaring looks at her rear end. From where his evening started with his Captain Morgan's and Lethal Lipps clip session, Marcus was getting more and more excited by the second. He only expected to be in such long running corridors when accompanied by a tour guide explaining which monarchs and concubines used to roam the halls decades before.

"Okay boys... this is your room... there's an en-suite in there. Go nuts. How long do you need? Do you want a drink, suttin to eat?"

"Nah nah," Stephen replied, walking into the room with his eyes drinking in the regal décor of the room. "We've got everything we need, thank you."

"Alrighty then," Cleo said, knocking back her drink with a large hiccup. "The room we're all gonna be in is though that door. When you're ready, put a CD in that system over there and come out. We'll be ready."

"So will we!" Marcus added.

Cleo backed out through the other door, into the room where a hum of music and female laughter was coming from. Marcus looked behind her and saw a sea of women just as the door closed. And that's when the nerves kicked in.

"Dude, what the FUCK are we gonna do?" Marcus shrieked.

"Relax bredrin." Stephen replied, still taking in the décor of the room and unpacking his bag.

"I just saw a sea of black women out there. They won't eat us but they will bite and, you know if we're crap, they'll let us know."

"Just chill out. Your killing my high." "But I'm shitting myself right now." "Look, once your oiled up and got your outfit on, you'll feel better." Marcus was pacing and his nervousness was rising over the drink

and marijuana in his system. His armpits started to warm, his legs felt like jelly and the regal room started to spin.

He put his bag down and sat with his hands clapped together, taking in the sounds coming from behind the door. Women laughed, '90s jams blared, glasses clinked, someone screamed and Marcus got more nervous.

"I feel sick."

"Vomiting ain't a good tip collector, just FYI," Stephen said, taking his coat off and lining a side table with tools.

Marcus watched him pull out vaseline, a deodorant stick, a pack of baby wipes, a 50ml bottle of Diesel for men, baby oil and a few pairs of shorts.

"Suit up!" Stephen said.?" Is it that time?" "Time to make that money." The double act were dressed, ready and rehearsed in 10 minutes

flat. They'd both taken moments to peek through the door and spy at the crowd who were now chanting for the show to begin.

Stephen had his CD of music ready and slid it into the player, pausing the first track before it began.

In cotton soft terry cloth robes, Marcus and Stephen held their ears to the door as the chanting reached a crescendo.

"Remember: deep breaths, remember your steps, during solo time, make sure to remember your hips and waist, yeah? Can you actually do this Marc?" Stephen asked, looking at Marcus with concern.

"Bruv, I'm not gonna lie. I am BRICKING it. But, there's two things I am always ready for. Money and pussy. And dancing."

"That's three things bruh, can't you count?"

"I'm gonna be counting these tips tonight, that's what I can count. Bet I make more than you."

Stephen swivelled on his heels and looked back at Marcus who was looking at his outfit under his robe, making his pecs flex.

"Marcus! Listen. I get that your excited. You wanna get started and get it over with... I get that. You wanna get paid. But do

NOT think that you can do what I do. This is my job bitch boy. When it comes to fucking up relationships and doing some nasty shit between the sheets, you might beat me. But stripping? Dude, come on, it's your first time. You can't fuck with me at all!"

"Wanna bet?"

Stephen froze. "For fuck sake, ok. Fine, whatever. By the end of the night, whoever has the most tips wins."

"Deal." "Rookies!" Stephen said then chuckled. "Alright, let's do this."

With one last application of baby oil to their torsos under their dressing gowns, Stephen and Marcus parted the door slightly and gave a thumbs up to Cleo, who was watching for their signal. He turned around to Marcus and gave him a handshake them a shoulder bump before pressing play on the CD player.

The music in the other room turned down and shrill screams began to erupt in the crowd. A voice took to a microphone.

"Evening ladies. Sorry about the wait but the entertainment is here and it is ready for your viewing and devouring. We have two fine, OH so fine, specimens of chocolate coming through to do a lil' dance for

the bride-to-be. Maybe you can get you some. So pull out ya notes ladies, it's about to get chocolate up in here."

Boyz II Men's Motown Philly started and the room broke out in loud excitement.

Marcus looked at Stephen with a confused look on his face. Stephen's face said 'this is a brilliant song to dance to. Don't judge me!'

They both took deep breaths then two-stepped through the door into the room full of women who gave them a drunken round of applause and broken voiced screams. From their changing room, it looked like a healthy crowd of 20-25 women of all shades, ages and waist sizes but as they cut through the crowd, the medium crowd opened to a larger group that looked more like 50-60 people.

Holding onto the game face he practised in the changing room, Marcus could feel his bravado dropping with every woman he skipped past. So many faces, so many lips being licked and all of them following behind the male duo who were making their way to the stage at the hall-sized room.

Stephen reached the stage, put two hands down and committed to an athletic and dramatic hop onto the stage while Marcus took the stairs to the side. In his mind, he could see himself trying that same hop and not making it look as professional.

Standing up on the stage and looking back at the crowd, Marcus could feel his flaccidity shrivelling further into his stomach. Scanning the excited women in front of him, he tried to pull Stephen to speak to him as he was touching the hands of the women at the front of the stage.

"Bredrin... when you came to my yard, you said this was gonna be a 'small and intimate' suttin?"

"Yeah, even I didn't expect this many people," Stephen said, letting go of his last hand. "This is aright though."

Marcus continued to panic. "This is opening day of the Peckham Primark sale! There's about 100 people up in here."

"Don't shrink on me now dude... just remember cha CHING!"

The deepest of sighs escaped Marcus and he followed Stephen to the back of the stage.

Boyz II Men lowered while Marcus was trying not to make eye contact with the many many women in front of him, folding notes into their cleavage. He suddenly felt physically and rhythmically inadequate with so many eyes on him. One on one, Marcus knew he could stare down and converse with any woman. He was a fan and firm believer in the power of a concentrated stare. There was something that warmed through him when he felt something inside him astrally project into the her of the moment. Eyes, to Marcus, truly were a window to the soul and he'd laid plenty pipe through those windows in the past.

But, standing on stage, in an extremely tight pair of shiny shorts, terry cloth robe and covered in oil like a fried dumpling, Marcus felt nervous with the many eyes baring down on him.

"GOOD EVENING LADIES!" Stephen said with a microphone in his hand. "We are your entertainment for the evening."

The crowd of women whoop whooped and applauded like a call and response.

"My name is Chocolate Lollipop and this is my partner in crime Lights Out."

Marcus turned to Stephen with a confused look on his face. His eyes were saying to him, 'when did I get the name Lights Out?'

The crowd laughed, as Stephen expected them to. "Now where is the bride to be?"

A sea of pointed fingers went into the air and landed above the head of a woman wearing a boob tube and leather mini skirt with angel wings and a policeman's hat on. Straight hair down to her shoulders and a drunken smile on her face, Federica hiccuped and cowered under the fingers pointing at her.

"There she is, let's get the bride on stage shall we?"

Marcus reached out for the Mediterranean-flavoured women who was giggling her way to the stage.

Handing her to Stephen, Marcus kept his back straight and his chest out, trying to shake off the inadequate feeling that was still coursing through him. It was the eyes he could feel that was making him so nervous. The sweat under his armpits was sliding into the material of his robe.

Stephen pulled a chair and placed Federica in the seat, kneeling next to her ear and whispering something. He then looked up at Marcus and asked him if he was ready.

"Let's do this!"

"LADIES and... LADIES! Let's give you something to scream about." Stephen said before before the intro to The Jones Girls' Nights Over Egypt kicked in and the crowd hummed as they recognised the song while, on stage, Marcus and Stephen got into position.

They stood either side of Federica and held their statue pose while the song continued to build. When the drums rolled in and led the song into the melody, Stephen broke formation first. One arm shot out to the side and the other followed then they both reach to the ceiling then down his body and below his waist. He then pointed over Federica's head and she ducked as he aimed his finger at Marcus.

"This is it," Marcus said under his breath.

He stuck his arms out to the side then to the front and rolled them like ocean waves before separating his legs in a basketball defence stance and rolled his chest and his stomach into a smooth grind. The crowd went ballistic and Marcus' first £5 note hit him on his ankle and he smiled.

Pulling back on the bride's chair, Marcus and Stephen stood in front of her and began their practised in the limo and backroom routine. Borrowing heavily from their memories of 90's dance steps, Marcus and Stephen went through their routine with slow but precise movements. Marcus was watching Stephen for the changes but trying to keep his movements smooth enough that he didn't look as amateur

as he felt. The routine Stephen ran him through in the back room was steeped in New Jack swing thrusts with dancehall swag and a hint of stripper flavour. Stephen made sure to keep the routine short and sweet before each of them took centre stage and did their solo sets.

The eyes Marcus felt all over weren't feeling as intrusive as he began to enjoy the hands in the air, reaching out for him, trying to undo his robe. He locked eyes with a few women in the crowd and was enjoying the smiles and excitement they showed with drunken smiles and screams of 'TAKE OFF THE FUCKING ROBES!' And with Federica reaching out for the male cheeks dancing in front of her, Marcus looked back at her and smiled.

Federica suddenly stumbled to her feet, picked up the microphone and raised her hand.

"I want a lap dance and one of you is gonna give it to me!" Her crowd of friends gave the loudest cheer of the evening. Slipping into the background and standing next Federica, who was

sipping a drink and swaying to the music, Marcus watched Stephen stand wide-legged and freeze before slowly undoing his robe as R.Kelly's Bump and Grind mixed in and driving the crowd wild.

With his arms by his side and his back straight, Stephen took off his robe in one slick swift movement that made the crowd lose their minds. Hands and money flew in the air towards the stage and the crowd rushed towards the stage, reaching for Stephen's glistening torso.

The muscular black man in the short shorts with the robe at his feet and the black Nike Air Max turned to Marcus and smiled as a sea of hands ran up and down his shiny torso while grinding his hips to the brave fingers that dared to grab his privates.

Mouthing the words as he watched Stephen work through his routine of street dancing and straight hip and waist movements, Marcus took notes. In his mind, he had a rough idea of what he was going to do but it was the 'doing' that had him shaking where he stood.

"You enjoying yourself?" Marcus asked Federica, leaning into her ear.

"I don't think your gonna be able to give me a dance tonight sir," Federica replied, looking at Stephen's ass move in front of her.

It was then that she stood up shakily and walked up to Stephen who was face down on the ground swirling his hips in a humping motion. Giggling foolishly while trying to hold a straight walk, Federica stumbled until she fell back onto Stephen who was mid-press-up. He held her weight and continued his rise and fall while the crowd cheered him on and counted with him.

"LADIES, WE HAVE A WINNER!" Federica shouted into the microphone.

Marcus could only watch with his arms across his chest. His robe now felt stifling as he watched Stephen make it to his feet as £5 and £10 notes rained down on him from the crowd.

If Marcus didn't feel inadequate before, he well and truly did now. He didn't even get to perform his freestyle set that was going to be filled

with old school moves and ragga waist movements as Xscape's Just Kicking started.

Stephen stood up while collecting money that was peppered across the stage and his body.

"I think you owe me some money bitch!" Stephen said, peeling a £20 note from his inner thigh.

"Nah, I didn't even get my chance to..."

"LET'S GO!" Federica said, grabbing Stephen by the arm and pulling him off the stage. "LADIES... THE OTHER ONE IS ALL YOURS! WE'LL BE BACK IN A MINUTE!"

With one hand being pulled by the tipsy bride, and the other handing Marcus a crumpled wad of money, Stephen left the stage and mouthed to Marcus, 'handle that'. The crowd was roaring with laughter as Federica and Stephen disappeared through the crowd into their changing room, leaving Marcus on stage.

"GOOD LUCK LIGHTS..." was the last thing Marcus heard as the door closed and the introduction to Chaka Khan's I Feel For You kicked in.

As the intro kicked in to the first beat drop, Marcus thought to himself, 'fuck it, let's do it!'

His arms became robotic and he rocked to each beat as the song began and the crowd responded with whoops and progressive cheers. The sound and vision of the crowd rising to his occasion as he moved his arms and legs and reached for the bow he'd tied in the front of his robe. Dancing and flexing on stage with one side of his robe flashing open, Marcus's heartbeat was in his throat as he looked over the crowd of women, trying not to make eye contact with anyone who's hands were reaching out for him. Marcus slid the robe down to his waist and flexed his glistening pecs as a chorus of screams responded to his chocolate skin shining in the spotlights.

A woman in a long black maxi dress reached out for the bottom of his robe and Marcus danced out of it, letting it fall to the floor.

The music switched to Total's Can't You See and Marcus began to enjoy himself as he walked the length of the stage, letting hands drift across his skin, leaving the hands wanting more.

"Oh yeah," Marcus said to himself as he walked up and down the stage, letting the music lead his body to do his bidding.

He stopped to the left of the stage and began to grind while getting lower and lower while the crowd got louder and balls of money began to hit him on hi chest.

Finally feeling brave enough to look into the eyes of the women in the crowd, Marcus moved to within arms reach of the crowd and let hands run all over him.

With his body rolling to the beat, he felt hands on his chest, his stomach and inner thighs. It was then that he saw Cleo, the maid of honour, behind the front row of hands, staring at him while sipping a large glass of something. She wasn't moving to the music or cheering him on to take off more, she was just staring at him folding notes and throwing them at him with sensual eyes.

Get it on tonight by Montell Jordan, Only You by 112 and I Get Lonely by Janet Jackson had the stage peppered with notes. Hands were a lot more grabby and he the shouted comments made him mentally note possible the women who he'd be talking to after his performance. Whatever he was doing was working because the crowd was singing along to his background music and money was hitting him in little balls. In between steps, Marcus could see a few corners of £20 and £10 notes with a possible £50 on the left side of the stage.

While Bell Biv Devoe's Poison played and Marcus was deep in his last round of hip swirling and dick thrusting in his short shorts, from the corner of his eye he could feel a presence coming up the stairs of the stage to his right. Thinking it was Stephen returning from his private dance, Marcus made his right arm flow to this right and he ended with his index finger pointing to Stephen. But as he looked at the end of his finger, he saw it wasn't Stephen who was on the stage but Cleo in her sparkly floor-length dress.

She stood there with her weight balanced on one leg and her arms folded, while sipping her wine and staring at Marcus with eyes full of intent. Her eyes were focussed on the bulge in the front of his shorts and the rise he felt was his response.

The crowd slapped the front of the stage, making it vibrate under his feet as Cleo slow walked towards him.

"OoOoOoOoOooo... Cleo's gonna get him... don't give him a chance Cleo... that's that Cleo slutty look..."

Marcus could hear members of the audience egging Cleo on as she walked towards him, taking longer sips of her drink and her eyes undressing him more and more. For the majority of the performance, being on stage above everyone else helped Marcus gain enough confidence that his heart wasn't beating as fast and his legs didn't feel as heavy as they did in the changing room. But now, with Cleo on stage staring at him like she was about to take a bite out of him, Marcus suddenly felt nervous all over again.

Her clothed presence, coming so close to his semi-nakedness made him suddenly feel conscious of his body and his movement relaxed slightly. He licked his lips and turned to Cleo, who was only yards away from him as Janet Jackson's Rope Burn mixed in and the crowd oooh'ed and aahhhh'ed, anticipating sexiness on stage.

Looking her up and down, Marcus held his hand out to her and the crowd cheered her on to take it. She brushed her hair away from her face and looked at the crowd with a dirty smile. Her eyes met with a group in the crowd who were screaming for her to 'do it'.

Cleo looked back at Marcus, finished her drink and gave the glass to a woman in the crowd who was two hops away from bouncing free of her tube top. She was handed a chair which she put on the stage.

She began to walk with him, with the crowd giving them a round of applause, when she stopped dead, ran her hands up her thighs, hooked her thumbs into her panties and slid them to the ground under her dress to the beat of Janet's sultry vocals.

Marcus found himself mesmerised and the crowd was going bananas with hands slapping the stage.

"Get him Cleo..." shouted a shrill, drunk voice from the crowd.

Cleo, the sexy maid of honour, was upright and looking Marcus dead in his eyes with no smile on her face. An air of ice cold washed over him as she looked him up and down, put a hand on his chest and pushed him back into the chair on the stage.

Turning to the crowd, playing up to the act, Marcus looked wide eyed and confused. He shrugged his shoulders and looked at her, returning the up and down look, before mouthing to her.

"So what you wanna do?"

Each step Cleo took closer to Marcus was on beat and made her body ripple with every extra instrument in the song. His erection which was sticking and growing to the left inside his shorts was growing and felt stifled by the tight material. Marcus adjusted himself and the crowd went crazy.

"WHIP IT OUT LIGHTS OUT!"

Marcus laughed before waving off the request. He knew it'd probably be a flaccid reception if he was to whip out his manhood in front of all those women. The amount of eyes in that room would make his erection droop quickly and immediately. The pressure of having so many eyes on his stuff was making him shrink just thinking about it.

Suddenly, Prince's If I Was Your Girlfriend came on through the speakers and the crowd groaned while Cleo looked towards the heavens. Marcus could tell this was her song the way her arms went over her head and came down with her hands tracing the curves of her hips while her waist was moving in slow circles.

She turned around and pushed Marcus onto the chair while giving him her back to stare at. His eyes started at her neck and made their way down her shimmying back to her backside which was moving towards him.

"Give him the move Cleo... do it Cleo... you dutty bongle, you're gonna have another man hooked on you..."

Marcus AKA Lights Out felt like his bump and grind show had slowly become the Cleo show as he felt the material from her dress graze the front of his shorts. She slowly swayed her hips from the left to the right and his erection had a mind of its own as it moved along the inside of his shorts.

Cleo must've felt the movement because she spun around and looked at Marcus' groin while her waist was wining towards the crowd. He shared the smile with his hands holding on to the chair, impressed at his own growth and equally impressed with the look of kudos he was getting from Cleo. She stared at his groin then looked back to the crowd and back again, clicking her fingers.

Marcus caught Cleo's eyes and searched for intention. He'd been in enough situations to know when he had a woman in front of him who would eventually have his penis in her mouth. He knew the look in her

eyes, the body language and he knew the subtle transitions a woman went through before she made her way to her knees. However this dance was going to end, Marcus knew he'd soon have Cleo on her knees sucking his dick.

He was suddenly very aware of where he was and the amount of eyes that were on him suddenly made him feel inadequate all over again. His skin felt like a breeze of cold judgement was covering him from the eyes in the crowd. But the closer Cleo got to his dick, the more whooping and hollering erupted from the crowd.

Money was still raining down on them and Cleo was so close, he could feel her breath on his shorts. His instinct told him that Cleo was a tease; someone who would make all the right moves towards good head but then be a one suck pony in the end. And after all this build up, Marcus decided that was not going to happen to him.

With his shorts rolled down to his ankles by Cleo – which drew a huge cheer – and one leg out, Marcus made an attempt to gain control over the show, which was taking a turn for the sexual.

Suddenly, the music stopped.

It was that moment, with the crowd groaning, that she took his dick and managed to get it three quarters of the way into her throat without pre-moistening.

Shock made Marcus lift himself off the chair and into the rest of Cleo's mouth. She gagged at first but instantly adjusted and held him there as he lowered back to the chair. The crowd exploded, more money flew onto the stage and Marcus couldn't believe just how amazing his Saturday night had become. He wiped beads of sweat from his brow as Cleo rested her arms on his thighs and looked up at him with the head of his dick in her mouth.

"GO CLEO GO!!!" someone shouted from the crowd of hype women who were reaching out for Marcus' leg.

He looked straight up, catching sounds of Cleo's wet mouth in between the whoops and the cheers. The baby oil he covered himself in was making him sweat as she bobbed and weaved in his lap, thrashing her head from side-to-side, catching his stray hairs in her teeth. Each catch made him wince but he hid it from view of the crowd and began to work his hips to the rhythm of the crowd's noise.

He wanted to look down and watch what she was doing but there was a chance that looking and feeling at the same time could make him cum before he was ready. And with all eyes on him, he wanted to put in a timely performance.

"SUCK IT CLEO," a woman's voice said from the middle of the crowd.

Marcus looked for the owner of the voice but the music started up again with KP and Envy's Shorty Swing My Way and Marcus made the mistake of looking down at Cleo, who's hair was draped over her face. His dick felt warm and extremely moist in her cave of hair as a train of

saliva dripped down his testicles and onto the chair beneath him. He put one hand on her head and controlled her.?With his hips thrusting, her throat surrounding and the crowd enjoying, Marcus felt his toes flex and crack.

"Shiiiiiiiiiiiit," he said under the music, trying to hold his facial expressions.

His eyes looked down at the notes that were continually landing on the stage around Cleo's kneeling body.

The pressure became too much for him and any resolve he had began to leave when Cleo took him deep into her mouth while sticking her tongue out and licking his testicles.

Marcus grabbed the chair with one hand and a handful of her hair with the other. He knew he only needed thirty more seconds before he'd be exploding in her mouth. And with mental calculation he had done in his head of the money on stage, he was about to cum amongst £500 in £5, £10, £20and the odd £50.

With his eyes back to the ceiling and Ghost Town DJs singing My Boo through the speakers, Marcus was more than happy he answered the door to Stephen.

That was when, out of the corner of his eye, Marcus could see something moving quickly through the crowd. With Cleo's hair in his hand and her mouth making deliciously wet sounds, Marcus looked down at the figure that was cutting through the women like a hot comb through tough hair.

Cleo had Marcus at the back of her throat and was pushing him further, her tongue slow stroking against her testicles.

His hazy eyes caught sight of Stephen pushing through the crowd, bouncing off dancing women, giving them dirty looks, with a majorly worried frown on his face.

"Oh fuuuuuuuuck, don't stop, don't stop, doooon't stooooop..."

Stephen was now at the front of the stage trying to get Marcus' heavy-eyed attention. He waved his arms and slapped the stage with both hands and was mouthing something as Marcus shrugged his shoulders and pointed at Cleo with two thumbs up of pride.

His body began to jerk and he knew his thirty seconds was over. A ripple of a wave began to surge from his toes as he continued to fuck Cleo's mouth. He pulled all hair away from her face so he could watch her work.

Saliva had frothed up around the base of his dick and the sight of it was all Marcus could take.

Stephen was waving his arms and rubbing his neck while the good feeling of an orgasm traveled up Marcus' thighs. There was something about the look on his friend's sweaty face that made him open his eyes more but Cleo was making it hard as she dipped her throat repeatdly.

Marcus' toes twitched as the crowd cheered on.?" GO CLEO GO CLEO GO MAKE THAT DICK MAKE THAT DICK BLOW!" Arms were high in the air, including Stephen's, joy and jubilation

was all over the place and Marcus felt like a king as his cheeks clenched and he pushed Cleo's head down as far as she was willing to go.

"Oh God... I'm gonna cum," Marcus said, standing up.

Cleo tilted her head back with her mouth and eyes wide open and, for the first time, Marcus noticed the lump in her throat. He frowned and squinted at it while euphoria reached the top of his scalp and he began to masturbate in front of Cleo's face.

To his right, he could hear Stephen's voice just under the screaming crowd.

"They're... all... men!"

Marcus' eyes shot back to Cleo on his knees as the first stream of cum hit him in his face. He reacted by rubbing it in his face and welcoming the following streams that Marcus could do nothing to halt.

"No... NOOOOOO!" Marcus yelled as he pulled his hips back but his dick was pulsating, shooting stream of sperm on Cleo's Adam's Apple.

He fell back into the chair, looking at Cleo on his knees, licking his lips and the back of his hand. Stephen made it to the stage at the same time and looked down at the conclusion on the stage while giving Marcus wincing eyes.

Cleo stood up, looking at the creamy splats of Marcus on her outfit and raised her arms in victory. She picked up someone's glass of champagne at the front of the stage and knocked it straight back.

Federica made it back to the stage and was naked except for his veil.

"Am I gonna be a dirty wife or what? That old man ain't ready for me tomorrow," Cleo said to the crowd of transvestites, transsexuals and lady boys who cheered the loudest they'd been all night.

"I got my something old. That's my something borrowed and new. Well, that's my something borrowed and new. Just need something blue."

Marcus' stoic face couldn't leave Cleo, the womanly shaped man, who'd just given him a blowjob. He was scanning the crowd and could see the same lumps in the throats of the women he previously thought were women. They looked like women.

Stephen was already scooping the money from the stage into a black bag as Marcus could only look at the ceiling and sigh heavily.

He should've looked at the corner of the room where the security camera blinked three times then turned off as Quincy burned the night's footage to a DVD and dialed the last person on his call list.

"Hello? Tat, you busy?" "Not really, why?"
Wanna catch a movie or watch a DVD?!"

KIKI PEACHY, RORO THE LADY & CHARM THE DETECTIVE – C.L.I.T.S

A bright spot light fell on Lamar.?" Lamar? Lammmmmmmmar?" "Someone slap him please?!" "He's already seen Becky Becky, Miss D and Butterfly... you know he's been slapped enough!" "LAMAR?" He woke up instantly, his eyes fighting the brightness that was bathing him in light while darkness surrounded everywhere else. He looked around, trying to see through the pitch blackness breathing heavily.

"Morning sleepy head," said a voice from the darkness.?" Sleep well?" asked another.?" Let's hurry this up, I got dick waiting for me at home!" said a third. "Who's there?" Lamar begged, following the sound of the voices. Three spotlights shone before him over three women in dressing gowns sitting in comfy chairs, separated from him by darkness.?" Hi, how you doing?" said the first of the three?" How many more of you cun..." "It was a rhetorical question sir. To be honest I don't give a fuck. My name is Charm The Detective. Wassup. This ridiculously chocolatey lady next to me is Kiki Peachy, with the ass so meaty, and...."

The woman in the middle gave Charm a playful slap on the arm then raised a finger to Lamar.

"And the serious faced lady with the nice rack on the end is Roro The Lady. Worst thing you can do is call her out of her name. You've been warned."

The last woman in the panel didn't look up from her phone.?" Ro?" "Oh yeah," she mumbled. "Sorry. Yeah, hi. Alright, let's do this." "Do what? I don't even know where to start on how illegal this all is, what else do you lot wanna do? Who the fuck are you even?" The women looked at each other with puzzlement and confusion.

Roro raised her hand.?" I'll take this. Lamar, we are the C.L.I.T.S. It says so on the dressing

gowns." "Okay, okay, forget that. If he doesn't know by now, I'm sure

Pandora will tell him." Kiki sat up in her seat and leaned forward.?" Lamar, have you figured out why you're here yet?" "Do I look like I have? How could a bunch of women done this?"

The three women looked at each other and gave Lamar three different versions of offended on their faces. He wasn't sure where he went wrong but something had pissed them off.

Charm took a long breath before raising her finger at him.

"Lamar... damn you men are stupid. Look, do you remember the list Keisha gave you just before we borrowed you?"

He sighed. "Yeah, whatever."

"He remembers," Roro jumped in. "If my man told me I was basically shit at EVERYTHING, I'd damn sure remember everything in that bloody list that's for sure."

"What makes you think I'm shit at everything?"

Lamar raised his hands, realising for the first time he wasn't restrained by his wrists. He rubbed and rolled his wrists and rubbed the back of his neck. He tried to slide his feet forward but they stopped short and chains rattled.

"Hey, HELLO? Can we have some focus please? I see Kwamè didn't teach you anything. Anyway, let's go through that list shall we?"

One of the three women clicked her fingers in the dark and Keisha's entire ten list rant appeared – word for word and bullet pointed – in the darkness between them.

Lamar did a double take, to make sure he was seeing what was right in front of his eyes. Reading and remembering, he reached out for the words but his hands had no effect on them.

"Cool right?" Kiki giggled. "I love this lil' play thing. Marquita and Pandora came up with this. Anyway, let's go."

Charm swiped her finger in his direction and the first sentence highlighted before him.

"Lamar, would you say you've lost track of what Keisha likes and how she likes it?"

He frowned. "No. I know exactly what she likes and how she likes it. When she's screaming my name and having multiple orgasms, yeah, she likes it."

"Are you sure about that Lamar?" Roro asked sarcastically. "Yeah," he replied equally sarcastically.?" Okay, then," she fired back. "Let's see." She clicked her fingers and a paused CCTV screen appeared in the

darkness to the left of Charm the Detective and started playing. It took him three seconds to realise it was himself and Keisha in bed. He recognised his back and cheeks as Keisha lifted her legs.

The camera zoomed in on Keisha's face and paused.

Roro sat up. "Oh yeah, look at that face right there. Come ladies, tell me that's the face of a woman who looks like she's getting what she likes and how she likes it."

Lamar looked at Keisha's face on pause, full of annoyance, irritation and a classic roll of the eyes.

"Woooooow... hands up ladies if you've ever made that face?" Lamar looked at three hands go up.

"Don't try it ladies, that is just a pause at a random moment. Play it and watch her."

The clip played and the volume turned up. Lamar was moaning and talking while Keisha was looking at her fingernails, looking at the side of his head and throwing in random moans and potential orgasm arrivals.

"Oh Lamar Lamar Lamar... you are NOT representing for the team my brother," Charm chuckled and shared a high five with Kiki, who shared her own high five with Roro who was bent over in laughter.

"OH my God... that face is killing me... OH SHIT... she's mocking him, look."

Lamar looked. There was no way he could deny the absolute boredom on Keisha's face.

"Stop the tape. Oh my stomach is killing me. That is too much," Charm said, dabbing a tissue at the tears of laughter from the corner of her eyes.

"Okay," Kiki chuckled, folding a tissue and dabbing at her mascara.

"This is gonna be a good one. Okay, what was next on the list? Oh, first of all, do we all agree that Lamar needs to work on things in the bedroom department, based on video evidence?"

Charm and Roro agreed while still laughing and sharing a joke amongst themselves.

"Okay, I'm next," Kiki chimed in, swiped her finger and highlighted the second part of Keisha's rant. "10% Lamar? Really?"

"What do you men think foreplay is?" Roro asked.

He looked down into the darkness. "Are you seriously asking me that? Or do you have evidence of how shit I am at that too?"

Kiki swiped her finger. "We do actually. Multiple clips actually. It's a shame we had so many clips to choose from actually."

The other girls sniggered.?" Is laughing at me teaching me something?" "Depends on how you look at it," Charm said. "It sure is enlightening

though, wouldn't you agree?" "How did you get a camera into my bedroom first of all? Fuck all

these questions and videos and shit, you guys are just racking up a whole list of crimes. I've had all your fingers over me, there's DNA all over. That's if I decide to go to the police about this. And I'm not feeling to do that. I'm gonna call some friends and they..."

"Please put your dick away Lamar," Charm giggled. "We don't have a lot of time with you and we have a LOT to go through. Apparently, there's a lot wrong with you!"

"Fuck you! Fuck you lady and fuck you Kiki-Coko Coca-Cola or whatever the fuck your name is. You lot might be able to pull this off on some weak ass men but I'm not one of 'em."

"Okay, let's get one thing straight Lamar." "Is this no attention-paying wretch trying to..." "Whoa whoa, let me take this one HERE... Whoooooo..."

"I'm done with you lot." Lamar turned his head and gritted his teeth, exhaling hard and long. "Well," Roro said, clearing her throat. "I like Lamar a little bit more.

But, unfortunately sir, I have to let you know something. Not one of us here are saying that you are weak in any way, but, as a boyfriend – and lover – you suck! Which is actually number four on the list."

"My head is top notch darling!"

All three ladies froze, looked at each other in shock and swiped their fingers at the same time.

Suddenly, video clips appeared in every piece of darkness between them. Lamar's eyes swung from each playing clip. Every clip showed him giving head under his covers on his bed. One clip showed Keisha reaching under her pillow for a magazine while throwing random moans and groans his way. Another video showed her reaching for a book, another video had her reaching for her Kindle, book, phone and even a Rubix cube.

"Say something now sir top notch!?"

Lamar's eyes were overloaded with the visions of him working his ass off trying to get her off and she wasn't even enjoying it. He remembered that every time he went to give her head, she covered his head because she didn't like to watch him eating her out. Apparently she was hiding what she was really thinking and feeling, which was nothing.

He looked at the women, who were showing grimace and embarrassment while looking at the different videos playing. Kiki covered her mouth.

"Dude, this isn't even funny to watch. This is cringe-worthy. Are you really thinking this is top notch? Hold on, what are you doing in that one? Look like you're nibbling corn in that one."

"Anything to say on that one?" Roro asked him with her eyebrows up.

He chuckled. "I don't even know what to say on that one. Even I'm a little shocked."

"Oh, have we managed to get through to him?" Charm laughed.

"LADIES: Sorry to interrupt but we have to keep Mr Lamar moving. He has a few more visits coming his way and he has to see the Nurse."

Everyone looked up at the voice that came out of nowhere.

"Oh come on," Roro moaned. "I was just starting to enjoy this lil' thing here. And we were starting to get somewhere."

"Really P?" Charm looked up. "Give us at least ten more minutes. This was getting interesting. We didn't even scratch half of the list."

"Whoa, wait, he's going to see the Nurse?" Kiki looked at the other ladies. "Yeah, remember how she looked earlier? She is NOT in a good mood."

"What nurse?" Lamar asked the darkness.

"And Zeah!"

"Oh shit, Lamar, don't let us keep you. You've got a long night ahead of you. We'll just watch the videos without you," Charm laughed, tucking her feet under her.

"Look, I don't know who the fuck you are, but you need to let me go!" Lamar shouted.

"Ain't nuttin' butter muffin. We got a lotta butter to go!"

"I hate when she says that," Charm said. "I don't even know what the fuck it means."

"Right, I've got a date on some dick," Roro said preparing to stand up. "Lamar, nice to meet you. Good luck, hope you learn something."

A finger in the dark pressed a button on his neck and he blacked out.

POWER OVER THE POWERFUL

A dull ache was growing in Nathan's wrist as he tossed the metal fries bin into the air making fries dance and fall dripping oil. He used both hands to drop the fries into the fries bin, added salt and shouted, "FRIES UP!"

Then he slid over to the freezer, refilled the fries bin and dipped it back into the boiling oil that secreted a scent that stuck on his clothes all the way through his shift. But he wasn't bothered about that. He was just happy to be working and earning again. He'd been used to collecting funds in other unethical and illegal ways but he was happy to start at the bottom and grow from there. Even it was in McDonalds working the fries.

Today was the sunny day where Nathan passed his three month probation period and he was tossing the fries knowing he'd secured the job. Since the start of his tenure, he hadn't put a foot wrong, learned the systems of the food production very quickly and worked like he enjoyed it. With a new batch of fries dancing in the oil, Nathan started to drift away in his mind, reminiscing about his old days of trouble when a hand on his shoulder woke him up.

Godfrey, the chunky supervisor with the beady eyes, had a hand on his shoulder. "Hey Nathan, can I see you in the office for a minute please?"

"Yeah, sure erm, what about..."

"Don't worry about the fries, I'll get Matthew on 'em. HEY MATTHEW WATCH THE FRIES!"

Nathan followed his rotund manager to his office and closed the door behind him. He stood with his hat off.

"Sit down, sit down, relax," Godfrey hissed, assessing Nathan's physique as he took the chair. "SO Nathan. Today's the day. Three months. How'd you think you did up to now?"

Nathan sighed. "To be honest, I think I've done quite well. Up to speed on all current work practices and systems in place. Get on well with the staff and..."

"Exactly what I was thinking! Congratulations and welcome to the McDonalds family."

"Oh shit, don't lie? Awww sweeeet..." Nathan punched his fist into the air and mumbled to himself.

"I take it you accept the job then?"

"Hell yes. Every time and twice on Sunday. Thank you so much Godfrey, I swear you won't regret it."

They shook hands strongly across Godfrey's cluttered desk. Nathan wiped his sweaty hand on his work t-shirt when he leaned back, hoping he didn't see it.

"Good good good. Now, we have to celebrate. What you doing later?"

"I'm working until six and then..."

"Me too! Actually I'm working 'til seven but I'm leaving early. Right, I'm inviting you for dinner and I won't take no for an answer."

Nathan sighed again, feeling between a rock and a hard place. He wanted to go home, drink a Desperado, find some high grade and celebrate in his own way. But he'd just been given a job by the sweaty wide man sitting across from him in an extra large t-shirt with damp patches linking with sweat from under his man boobs.

"I guess I'll see you at six then."

Nathan got up to leave and they shook hands again, this time with Godfrey stroking the back of his hand with his thumb. Nathan was sure he did it because he felt it but Godfrey continued as if nothing happened.

"OoOoOoookay," Nathan mumbled returning to his station.

Nathan clocked out, had his things and was standing outside the main entrance with an autumn breeze blowing a strong wind against his slender frame. He turned up the collar of his jacket and thrust his hands in his pocket, watching Brixton high road bustle around him. For the second time today, Godfrey managed to sneak up behind him and put a meaty hand on his shoulder.

"Ready?" "You know, for a portly gentleman, you move very silently." "Thanks, I think." Godfrey laughed. "Let's go, got a cab waiting." They shuffled to a cab parked outside HSBC bank with it's hazard

lights on and they got in.?" My wife has gone to a lot of trouble for dinner so even if you don't

like it, act like it's the best thing you've ever tasted, deal?" "Deal!" Nathan murmured as Godfrey shuffled into the cab with his

shoulder covering half of Nathan's chest. He moved up to accommodate his size but there wasn't much space to move into.

"28 Angell street please boss."

With the essence of chip grease on his skin, covered with a quick spray of Lynx Africa and a fresh t-shirt and Nathan was ready for the awkward night ahead of him. He was hoping some act of God would cancel the evening and he could celebrate the way he wanted to. But Godfrey seemed more excited now than he did before.

The cab driver knew the streets and was taking sharp turns down back streets, cursing other drivers in a language Nathan didn't recognise. But it didn't sound like a happy dialect.

"Fucking women drivers. Should've never let them vote!" The cab driver yelled with an angry fist pump.

With houses and cars blurring past, Nathan turned away from the window and caught Godfrey looking him up and down with strange eyes. When their eyes met, he looked away, then looked back.

"Oh yeah, I wanted to ask, do you eat chicken? 'Cuz my wife is making chicken tonight."

Nathan scowled. "Why in the hell would you think that I don't eat chicken? Like seriously? You know I'm black right?"

He offered Godfrey a nervous laugh, wondering why the hell he would ask that question and why the hell was he looking at him like he was about to lick him.

A few quick left turns and a couple rights and the driver pulled up abruptly. "£8 boss," he spat out while turning the internal car light on.

Godfrey gave him a £10 note and told him to keep the change.

Hopping out of different sides, Nathan looked at the houses, wondering how in the hell the manager of McDonalds in Brixton could afford to live in a house on this street. He waited to see which house he would walk into.

A three-floor Victorian with basement, beautiful garden display in the front and a massive front door.

"Come, dinner is almost ready."

Nathan walked with his face up, imagining owning a property like this for himself. The idea of having so much space to himself freaked out his thoughts and he shook them off.

"Hey honey, we're home..." Godfrey charged as he swung the dungeon-like front door open.

"Kitchen you fat fucker..." a voice replied and Nathan raised his eyebrows, unprepared for such a sharp response.

Godfrey turned around and smiled while ushering Nathan into a beautiful foyer of pine wood floors, art on the walls and a scent of incense in the air. His eyes followed the stairs, his mind wondering how many stairs were in the whole house.

"Damn!"

"Not bad for a manager right?" Godfrey giggled proudly as he walked towards the kitchen.

"That's because you couldn't get this on a manager's salary. I could but you couldn't."

"Nathan, I'd like you to meet my lovely and very outspoken wife Asitah... honey, this is..."

A sturdy woman standing at roughly five foot ten in a thigh-length burgundy Chiffon dress looked up from a plate of savoury pastry starters and tilted her head to the right. She looked about the age of some of his aunties but even then, he could see how his aunties stayed having various issues with men harassing them. He'd never admit out loud that they were pretty or had sexy shapes for their ages but he couldn't act like he couldn't see it either.

"Chocolate in a box... good evening young man."

"Hey, how are you?" Nathan offered his hand out but the woman with the strong arms looked back at him.

She wiped her hands on a towel she had draped over her shoulder before walking round a massive breakfast bar towards Nathan and his out-stretched hand. Her full figure was hidden by the granite-covered breakfast bar that was decorated with trays of little nibbles and bottles of alcohol.

Asitah walked towards him while licking something off her finger and looking him straight in the eyes. He pulled his hand back before her

full, eye-catching cleavage made contact. She was so close to him and hadn't raised her hands or anything and he started to back up.

Just as her breasts made contact with his chest, her arms went up around him and pulled him into a very close hug with a kiss on both of his cheeks. He tried not to look at the thick meaty line down the middle of her cleavage but his face was mushed against them and he had no choice.

"I'm doing just fine sweetheart, take your coat off, get comfortable. Dinner is almost done. Hey, fat boy, go and change."

There it was again. A straight slap shot to the heart of Godfrey's weight problem. The first time Nathan heard it, he registered it but that was it. He put it down to married couple banter who were open enough to joke about those types of things. But now, it sounded like a regular thing and the way Godfrey shook it off made him raise his eyebrows even higher.

With Godfrey stomping up the stairs, Nathan turned to the woman who turned her back to him, making his eyes drift down to a beautiful backside that hitched the back of her dress up high on her thighs.

"You have, erm, a lovely home."

"I do don't I?" she gushed spinning in her heels behind the breakfast bar. "Decorated myself. I wouldn't trust that dipshit to decorate a hostel. He'd probably eat the house before decorating it. Drink?"

Nathan approached the breakfast bar and looked at the bottles. "Yeah, I'll have a..." "Make sure it's a strong one. That's the only rule for drinks tonight." "Okay," Nathan smiled. "I'll have a Wray and ginger beer." "Hmmm..." Asitah smiled to herself and started his drink.

"So, Mr Nathan, congratulations are in order I hear. You passed your three months. Well done young sir."

"Thank you Asitah. That's a nice name, where's it from?"

"It's sexy innit?" she chuckled while popping a cherry into her mouth. "It's from a small island off Madagascar where the women make love on shields."

"Really? Wow, that's exotic."

"That's bollocks too. I have no idea where the name comes from but it is sexy though."

A bit too sexy for Godfrey, Nathan thought to himself. With the way her legs looked and her waist looked almost cinched in as well as the past behind her, he couldn't understand how someone as sweaty as Godfrey could end up with such a beautiful wife.

"It is the kind of name where you'd say, 'oh, that's different'."

"Oh I sure am different. Anyway, take a seat at the table, get comfortable."

Nathan sat down while Asitah cut across her kitchen, lifting trays of food from her oven, splashing a shot of wine in a pan which made a massive ball of fire jump into the air, while draining a mixed leaf salad and stirring a creamy sauce that she tasted with a deep "hmmmm..."

"Yeah, every time one of the new boys pass a probation period, we invite them for dinner," she started. "It's just a way of saying congratulations and welcome to the company. I know I don't work there but I like to make sure that people know they are appreciated, ya know?"

"I can understand that."

In his head, he couldn't understand that. If he was the manager of a business, he wouldn't have any and every rookie in his house eating dinner off his plates. But to each their own.

"So, what is smelling so good in here?" Godfrey chortled while walking into the kitchen diner and clapping his hands together.

"Not your last cholesterol reading," Asitah muttered loud enough for both of them to hear.

Nathan was mid-sip when the comment landed and he choked on his drink but kept the glass in his mouth, not even daring to act like he heard the biting retort.

""Whatever Anna-Mae... least I'm not gonna end up looking like my mother!"

The look Asitah gave Godfrey was enough to make Nathan look straight ahead at a picture on a side table of Asitah with her arms around an older woman of the same chocolate shade with a strong face.

"Anyway," she said with a full curse on her face. "For dinner tonight, we are having asparagus, ham and chive filo tartlets, spiced chicken ballotines with wild roasted vegetables, pink grapefruit and honey sauce and for dessert, oh boy, we're having hot banana souffles with caramelised rum bananas."

"Oh, okay," Nathan replied licking his lips in his mind. "Got a Jamie Olivier in the kitchen complex have you?"

"If you mean am I a Don in the kitchen? Yes I fucking am!" Asitah took a long swig from a wine glass and finished her drink, catching her breath and looking at Nathan with funny eyes.

"Right, here we go," Asitah shuffled around the breakfast bar with a tray of pastry tartlets.

Godfrey had his hand in first and pulled it away with three tartlets leaving with him as he fell back into his seat.

"This negro has no home training. We've got a guest for fuck sake." "Well my guest should've been quick enough to get there first." "Sorry about my jackass of a husband. Please, take one." Nathan reached for one and nibbled it quickly, trying to hide the grin

that was growing on his face. The interaction between the two of them was making him laugh.

He looked at the pastry a second time when his taste buds woke up. A far cry from the lack of herbs and spices on McDonalds food.

"Right, enjoy those, I'll dish up dinner." "Excuse me Mrs... erm..." "Lupalinda." Nathan stopped and pointed at Godfrey. "But your surname is..."

"Yeah I know, she wanted to keep her family name. Only child and all that so she wants to keep her name alive. Dunno why, it sounds like..."

Asitah looked up from the plates of food she was preparing with an oily spatula pointed at her husband. "GO on... say it, I dare you. See who licks your balls after that."

Nathan choked again, this time needing a napkin as liquid rang down his cheeks. Asitah looked at him and winked then went back to serving the food while Godfrey sat angry with pastry crumbs around his mouth.

"Well, it all smells delicious," Nathan interjected, trying to break the pressurising tension in the room.

"And dinner is served."

Asitah brought out two plates for Nathan and Godfrey and slid them on the table. The food looked so good, Nathan didn't want to touch it. He stared at the different colours on the plate, the way the food was laid out and arranged then he looked at Godfrey's plate which was less arranged than his.

She returned to the table with her plate and sat down across from Nathan. Pulling her chair in, her chest bounced and he couldn't help but look.

"Dig in fellas."

Nathan waited until they picked up their cutlery and laid their napkins on their laps before he reached for his cutlery. Armed with his knife and fork, he cut into a slice of the chicken ballotine and tasted it, hoping the look of 'I hope this tastes nice' wasn't written on his face. The spice danced on the curve of his lips before the flavour of the seasoned chicken shimmed through and he was content. He had a taste of the vegetables, grapefuit on the side and the honey sauce, all individually, before combining his fork with different flavours.

He looked up with a mouthful of food and was drawn right into Asitah's stare. She didn't look away as he met her eyes while she chewed slowly and rested her face on her hand.

"So Nathan, what's up?"

"Nothing. I can't talk at the moment because this food is too damn delicious."

"Eat up!" Asitah whispered before taking a sip of her drink, her eyes still locked on him.

"Stop it Asi." Godfrey groaned with a mouthful of vegetables. "What is it now dump truck?" "I know what your doing so just stop it!" Asitah took a long sip of he drink and finished it. "Why don't you go

to the toilet for a minute or two?" Godfrey sighed. "For fuck sake." He got up from the table grumbling while walking away from the

table with his plate of food in his hand.?Nathan was trying to ignore what was going on round him as the

couple spoke with frowned faces and cold voices. His face was pointing towards his food but his eyes were watching them, thinking he couldn't

take a lot more of this tension but he wanted to finish his meal and he definitely wanted to stay for dessert.

Watching Godfrey shuffle out of the room, Nathan looked back at his food and poked at it for a while.

"Nathan, do you think you could fuck me better than him if you had the chance?"

He couldn't stop the flecks of food that flew out of his mouth before his hand covered his lips. He inhaled deeply to cough while beating his chest and sipping his drink.

"You what?!"

"Honestly, if you had the chance, do you think you could make me cum more than eight times? That's my record at the moment."

Still coughing, Nathan dropped his fork and pushed away from the table to give him space.

"I'm sorry," he giggled. "I just wasn't expecting that." "Well, I have now, so what'd you think?" Nathan turned around. "What about your husband?" "I'd like him to watch if that's okay with you."

"Oh shiiiiiit..." Nathan slipped into another coughing fit and tried to keep his eyes on Asitah who was eating her food as normal.

He was thinking about it. He'd been thinking about it ever since he arrived but he didn't think such an offer would be thrown on the table with the second course.

Constantly looking at Godfrey's empty seat, Nathan dared to stare at Asitah's cleavage imagining his dick sliding between them with a slop and a squelch. Then he shook his head to discard the daydream.

"Okay, well here's the offer I'm putting on the table. My husband, your manager, is a submissive. He likes to be told what to do. For some reason it turns him on. It turns him on much more when he is disrespected or treated like shit. Oh he loves that. So that's what we do. I fuck other men in front of him and he let's me."

Nathan was eating while paying extreme attention. It was fun to be learning about his boss and his personal shit from the one woman who probably had the most information about him. The conversations and interactions between the pair of them made perfect sense and Nathan relaxed, even though he was being groomed.

He packed vegetables and chicken on his fork and swallowed hard while taking her offer into account. He was thinking he could easily have sex with Asitah and go for as many orgasms as possible. In his mind and his libido, he knew he was capable of triple figure orgasms so the challenge, to him, seemed doable.

"Are you serious?" Nathan wondered.

"Very serious. I didn't shave for nothing so might as well have someone take care of it properly, not just sweat on it like that chunky butt does."

Nathan felt like he walked into the Twilight zone with delicious food leading him there. He took an extra long sip of his drink.

"Here it is. I want to have sex with you Nathan. Not like a nice love making session. I wanna fuck! After dinner and dessert, I wanna take you upstairs and fuck the shit out of you. And I'm going to put my husband in the corner like a good little boy and I want him to watch. I want him to learn how pussy this good should be treated. So, I'm gonna need you to join me upstairs after dessert, okay?"

Asitah slipped a forkful of food into her mouth and looked up at Nathan while reaching for her glass, her face alive with a devious smile.

Nathan didn't know what to say. He was holding a fork of food up to his lips but couldn't seem to follow through.

"Erm... listen..." he started.

If you think Nathan should say yes to Asitah's offer, read Power over the powerful part A

If you think Nathan should say no to Asitah's offer, read Power over the powerful part B.

DID YOU CUM?

Tyrone took slow sips while undressing Tunisia with his eyes. He was resting against her kitchen counter, enjoying the sexy simplicity of her clothes which was black leggings and white wife beater.

She didn't take any notice of him staring as she was engaged in a hilarious conversation about men and how they will never truly understand women. But she felt eyes on her and turned to catch him looking at her rear.

Tyrone winked at her and she felt her skin flushing over. Reaching for her drink, she took a nervous sip trying not to smile uncontrollably. This wasn't the first time she caught him smiling at her like that but it was going to be the last.

By the end of the night, Tunisia had tasted every drink bought for her leaving party and was well and truly white girl wasted. Carrying a tray of plates and empty glasses to the kitchen, she balanced herself on the counter as a wave of tipsy washed over her. With her head down resting on her hands, she took a long breath and felt fingers sneaking around her ribs, slowly climbing to her breasts.

She turned around. "Who the fuck is..."

By the time she turned, she was face-to-face with Tyrone who had his t-shirt off. His skin was radiating heat through her vest and she didn't know whether to voice her discomfort or submit to the animal feeling inside that was begging him to turn her back around, pull her leggings down and do whatever he wanted back there.

"Hey, I thought you left," she said, looking down at his man boobs. His stomach was out-stretched thanks to a delicious dinner and was pressed against her nipples, which were protruding from her vest.

"Apparently I forgot something!"

He looked down at the connection his stomach was making and reached underneath to sneak his hand into the waistband of her leggings. His hand was cold against her skin and she inhaled by sucking air through her teeth.

"Oh!"

Tunisia didn't get to finish making the sound she wanted to as he grabbed the back of her head and pulled her into a deep kiss that took her by surprise. Her eyes widened then closed as his hand danced between her thick thighs and unfolded her lips, searching for her clitoris.

"Don't start something you can't finish!" "Deal!"

Tyrone wasted no time and spun her around, making her hands slam on the counter. He ran a strong hand from her neck to the base of her spine, pulling her leggings to her ankles. She tried to turn around and watch but she was forced to look straight and keep her hands on the counter.

"Like that then huh?" she said as a 144 bus heading to Edmonton drove past her window.

Tyrone responded with a deep grunt and pulled the back of her vest over her head. The tray of plates and glasses clattered to the floor as Tyrone tightened a hand around her neck and fully bent her over the counter.

Tunisia was warming below at the fact that she couldn't see what he was doing but could feel her legs being separated and the sound of the zip on his trousers opening.

"Tyrone, look, we can't..." "Yes we fucking can!" he replied angrily.?She heard him spit as he slapped her backside and watched it

wobble before running the head of his dick up and down her opening. The initial contact was electric and every hair on her body stood on end, waiting for the moment he broke through and slipped inside her.

She tried to turn her head again but Tyrone had her braids wrapped around his hand. "Eyes forward! Don't worry about what I'm doing back here!"

His other hand held a cheek open and he pushed himself all the way inside her until he had nowhere else to go. Her mouth opened and she looked at the mess of broken plates and glasses on the floor before slapping the counter.

Her grunt was deeper than his as he withdrew and followed with another long deep push.

Tunisia reached around and began to slap his thighs as she tried to latch onto something before the orgasm hit her.

Her back curved and her legs shook so much he put an arm around her waist to hold her up.

"No no no noooo..." she moaned.?" Yeaaaaah, tell me I can't have it!" he replied while wiggling his hips. "Fuuuuuuuc..." Another two orgasms followed before he even delivered a third

thrust and Tunisia grabbed a ladle and began to whip him with it. The sting of the plastic on his skin only seemed to spur him on and he thrust faster and faster.

Rocking on the counter with her face against the cold granite, Tunisia was happy to be taking sure punishment for no reason and was definitely enjoying telling him no while being ignored.

"Stop it Tyrone..." "Make me!" He opened her ass and spat a white glob on her anus which made a

large splat sound.?" Oh God... no... I don't do..." "Shut the fuck up bitch!" Tyrone's index finger disappeared slowly in her ass and she

screamed louder than she'd ever screamed before. "SMELLLLLY FUCKKKING CAAAAAAAAAT!!!!"

"Huh?!" "Are you okay babe?" Andre asked, sitting on the sofa next to her. Tunisia looked up from her drink and scanned the room. Her

husband was sitting next to her with a confused look on his face. "What?" "You just randomly screamed out SMELLY FUCKING CAT?!" "No I didn't!" she said, still looking around the room.

"Yeah you did sis." Tyrone said, taking a bite out of a Jamaican pattie.

"Are you sure?" "Yeah, we were talking about football and..." Tunisia tuned out while shaking her head and going to the kitchen for another drink.?She stood in the doorway, staring at the counter and the tray and the ladle. She held a hand over her eyes, feeling her flushed cheeks as she poured an extra large glass of wine.

"Well that's definitely a new one!" she said after a long sip. She touched her pussy over her leggings and moved her hand instantly as her clit responded with a throb, "Tyrone huh?"

"Wassup sis?" he said, sliding past her, moving to the spirits and pouring a drink.

"Nothing, I was just talking to my mum and she told me to tell you to say hi to your mum," she lied.

"Oh, okay, tell her I said hi," he replied.

Tunisia stood behind him and watched him turn around, looking at him intently.

"What?" he asked.?" Nothing! Nothing at all!" Tunisia lied.

NURSE GRIMY CORE – C.L.I.T.S

"WAKE THE FUCK UP! NHS SERVICE BITCH!"

Lamar jumped awake. He couldn't remember the last place he closed his eyes but the sound of a woman screaming hoarse obscenities at him made his body jolt.

"YOU AWAKE YOU USELESS PIECE OF SHIT? GOOD... LET'S GET TO WORK!"

He tried to lift his head but found that he was more tied down than he had been throughout his entire ordeal. Something was holding his head down from his forehead, at his neck and his shoulders. He could turn his head to the left, which showed him that he was in a makeshift operating room. He turned his head to the right and he saw the back of a shape in a nurse's uniform.

"I'll be with you in a minute cunt face." "Oh for fuck sake. Another crazy one!" "Oh no sweetheart, the CRAZIEST one." She turned around and a woman in a hospital face mask walked towards him carrying a metal tray." Oh shiiiit..." "Hi! You alright?" she replied putting the tray down next to his head. "Look... I don't know what the hell I'm supposed to be doing here or why you lot think I need to LEARN something but..." "Shhh shhh shhhhhh... you know why you're here. 'Because you suck! Didn't you know?" "Fuck off... man don't do them tings deh!" The nurse sighed heavily. "If only you knew how many ways that sentence was wrong." "What?" "Forget it... now where is my scalpel? Silly me, I left it in the other guy." The nurse laughed raucously to herself before walking away from where Lamar was now sweating.?" So, lemme ask you a question Lamar. Do you engage in bamb? "The fuck is that?" "Bamb?

275

Bitch ass man behaviour?" "Bitch ass what?" The nurse appeared over his face, looking down on him. "Bitch ass man behaviour?" "What's that?" "You know what it is." "I really fucking don't." "Oh really? Not you don't, you FUCKING don't!?" The nurse tapped a scalpel on his forehead.?" Look, I'm not even pissed off anymore, just take me back to my yard innnit?" "OoOoOoOooo and a road talker too? Frigging great!" "Look you fucking retard, I swear if you..."

The nurse's eyes squinted. "No wonder Butterfly almost fucked you up. You got some mouth on you."

"Who that bitch with the steak knife? Fuck her."

"I'll make sure I tell her that... Remember we know where you live ya know and that is one woman you do NOT wanna piss off."

"I don't give a fuck who..." "Have you got a small dick Lamar?" He recoiled. "Why the fuck would you think that?" The scalpel dropped out of her hand and the end bounced on his chest as he inhaled deeply. Lamar watched it fall blade side up and trickle down his chest.

"Pheeeeew, that was close... I almost cut ya. So anyway, you look and sound like you have a small dick, that's why I'm asking."

"Why don't you take your mouth and find out?"

The nurse exploded in anger. "SEE... this is the bitch ass man behaviour I'm talking about. Why are you here Lamar? Huh? Why are you here? You're here because you're a shit boyfriend and this is the last stop on your train before splitsville. But instead of you trying to make yourself better, you're trying to get some head from a woman with a scalpel in her hand. Do you even love Keisha?"

"You don't know me and you don't know..."

"I actually do know you and I DO know Keisha. Personally. So I know for a fact you've got a small dick! She told me. Apparently you don't, how did she put it, measure up."

Lamar tried to move his head and look into the eyes of the woman behind the nurse's mask. "Who the fuck are you?"

"Don't worry about who I am... worry about the fact you just asked me to suck your dick and I know you're girl properly. I've been in your house sir!"

Lamar frowned while trying to figure out who she was.?" Cree? Is that you?" "Who? What kind of fucking name is that? Thank God that's not my

name. Anyway, I'm Nurse Grimy Core and I was supposed to be talking to you about your bitch ass man behaviour but fuck that, I need to have stronger words with you."

She walked away and moved to her tray of tools and 'toys' and came back with a syringe filled with clear liquid.

"Now this is a liquid I love. It's 200cc of the best shit in the world. It will make you fall asleep and wake up in the most excruciating pain ever. I've been waiting to use this on someone for ages. I want you to enjoy this."

"Look, whatever your name is nurse gritty, nurse lime and grime cleaner... I'm sorry okay?"

"What'd you just call me?" Nurse said.?" Erm... please..."
"Shhh... shhh... Let this be a reminder that bamb won't be tolerated

in any way shape or form so FIX THE FUCK UP!!!"

"I will I swear I will..."

Holding a scalpel in one hand and a full syringe in the other, Nurse Grimy Core removed her face mask. "This ain't no Keith Sweat tune with all that begging. Just fix up and go to sleep. Night night nigga!"

"When? Where? Hold on, lemme' see..."

Billie Baatin rushed out of her toilet without washing her hands and with her panties and tracksuit bottoms around her knees. She was shuffling them up her thighs while she was running to her living room.

Her laptop was open on the sofa while her three month old daughter Tammy was laying on her back on a play mat on the floor, lost in her own hands.

Billie sat down, unlatched the footrest attached to her sofa and put her laptop on her legs as she changed the channel to music television.

"Did you send me the link?" Billie asked." Yeah, it should be in your inbox," Lydia her neighbour said. "What's his name again?" "I don't know his name but he used to hang around with Wiley and

Kano and Wretch and them. He was on that track with Bashy back in the day."

"How many pictures did he send you?" Billie said, getting comfortable in her seat and lighting a cigarette.

"About six and a video..."

"Reeeeh, he must really think your gonna go down there and give him some?"

"Who said I wasn't gonna give him some?" Lydia said. "That's a sexy brother right there."

Billie opened a tab for her e-mail and opened the message. Clicking on the first message, she selected the first of six pictures, blowing smoke out of the open window behind her.

"Alright alright ALRIGHT... well you better give him some otherwise I will," Billie said, scratching her dry scalp with a finger.

"You wish... like Ohren would ever let you fuck anyone else."

"Fuck him... you know what that fucking waste of fucking space did now?"

"There's more?"

"Yeah, he... whoa... that's a nice looking dick right there..." Billie said, turning her head to the side to take the dick picture all in.

"What did your dickhead of a babyfather do now?"

"You know him and that 18-wheeler of a girlfriend have been trying to claim benefits in my name."

Lydia went silent. "HE DID WHAT?!"

"Yeah... I dunno if he did it or that fat ugly bitch of a heffer did it but they tried to apply for suttin' in my name, she must've said she was me. He had my National Insurance number and my benefits info and he tried to get a flat."

"But you already have a flat so how..." "Exactly!" Billie exhaled angrily while glancing at the letter she received from

her local authority, letting her know that all her benefits had been frozen until further notice. The letter was discarded on the floor amongst children's toys, wet wipes and clothes that were yet to be folded.

Billie changed the channel onto X Factor.?" I know this isn't the time to tell you I told you so but I DID tell you

not to have a baby with that man." "Yeah, yeah I know," Billie exhaled putting her cigarette out. "I fell

for those lips." "Yeah, he fell for yours too. When you two used to kiss was it like

Pinky and Cherokee standing butt-to-butt?" Lydia burst out laughing while Billie imagined such a picture in her

head.?" Piss off you trollop, my lips ain't that big." "From time Lethal Lipps says to you on Twitter that you got some big

ass lips then you got some big ass lips woman!" "Anyway," Billie said, changing the subject. "You gonna fuck this

dude or what? 'Cuz looking from his dick pics, he might be a good ride. Long as he can hold off premature ejaculation, you're good."

"Hmmm, I dunno. So what are you gonna do for money?"

"Babe, I don't even know ya know. Like, I've got enough to get Tams her food and nappies and ting but after that I don't know. Might have to hit the corner, see if these lips can make me some money."

"At least go on Twitter and sell that mouth, a lot of thirsty niggas there and fools with more money than sense."

Billie recoiled. "I was just joking." "Shit, I wasn't. There's money out there, you just gotta find it." "Nah, not me. Anywhoo, I can smell madame's nappy so lemme go

and I'll holla at you on What's App." "Alright love, later." Lydia hung up first. Billie looked around her living room at another

lonely and boring Saturday night. Not enough food in her kitchen to make a meal, yet just enough to knock something together if she wanted. Tammy was okay as far as food and care were concerned but Billie was used to having enough food and enough biscuits and sweet things so she'd never run out. Now, with her benefits cut, she was struggling and she'd only just received the letter.

She went back to her laptop, imagining sucking a dick that size and making money from it. She'd seen people on Twitter who sold 'services' but she never thought they made that much money. But the way Lydia spoke, it was like she knew something she didn't.

"Like I'd fucking do it anyway, this ain't Pretty Woman and yo' mama ain't no hoe!" Billie said to Tammy who was falling asleep on her back. Scooping her daughter from the floor, Billie changed her and made a

bottle, before rocking her to sleep singing Rihanna's Birthday Cake. Her daughter fell asleep before she reached the chorus and was

snoring softly as Billie put her down and backed out of the room, singing lightly.

She closed the door, but not all the way, as she shuffled in her house slippers back to her throne. With her laptop back in her lap, flicking through hundreds of Sky channels and smoking a high grade spliff given to her by Lydia, Billie exhaled while staring at the ceiling.

"Is this it for me?" she asked herself.

Billie loved her daughter and would not take her back for the world but the way Ohren left her to fend for herself then went and made another family with someone else left her confused and very alone. He didn't come round to see the daughter he begged her to keep, nor did he contribute to her upkeep. But that didn't mean he didn't have a lot to say on social media about Billie and her 'babymamma' ways.

'@badman4ward the day @singlemamasexy can stand on her own two feet without me will be a great day.'

'Hey @singlemamasexy I know u miss the D but stop ringin' my phone innit? Ur old news'

'I done told u @singlemamasexy u and ur bowlegged pickney can fuck off. She dnt look like me. Put an ad in the Metro and find ya baby daddy! #BitchesOnMyDick

Billie didn't have the energy to play games whether it be on social media or in real life. She had phone bills, gas and electric to top up, weed and drink money to find before things started getting on top of her. And being alone and handling all baby duties by herself, the pressure was beginning to tell through the random grey hairs she started to find below her navel.

Opening a tab on her laptop for Twitter, FaceBook, Tumblr with Instagram on her phone, Billie was ready for an exciting night of commenting on people's pictures, jumping into conversations and bashing the hell out of men who weren't handling their business with their women or their children.

She changed the channel as an advert with Arsenal footballer Ricardo Reed came on the TV. He was topless and running through a field, holding a bottle of men's aftershave, with a deep voice over saying the cheesy tag line, 'live life lovely', and held a pose that showed off every muscle in his torso.

She switched to another channel showing Spike Lee's Jungle Fever and tossed the remote. "I haven't seen the Gator dance in years."

Her first stop was Twitter to let her tweeps know she was going to be on and ranting tonight. Then to FaceBook, Instagram and Tumblr to do the same.

She scrolled her timelines, leaving comments on statuses that allowed her to vent and swerve the subject towards her and the way Ohren has been treating her.

Twitter and Tumblr were quiet and Instagram seemed to be flooded with followers who were out for the night, taking pictures in bars and in drunken huddles with friends. Her FaceBook timeline was rammed with people posting positive messages from the world's great thinkers when really she wanted to vent and curse men out for Ohren's mistakes.

As she was about to change tabs and go back to her Tumblr, the icon at the top of her FaceBook said she had a new follower waiting for her approval.

"Who the fuck is this?" Billie said to herself. "No fucking way!"

The man she'd just seen on the TV running through a field looking all glistening and yummy was apparently now trying to add her to his friends list.

"Ricardo Reed wants to add ME on FaceBook? Don't fucking lie!"

She went into investigation mode. She clicked on his page and began to analyse whether or not the real deal was trying to add her.

His followers were in the six figures, his club was the same, his picture was one of him celebrating the goal that won Arsenal the league title and his birth place was the same as his real one.

She typed his name into the search box, looking to see how many other Ricardo Reeds were on FaceBook and how many of them were supposedly him. Her results came back with over 200 possibilities and she sighed.

"Fuck it." She clicked Accept.

She sparked her spliff and watched the screen do nothing until she looked away from it. A message box popped up as soon as she flicked to her Twitter page and she flicked back.

It was Ricardo Reed.?" No fucking way!" she said to herself again.?With his name flashing at the bottom of her page, Billie picked up

her phone to send a What's App message to Lydia.

'Oiii, guess who just added me on FaceBook? Ricardo Reed.'

She pressed send and waited for the two ticks to appear but her friend replied instantly.

'I know. Who'd you think sent him?'

With that information in her mind, Billie put her phone on the cushion next to her and moved the cursor over the blinking name. The message opened up and Billie couldn't understand what was going on.

Why would Lydia give him her FaceBook? How the fuck did Lydia know him in the first place? What the fuck did he want?

These were questions running through Billie's mind as she read the first message.

'Hi Billie, it's RR, how are you?'

Her fingers wanted to type 'no fucking way' but her digits were frozen. There was no way in the world that one of the highest paid footballers in the country wanted to spend a Saturday night talking to her on FaceBook when just last week he was in the newspapers rumoured to be sleeping with Katy Perry, Rihanna, Jordan Sparks and one or two of the Kardashians.

She looked down at her clothes: tatty Fido Dido t-shirt, Bermuda shorts and slippers. Not exactly clothing on the level of those Ricardo had been rumoured to be sneaking out of hotels in newspaper snaps.

Her fingers unfroze and burned across the screen.

'RR, huh? Really? This is the REAL Ricardo Reed? 30 goals a season Ricardo Reed? Centre forward but prefers to play behind the main strikers Ricardo Reed? £50,000 a week Ricardo Reed? Prove it.'

She pressed send and folded her arms with a massive grin spreading across her face. She was not about to be Catfished or set up by anyone. Even though the link came from one of her best friends, she was still cautious.

Her phone buzzed.

'Gimme your phone number and I'll prove it to you.'

She froze again. If this was a fake someone pretending to be the real Ricardo Reed then she was giving her number out to a complete stranger and that did not sit well in her soul. Just the fact he was asking for her number so quickly before they'd said anything to each other was also making her nervous.

She was thinking she'd never been so lucky to have such straight contact with someone so famous so it had to be a fake.

"But what if it's really him?" she mumbled to herself. "I have no idea what the fuck he'd want with me but what if it is him?"

She rubbed her hands together and began to type slowly, not sure what she was going to say, just letting her fingers figure it out.

'My phone number? Already? You don't even know me and you want my number already? Nah fam. Not yet.'

'Alright then, call me then. My number is...'

"Whoa," Billie said to herself, feeling her armpits getting sweaty. She thought she'd caught a fake by not giving out her number but the willingness to provide his number made her all the more nervous.

"Must think I'm a dickhead. A'ight, watch!"

She typed the number into her phone and video called it straight away. Then hung up, looking down at her clothes. She ran a hand over her head, thinking about how she'd look on camera.

In the mood she was in, with Ohren still jarring her thoughts, anybody could get cursed out.

Picking up an old t-shirt and wrapping it over her undone hair and sliding lip gloss on her lips, she set her number to private and called again.

"Go on then, answer it," she said looking at her phone. "'Bout ya tryna catfish me!"

The ringing stopped and the screen went blank before exploding in Blair Witch style shaking and loud music. She pulled the phone back and turned her volume down, hearing someone apologising.

Then his face appeared on the screen.?" Believe me now?" Ricardo Reed said.?" Oh shit!" Billie screamed, dropping her phone on her laptop.?It was him. The handsome, multi-millionaire face of every famous

brand from Nike to YvesSaintLaurent and Cillit Bang who was in the news every week for either his football or his womanising. The same face that ran up to the camera after his match-winning volley against Barcelona in the Champions League final and put his delectable lips on the camera screen.

Billie was a die-hard Arsenal fan and knew every player from the George Graham era, through the switch from Highbury to the Emirates and she knew Ricardo Reed inside out. He was the highest goal- scoring striker in the club's history and he took the plaudits with Kanye-style attitude and believed he was as good as he was. What seemed to irritate everyone from managers to other players and even the F.A was the fact that he talked a lot but he also scored a lot and was an all-round team player that people loved to hate.

"Hello? Is anyone there?" he shouted at a blank screen. "I can't see you. HELLOOOO?"

Billie caught herself with her hand over her mouth. "Hold on a minute."

She hopped off the sofa and went to work fast. At the same time she got up, she picked a brush out of her handbag, and pulled up in front of a mirror. Crumbs were brushed away from her face, Tammy's spit up that dried on her t-shirt was scratched away and her brush tried to traverse the rough terrain of her tangled relaxed hair. Thinking quickly, she brushed her hair halfway and tied the rest behind her hair while putting applying another coat of lip gloss.

"That'll do."

Back on her throne with her laptop next to her, her phone on the sofa, Billie ran a hand over her hair before taking her finger off the front-facing camera.

"Oooo hello!" Ricardo said in the camera. "Lydia was right!"

"About what?" Billie said, raising an eyebrow. "What'd that teeny bitch tell you?"

"Nothing bad, nothing bad at all. She just said you're very pretty that's all. And she's right."

"Oh," she said, blushing while giggling and covering her mouth. "Well thank you. And just so I don't come off like some sort of groupie, lemme' just say this now. You are a fucking nuts footballer."

He looked down and smiled. "Thank you."

"Nah, for real. I've been a Gooner for the longest time and I swear, if you help us win the title, I'm gonna scream my fucking head off!"

"We're trying. Long as I keep scoring those sexy ass goals, we'll win it. We're in the best position to do it so let's see where we go."

"We're gonna do it," Billie shouted.

"Are we?" he said with an arched eyebrow.

"Yeah, we're gonna take the whole thing. Champions league, title, F.A cup, all of it."

"Oh." "What?" she said blowing a smoke ring in the air.?" When you said we're gonna do it, I thought something else." Billie smiled. "REALLY? And what did you think?" "Alright, look, I'm gonna be honest with you. I think I've been

looking for you."

Billie was taken aback but tried not to show it. She was still struggling to hide the excitement on her face that she had Ricardo Reed talking to her on the phone. Her legs were kicking out and she struggled to stifle her grin as a McDonalds advert popped up on the screen where Ricardo bit into a Big Mac with a cheesy, satisfied grin.

"Didn't I see you in the paper with Paula Patton the other day about you're looking for me?"

"That's my friend," Ricardo said, failing to cover his smile. "We were just hanging out. But that's not what I'm looking for."

Her voice got seductive. "Well what are you looking for?"

He brought his face closer to the screen. "To be honest, I'm looking for that mouth."

"Excuse you?!" she replied with her eyebrows fully arched.

In her mind, she thought she heard him say he was looking for 'that mouth' but she didn't think he was being that brazen.

"I can see from here that you've got the mouth I'm looking for."

"Yeah, I don't think I'm the one for you... who exactly do you think I am? About!"

She watched him get into a car and the thumping bass line behind him dulled to a muted hum.

"I think your a friend of someone who knows someone I know." "And who the fuck do you know who I know?" Billie yelled.?" My brother knows Lydia and she knows you." "Who's your fucking brother?"

"He's a policeman. Anyway, that's not the point. The point is I wanna see what that mouth do and I'm willing to pay for it."

Billie dropped the spliff from between her fingers. "The fuck you just say?"

"Look..."

"Oh no, YOU look..." Billie picked up the spliff from that was burning on her laptop. "I know your some millionaire footballer dude and I know you probably have bitches hanging off your dick everyday but I'm not one of these any hoes who..."

Ricardo brought the camera close to his face. "Have you finished?" "What'd you mean 'have I finished'?" "I want some head. And I'll pay you £1,000 for it." "You must really think that... hold on, what?"

Billie hung up the phone and tossed, mumbling to herself.

"This cunt must really think I'm some any little bitch he can call and think I'm gonna suck his dick... what the fuck? I can't believe this fuckin' guy... what the fuck is Lydia doing giving my... you know what..."

She picked up her phone and was about to call Lydia and curse her neighbour for giving her number out when her phone rang with a video call.

"This fucking..." Billie looked at her phone and answered while inhaling three tokes and holding them in her lungs. "Look, I don't know who you think you are..."

"Is £1,000 a piss take? How 'bout £5,000?" "Is this your life? You just throw money at women and they..." "£10,000 then." Ricardo said sipping from a drink while driving. "This is fucking ridiculous, you can't just..." "£20,000?" "Stop saying num..." "£30,000?" Billie paused. "You mean to tell me you're willing to give me £30,000

just to give you head?" "Yessur I am. I've been looking for the most righteous head game

and, yes, I'm willing to pay for it. If it's good enough then the head will pay for itself."

Billie could feel her anger washing away as she mentally spent £30,000 in her mind.

"Yeah, but £30 grand though? Are you really serious?"

"Cash even," he said. "Honestly, I have more money than I know what to do with. I ain't got no kids, no girlfriend to waste it on... so I spend it. Plus, I can tell good head just from looking at a pair of lips. Why you think you don't see me with white women in the papers?"

She stopped spending money in her head. "Erm, Katy Perry is white?"

"Yeah, but she's one of those special white women. She gets an allowance. Not bad to be honest but meh."

"So you want me to suck your dick for £30,000? Are you serious?"

"I'm as serious as a ligament injury and I don't want one of them, so what you saying?"

Billie wasn't sure what he was reading from her face but in her mind, she was weighing up the pros and cons. The idea of giving head to a stranger didn't freak her out as much as she thought it would but she still felt the shade of prostitution creeping in her mind. And that didn't sit well with her. Though her past was chequered with numerous questionable moments of sexual gratification, getting paid for directly doing something made her feel dirty. But on the other hand, her mind was thinking about how comfortable she would be with £30,000 in her pocket, tax free.

"I'll give you a few minutes to think about it and I'll call you back." Ricardo hung up the phone and the screen went black.?" Like anyone would pay someone such a ridiculous amount of money

for some head. Even though, I do suck a good dick."

288

She couldn't help but wonder if she earned £30,000 for every penis her lips pulled to the precipice of pleasure, she'd be holidaying with the Hollywood elite in the Hamptons, lunching in Harrods and burning £20 notes to light her spliffs. Then she began to think about the dicks she'd sucked for nothing other than lust, boredom, to get something or just to shut them up. Her lovers reached the same precipice but she was a lot more broke by the end of it.

Her phone vibrated and she had a new message. While still contemplating what was going on in her mind, she opened a message from Ricardo's number and received two pictures. The first was an image of £50 notes separated by money wrappers in six piles of five stacks. Billie's eyes smiled and her whole face lit up as her pupils counted the stacks individually.

"That can't be £30,000!?"

She scrolled down to the second picture and tilted her head to the side as Ricardo's dick popped up on her phone.

"FUCK! A lot more than I thought he'd have. I've deepthroated longer... Shut up, talking like you're actually gonna do this..."

She twisted her phone and turned her head, sucking in air through her puckered lips.

Her phone rang next to her with the same number.

"That wasn't a few minutes," she said, still thinking about how far her lips could fit down his shaft.

"Oh, sorry, do you want me to call you back?" "No, no. I don't think so." "Okay, here's how we're gonna do this. You're gonna text me your

address in two minutes and I'm gonna send a car for you. This car will bring you to me and drop you home. If you don't send me your address then I'll assume your not coming and I won't call you again. Deal?"

Billie felt pressured. "I know I keep asking but are you seriously gonna give me £30,000 to suck your dick?"

"Yes, why is that so mad?" he asked.?" More money than sense!" she said to herself.?" Exactly. I could give this money to some expensive bar for bottles

of shit that's gonna pee out my dick in a few hours or I could give the money to someone who could do with it."

Billie frowned. "Who said I need the money?"

"Look," Ricardo ignored her question. "I'm just getting home so either text me or don't. See you soon. Or not."

"Oh, okay," Billie stuttered. "Peace." The phone hung up.

Sitting in front of a stream of adverts on TV, looking down at her Bermuda shorts and chipped toe nails, Billie sighed fighting with herself. She played with her phone, spinning it between her fingers, locking and unlocking the screen, unsure of what she was going to do.

She knew that much money would do her for a very long time. She wouldn't claim it, which meant it was free from the government's greedy fingers and she could still claim her benefits, as soon as they were reinstated.

"What am I going to wear?" she said to herself, jumping up from the sofa and marching to her bedroom while sending a text message with her address followed by a text to Lydia asking her to babysit.

Straight into her wardrobe, Billie chose a simple but effective outfit that accentuated her D cups and her shapely behind in one fell swoop. Extremely fitted t-shirt, which would rise above her waist when bent over on her knees and knee-length summer skirt that could easily be lifted if lying down.

With the text sent, Lydia agreeing to look after Tammy and her outfit completed with a yet-to-be-worn pair of Primark heels, Billie looked at herself in the mirror while pulling moisturiser through her hair and adding curling spray to make her hair easier to brush.

"It'll do," she scrutinised her make up in a hand mirror. The lips in her reflection caught the light in numerous spots and she pouted.

"Yeah, totally worth it." Her phone vibrated with message from Ricardo.?" Driver is downstairs." She hooked her jeans jacket over her arm as Lydia knocked softly on

the front door. Billie picked up her keys, phone and purse, just in case she needed loose change for anything.

She opened the door to Lydia's annoying grin. "So where you going?"

"Don't worry about where I'm going."

"Like I don't already know. Enjoy your night. Or morning." Lydia grinned while looking at the time on her phone.

"You're such a dick! Tammy had a bottle about 20 minutes ago so she should sleep throughout. I don't know how long I'll be to be honest."

"Yeah I bet you don't!"

Billie rolled her eyes and pushed past her friend. "Don't eat out all my food! Later!"

Down in the lift and out on the pavement with a slight breeze nipping at her heels, Billie saw a black Jaguar XJR with tinted windows humming across the road. She didn't think the car was for her, again not thinking she was that lucky that such a car was there for her.

The driver got out and made his way to her. "Good morning Billie." "Erm, hello. Is it morning?" she replied nervously.?" Yeah, technically." He opened the door for her, she thanked him and she slid into the

back seat, looking around and taking in the delicious fresh car smell as the engine vibrated silently.

The salt and pepper haired driver got in, put his seatbelt on and pulled out onto New Cross road. With her own seatbelt on, Billie looked

out of tinted windows, stroking the armrests and wiggling her hips in her seat.

"Oh yeah, this is the shit!" Billie said under her breath. "Excuse me, where are we going?"

"Claridges," the driver said, looking in his rear view mirror.?" Oh, okay, thank you." She heard of the hotel mentioned in a number of magazine articles

that included pictures of random women taking the walk of shame out of a random celebrity's hotel room with odd items covering their faces. Not the kind of place she would find herself.

"Claridges huh?" she mumbled.?" Yep," the driver replied. "The Diane Von Furstenberg suite." "Oh, wow." She'd never heard of that name before but it sounded important so

she threw in the appropriate 'wow'.?With her thoughts switching between Tammy asleep at home, Lydia

finding her secret stash of Ferrero Rocher in the vegetable section of her fridge, the warm air blowing between her thighs and the scenery tearing past her at a blistering pace, Billie exhaled heavily. She was flicking through the possible scenarios she could encounter meeting a footballer for the first time. Of what she knew of Ricardo Reed from Match Of The Day pundits to newspaper and magazine articles, he was egotistical which meant he could hold a serious power complex. Someone who was used to women bending over at the sound of his voice or licking his ass for the price of a bottle of champagne. Maybe he was one of those super controlling 'sit-back-and-watch-and- command-while-smoking-a-cigar' types.

So consumed were her thoughts, she didn't realise the car had come to a stop. She looked up from her last life in Candy Crush and saw a brightly lit doorway and doorman, who was opening her door.

Offering his hand, the doorman grinned at Billie as she protected her modesty with a hand over her lap and got out of the car, nodding her thanks.

The driver came round and met her at the door. "The room number is 1624, here's the room key. When you walk in, just walk straight to the lifts on the right. Fifth floor. I'll be right out here when you're ready to leave."

"Oh, okay, erm, thank you..." "Leonard." "Thank you Leonard." "No problem. You're much more polite than the other ones," he said while lightly pushing Billie towards the reception area.?Billie looked around at the chandeliers above her head, the dark

wooden pillars in the middle of the reception and the general flavour of decadence that she was used to seeing in gossip mags.

Remembering Leonard's advice, she rubbed the credit-card looking room key in her hand and walked straight to the lift without looking at anyone. Random folk were walking through the reception and the sharp dresser behind the desk was dealing with a family which allowed

her to breeze right past. Her nerves were tingling and she remembered her days of jumping the barriers at train stations with the same feeling coursing through her.

"Don't say shit to me, just don't say shit to me... come on lift," she mumbled as she pressed the Up button repeatedly.

Turning once to see if anyone was looking her way, Billie kept her head in the direction of the shiny marble floor that made her heels click with perfect resonance.

The lift door opened and she walked straight into a couple in black tie. "Oh shit, sorry."

They both gave her the 'are you in the right hotel' look as they past her and disappeared into the lobby.

Billie didn't have time to be offended, she just wanted the doors to close so she wouldn't have to answer anyone's questions.

It wasn't like she was a pro at visiting men in hotel rooms so she wasn't sure if she was allowed to just walk in the way she did. And with Leonard's extra advice, she knew once she was in the lift she was okay.

Soft classical versions of pop hits played in the gold carriage that lifted her softly to the fifth floor. Looking at her reflection in the mirrors on all sides, Billie straightened a leg and began to worry that her outfit wasn't enticing enough.

"This is a man who's banged actresses so me and my little Primark heels ain't shit," she said to her reflection. "But they ain't got lips like these. Well, maybe Jill Marie Jones but I don't think she's fucked him."

The lift came to a slow stop and Billie stopped talking as the doors opened. "Fuck, fuck, fuck..."

Looking for room numbers as the corridor split into three directions, she chose the middle and walked in her heels like she was the first model sent down the runway of a catwalk show.

She counted room numbers. "1616... 1618... 1620... 1622... 1624..."

Billie stopped and sighed. She stared at the door, daring herself to knock. One more check of her outfit, which she hated more and more, one more application of her lip gloss and she was as ready as she was ever going to be.?" Alright girls, let's get a quick one and be out." she said to her lips and knocked the door three times.

The following silence felt like waiting for death. Looking up and down the corridor, waiting for the receptionist to come tearing behind her with security behind him, Billie got closer to the door, planning to slide in as soon as it opened. But it didn't open.

She knocked again, this time with a harder three.

Every silent second in her mind was a moment she was closer to being discovered and thrown out as a non-guest.

The door slowly opened, followed by a wave of smoke that slithered into the corridor. With her eyes on the smoke, Billie didn't see the hand grabbing her wrist.

Billie spun into a full-length mirror and almost fell onto a tray of tea and coffee sachets. Her handbag swung off her shoulder and she stretched an arm to balance herself on the bed.

"What the..." "Sorry, I don't want the smell to get out." Billie stood upright and couldn't help the laugh that exploded from

her stomach. She covered her mouth as Ricardo pushed a wet towel against the bottom of the door with slippers on his feet. And nothing else on. Her eyes didn't need to undress him in his Arsenal kit as she always did because every part of his chocolate was on display. Her eyes were up and down then up and down again, taking in every part of his deliciously toned torso. He wasn't rippled with muscle but what he had was nicely cut as he walked past her like he didn't notice he was naked.

"Your lips are a lot bigger than they looked on the phone."

Billie caught herself staring in awe. "Wha... oh yeah, erm... thanks. I think. Sorry, I just can't believe I'm standing in front of Ricardo fucking Reed. When I say I'm a die hard Gooner..."

"Yeah, I am the shit ain't I?" he laughed as he jumped on a massive four-poster bed, with his back against the headboard under a colourful art piece.

He reached over for an ashtray and picked up a roll up.?" I'm sorry," Billie said, still in awe of the naked presence before her. "I know high grade when I smell it. How the hell can you smoke weed and still be one of the biggest strikers in the league?"

Ricardo leaned over to a duffle bag and flicked it open. "Well it's off-season so I'm good as far as pee tests but, in general, urine off eBay. I got a lifetime supply. I remember how they did Rio back during his pee test drama so I bought in bulk."

Billie laughed. She felt like she was learning so much about one of her heroes just by being in his presence. The more she stared the less awe she was in and the more aroused she became.

"And since you know the smell, I imagine you toke too?"

Ricardo held his arm out towards Billie, who put put her handbag on the end of the bed and sat down, taking the spliff from him.

"Thank you. I've just been passed a spliff from Ricardo Reed." She couldn't hold the laugh as she looked around the room.?" The Diane Von Furstenberg room. Sexy ain't it? Two king size beds, roll top bath, butler service, wide screen TV, oh yeah... I fucking love this room. Get it every time I come here."

"It's... too sexy in here," Billie said, looking at the spliff as a deep sour taste sucked into her lungs. "Geeeeeez, this is high grade for real innit?"

"I know. Right, just so you don't think I'm trying to run any type of game on you, your money is over there on the table."

Her head turned and she was quick to her feet and walking in the direction of the money. The cash was in the same stacks as the picture he sent and she rubbed her hands together, thinking of hiding places at home for her money.

"Right, so put that away. That's yours. I know I definitely paid good money from what I can see."

She picked up a stack of notes and held it in her hand for a moment, looking at the number of notes, trying to count them as she thumbed them in her face with her eyes closed. The wind from the wad of cash smelled like fresh notes and she inhaled and exhaled with a smile. She'd never seen such an amount of money in one place at one time that she was allowed to touch.

Her local Londoner instincts kicked in and she started putting the notes in her handbag stack by stack. When that seemed like it would take forever, she took another toke of the spliff before giving it back to Ricardo, opening her handbag and using an arm to wave it all in.

Notes fell to the floor but Billie's eyes followed each one to the ground, making sure she got everything she came for.

"Can finally finish decorating Tammy's room... Costco visit for nappies, wipes and all that shit... Tesco deliveries, no Waitrose deliveries... Q of high grade... oh yeah baby, we're going on holiday... fuck Ohren and his fat bitch and her stretch mark face..."

With her back to Ricardo, she hugged her handbag tight and swayed from side-to-side.

"Right, we ready to do this?"

Billie turned to face him as he was drinking Patron straight from the bottle. His dick was between semi flaccid and growing as she took her jacket off and folded it on top of her handbag.

"Okay," Billie sighed. "Let's do this."

He finished the spliff and the Patron, wincing as the alcohol burned his chest.

"Yeah, yeah, you got any lip gloss? I wanna see those lips shine. And I like it really sloppy as well... and deepthroat? Oh yeah I like that... "

"Shush..." she said, reaching back and tying her hair. "I've never once been told how to suck a dick, yeah?"

She stepped out of her heels, added a fresh coat of lip gloss and climbed on the bed on her hands and knees, spreading his legs and watching him rise before her.

"I got good stamina ya know," Ricardo said, looking proud of himself.

"I got good lips too so let's see!"

Billie lay down flat on her stomach and slithered her dripping mouth onto his dick and had him in her throat with the first stroke of her lips. She slid up to his head and left him with a sheen as she dropped her mouth on his dick again while looking in his eyes.

The first stroke in her mouth was filled with disgust. This was the first time she'd ever sucked a dick having so little interaction with its owner.

He smiled with his pupils while drifting off and throwing his head back in extreme pleasure. His hands stroked down her arms and ventured to her head as she opened her mouth and took him in, allowing her mouth water to slide out with her movement.

"FUUUUUUUUUCK..." Ricardo shouted.?Billie popped his dick out of her mouth. "I ain't even started yet!" She removed her moist hands and took him back in, holding his dick

up with her mouth. Every movement was emphasised with a sloppy, sucking sound and Ricardo was slapping the bed. He had his hands in her hair as her tongue tickled the base of his helmet, driving him crazy. His hips were humping up to her mouth and she met him and took him throat deep.

"Ohhhhhh shit.... no fucking way..." Ricardo moaned pitifully. Billie was warming up with her eyes closed, focussed on the best

way to purse and pout her lips in order to get him the maximum pleasure in the smallest amount of time.

Moaning from her throat, Billie opened her eyes to see Ricardo making fists with his hands and clenching his teeth.

"DON'T FUCK ABOUT!" Ricardo shouted out loud as he held Billie's head and pumped his dick into her mouth.

Billie didn't expect him to start cumming as soon as he did. She was literally just warming up, getting used to the smell of her saliva and his dick in her mouth. The stigma she tried to ignore that was still in the back of her mind was drifting away every time he moaned in pleasure and she remembered the money in her handbag.

His dick throbbed with his orgasm. She clamped her mouth around him with her eyebrows raised, sucking, swallowing and being confused all at the same time. She didn't have any expectations going into this about his stamina or his prowess but she did wonder just where the stamina was as his jerking body slowly calmed down.

"That's a fucking record!!! Oh fuck YEAH!!!" Ricardo shouted while punching the air. "Best head ever!"

From out of nowhere he threw a hand into the air and money rained down on her from out of nowhere. She wasn't sure where the money came from and watched it fall while he began to shrink in her mouth.

"Did you just make it rain?" Billie laughed, pulling a tissue from the bedside table.

"No, YOU made it rain. I just had to throw some respect at some bad boy dick sucking. I hope I'm not objectifying you when I say this but you can take this money with you as well. Believe me its worth it."

Billie frowned, suddenly feeling used. "I... erm... I'm not sure if..." "Just take it. What am I gonna do with it? Buy another Bugatti..." Ricardo yawned once and twice before closing his eyes. His snoring started before Billie had the chance to get off her stomach and hop off the bed.

"You got knocked the fuck out!" Billie giggled.

"I know... I told you those lips of yours were something else! Please feel free to hangout if you want, order some food, watch suttin', have a shower, whatever you want..."

Ricardo drifted off into sleep again and his snoring kicked in, heavier and with more bass than before.

She let his drained dick slip out of her mouth and watched him flinch before going back to sleep. Trying not to make the mattress move as

she got up, Billie slid off the bed and stood over him as she snored with his flaccid penis leaking between his thighs.

298

"More moolah baby!"

Counting as she picked up the £20 and £50 notes from the floor and the bed, stuffing the notes into her hand bag while mentally spending, Billie could taste him behind her teeth. But she continued picking money up, swallowing heavily.

"I can buy a bottle of Ace of Spades just to see what all the fuss is about... savings for Tammy, rent arrears can suck my battyhole... but we gotta be slick with it..."

Her mind was flashing between spending frugally and going on a rampage of receipts and irresponsible spending that her neighbours and friends would notice straight away.

With the extra £7,350 she picked from the floor, Billie stood up and looked over Ricardo with her handbag on her shoulder and a smile on her face. She reached into her bag and pulled her phone out, put it on silent and took a picture of Ricardo's naked body as he slept.

"For memory sake," she said, holding her phone to her chest. "Come we go... let's get this money home..."

Billie looked around the room, and her eyes locked on to the very large block of unwrapped marijuana that sat under the wide-screen TV. Even though she'd been a smoker for many years, she'd never seen a block of weed so big. A corner of the block, which was the size of a PS3, looked picked at.

"I'll just take a little bit from the corner," Billie mumbled, while shuffling to the TV.

She pulled out her nail file and stuck it in the corner of the block, sawing her way to the bottom and a nice corner chunk fell away.

"That's more than a Q," she said weighing it in her hand. She ripped some cling film off the main block, wrapped it and slid it in her purse.

Taking a few more pictures of Ricardo in his state of knocked the fuck out, Billie picked up her heels and walked on her tip toes to the door, pausing each time she stepped on a creaky floorboard. She stopped to take a large sip of his Patron from the bottle, washing the taste from her mouth and opened the door silently. Carefully and quietly, she took over a minute making sure the door was closed properly, hoping he wouldn't wake up.

Back in the corridor, less than 20 minutes after she arrived, Billie was back in the lift and on her way down to the ground floor and on her way home.

"Please be there Leonard, please be there," she mumbled as she walked proudly through the reception area, nodding at the employee behind the desk.

With every step she took, she could feel money moving in her bag and that thought kept a smile on her face all the way out to the street, where she scanned the pavement for Leonard's black Jaguar.

He flashed his lights at her and she waved and ran to him. She got in gracefully and closed the door softly.

"Hey Leonard. I didn't think you'd be here."

"Told you I would be. Ready to go home?" he asked starting the engine and strapping on his seat belt. She caught his eyes in the rear view mirror, giving her the look of 'that was a quick one'.

"Yes sir," she said looking in her handbag. "I'm ready to go all the way home!"

Leonard drove quicker than before with his eyes flicking between the road and his rear view. She wasn't paying him any attention as the scenery of London passed her by in between thoughts of Ricardo's hands in her hair and his last goal of the season which won the game and brought Arsenal their first Premier League title in years and was voted goal of the season by Alan Hansen, Gary Linekear and Alan Shearer on Match Of The Day.

She put her hand in her bag and giggled to herself, wondering if it was worth it.

"I've sucked dicks of dudes I don't like for less so, fuck it!"

Leonard made the journey in less than 15 minutes. He came round to open her door and Billie waited for him to do so, soaking in the last moments of opulence.

He shook her hand. "I hope to never see you again!"

While that played in her mind and £37,350 was secure under her arm, Billie didn't take the lift and climbed the stairs to her flat, breathing and tensing the muscle in her bag arm, just to make sure she was in fact holding the money and not imagining it.

She walked in to find Lydia on the sofa with Ferroro Rocher foil littered around her chest and between her thighs.

"Bitch," she muttered. "I'll get some more."

Billie sniggered, walked quickly to her room and closed the door. She let out a hefty She took out one wad of notes and put her bag in her wardrobe. Staring at the money as she got naked, Billie started spending in her mind.

"We won't buy a car, that's stupid... hire one... let's buy a house... come on now Bill... it's only £30 grand, it's not millions..."

She talked to herself in her head while massaging the money until she fell asleep.

Grey clouds rolled over her flat as she stirred for the first time. She wasn't sure when she fell asleep but she remembered spending money in her mind. Before she could start looking around the bed for the cash she was playing with, Lydia burst into her room and scared her out of her sleep.

"WHOA, HEY, WHOA... WHAT THE FUCK IS WRONG WITH YOU?"

"Please tell me that isn't you sneaking out of Claridges hotel this morning? Puhleezzzze say it's not you!?"

Billie was still waking up as Lydia thrust a copy of The Metro in her face. The paper was open to the Guilty Pleasures page and on one full page was a picture of a woman wearing a very similar outfit, same shoes and same chunky handbag getting into a very similar car.

The headline read: Straight in, straight out: Ricardo's converyor belt of beauties continues...

"You are EVERYWHERE babe... they got your face and everything."

"Oh shiiiiiiiiiiiiiiit," Billie mumbled to herself while reading the article and cursing.

WATER

Rosa was having one of the worst nights sleep ever.

Every time she felt herself drifting off, she jolted out of her light slumber and would have to fall asleep all over again. She tossed and turned and could feel herself attempting to sleep but failing miserably.

She could hear traffic on Drayton park road creeping past her window while Corrina lay next to her sound asleep. But on this night, Corrina wasn't asleep. She was laying with her back to her partner of six years but she was wide awake. Even if she was asleep, Rosa's constant fish flopping would wake her up and keep her there.

"For fucks sake," Rosa said into her pillow while swinging her legs out of bed. She ran her hands into her hair and stretched her back, groaning miserably and reaching for a bottle of water she left on her side table.

Behind her, Corrina was staring at a spot on the wall. She was curious to find out what was keeping her bi-sexual long-term lover awake. She had an idea what it could be and refused to be told otherwise, although Rosa continued to deny said idea.

It was this idea that had them arguing late last night and early into the morning. Shouting at each other, pouring extra large glasses of wine and taking the argument into each room of their flat.

Corrina was the one throwing the accusation while Rosa defended herself against her lesbian partner who thought she was tired of her and in need of a man.

These arguments, as well as Rosa's sleepless nights, began when the half Moroccan, half Jamaican lady with the extremely long curly hair started her job as a PA for the MD of Creative Minds Unite Consultancy (CMUC) company based in Covent Garden.

"Morning," Corrina said without turning.

"Hey babe, I didn't realise you were awake." Rosa said, turning her head to give a portion of her attention. "You alright?"

"Yeah, I couldn't sleep." "How come?" "Are you seriously gonna ask why I can't sleep??Rosa sighed as she stood up. "Oh Rina, let's not do this now." "But its okay for you to go to work and see him and... I bet you've

thought about fucking him haven't you?" "You can be so crass when you're ready you know. This is my job

Corrina. I work with this man." "And you wanna fuck him, I understand. If men did it for me, I could

see how he's attractive but..." Rosa slammed the door to their en-suite bathroom and sighed as

she put her hands on the cold sink and looked back at her reflection. Corrina was still talking through the door.

"Do you?"

"Do I what?" Rosa asked back, running her toothbrush under the flowing water.

"Do you wannna fuck Thornton?" "Rina... just... leave me alone."

Brushing her teeth and running through her mental wardrobe, connecting and disconnecting work outfits in her mind, Rosa looked at her reflection and frowned.

She hoped last night's argument would get left there... last night. The furore, the verbal violence, the volume, the hole in the wall, the broken glass in the kitchen, all culminated in a toss and turning night's sleep where the argument was not resolved before both heads hit their respective pillows.

Corrina was on Rosa as soon as she got back from work after another late night with boss and the team. The curly-haired PA had barely put her bag down and kicked off her shoes before she spotted Corrina's angry face and burrowing eyebrows sitting in the living room with a glass of wine. Rosa hit the kitchen first and made herself a brandy and coke, knowing that a quiet evening was out of the question.

Rosa took slow steps to the living room where her partner was sitting on the floor watching TV, tapping the keyboard on her laptop and running her fingers around the edge of the glass. That was Rosa's cue to know that Corrina was pissed about something.

She walked into the living room and she could feel Corrina's negative energy radiating towards her.

"Hello BABY!" Corrina said sarcastically, turning her laptop screen so Rosa could see what she was looking at.

"Hey, how are you?" Rosa replied, waiting for the argument to begin.

On her Apple Mac screen was a picture of Rosa and her manager with his arms around her and her working team at a party.

"I'm fine, just don't understand why he's always touching you like that."

"Who's touching me? When was this?" And that was the start of last night's argument.

By the time Rosa was dressed, Corrina was halfway through a very large tobacco roll-up when Rosa walked out of the bathroom in a black pinstripe suit with pencil skirt and black and white patent leather heels. She looked herself over in the floor-length mirror and looked at herself from the back.

"Making sure your ass looks good for your man, yeah?" Corrina said through a cloud of smoke.

"You really are stupid aren't you?" Rosa said dismissively.

"Don't call me stupid Rosa, you know I don't like that. And I'm not being stupid, I can tell."

"You can tell that I'm making myself sexy for my boss in a suit I've worn many times before? Can you even hear yourself?"

Taking a long pull of her roll-up, Corrina squinted evil eyes at Rosa. "I know you wanna fuck him! I can smell it on your pussy."

Rosa was taking a long sip of her Evian when she spat some out through the sides of her mouth and started choking. Coughing and slapping her chest, she looked at Corrina who was just watching her. She wanted to say something but the water was still irritating her throat.

"Best thing you can do is finish your smoke and go create something 'cuz your being ridiculous. I told you last night, and I've told you a hundred times before, I don't fancy Thorton, I don't want Thorton, he's just my manager that's it, okay?"

"Does he make you take dictation?"

Rosa frowned as she took another sip of water. "You can be such a bitch sometimes you know that?"

With her bag on her shoulder, Rosa stormed out of the bedroom while Corrina was laughing and saying something. Walking through their flat with angry feet, Rosa was feeling herself getting more and more angry as she slammed the front door and watched the sun rise over the Emirates Stadium. She was angry over the accusation that was thrown at her but she was also angry that Corrina was right.

Thorton was the biggest, baddest, sexiest, most handsome man she had ever seen in a suit. Six foot sky bound, pure chocolate, sturdy, worked out so looked nice and tight in a shirt, salt and pepper goatee and incredibly powerful. How could she not want him?

In the office, he did everything and was hands on with every department of Creative Minds Unite Consultancy. Marketing and promotion, legal, design, they all came to him for final approval and corrections. He was technically the GM of the company considering it was his family money that he put into the business but he wanted to be close to the network of the business by working as a manager. And he balanced both roles effortlessly and that's what turned Rosa on the most.

The sound of his voice during a business meeting when he is not getting the results he expects, watching him scribble across reports when an employee gets something wrong, his wry smile when he is conducting a sneaky business transaction, the ripple of arm muscle by her head when he was looking at something on her computer.

Thorton Mornington was married with three children and he happily displayed his family around his office and they visited the office so much, it was as if they worked there. But that didn't stop Rosa from taking lengthy trips to the toilet to break out her miniature wand vibrator which was disguised as her lipstick. The gold and mauve vibrator had a lipstick lid but was designed for her other lips and was bought for her by Corrina as a joke birthday present. But she was finding a use for it; spending time at her desk in front of Thorton's office with one hand under her desk and her thighs slightly ajar as she listened to recordings of his voice that she was to translate into letter form.

Switching to the Northern Line while listening to his voice on her Dictaphone, Rosa could feel her nipples rising. He was dictating a

letter to his arch-rival Naomi, who worked in a company across the road and he was being condescending as hell. The tone of his voice, his cadence, his flavour of condescension had Rosa stupidly aroused while her nipples were pressed against a pane of glass in an extremely packed train carriage.

She brushed her hair away from her face as his voice travelled through her ears, down her spine between her cheeks and through her lips, which she knew she'd be playing with as soon as she saw him. She always did.

Sipping water slowly, trying to counteract the movement of the train, Rosa swallowed and enjoyed the tickle as a drop of water trickled down her chin.

Being an avid fan and consumer of water, Rosa loved the way it tasted. For many who would say water had no taste, Rosa would say "taste it after Corrina has just eaten you out."

Whenever her lover would look up from between her thighs after a mammoth session of eating, Rosa's first sip of water would feel like alcohol to a recovering alcoholic. And since Rosa had been teetotal for six years, she knew the feeling well.

But recently, her water has tasted like Thorton and she didn't know why. Well she did but she was happy to live in the denial because she wasn't hurting anyone by fantasizing. Just enjoying the benefits her job put on a visual platter for her.

Rosa emerged from the maze of tunnels that was the London Underground feeling like nature left the radiator on overnight. Beads of sweat snuck down her temples and her thighs slid past each other with moist ease. She welcomed the heat on her skin as she stopped at Starbucks for a frappuccino, with Thorton's voice still creeping down her spine.

"Make sure MAKE SURE you add the 'fuck you very much' at the end. Don't forget because that's the most important. Thank you Rose."

"Ooooo..." Rosa said to herself, walking into her office building. "the way he says FUCK... good God!"

Suddenly her phone vibrated and she checked it as she got into the lift to her floor, ignoring hellos from workmates as Thorton gave her good aural while a Corrina text message gave her the visual.

'Hey... tell your man to stay the away from my girl. And you forgot your keys Miss D Nile.'

Strangely, Rosa felt annoyance creeping over her at Corrina's attitude to all of this. Even if she did want Thorton to take her roughly and with full malice over his dark brown oak desk, she didn't take it past a fantasy.

"D Nile? So stupid you are," Rosa said to the message and put her phone back in her bag. "So what if I wanna fuck him? Doesn't mean

I'm gonna," she said to herself in the empty lift carriage, feeling her nipples rise.

This was the regular dance she experienced every day beneath her bra. As soon as she got to within two floors of her office, she would feel her nipples begin to rise in anticipation. Her body knew she would be in close contact with a powerhouse of a man who could pick her up and have his wicked way with her if he wanted to. He would lean over her shoulder to look at something on her screen and his chewing gum minty breath would tickle her neck and make her think of their bodies sweating together as he moaned in her neck.

"ROSA!" a voice bellowed from the office as the lift doors opened. She knew whose voice it was. She worked with it every day and knew every nuance of its sound, its cadence, its tone.

Made her shiver every time he called her name with such authority and urgency.

She kicked up her speed and walked faster to her desk, where Thorton was sitting, looking bemused and confused.

"Morning Rosa... I was looking for the minutes from our last staff meeting and I couldn't remember your password. What is it?"

"Erm... why would I tell you my password boss? Wouldn't that defeat the purpose of a password?"

"Whatever smart ass," Thorton replied, his sky blue shirt tensing against his muscular upper body as he got up from Rosa chair. "When you've settled, could you send me those minutes please? I need them before the staff meeting."

"Oh yeah... I forgot about that."

It was Thorton's voice that made her forget about their monthly performance meeting that was held with the entire staff team. Mainly looking at performance and positive output, the meeting was usually an all day thing with food and drinks usually running into the early evening.

"Is it gonna be a long one?" Rosa asked.

"I think so... there's a lot to go over, what with Naomi getting arrested for sexual harassment and her company flopping. We need to capitalise on that and make that work to our advantage."

"You could sexually harass me any time!"

"What'd you say?" Thorton said, with his nose in a particularly thick file and his eyes scanning.

"Nothing... am I taking the minutes again?"

"I'd have it no other way!" Thorton said with a wink as he went into his office and closed the door.

Rosa sat at her desk; her handbag in her draw, bottle of water on the desk and her suit jacket behind her chair when a massive shiver ran through her.

"Why is he saying shit like that to me? Doesn't he know I'd kill him with the pussy?" Rosa said to herself then laughed. "He has no idea. I'd kill him with it."

Her morning consisted of emails, switching music choices multiple times, checking her phone for messages from Corrina, coffee, quick two pancakes she left in the staff fridge and the pleasure of having solo moments in Thorton's presence when he called her into his office.

At 11:30, everyone in the office got an email to let them know it was meeting time. Rosa enjoyed these meetings as it gave her a chance to see faces from the office she didn't see everyday like beautiful and voluptuous Roni from I.T., the short woman with the roundest breasts Rosa had ever seen and the cuddly Greek guy with the extremely long name she couldn't remember who made her laugh so hard, water came out of her nose.

Converging in the large conference room, Rosa walked in and saw staff had already found and devoured most of the Krispy Kreme doughnuts she ordered. The cling film over the snacks were ripped to shreds and crumbs and icing showed a trail of who the quick-fingered culprits were.

"You lot are too craven. Meeting hasn't even started yet," Rosa said to the room of chewing, laughing faces.

Thorton wasn't far behind and walked into the room, brushing past Rosa as he went. "Wow... nice to see everyone found the snacks before the meeting even started."

"I just said the same thing. You got a famished staff team here." "Let's hope their as craven for success."

Thorton took his suit jacket off and draped it over the chair at the head of the large table. Rosa took the seat next to him with her handbag at her feet, her bottle of water and a writing pad, ready to take minutes. She stole one look at Thorton as he waited for the room to fall into silence. His brick wall of a chest was imposing from the side and made Rosa take a very long sip of water.

She asked the man next to her to pass the cravat of water and a plastic cup as Thorton cleared his throat and rubbed his hands together.

"Alright people. Thanks for coming. First things first... we are the shit! And don't ever forget that. We've been hot at what we do for a long time but now, with our competition under investigation for sexual harassment, it's time for us to get white hot on 'em..."

As Thorton spoke, Rosa poured and took a sip of the ice cold water. Her chair, the room, the staff, the doughnuts, everything disappeared. She rubbed her eyes to make sure what she was seeing was real but

she knew what was happening. The melody of Thorton's voice made her drift again away into fantasy land.

An elbow in her ribs from the guy next to her woke her out of it and she was steamed. There was never a time where a good Thorton fantasy wasn't accepted and appreciated, especially when he spoke on a grand scale.

On the outside it may have looked like she was asleep, but she still managed to write the minutes down and paraphrase his speech with eerie accuracy.

But now she'd have to do it looking right at him. And that was going to be a problem.

Another sip of water slid down her throat and cooled her rising heat as she watched him walk around the room, looking at each person in their eyes, making sure what he was saying applied to everyone individually.

Watching him touch people on the shoulders, pointing at them, making sure his words put a smile on their faces made Rosa stop writing for a moment and watch him work. The awe on her face must've been visible as she felt like she was drooling at one point.

"...we have to be the market leaders, we ARE the market leaders. 100% positive output from all departments, extremely intelligent staff team. We just need to go further. We need to show everyone that they need Creative Minds Unit Consultancy in order for their career to truly take off..."

Rosa was struck dumb by him.

He had the entire room hooked on his every word thanks to a squeeze of Barry White's tone in his voice. Personable and approachable, handsome and an astute business man, Thorton Mornington had every eye on him, especially Rosa, who was onto her second glass of water as she felt heat rising throughout her body. She wanted to reach for a doughnut but, as she looked at the tray of delectables, she watched the last one get picked up and stuffed into a mouth.

"Fuck," she mumbled to herself.

With everyone in the room hanging on Thorton's every word as he filled everyone with promise and optimism that they can excel as the market's supreme black media consultancy company, Rosa never blinked or took her eyes off him. The only movement from her was to lift the plastic cup of water to her lips. Her last sip came with an added surprise and she felt an extra special heat began to emanate from between her thighs.

With one hand slowly sliding off the table and underneath it, Rosa ran the hand up her legs and she felt a sticky single stretch of liquid between her finger and her thigh.

She tried to hide the look of surprise on her face by merging her shock with a roar of laughter that went up in the room as Thornton made a joke.

She feigned laughter while feeling the part of her panties that covered her lips. The warm moisture was bemusing and confusing as well as enthralling and electric. Something about being in a room of full of professional people while her pussy was reacting to her boss was a naughty feeling she liked.

In the laughter, she took a wet wipe out of her bag and wiped her hand under the table so her scent didn't fill the room.

"...I want you all to leave this room after this meeting and I want you to feel great. I want you to work like you run shit. Work like you know you are the market leader. Work like you are the top of your field because you are, did you know that? This company is..."

Rosa brushed her curls behind her ear and tried to regulate her breathing and calm the flushed feeling that was washing over her from her head to her heeled feet. Thornton's pacing was making her dizzy as she couldn't keep her eyes off him. And now she was starting to feel a patch of cool growing under her cheeks and through her skirt.

He walked past and touched her on the shoulder and she poured another glass of water, leaving the cravat within reach, while her other hand was writing furiously. Longer sips meant she was getting hotter and hotter.

Thornton slammed a fist on the table and Rosa jumped, making everyone laugh at her. During the big chuckle, Rosa was more concerned with the heat she hoped wasn't displayed across her skin tone.

"Sorry, that scared me," she said to everyone. Thornton was looking at her and smiling.

Right then and there, Rosa made a dangerous decision.

With attention falling off her and back onto Thornton, who had growing sweat patches under his arms, Rosa looked around the room. Something about watching him perspire further made the decision easier for her.

"Just wanna lick him..." she whispered to herself.?He walked to the head of the table and raised his hands.

"Listen, I know its been hard for us to get off the ground but we have and we're flying high right now and that's because of the people in this room. You guys have put in the work and made this company what it is..."

She took one last look at the people in the room, who were all staring at Thornton, before reaching slowly into her handbag. Her mind was connecting with what she was feeling as she rifled through her bag, trying to find her lipstick. She needed it. And she needed it now.

Running fingers over her phone, purse, Oyster card, tissue, phone bill, wet wipes, chewing gum and Vaseline tin, Rosa remembered she put it in the side compartment. A quick unzip and she found her lipstick, which she slid into her lap as she sat up straight.

Another look at the staff team, who were hanging on Thornton's every word, and Rosa adjusted herself in her seat. She was trying not to smile too much over what she was about to do and thus draw

attention from someone in the room who'd wanna know what she was smiling about.

She slowly opened her thighs and picked up her pen and began to write random words. She'd already noted most of what Thornton said, but she began writing random words she remembered him saying while her other hand was in her lap pulling off the top of her lipstick.

"...We're at a stage where we need all hands on deck because there's a few major contracts coming in that we need to secure and prove that we are not a flash in the pan company or some fly by night quick start company. We are about to go into league with the big boys and become big boys ourselves and that..."

One click on the end of her lipstick and it began to vibrate in her lap. She squeezed her thighs around it at first to muffle the sound and see if anyone sitting next to her would hear it. She took another look around the room and they were still sucked in to the boss.

With no sign of acknowledgement from her peripheral vision, Rosa opened her thighs and held the wand between her forefinger, middle finger and thumb before dabbing it on her clit. She knew that was the wrong thing to do as she inhaled a sudden breath that made Thornton give her a quick look.

She threw out a quick cough to cover the surprise between her thighs. The initial dabs weren't quick enough and the contact on her already excited clitoris was a shock to her system.

Breathing quickly, she wrote more words on the paper to give the illusion of not doing what she was actually doing. The vibration travelled along the fabric of her panties and along the elastic, making her moist lower half come alive.

She dropped the pen and looked up at the man who was making her masturbate under the table in a meeting full of over 40 colleagues and work people. The more she thought about it, the more wrong it felt, which made it feel so right.

The lights from the ceiling were making him look almost regal as her hand under the table imagined him using his tongue to slide up and down her lips. His strong shoulders sliding under her legs and his arms reaching up to play with her nipples and wrap around her neck. With every word he spoke, Rosa matched the melody of his voice to the movement of her hand. When his voice got low and stern, she ran the bullet between her lips and when he got loud and excited, she held it on her clit. With the rise and fall of his tone, Rosa felt her face twitching and her eyes squinting. Her bum cheeks were clenching with each loud word he spoke. She picked up the pen and clenched in tight in a fist while gritting her teeth. Her heart was beating quickly and she licked her lips, with her hand imagining Thornton picking her up, putting her against the wall and lifting her onto his shoulders to eat her pussy. Being able to look down at his strong arms holding her up and his beautiful face between her thighs, eating her the way she knew he could.

Her hand was making a small circle over her pussy and she opened her thighs wider as her nipples rose. She looked down and watched them poke through her shirt with a grimace due to the increasingly pleasurable feeling going on beneath the solid oak conference table.

"I don't know about you lot but I'm not struggling any more. I put everything I have to make this company work and I'll be damned if I'm not going to put 100% effort in. And as long as I've got a team around me who are willing to put in 110%, there's no way we can't win..."

Rosa was hanging onto every word. Her hand above began to crack the pen under such a tight grip while the hand below was somewhere between Thornton turning her over and pulling her hair.

The circles she was making got faster and her hips began to jerk in her seat. In her mind, she was moaning like she'd just been shot. Her voice was breaking and cutting out because she was screaming so loud. Physically, she was the picture of calm, although a tint of flush red was washing over and her left eye was in a permanent squint.

She knew she was about 20 seconds away from having an orgasm in her seat. She could feel liquid spreading through the material of her skirt and her clit throbbed on a different melody.

"...I don't know about you, but I'm out here to build something out of nothing and be successful doing it. Fuck working for some big corporation, let's BE the corporation! I know you guys heard about the shit that went down at Naomi's across the street... I'm not going out like that. Let's keep it professional at all times, get those contracts, build brands and let's make greatness!"

Rosa was breathing like she was chasing a sneeze. The pen snapped in half and her wand was lodged firmly to the left of her clit.

The orgasm started and ended before she knew it. She frowned and opened her mouth slightly while closing her eyes as the room erupted in a round of applause and whistles. The sudden eruption of noise took her by surprise and she dropped her lipstick wand while her pussy was still throbbing in orgasm.

"Fuck!" Rosa shouted instinctively. "Yeah! Fuck yeah!"

She discarded the broken pen and raised her free hand in the air while the other was lodged firmly between her thighs.

Dropping her head so she could let her face truly express what she was feeling, Rosa kept her one hand in the air as the room began to empty. She looked up to see Thornton gathering papers together.

"You okay Rose? You look a little flushed?"

"Nah, I'm good, thank you. That was one hell of a speech. You spend all night practising that?"

"A few hours here and there. Okay, I was up for two nights straight."

He put up his hands in surrender, smiled a dangerous smile then put a hand on her shoulder as he walked to the door.

"I'll meet you in my office, I just need to make a call."

"No biggie smalls," Rosa mumbled. "I need to call the missus anyway so take your time."

"Will do." Her head fell as she watched his back move towards the door to the

conference room. She rested her head on the table and let out a long sigh.

Rosa was glad she was alone because she didn't want anyone to see the smile on her face. She wanted to enjoy that by herself.

"Speak of the devil and they shall appear! Hello Corrina... she was just about to call you."

Rosa's head shot up so fast, her momentum made her chair slide back on its wheels. She watched Thornton hold the door open for Corrina and instead of a thank you, she gave him a stare followed by a wry grin.

"Was she?" Corrina said.

"Well I'll leave you ladies to it. Corrina, nice to see you again. Rosa, I'll see you in a minute."

"That was a nice speech you gave. Real motivational," Corrina said sarcastically.

She looked at Rosa with eyes that spoke volumes. Sitting in her own joy juice, with her girlfriend and the desire of her fantasies having a conversation made her uncomfortable but the look Corrina was giving her said that she heard and saw more than just a bouncy pep talk.

"Thanks, gotta rally the troops sometimes, ya know? Anyway, got a lot of phone calls to make. Nice to see ya, take care."

Thornton left the room as Corrina stood in the doorway, looking at Rosa but saying nothing.

The former silence she was enjoying for the come down of her orgasm was now eerie as they stared at each other. Each waiting for the other to say something.

"I only came here to bring you your house keys 'cuz you forgot them, remember? Or were you too BUSY to remember you forgot them? And with the toy that I got you as well?" Corrina said, throwing Rosa's keys at her.

Rosa flinched and ducked as they flew towards her face. She looked up from her recovery position to see Corrina leave the room without saying another word.

"Fuck," she said to herself, pouring another cup of water and knocking it back in three large gulps. "Fuck, fuck, fuuuuuuuuuuck!"

POWER OVER THE POWERFUL PART A

"I don't think..." Nathan laughed, looking down at his plate. "What?" "It's just... you just never know about what people are like when

they're at home. At work, Godfrey can be a real..." Nathan froze and began to play with his food.?" A real dick right? Yeah I know. He's got a fat boy complex. Hates

people who can see their dick." They shared a laugh and for a second, Nathan forgot where he was.

In front of him was a beautiful, completely fuckable yet slightly older woman who was obviously flirting with him. She even went one step further and put her married cuckolding cards on the table beside a delicious dinner and chest stinging alcohol.

He finished his drink with a silent burp as Asitah got up from her seat and walked towards him. His entire body tensed up as she reached for his glass and went back to the breakfast bar of drinks.

"Let's make it a little stronger shall we?" Asitah murmured with a sexy chuckle.

"Sure, why not," he replied, watching her hum like the world was kneeling at her feet.

She put his glass of fresh liquid next to his plate before running her hand from the top to the bottom while looking in his eyes. Three quarters of the way through his meal and Nathan still hadn't answered the question. His drink was placed next to him as he watched her hips sway back to her seat.

"So, what you saying Nathan? Did I get that right? I hear a lot of young people saying it. Was I close? What you saying?"

He laughed and stuttered. "Yeah, that wasn't bad. Erm, alright then yeah I'm cool with it."

The answer left his lips before he'd fully decided what he wanted to do. It was the last look at her lovely shape that made the decision for him and he stared back at her, feeling his mojo wake up.

"Oh goodie goodie... there's a fat bastard licking a plate that owes me £20."

She went back to her plate with a huge smile on her face, gathering the rest of her food in a pile.

"Oh, okay," Nathan replied confused. "So, how does it..."

"Don't worry, we'll get to the rules after dessert. And you've got to try my banana soufflés with caramelised rum bananas. Trust me, you'll wanna fuck me on the table after tasting this."

The vision of Asitah on the table with her legs spread to the heavens clouded Nathan's mind and made him look at his last few forks of food on his plate. In his fantasy, he said fuck it to the food and cleared the table with one swipe of his arm. The commotion of plates breaking would make her look up at him but it'd be too late because Nathan would be in her personal space and ready to pull her by the hair. Slam her down and bend her over like he didn't give a fuck, lift her dress, pour wine down the crack of her ass and totally abuse her pussy. She doesn't scream because he's covered her mouth to stop any hope of Godfrey hearing her. Then he'd remove his hand because he'd want

Godfrey to hear what was happening to his wife while he was off somewhere licking gravy from a plate. Nathan would want him to hear the table scooting across the floor, knives and forks falling to the ground and the drinking glasses clashing to the ground.

"Sounds like I'm gonna like whatever you put on the table."
"OoOoOookay..." Asitah giggled taking her plate to the kitchen. Nathan sipped his stronger drink and stared at the outline of Asitah's

shape as she bent over the oven, checking her soufflés. He'd spent the whole night trying not to imagine her moaning while grinding her hips on his dick. He imagined she had the most chocolate of breasts with dark chocolate areola that covered her breasts with double D curves . Hips probably had a few stretch marks which were a sign of good growth and legs that looked beautiful whether she was in heels or not.

She picked up a bottle of Wray and Nephews, held her thumb over it and drizzled the clear liquid into the pan. A fierce sudden flame jumped into the air but Nathan had his eyes locked on Asitah and the cool, calm way she shook the pan until the fire died.

She moved the pan off the fire and scooped slices of browned bananas on a side plate next to an individual soufflé.

"Tastiest thing on earth besides me!" she said, sliding the plate in front of him.

Yet again, Nathan looked at the food n front of him like it was made for someone else. He didn't know where to start due to the fact that the food looked of restaurant quality.

"Start from the top and work your way down!" Nathan looked up from the steam rising from his plate.?" I like to start at the bottom. That's how Drake said he started." "Who?" "Oh, this rapper..." "I can't stand rap music. So much misogyny. It's not about the art of

it any more, just money and bitches. Anyway, you gotta eat this in silence. Just watch."

Picking up his spoon, he couldn't decide where to start. The bananas were browned on the edges and sending trails of rum streaks into the air and oven heat was still pouring off the edges of the ramekin. He looked up to see Asitah staring at him while chewing slowly, her eyes dipping up and down in his direction.

"Oh shiiii... where's Godfrey?" "Don't worry about him, he's getting ready. Eat up."

They ate the rest of their dessert in silence. Asitah took every mouthful with flirtatious pleasure while Nathan was imagining being in control of such a powerful woman who had her husband eating somewhere else in the house like a house servant. With every other scrape of his plate, Nathan wanted to ask something but every swallow made him feel more intoxicated.

His last piece of banana and soufflé was gone and he dropped his spoon and clapped his hands. "That was one of the tastiest things I've ever eaten."

"Yessur... but I taste better."

Asitah picked her last piece of banana with her fingers and dangled it over her mouth, liquid droplets hanging before falling between her lips and down her chin. "Actually, we probably taste the same which is damn good!"

Nathan was telling himself to relax and play with the flirtations but he was still dubious that Godfrey was somewhere in the house.

He knocked back his drink. "Can I use your bathroom please?"

"Yeah, good idea, get it out of the way. In the hallway, under the stairs."

"Thanks."

Following her directions, he found the toilet and locked the door behind him. He turned on the light and sat on the seat smiling to himself.

"Oh my God... what the hell kinda relationship is this... she really wants me to... fucking hell..."

He jumped to his feet and spun around with his hands covering his face. Then he remembered why he came into the toilet.

"Oh yeah!"

He finished and flushed, making sure he shook the remnants and wiped with a tissue. Washed his hands, dried and started to feel ready.

His reflection stared back at him, not sure what to say, just smiling. "Let's go handle that!" he said to himself.?He turned the light off and opened the door to Asitah, who was

standing in front of the door. Before he could even register the fact she was there, she put an arm around his head and pressed her lips against his. Her mouth tasted like Malibu and her moan vibrated from her throat while her other hand grabbed his behind.

"Yummy yummy... okay, just needed to find out. Let's go. GODFREY, GET IN YOUR PLACE!"

Asitah took Nathan by the hand and walked ahead of him while humming. She picked up a glass full of something and didn't stop moving up the stairs with Nathan trailing behind her with his eyes on her ass. Each cheek had a mind of its own and didn't shake like it's neighbour. Her left cheek rose, tensed and then wobbled while her right cheek wobbled, tensed then rose.

"YOU READY?" Asitah screamed as they got to the top of the stairs.

"YES I'M READY!" Godfrey shouted back from somewhere ahead of them.

Due to the fact that he hadn't heard his manager's voice for such a long time, and he was lost in hypnotising glaze of Asitah's shape, Nathan forgot Godfrey was even there. He shook his head, trying to get his game face back on when he looked up and saw Asitah facing him.

"Come here... just one more time."

She grabbed the back of his head and kissed him again. This kiss was deeper than the last and made him close his eyes, working his lips and wrapping his hands around his hips, moving slowly down to her ass.

He sang a song in his soul as his hands reached the apex of her behind and he squeezed as strong as he could. Pulling her into him, Nathan felt his dick rise against her groin, the taste of banana and rum on her tongue.

They parted with a single line of saliva stretching between their lips and she licked her tongue between them.

"Oh HELL yes!" she said lowly.

She pulled him by the arm, walked three steps and kicked a door open while kicking her heels off in front of her.

"You, stand there!" she pointed at Nathan without looking at him and walked towards one hell of a four-poster bed. Sheets were hiked up around the top of the bed and a massive burgundy duvet and perfectly arranged pillows.

Nathan couldn't see much in the room except for the massive bed. He looked around, trying to see the intricacies of their bedroom, but the only light was from a small, energy saving lamp at the side of the bed.

Looking around, he grabbed his dick, enjoying the anticipation of getting behind Asitah and working her until the sun came up. That was until he saw something that made him take a few steps back.

In the corner of the room, with his own lamp at his feet, stood a naked Godfrey with his head buried in the corner.

"How was dinner?" Godfrey asked without turning around.

Nathan didn't know what to say to someone he'd always seen drilling instructions at him or his co-workers or cussing for some reason. Beads of sweat were dripping down his large hairy back and into the crack of his behind.

"It was... nice. Thank you."

"What you thanking him for? He didn't cook shit. All he's gonna do is shit it out and probably block the toilet again." Asitah shrieked. Nathan looked at her and she was standing with one leg forward, model style, in nothing but a smile.

His head turned from her to him, back to her then quickly back to him and third take at her and his eyes widened.

However shapely Asitah looked in her dress, the truth of her curves was hidden because Nathan had never seen such perfect thickness except online. Video and magazine models came built or paid for like this but he had never seen it with his own eyes. The light behind her eased around her curves and Nathan was enjoying every contour while Godfrey was heavy breathing in the corner behind him.

"Fucking hell!" Nathan mumbled.?" Hey, that's my wife you're talking to. Show some..." "Absolute and utter disrespect! You see Godfrey, that's exactly the

problem right there!" Asitah walked up to Nathan with everything shaking and turned him

to face her husband. "Look fat boy."

Godfrey turned around with his head down and a Hello Kitty ball-gag in his mouth. She took Nathan's hands and placed them on her ass and he automatically squeezed.

"See, THIS is how I like my shit squeezed! Just like this, squeezed like it matters! Turn your fucking head around."

Godfrey did as he was told and turned back to the corner while Nathan watched with his mouth open and another erection growing.

It was weird because he was getting aroused watching Asitah dress Godfrey down and was getting excited at the prospect of fucking her and making him watch.

"Come on young stud, let's show him how fucking should look."

She walked backwards towards the bed and sat down in front of him unbuckling his jeans.

"Now," Asitah said looking up at him. "I'm gonna need YOU young sir to fuck the SHIT out of me. I'm talking no holds barred, pull my hair, spit in my mouth, finger in my ass, choke me out, leave a bruise, fuck the dog shit out of me. D'you think you can do that? I know he can't."

Nathan looked back at Godfrey then back at Asitah who was pushing his jeans down to his knees.

"Can you do that Nathan?" she asked holding his dick in her hand. "Yeah, no, sure no problem. It's nothing." She smiled sweetly. "That's what I wanna hear. And that's what he'll

hear!" Her lips danced together before she spat on Nathan's limp dick and

followed with her mouth. She took to one knee and made him step out of his jeans. His back arched as her warmth enveloped him and he felt himself growing in her mouth. Every inch of his dick was taken by her mouth which was something he'd never felt before. Her throat took him in as he grew instantly, put his hands on the top of her head and began to enjoy.

"Slow and sloppy?" Asitah asked. "It's never anything else!"

A thick, long line of saliva dripped between her breasts. She rubbed it in her cleavage and turned her head from the left to the right, showing amazing technique. Every gamut of perfect head was flashing before Nathan's eyes and he didn't know what to do with himself. His hands weren't controlling her head, just resting as she had everything under control with her mouth. She moaned ravenously as if she was searching for the truth and the answer was waiting to erupt from inside him.

Nathan wondered if the loud sounds were for Godfrey's benefit or if they were her own regular grooves. Not that he cared as he looked at Godfrey's back, watching him face the corner and scratching his hips.

"Suck that dick!" Nathan said, still looking at Godfrey's back. Down below, Asitah was following instructions and had both her arms out to the side and was making saliva drip from every inch of him. It was such a nice feeling, Nathan didn't want to watch. He wanted to but the sight before his eyes was too much to enjoy without enjoying it too

much. The muscles in his fingers flexed as he cupped her head and pulled her into his groin, admiring the lashing of frothy bubbles that slid off his dick and splattered on the floor.

"Oh that's it fuck my face!" Asitah mumbled then looking towards Godfrey. "Hear that? It's called face fucking!"

"Yeah I hear," Godfrey quipped in the corner. "Good... make sure you pay attention."

Asitah jumped up from her knees with her neck, chest and shoulders glazed in saliva and got on all fours on the bed, her eyes leading Nathan to follow. He pulled his t-shirt over his head and discarded it somewhere in the darkness. He didn't need an invitation to be told what to do and, with the spit still dripping down his dick, Nathan was naked and setting his hands on Asitah's waist as she arched her back, putting her ass high in the air.

"OoOoOooo... he really is naughty baby," Asitah said looking into the corner. "He tried to slip it in."

"No, I didn't, I just..."

"He did honey. He tried to fuck me without a condom. Oh baby, you're gonna have to watch him. He's sneaky."

"Are you serious?!" Godfrey started to say.

By the time he turned around, Asitah reached back, grabbed Nathan's dick and ran it up and down her lips before sliding him in with a pleasurable sigh.

"OH GOD! Are you watching Godfrey? ARE YOU? WHO TOLD YOU TO TURN AROUND AND WATCH? DID I? HUH? FINE! NOW YOU HAVE TO WATCH!"

Playing with the handfuls of her ass, Nathan looked up to see Godfrey standing with his arms crossed in front of his penis watching his wife grind on the unsheathed dick inside her.

"Come on... don't fuck about back there..." Asitah started to say.

Nathan pushed himself deep until there was no where for him to go inside her. Her walls clamped onto him and created a slow drag as he pulled out, infusing a slow drag and a slick push with each thrust.

"You fuck..." Nathan moaned, parting her cheeks and staring at her anus with wonder. He didn't have long to stare as the rest of her behind jiggled as she fucked him back. The bed legs could be heard scooting against the wood floor as Asitah threw her all into pushing back on Nathan but he held strong and pushed back. Each movement made her moan and scream and, without realising it, Nathan had danced too close to the sun. The force of her movement, the moan that made her whole body shimmer, the slickness of her walls, the anger on Godfrey's face, all felt too good.

He was trying to hold on, trying to slow down and withstand the movement that her body was making but he didn't pace himself, instead going for the short con as opposed to the long one.

"Oh shiiit..." Nathan moaned.?" Yes baby... that's it don't stop tearing up this pussy!"

"Fuck you, don't say shit!" Nathan mumbled, wiping his forehead with the back of his hand.

He wasn't ready for such a feat of wet, slick walls and great sex and was losing to everything she threw at him. The way her ass bounced off his stomach and giggled for a few seconds, the quick peak of her asshole, the moan she secreted, Godfrey in the corner watching with a major scowl on his face.

Asitah looked back at him. "What are you doing? Why you slowing... oh no... no no no... not yet... it can't be..."

Nathan was holding onto her hips and pumping furiously inside her, trying to hold off until the last possible second before pulling out.

"I'm sooooorry..." He moaned as his seed began to shoot.

He'd pulled out just as his first spurt flew into the air and landed on her back.

"Really Nathan?"

His dick was spraying all over the place due to the sweetness of the orgsam. Each squirt seemingly pushed harder than the last and flew onto her back, her neck, in her hair and over the bed.

"Geeeezuuuus..." he shouted while working the last strains of white liquid from the head of his dick.

"Really Nathan? If I wanted quick sex, I would've gotten.... oh for fuck sake."

Still on his knees, Nathan watched Asitah get up off the bed with a strong huff and walk towards her husband.

"Clean this off!" she said strongly, turning her back to her husband.

Nathan couldn't hide the horror that crept across his face while Asitah was looking at him with the corner of her lip curled. Godfrey's head could been seen bobbing up and down behind her shoulders slurping with his tongue.

"You know you can't leave yet right? Not until I get my pussy seen to. That was looked at but not seen to. You eat pussy Nathan? Or are you EXACTLY like this Michellin man back here? MAKE SURE YOU LICK IT ALL UP!"

"Yes Asitah." "So, Nathan, do you eat pussy?" "No, I don't." Asitah looked up with shock covering her face. "Erm, what the fuck did you say? Godfrey? Get my knuckle dusters please. What'd you mean you don't eat pussy? You know you ain't leaving until..."

Asitah didn't finish her sentence, she just whistled and pointed at her pussy as Godfrey returned and handed her a pair of knuckle dusters.

Nathan, with his dick shrinking and leaking, raised an eyebrow. "Are you serious?" Nathan asked, looking for his clothes.?" I REALLY WOULD use these on you if you didn't eat my pussy.

Wouldn't I darling?" Godfrey looked over her shoulder with a dab of white liquid smeared

across his mouth. "She would." Nathan frowned as Asitah put the brass knuckles on and pointed to

her pussy. "Quickly then."

I WILL CUT YOU & ZEAH THE BALL CRUSHER – C.L.I.T.S

"Nah, but look at him though, he walked right into that one."

"Yeah I know, that's a man thing though. Then I bet he... see, I knew it. He'd act like he didn't know how it kicked... Oh awake are we?"

With his head dropped back, Lamar looked forward and blinked hard, trying to get his eyes to focus. He knew there were two women with him but he couldn't see them as his eyes hazed over.

"We don't time for you to be all confused... HEY... FUCKER..." "Be easy with this one You." "I can't promise anything in the mood I'm in Zeah, like seriously. I

don't know why but he's already pissed me off." Still trying to gain some equilibrium, Lamar rubbed his nose and

realised his arms weren't held down like they had been. He tried to move his feet and that was when he was given a hefty backhand slap that woke him up instantly.

"ONE OF YOU FUCKING SLAGS HIT ME AGAIN AND I SWEAR I'M BURNING THIS PLACE TO THE FUCKING GROUND!"

Zeah stood up from her seat so fast, the chair fell backwards. She rushed into his space and thrust her hand between his legs with a strong grip that made him wince.

"Oh fuuuuuuuuc..."

"Okay, now we're gonna try this again. Hi, my name is Zeah. Zeah the Ball Crusher. You can imagine why that's my name, right?"

Lamar was about to say something as her grip got tighter and he nodded while holding his breath and beginning to sweat.

"Good... and that lovely piece of caramel over there is I WILL Cut You."

Lamar looked at the woman with the statement name sitting back on a chair with her feet up on another chair, grinning manically.

"Yes, that is her actual name. And the worst thing is, she WILL cut you! Best thing to do is not call us bitches, slags, sluts, hoes, thots or anything like that. She hasn't cut anyone in a while so don't aggravate please?"

Zeah let go of his testicles and sat back down. "Hello Lamar," I WILL said very calmly. "What'd you want?" "Watch this!"

A large screen on the wall that skipped his attention previously lit up and showed him CCTV footage of a man cleaning a flat that looked a lot like the one he shared with Keisha. It took him a moment to realise it was him cleaning and putting Keisha's make up bag away. The video then cut to the moment Keisha was looking for the make-up bag and the argument that followed.

The video paused and I WILL Cut You looked at him. "What did you do wrong there Lamar?"

"Nothing. I fucking remember this. I was like, 'what is she pissed for?' Bare women complain men are lazy and don't do anything and I was cleaning for fuck sake. Then she wants to come and argue with

me 'cuz she couldn't find her make-up bag? That's it? Is that worth an argument?"

"Yes," the duo said together.?" Why?" I WILL jumped forward and Lamar flinched. "Because, dipshit,

women know where their shit is. All the time. Even in a mess, a woman knows where her shit is. And when you move out shit without telling us, that creates an argument. Think about it. Lemme show you another one."

The video changed to more CCTV footage of Lamar sitting at home watching TV. Keisha walked in with a brand new hairstyle and she tried to show it off to him but he was engrossed in whatever was happening on the screen.

"Now this is my personal piss take. You didn't even look up from the screen to look at her. You just said some shit and that was it. All you had to do was PAUSE the TV, look at her, say something and then back to what you were watching. You've got Sky Plus, you could've paused it."

"Zeah yeah? That's your name yeah?" Lamar said with an air of frustration in his voice.

"Yep."

"I remember when this happened but, lemme ask, where did the camera come from? We ain't got no cameras in the flat so where did that come from?"

"Good question Lamar. But is THAT the question you should be asking after the night you've just had or should you, at this point, be paying attention to what the fuck we're trying to teach you?"

"Alright," he mumbled, thinking about the argument he had when Keisha went to bed with her new hairstyle and he ran his fingers through it while laying next to her.

"This last one, I can't even believe you couldn't see where you were in the wrong," I Will shouted. "Play that shit Zeah."

The ball crusher pressed the remote control but nothing happened. "I think we lost that footage." "Shiiit, I really wanted him to see that one." "Excuse me, how the fuck did you guys get a camera into my yard?"

Lamar said with a raised voice.?" This guy," Zeah giggled. "THAT's what you wanna know?" "You don't wanna know how we know so much about your life?" I

WILL added.?" Or how we got into your flat?" "Or how we know how much of a shit boyfriend you are?" "Or how long we've been watching you??" Or how we got you out of your bedroom and here right now?" "Men are so close-minded," Zeah moaned.?" Should've let me cut him, that would've taught him." Zeah pressed the button on his neck and he drifted out of

consciousness, watching himself on screen arguing with Keisha. "I think he'll be alright," Zeah said.

"I wanna give him a smile on his neck." "You really need to see someone about this cutting people fetish!" Lamar could barely hear them talking as he drifted out of consciousness wondering, 'what the fuck is this thing on my neck they keep pressing?'

KEEPING IT COOL & CHRISTIAN

"Right... where is it?"

Shaun went rifling through his shoulder bag, flicking through folders, shuffling papers and throwing random bits into the street.

"Babe... aren't we supposed to be somewhere? Cold feet?"

Shaun scoffed. "ME? This was MY idea and you think I'm gonna pussy out."

"You did last time," Gloria added, crossing her leg, letting her tan mac fall open.

Shaun had a 'VOILA' moment on his face and pulled out a cigarette box from his bag.

"First of all," he started. "I didn't pussy out last time. I was CAUTIOUS last time. Look at where we were?! Someone else's house, loud music, it wasn't even our party... but we still pulled it off."

Gloria laughed while criss-crossing her legs, giving him just enough thigh to look at. Shaun tilted his head to catch a long, lingering look between her legs.

"Oi..." Gloria grinned and snapped her fingers. "Weren't you looking for something?"

"I found it," Shaun responded by sitting down next to her and pulling a spliff from his cigarette box.

She pulled a lighter from her pocket and he made magic with the two. He passed it to her while taking a look around, making sure they weren't being watched.

"Take two tokes of that and call me in the morning.."

Gloria took the roll up, handled it and rolled it between her fingers before pulling it to her lips. She inhaled slowly, closing her eyes, dancing with the influence that instantly washed over.

Sitting on a broken wall, Shaun and Gloria sat in a moment of silence.

Leaning on his knees, Shaun looked at his wife and smiled as she passed it back to him.

"So," he said, tapping thick ash from the end. "How are you baby?"

"Don't be stupid Shaun. Everytime we do this, it's like you wanna have small talk. What the fuck is there to talk about?"

"OoOoOo... nervous are we? You don't have to do this if you don't want to ya know? We can just go home and..."

"Fuck you," Gloria said, making a perfect smoke bubble. "I bet you'd LIKE me to go home."

Shaun burst into a fit of laughter and paced in front of her.?" Nah babe, seriously, we don't have to do this." Gloria giggled and shuffled her heels on the ground so they clapped

together.?" Don't worry sugar... we're doing this!" Shaun took the spliff from her and smiled.?A smile she was used to seeing when he had an interesting idea for

them to spice up their sex life. Whether it was the time they went to support a friend in Stratford Magistrates court and ended up having

anal sex in the public gallery or the time she gave him a blowjob under his desk at home while he was being interviewed about his job on BBC News. Or the time they managed to have sex on London Bridge during rush hour. Her personal favourite was the out of this world moment when they got tickets to the Olympics and they managed to pull off a seated reverse cowgirl while Mo Farrah won his second gold medal with the crowd going wild around them.

Gloria was a thrill-seeker and Shaun had a taste for pushing her thrill-seeking to its limits. There was nothing too crazy for them. The heights of Canary Wharf and the lows of underground after-hours clubs in Shoreditch; the bright lights of a Chelsea rented apartment and the dark cubbyholes of sex clubs in Ealing.

As a couple they left their mark up and down the country and today was another game for them to play.

"So, how we gonna do this?" Shaun asked exhaling into the air. "Don't try it. You do you and I'll do me. Isn't that what we agreed?" "Yeah but..." "Shhh..." Gloria said taking three successive tokes then holding her breath.?Shaun knew that when Gloria took a triple toke, she was preparing to change into character. A touch of Mary Jane usually helped the metamorphosis. She was looking down at the ground, listening to the sounds of the estate they were sitting in as the sun went down in the distance.

Still pacing in his suit in front of her, Shaun bent down, taking the spliff from her and kissing her at the same time

"You ready?" Shaun said, looking at the two puffs left.

Gloria stood up, brushed herself down and sighed heavily. "I'm more ready than you are."

"I seriously doubt that."

"Wanna bet? I'd like to add an addition to this then. I bet not only do I come first, but I'll do it in such a way that you won't be able to help but give me props for the rest of my life."

Shaun smiled, "I'll take that bet. And if you lose, I get to choose a forfeit for you to suck on."

Brushing her hair out of her face, Gloria laughed to herself. "Yeah... whatever. You ready to do this?"

"Come we go."

Shaun held his arm out and led the way for Gloria to walk on.

She interlocked her arm in his and they walked quickly, huddled together as an autumn breeze blew over them.

Walking through the miscellaneous estate, Shaun and Gloria were both getting nervous. Her legs weren't as sturdy in her heels and blood was coursing through his veins particularly fast as they crossed a busy road.

Cutting through Stratford streets, the couple slowed their steps as they reached the shabby building with the peeling paint, mesh-covered windows and faded Great Britain flags left over from the Jubilee celebrations.

"You're nervous aren't you babe?" Gloria said with a giggle.?" Like I haven't noticed that you've been walking extra slow." "It's these heels you made me wear. You KNOW these shoes hurt my feet... maybe that was your plan." "I don't need tricks to beat you. I'm winning 38-37." "Whoaaaaaa, wait a minute, hold the fuck up. What's the score?" Shaun felt her eyes on the back of his neck, "It's 38-37 to me." "Excuse me?" Gloria said sliding her head to the left.?" It's 38-37." "Say that again?" Gloria whispered, sliding her head to the right and squinting.?" IT IS 38 points to me and 37 points to you." "Are you SURE Shaun? 'Cuz that sounds like absolute bollocks to me!" Gloria shouted with her eyes as wide as clock faces.?" Yes, it was 36 to me then I got two points last week at the back of that Gordon Ramsey restaurant." "Yeah but didn't I get two points at the... you know what? It's ALL good. Let's go... let's just go. It's 38-37 to you!" Looking at their destination, then back at Gloria, who broke out her hand sanitizer with annoyance seeping out the top of her head, Shaun giggled because he knew he was talking about a contestable two points.

"Don't be mad at me 'cuz you're losing!" Shaun rubbed it in.

"If you say so, let's see what the score is when we're done in here." Gloria said, rubbing her hands.

Shaun growled. "God, I love you woman."

He kissed her passionately, pulling her into his body, his hands sliding into the small of her back.

Gloria moaned in her throat as Shaun's warm lips met hers. Then she felt his fingers flex and begin to investigate her shape.

"Erm babe," he said, with his fingers feeling more of her shape through her mac. "Are you..."

"So let's go then." Gloria replied quickly, backing out of his grasp.

Two couples and a family of six walked past them and went into the building, where music and voices could be heard.

Shaun and Gloria followed behind them, interlocking their fingers. Gloria stopped. "Oh shit, I forgot my thing..." "What thing?" Reaching into her giant shoulder bag, she pulled out a piece of

material and began to fold it into a shape.?Shaun watched her with confusion written all over his face. He had

no idea what the hell she was doing but the look on her face was one of expert precision.

She folded the material into a triangle, tied both ends together, put it over her shoulder and tucked it into her mac, adjusting her arm uncomfortably.

"You ready?" Gloria asked.?" What's that for?" "What's what for?" she replied with a devilish smile of her own. Shaun shook his head. "That's cheating." "Don't watch me, watch TV!" "Where's the TV?" "It's me! About 37-38? You must have me all fucked up round here.

Come we go."

Walking to the doors of the building, Shaun looked at Gloria and tried to deliver his trademark sinister smile but he was shaken by her introduction of a sling. He was confused because he had no idea what it was for or how it would help her to defeat him.?And the more he couldn't figure it out the more nervous he got.

He popped a tab of chewing gum in his mouth.?She flicked a crumble of ash from her mac.?He sprayed deodorant under his arms.?She squirted a quick hit of Elizabeth Arden's White Diamonds on her

fingers before dabbing her wrist, neck and behind her ears.?He adjusted his shrinking erection that arose when he kissed her. She looked at him with a wink.?They approached the doors together and sighed in unison before

sharing a giggle. Shaun put his hands on both doors and pushed them open at the same time for effect.

The instant smell of Black Coconut and Frankincense incense splashed over them, followed by a roar of sound.

To Gloria, the smell and the sound like static white noise and made her neck snap back. Shaun took it better and wrinkled his nostrils and popped his ears as the noise came into focus.

"AMEN AMEN HALLEUIA... BLESSED IS THE LORD IN THE HIGHEST..."

The church of Kinship in Christian & Contact was in full swing with their Friday night sermon.

A six-part choir of full-figured women with no microphones were filling the room with off-key vocals that excited multiple rows of worshipping white garment patrons.

A stage up front held the choir and their combined weight with a drummer, keyboardist, bass player and a makeshift pulpit.

Incense smoke was thick in the air, hands were raised and the room was seemingly moving in a wave of happiness.

Shaun and Gloria were stuck in the doorway, watching the happy, clapping, singing congregation, not sure what to do or where to go.

A member of the congregation looked back at them and stepped out from his seat and approached them with wonder.

"Hello, can I help you?"

"We're just here for the 'sex and sin in society' sermon, have we missed it?" Gloria asked, making her voice as soft as possible.

"Ah no," the man replied with a thick African accent. "It's about to start. Go and find a seat... bless you."

Shaun set off down the centre aisle of the congregation with Gloria holding his hand and walking behind him. Eyes from both sides of the aisle were on them as they searched the rows of seats trying to find a pair of empty ones for them to occupy.

Gloria felt like all eyes were on her. Her feet were starting to burn, the incense was making her eyes water, the vocals were starting to give her a headache and there was a warm draft wafting up the front of her mac. Nerves were tearing through her but the marijuana in her system was increasing her bravery .

She walked in time with Shaun in front of her, trying to avoid eye contact with the white-garmented worshippers who were standing and singing the Lord's praise while watching her saunter through their church.

Shaun could detect judgemental stares coming their way as he gripped Gloria's hand tightly as he spotted two seats up front.

Turning to her, Shaun moved to her ear.

"Wanna go up front?" he said, daring her in his question with his right eyebrow raised.

"Can you handle the spirit upfront?" Gloria retorted with her own eyebrow raised.

Shaun walked to the front where the choir was in full swing, pulling Gloria with him. They moved towards two seats, passing two aunties and a grandmother as they went.

Shaun made eye contact and nodded to them but they did not return the gesture. Instead they looked at Gloria's legs and heels as she moved smoothly behind him.

One of the aunties was first to speak over the music. "Someone is sitting there." "Where?" Gloria replied as Shaun sat down.?" There, there, THERE!" the woman replied, pointing at the two

empty seats with her lips.?" But there's no-one sitting there." "Well they're on their way." "Well when they find their way, they can make their way to different

seats." The aunty exclaimed in shock before huddling with the woman next

to her. "Cha... gwan about ya business..." Gloria said to herself as she sat down, wriggling in her seat to drill the point home.

"What was that all about?" Shaun asked, sensing a verbal altercation.

"Someone's aunty tried to hold seats for her bredrins like this is secondary school assembly. Told her to gwan with herself."

"You are something else, you know that? How you gonna walk into church cussing?" Shaun laughed

"You've got bigger things to worry about son, you about to lose right now. It's about to be 40-38 in this piece!" Gloria replied, waving her hand that hung limply from her sling.

The church band was bringing the song to a crescendo as the couple got comfortable in their plastic-backed chairs.

The congregation were cheering and clapping while others were talking an unknown language that, to Shaun, sounded like Twista and Chris Tucker were having an argument with Bone Thugs n Harmony.

Some of them were shaking like electricity was coursing through their veins instead of blood while one member moved his shoulders like the Harlem Shake.

Gloria adjusted her arm in the sling, watching a couple in power suits to the side of the stage holding hands. As they reached the pulpit, the couple raised their held hands and the congregation came to life again.

Shaun nudged Gloria who was still adjusting her sling. "It's about that time bitch face."

"Whatever dick lips, just make sure you got my prize ready 'cuz I'm going for the title." Gloria laughed.

The amorous couple nudged each other with smiles as they felt eyes on them from all angles. They watched as the couple on stage waved to the congregation and turned on their microphones.

"Praise the Lord, praise the LORD, PRAISE THE LORD!"

The man on stage, Joseph Ocuyemi, was wearing an oversized grey suit with an orange tie. He was bald on top with a Homer Simpson wall around the sides and a middle-aged spread pressing against his shirt.

"God is good..." he said, holding the microphone out. "ALL THE TIME..." the church replied.?" And all the time?" "GOD IS GOOD!"

"Thank the Lord for our wonderful choir. Thank the Lord for my wonderful wife. Thank the Lord for you."

The church repeated his words as Gloria looked around, unsure of what to say and when to say it. Then she remembered she was not sitting there in order to find spiritual guidance, she was trying to win points.

She buttoned up her mac and adjusted her arm in the sling so her hand was able to reach below her waist.

"Today we are here to talk about the world. And the world that we need to save, amen?"

"Amin," the group replied.

" The Lord lives and he lives in all of us. The Lord has created all of us in his own image and it is up to us to save those who are not looking after themselves the way they should.

"The new fashion is going out, getting drunk, aiming to be rich and famous. But the only fashion they need is the Lord. Disrespecting the

vessel the Creator has bestowed upon you in order to achieve cheap pleasure. We're talking about sex ladies and gentlemen."

Gloria kicked Shaun at the mention of sex and looked across at him to see that he had pulled out a cover from his bag and draped it over his lap. The couple made eye contact and Gloria commended him with her eyes.

Good thinking hubby, she thought. You got tricks too.

Shaun was watching the outline of her arm under her coat and could see it moving slowly down towards her thighs and he finally caught on to the reason she wearing a sling.

On stage, Joseph handed the microphone to the woman standing next to him.

Jillian Ocuyemi was the Eve to Joseph's African Adam. In a matching grey skirt suit with the sleeves pulled up and an orange head wrap, Jillian's thick frame commanded attention as she spoke with her mouth too close to the microphone.

"If you'll turn to Genesis 1:27,28, it reads "God created man in his own image, in the image of God he created him; male and female he created them. And God blessed them and said to them, 'Be fruitful and multiply and fill the earth and subdue it.'

"Sex is meant for nothing but procreation and reproduction to ensure the survival of the human race. To ensure that God's people continue to fill the earth and protect the work that people like us in this church have done, amen?"

"AMIN!"

From the corner of his eye, Shaun could see the outline of Gloria's elbow moving repeatedly.

Her eyes were directed towards the stage but her hands and breathing were speeding up and her eyebrows were arched.

She had her free hand over her waist and made it look like all her attention was on the couple on the stage.

She looked quickly at Shaun's lap and thought she could see the peak of his dick poking out through his cover. His fingers were massaging the sides, trying to get himself up and challenging for the points.

With the incense hazing overhead and Jillian's voice becoming a low murmur, Gloria found it hard to concentrate on her surroundings.

The aunties on her left were highlighting passages in their Bibles, paying the couple no mind as they shot side eye looks at each other and grinning slyly.

Withdrawing her fingers from between her thighs, Gloria's sticky fingers reached into her inside pocket as Jillian continued to speak.

"We in this church know and understand about the sanctity of sex after marriage. We in this church know that the Lord created sexual pleasure for his subjects alone. To create life and repopulate the world and keep it in his image but many who are not of the faith are taking

his gifts and using them as tools for the destruction of the world.

"The Devil is out there polluting the minds of the people who we are trying to make pure and in his image. We see it everyday. We hear it. It's on our TVs, our music, our books, our magazines and newspapers, our films. Sex is everywhere. And God is watching. And he is not happy. He is not happy with them. And he is going to deal with them and the Holy Spirit will come and surround them and make them see the error of there ways. Amen."

"AMIN!"

Under the cover of her mac, Gloria pulled out a silver bullet she nicknamed Neo because it always delivered the one orgasm she needed.

Looking at Shaun, who was still eyes forward but working his fingers faster than before, she took a long look at the congregation, worried about the noise she was about to make.

Her arm slid through the sling and her thighs opened slowly, still worried about attracting attention.

She curved her fingers around Neo as it touched her thighs before then slid up to her clit. Her back straightened and she cleared her throat with a wiggle in her seat.

Jolting in her chair, knowing she would draw attention, Gloria raised her free hand to the ceiling.

"PRAISE THE LORD" she shouted.

Joseph and Jillian were taken aback by the sudden outburst but replied with a strong, "AMIN!"

The congregation followed.?Shaun couldn't help but smile, realising what she did.?Joseph took the distraction and ran with it.?" In Matthew 15:19 Jesus says, 'Out of the heart come evil thoughts,

murder, adultery, fornication.'?" It is this same heart that we here at Kinship in Christian and

Contact are trying to save." Gloria took the noise of the congregation to turn Neo on between her

thighs. To her it was the loudest noise in the room. The vibrations felt like they were shaking her entire body, travelling through her chair and connecting to every other chair in the room.

Taking a quick glance at the aunties beside her, Gloria began to enjoy the vibrations with a troubled grin on her face that drew Shaun's attention.

He leaned over with his hand still working under his cover. "What the FUCK was that?" "Bullet shock," Gloria replied with a whisper.?" You know toys are cheating? You can't have toys," Shaun said,

feeling his flaccid penis growing between his fingers.?" You never said we can't bring toys." Shaun leaned back and looked at his wife with a look of shock,

disgust and 'I can't believe she brought a toy with her' in his eyes.

Over Gloria's shoulders he could see the aunties staring at him and he scratched his nose with his middle finger.

The last look Gloria saw in his eyes was, 'alright then, game on'.

While Joseph and Jillian continued to tag team their sermon, Shaun and Gloria gave their attention back to the stage, with both of their hands submerged. They both looked attentively and hung off every word the couple on stage delivered through the speakers.

Folding her lips back, making sure Neo was pressed firmly on her clit, Gloria looked across at Shaun and gave him the wickedest smile. He smiled back then watched as she opened her thighs wider.

He was fully aware he couldn't be as free as he wanted with his dick in his hand. Really, he wanted to throw off the cover, slouch in his seat, open his thighs, lotion his hand with Astral and come quicker than an advert break. But the restraint of his predicament meant he had to work harder to find a good feeling then spend more time concentrating on that feeling to keep it bubbling.

For the first time since having the idea, Shaun did not feel confident about his chances of winning.

His bravery in choosing such a difficult setting made him feel like he had the upper hand. Even at work, while looking at incognito pages of Mz Deepthroat and Aries BBW, he felt confident about stacking more points onto his already winning score.

But now, with a picnic blanket draped across his lap and pre-cum making the tips of his fingers sticky, he was worried.

His eyes drifted to Gloria and he just didn't anticipate her bringing toys.

Shaun shook his head and tried to throw out the images of doubt and the negative thoughts that were causing his erection to shrink.

Shooting continual corner eyes at Gloria, he could see that she was fully in the zone. To those around her, she looked like a first-timer in a new church paying attention, searching for a message that would help her life make sense.

But to Shaun, she was concentrating on an orgasm. Whatever toy she brought with her was working nicely between her thighs.

Gloria's face was a picture of serenity but her body was something different. Her nipples stretched against the material of her mac, her sling arm was stretched downwards and her left leg was bouncing on a trip-hop beat.

"AMIN!"

"Aaaaaamen," Gloria replied with a heavy breath and slightly later than the rest of the congregation.

Realising he just spent the last few minutes focussed on her instead of trying to win, Shaun went back to work.

He fished in his pocket for a pocket-size Vaseline tub and dug two fingers in before reaching for his hidden flaccidity.

"Just last week I attended a function with my good friend the Nigerian High Commissioner for London. We were at a fund-raiser for the Nigerian Independence day event. And I went to the toilet. And in the cubicle next to me, I could hear noises. It sounded like two dogs nyaming a bone. And I could hear someone calling for God to help her."

Shaun distributed the Vaseline between his fingers and stroked his dick back to life.

Gloria had Neo on medium, buried deep under the hood of her clit.

Shaun locked eyes with Jillian and smiled, imagining taking her roughly against the pulpit without a condom.

Gloria twisted the end of Neo and closed her eyes in a fantasy of Joseph eating her pussy with her face down and her ass up while the congregation was watching.

As the amorous couple sat transfixed, Joseph continued his tale.

"Before I could wash my hands and make my presence known, this man walked out and left and, a few moments later, a woman walked out fixing her brassiere.

"I said to her, 'why are you treating the Lord's body with such disrespect?' and you know what she said to me? She said 'because I like it.' I knew it was the Devil talking through her."

Gloria winced and winked as she pressed Neo harder against her clit and straightened her back again, with her forehead scrunched.

Shaun made the Vulcan sign with his greasy fingers beneath the cover and slid his dick in the middle, still trying to rise.

Gloria turned Neo down to low.

Shaun turned two fingers into hooks and slid slowly up and down his dick.

Gloria crossed her legs, adjusting Neo so he stayed in place between her thighs, leaving her hands free.

Joseph had the congregation paying full attention with his story as Jillian took the mic.

"And when my husband came home and told me about the woman in the toilet, I could see how much it was affecting him. And we prayed together for her. We prayed and we prayed and we prayed and we prayed again.

"I could see her through his eyes. I could see her search for love and her need to be loved. Well the Lord loves her and so do we.

"No matter what she drinks or who she fornicates with or what sinful acts she engages in, the Lord still loves her. Hallelujah."

Shaun was hard and could feel pre-cum rising to the top of his erection.

Gloria had her sticky fingers circling her nipple and enjoyed the feeling of goosebumps rising all over her body.

Shaun worked his slickness, straightening his back while holding his cover above the tip of his dick.

Gloria turned Neo back up to high and enjoyed the sensation of the vibration travelling all the way through her body down to her chair.

Shaun watched Gloria's chest heave faster and faster, even though her hands were not moving.

Gloria sighed, nicely.

The choir and the band broke into a sudden rendition of The Lord is my Shepherd and the flock jumped to their feet, singing and filling the room with overwhelming sound.

Shaun and Gloria were both taken aback by the sudden explosion of sound and action and both covered themselves instinctively.

They looked at each other, both in different stages of arousal and majorly confused.

Joseph led the song which started and ended before it really got going, with his hand instructing the band to end it.

Church-goers stayed on their feet and raised their hands to the sky as Joseph held his own hand high.

"In Matthew 5:8, it says 'Blessed are the pure in heart, for they shall see God'. And you WILL see God my children. Every single one of you."

"AMIN!" the church replied.

"YES... PRAISE THE LORD!" Gloria shouted, her voice skating the thin ice line of enthusiastic and erotic.

Her voice distracted Shaun, who had found a nice space of concentration that kept his dick hard. He stared at her until she caught his eye and stared back. She was breathing heavily with one arm at her side and her other arm draped across her chest under her mac.

"I'm about to fuck you up," Gloria mouthed.?" Winner cums first," Shaun's lips replied.?" Watch this then." Jillian took the mic. "Turn to I Thessalonians 4: 3-5, 7 where it says,

'It is God's will that you would be sanctified; that you should avoid sexual immorality; that each of you should learn to control his own body in a way that is holy and honourable, not passionate lust like the heathen, who do not know God... For God did not call on us to be impure, but to live a holy life.' AMIN."

"PRAYER!" Joseph shouted.

Everyone in the church suddenly broke into their own individual prayer while Shaun and Gloria stayed seated.

Gloria reacted instinctively and threw herself to the ground during the loud collective murmur. Her arm in the sling held Neo and she pressed it harder against her clit while her facial muscles danced spasmodically.

A deep, throaty moan erupted from her stomach but was masked by the prayers of everyone around her. Shaun could only watch in awe as his wife bent over in front of him, faking a spiritual moment with her hand between her thighs.

Shaun would've done the same thing if he had a vagina.?Gloria mumbled loudly.?Shaun looked to the ceiling, hoping and praying for the return of his

concentration but the more he watched Gloria, the more he shrunk between his pasty fingers.

Gloria's back arched in a hump.?Shaun wanted to yell at his dick that was disobeying a direct order. Gloria screamed.

"PRAISE THE SPIRIT RUNNING THROUGH THAT WOMAN!" Joseph said on stage, pointing at Gloria.

All eyes fell on Gloria, who was holding herself up with one hand. She was facing the floor, mumbling inaudibly with the sound of collective prayer covering her naughtiness.

"PRAYER PRAYER PRAYER FOR THAT WOMAN WHO IS EXPERIENCING GOD RIGHT NOW!" Jillian said, breaking out of her own prayer.

Shaun was down to a stump and as the blood from his erection rushed to his head, he could feel defeat in his libido. The incense, coupled with the sound of collective prayer around him and Gloria going above and beyond to secure the win, had him majorly distracted.

Adding to that the fact that everyone in the room was praying for her, pushed him over the edge and he conceded defeat.

"PRAY FOR MY WIFE!" Shaun shouted, enjoying the show before him.

Joseph and Jillian joined hands and raised their free hands in the air. Taking the mic from his wife, Joseph kept the prayers going while Shaun put his dick away, removed his cover and dropped to his knees and rubbed Gloria's back as she was mumbling to herself. The congregation gathered around Gloria on her hands and her knees and were pumping open hands in her direction while chanting 'PRAYER'.

"Read I Corinthians 6:18-20 and it says 'FLEE from sexual immorality. All other sins a man commits are outside his body, but he who sins sexually sins against his own body. Do you now know that your body is a temple of the Holy spirit, who is in you..."

"JEEEEESUS..." Gloria groaned. "Feel it babe," Shaun said in her ear.

Gloria ground Neo between her thighs and felt the vibrations slow down. Her mouth opened but no sound escaped as it sucked back into her body. She breathed heavily, taking in the thick incense and tuning out the sound of the praying voices around her.

Her body told her she was closer than close and Neo had done his job as she dropped him on the floor, pulled her arm out of the sling and slipped two fingers inside herself and held them there.

Just where she needed them.

"PRAYER PRAYER PRAYER PRAYYYEEEEER..." Joseph shouted.

A rainfall of a feeling began to wash over her starting at her eyebrows, running down her spine and making her legs wobble under her. Shaun continued to rub her back, which kept the feeling going and the pastor's loud voice only amplified things.

She felt the squirt begin on her fingers and trickle down her thighs, rounding her knees and onto the carpet.

Whatever she was saying, Shaun could only make out 'Jesus' and 'fucking hell'. From the way everyone was still praying for her, he was the only one that heard.

Pursing her lips and attempting to control her trippy breathing, Gloria looked down between her thighs and could see a thin stream stretching from her labia to the floor.

She closed her eyes tightly, waiting for normality to return to her body as the congregation simmered down and returned to their seats.

The aunties next to her leaned down to see if she was okay but Shaun cut them off.

"Yeah, yeah she's fine... I think she just needs a minute."
"Water... can I have some water please?" Gloria whispered to Shaun. His gluey fingers reached into his bag and pulled out a bottle of

Evian which he handed to Gloria, who was upright on her knees with her mac covering the wet patch beneath her.

She sipped slowly, looking up at Joseph and Jillian who were watching her with concern.

Taking one long breath, she put the bottle on the floor and tried to stand up. With her left knee, she knocked the open bottle over and watched it spread over the floor.

Shaun picked the bottle up, sharing a smile with Gloria knowing exactly what she did and why she did it.

"HALLEUJAH!?" Joseph chanted. "HALLEUJAH AMIN!" the church replied. "HALLEUJAH!?" Jillian chanted. "HALLEUJAH AMIN!" "HALLEUJAH!?" the couple said together. "HALLEUJAH AMIN AMIN AAAAAMIN!"

Joseph started singing a song and the choir and the band caught on and kept it going as the collection bowls began to go round.

Sliding one hand under her armpit, Shaun helped Gloria back to her seat, staring at the patch below.

With her arm back in her jacket sleeve, feeling a moisture patch where she was sitting on her jacket, Gloria took a deep inhale and looked at the floor. The collection bag was passed in front of her but Shaun could see that she was somewhere else and didn't notice it. He reached into his back pocket for his wallet and put a £5 note in before passing it on.

"You okay babe?" Shaun asked, leaning closer to Gloria, who had a scent of pussy rising out of from her open lapels.

"Can we..erm... can we go please?"

Shaun looked at her properly, sensing something was wrong. "Yeah babe, let's... erm... of course we..."

Supporting her weight, Shaun helped her up out of her seat. Catching Joseph's eye, Gloria smiled and mouthed the words 'thank you' before shuffling out. Shaun walked closely behind her, hiding the wet patch on the back of her mac.

Looking down at the ground, Gloria couldn't wait to be out of the room. The taste of fresh air was delicious on her forehead and she walked faster, holding Shaun tight to her back.

"Thank you for coming," said the same man who welcomed them into the church.

"No problem," Gloria replied with a snide smile on her lips.

Shaun reached round her and pushed open the doors as Gloria sucked in the Stratford night air. She stopped walking and stretched her arms and legs, full blown smiling as she reached to the heavens.

"You okay G?" "Yeah, it's just..." She walked ahead of him a few steps before turning to face him with

a serious face.?" It's just that... I WON... I MOTHERFUCKING WON... YES I DID...

AND I DID IT IN STYLE..." "Oh God, I knew this was coming..." "No, I was cumming... did you see that babe? I was on FIRE... I

killed it in there..." "Yeah yeah yeah," Shaun said exasperated as he fished out another

spliff from his bag.?With her arms out in a beef stance, Gloria walked backwards. "Tell

me it's not 38-38 now!? Go on, I dare you. It's even 40-38." Snatching the spliff from his hand, Gloria walked off with her best

catwalk strut, leaving Shaun trailing behind.?" Tell me I'm the woMAN... go on baby, say it... in fact, I think you

should give me five extra points." "No way..." "Yep... come on... you JUST saw what I did... alright let's ask

THEM..." "You can't ask them... they're the readers..." Lighting the spliff, Gloria turned to you and said, "I don't give a

fuck... so what do you say person reading this? Yes YOU!! Was my performance worthy of two, five or ten points?"

TALK TO ME

I absolutely fucking hate bank holiday Monday!?Especially Carnival bank holiday.?Everyone is out drinking and grinding against each other, filling up

west London and making black people look like ignorant, tribal dancing monkeys.

Me? I did the smart thing and worked instead.

A full early until early evening shift on the London Underground, ferrying tourists, wine sippers and youngsters rolling deep and passing bottles to each other on their way to see the floats and half-naked women who spent spring and summer days in the gym just for this day.

Like I said... I did the smart thing.

Time and a half for the early shift and double time for the evening and an extra day off was worth it.

And now that long day was over.

Well almost over but I'm not home yet. Trust me to have a house smack dab in the middle of the longest fucking road in London is a bitch when you've had the long day that I've had. And it's about to get longer.

Because today is my anniversary!

Yay me. Two years with a beautiful, intelligent, warm-hearted, delectable, green-eyed, Coca-Cola bottle shaped, thick-thighed, slightly annoying, tight-fisted, bald patch hiding, negative, ugly on the inside woman who I'm surprised is still around. The past two years with Noraya have gone by like a fart in the wind and I haven't really been to bothered with remembering the smell.

I'm a busy man. Money to make, savings to save, goals to reach and all that. Sure I can make time for a woman and that's why Noraya is in my life. We met, ironically, at Carnival and from the moment I met her, I knew she was the one.

Yeah I know it sounds like some cheesy film shit but it's true. She is literally the prettiest woman I've ever seen in my life but, as the saying goes, 'show me a beautiful woman and I'll show you a guy who's tired of fucking her'.

Right now, I'm that guy.

My muscles felt like lead and I had a swirl of a headache rocking my medulla but the only thing that kept me going was the rum in my fridge and the nakedness I was going to display once I got in.

The path to my door felt like the last steps on the yellow brick road as I opened it, dumped my bag, put my dead phone on charge and sat down with a huge huff and a massive puff.

My eyes led to the clock and I sighed again. It was 19:48pm.

According to what I was supposed to do, I was 18 minutes late in calling Noraya and arranging our 'surprise' plans tonight. Honestly, I didn't plan anything. I was going to but, to be honest with you, I really couldn't be bothered.

If you can't already tell, I'm not exactly in a happy relationship. Yeah everything is fine, we get on, we work together, blah blah blah... but... there's something I just don't feel good about with her. I can't put my finger on it. It's like when you're having sex and you're happy your having sex but something about it feels... off.

And yes I'm basing the fact that I'm not happy in my relationship on the sex. What else is there?

Tonight, I just wanted some head, drink two drink and sleep my ass off. But, according to the 'relationship', I was meant to plan a romantic night that would basically save what we built together in the last two years. Which isn't much to be honest. I think she has more invested in this than me. I really wish I cared to be honest.

And that's why I didn't arrange anything. That's why you're reading this right now and I'm sitting in my favourite chair intent on doing fuck all.

With a spliff – rolled from this morning – staring at me in the ashtray, I charged my phone and waited for it to have enough juice that I could turn it on. Updates updated, messages I couldn't be bothered to open opened and calendar notifications beeped. But no messages from Noraya. She was either not bothered or extremely pissed off. I didn't give a fuck either way.

I changed into my tracksuit bottoms and Jordan Bulls jersey and exhaled at finally being home. The idea of calling her was not one I was looking forward to, but one I knew I had to get done and out the way, especially as 20:00pm was coming around.

Pressing each digit in her number slowly and deliberately, like I couldn't be bothered, I sighed and prepared my excuse for our celebration-less anniversary.

"I'm tired and I can't be bothered," I said to my phone, watching the marijuana and tobacco burn before my very eye.

The ringing continued, making me think she wouldn't answer. She was probably at home offended that I was over an hour late with my call and giving me the silent treatment. Like I give a shit.

In my favourite, weathered thick leather arm chair, I looked around, waiting for the phone to ring.

Few more rings and it'd go to voicemail, then I could leave some run of the mill message about work making me late, bish bash bosh, then wait for her to call.

One more ring and then...?" Hello?" Noraya said, dryly and with a massive yawn.?" Hello? Oh hi... I thought it'd go to voicemail." "Why would it do that? I've been waiting for you to call me since how

long and it's only now you call. No apology, no information on what we're doing, no nothing... I bet we're not even doing anything."

I rolled my eyes and lit my spliff. "Hold on, I haven't even said hello to you and already you're on my case... no how was work, no happy anniversary, nothing!"

"Oh Terrence, if your gonna be stupid about this then come off my phone, 'cuz I'm already pissed off at you..."

"I HAD TO WORK ALRIGHT?!" I shouted as the first touch of rum began to burn my throat.

"First of all, I don't know who you think your talking to but stop it, 'cuz I'm not a child or a dog so don't talk to me like one. Secondly, it's all good you had to work but did you tell me you were working today? Did you let me know you'd be finishing work late today? Did you tell me anything?"

"My battery died so I couldn't call out and you know how the underground is. Up then down then up then down. Reception then no reception."

I was travelling from annoyed to pissed off already and we hadn't said four sentences to each other. I felt like, 'who the hell are you to question me? Regardless of whether she had a point or not.'

I didn't wanna do anything on this fucking day anyway and here we are arguing about it.

"So, what are we doing then?" Noraya asked, sighing and sounding more than annoyed. "Fuck all the bullshit, are we doing anything tonight or not?"

I paused. Froze on the spot taking an extra long pull of my thai and cheese cocktail spliff. I was ready for more arguing and back chat between us before we got to the crux of the conversation.

"Well," I started. "It's late now, everywhere is closing or closed or not open because it's bank holiday and..."

Noraya cut me off, "So we're not going out to celebrate our anniversary then?"

"Why you saying it like that? It's not like we're weren't gonna do anything, it's just..."

"WHAT HUH? What the FUCK were we gonna do? What was your big, bad plan to take me out tonight?"

I knew what she was doing. Making me out to be a big talker with the idea that we were gonna do something great, only to flop.

Even though I did flop and we weren't doing anything, that wasn't the point.

"The plan WAS, actually, dinner at the Oxo Tower, then drinks at Smollensky's and finish at The Jazz Cafe," I lied. The plan was actually nothing, followed by nothing and finished with nothing. The sad thing was that the made-up plan I just gave her actually sounded like a great anniversary night.

I knew Noraya had never been to the Oxo Tower. And Smollensky's and The Jazz Cafe were two of her favourite haunts. But, as I said before, I couldn't be bothered.

"Really?" Noraya said, her voice sounding far away from the phone. "Oh whatever Terrence, that sounds like some perfect... bullshit! What, you think you can throw together all the things I like and say that's what we were gonna do? I'm not an idiot Terrence, you may like to treat me as one but I'm not. So, before we say anything else, are we going out tonight yes or no?"

"Like I said, it's too late to go anywhere now. The reservations I made have gone and there's just no..."

Suddenly, it sounded like the phone cut off. I wasn't sure at first as it happened so quickly but the dead tone sounding in my ears told me that I had just been hung up on.

"Hello? Hello? HELLO?! Did this bitch just hang up on me?" I said looking at my phone. Watching my handset cut the call and return to the home screen, I put my phone on the arm of the chair and just looked at it.

"Who the hell does she think she is about she's hanging up on ME? Is she fucking crazy?"

I picked up my phone in a fit of disbelief and was dialling her back. For her sake, I hope bad reception was the reason for the phone cutting off otherwise it'd be another issue on top of the one already in the air.

A quick succession of strong knocks on my front door drew my attention away from the phone as I looked at the time.

"For fuck sake..."

At that same exact moment, my phone rang with Noraya's ringtone. Lost Without You by Robin Thicke used to be my favourite song and now I can't stand the sound of it.

"For fuck sake..." I mumbled before answering the phone. "Hello?"

Pushing off my chair, listening to an awkward silence, I softly shuffled to my front door so my footsteps couldn't be heard over the phone. The closer I got, the more I could hear the soft rapping of a fingernail on my plastic door.

"Hello? SAY SOMETHING FOR FUCK SAKE!" Noraya shouted. "What'd you want me to say Nora?" "That's your problem TERRENCE... you don't know what to say or do

or anything. It's our fucking anniversary and you haven't even said 'happy anniversary'. No flowers, no card, no nothing from you. And this is from the guy who tells his friends that he's romantic and he does this and that for his girl blah blah FUCKING BLAH!"

"Okay," I said, squinting through my door. "Don't talk to me like that, yeah? I'm not a child. WHAT do you care what I say to my friends about you? Huh? Like I said before, I didn't even wanna celebrate this anniversary. I think they're stupid but nooooo... you just kept on and on and on and on..."

"And on..." Noraya added. "But if I don't go on then nothing gets done."

"Oh yeah sure, okay Nora... if you say so. The same way nothing got done for our first anniversary but we still ended up in Vegas right? That was all your planning wasn't it? Huh? All you? You booked it, you planned it, you arranged cover at work, you did it all didn't you?"

My sarcasm was climbing on top of my anger and I had to turn my volume down. With the door handle in my hand, I opened the door and Destiny looked back at me with her own phone on her ear, wearing the

same clothes she had on when I saw her on the train. Her handbag was balanced on her arm, her eyes were dressing me up and down and her thighs looked thicker than they did before in her short shorts.

She brushed her Poetic Justice braids out of her face, walked up to me with both of us on our phones, grabbed the outline of my dick and slid past me into my flat.

I gave her the silence signal with a finger over her lips as she passed me and she sucked my finger with a sultry grin.

"Hello? HELLO? You're not even fucking listening to me are you? OH MY GOD!"

With my attention completely stolen by the eye-catching, thicker than a sponge cake Destiny who looked as good from the back as she did from the front, I could hear Noraya reaching her livid point on the phone. I don't know what the hell she was doing but I could hear that she wasn't keeping still.

"OI OI OIIIII... don't shout at me!!! Yeah?! I get that your pissed off and I'm sorry I've messed up our anniversary but don't TALK TO ME like that!"

"Or what huh? What you gonna do? Fuck up the day even more? Promise to take me somewhere else then flop at the last minute? You're not even planning to come round and fuck me! God, you are well and truly shit!"

I sighed and closed the door softly, watching Destiny take her trainers off by bending at the hip.

"Yeah well, if I'm shit, then you appreciate shit 'cuz you've been with me and JUST found out I'm shit!"

"You know what Terrence, this is the last straw for me. I didn't want to say anything because I know how you get when you hear it but... I've fought off a lot of men to be with you. And I mean a LOT. I could be riding some Grade A chocolate dick on a private jet right now, but I chose to stay with your Oyster Card clart because I thought we were working to something..."

"Yeah uhh huh..." I replied, watching Destiny take my attention by grabbing my crotch and leading me.

"But, you don't wanna work to nothing do you? You seem content driving your little trains and smoking weed and doing fuck all. That's why I know you didn't plan anything for tonight. You're just..."

"Oh WHATEVER NORA... I'm always this and that and the other... if I'm all these fucking things then why are you even with me?"

"Because I fucking lo... you know what? I don't even know!"

The strength of her sigh went over my head because my erection was in the hands of another, who'd just taken my spliff out of my mouth and took a deep inhale.

Destiny was still on her phone as her handbag slid off her arm and she sat in my chair, while looking up at me with a smile of evil on her face.

"You know what Noraya, I'm tired of this. Always having something to say about me and my life and what I do. Always wanting to change

me, always wanting to tell me how to do things better... LEAVE ME THE FUCK ALONE INNIT?!"

With my voice all strong and full of anger, Destiny's eyes slanted and her grin went from evil to manic as she pulled my tracksuit bottoms to my ankles, waiting for me to continue on the phone.

"Is that my cousin?" Destiny mouthed.?I nodded. She smiled, looking at my naked thighs in front of her. "Well then," Noraya said. "Since you don't want my help making

changes in your life that would benefit you that YOU... you said you wanted to make then fuck you! I'm tired of feeling like I'm dumbing myself down and not aspiring as high just to make you feel better. If you're happy playing this middle fucking ground and not climbing higher then by all means do that! But I'm not gonna be here to watch!"

"Uhh huh sure..." I said, paying half the attention. My mind only caught half of her last tirade because Destiny spat on my dick and a long line of saliva stretched from her mouth to my groin.

I motioned her to shush again. If that sound was loud enough in my other ear then Noraya might've heard it too. And that would've had to have been a quick response of, 'oh it's the TV. Man vs Food is on.'

My eyes glanced to the ceiling. Whatever made me stutter was taking place in my groin area and was starting to feel wet and warm. I looked down at Destiny and had to cover my eyes. The way she was doing me so right it was wrong. My left knee buckled with the sound of slurping coming from her mouth but I couldn't watch. I had to remind myself not to moan too loudly as I listening to Noraya doing something while taking a sip of something. I could hear her clearing her throat and sighing heavily as I looked to the ceiling, counting the design grooves above the light. It was a necessary concentration switch as her lips gave me supreme V.I.P. Treatment.

She looked up at me with saliva and pre-cum dangling from her chin. Her eyes were extremely dreamy, denoting the pleasure she was getting from watching me in such a state of torture while trying to appear cool and calm to Noraya on the phone.

"You know what, lemme just say what needs to be said. Noraya... I don't wanna do this any more."

It was like Destiny was adapting her mouth to what I said on the phone as her lips parted and she opened her mouth and her throat to my dick. To anyone who's ever had a deepthroat to the point where your whole dick fills her throat, you know how hard it is to stay Mr Marcus calm.

I was punching the air, swinging my arms all over and gritting my teeth like new ones were about to grow underneath. My free hand slid into her hair and took control of the treatment.

"Yeah well, from the moment you didn't call me at 7:30pm, we were over, you just didn't know."

For a solo moment, I felt offended like, 'how can you say if I don't call you by a certain time then the relationship is over?'

Really, this was irrelevant because it was on it's way to being over and that's what I wanted more than anything. I wanted this relationship to be over, I wanted to get Destiny off her knees and fuck her like she owed me money and the cash was in her pussy. That's what I wanted to do. Throw off the shackles of this relationship, go out there as a single dog and do the dog catcher on some brand new delectable pussy that was out there with my name on it. But this conversation had to end first before I could begin with that list.

"Well whatever," I threw back at her, still feeling shades of indignation. "Well let's done then 'cuz I can't be bothered to be going back and forth with you over all your shit and..."

"MY shit?" she replied. "How you mean my shit? What have I done to..."

"Look Noraya, let's not okay, 'cuz this could go on and on and on. I'm done arguing with you okay?"

Destiny was seemingly done with being nice to my dick and began to slap it on her face with her tongue out, allowing saliva to slide down onto my hardwood floor with a splat. A sound Noraya used to make regularly until one day it felt like I was getting head from a squirrel eating a piece of corn on the cob.

Her eyes locked with mine at the same time Noraya went quiet and I felt mildly unsettled. It was as if they were both trying to listen out for each other.

Destiny responded first by whipping out one of her breasts and rubbing the head of my dick against her nipple, using the previously laid road of saliva to keep things smooth, wet and constantly arousing.

I held a hand over the phone and bent down so Destiny could hear me whisper, 'what THEE fuck?'

"SO... that's two years down the fucking drain, just like that?" Noraya asked, sniffing very hard.

"Do YOU want to done this Noraya?" "FUCK YES!" she half shouted, half screamed.?" Huh?" I asked. At the same time, I snatched my dick from Destiny's

mouth and gave her a full-fledged slap with it to which she moaned a delicious sound. Her face took the slap of meat and she looked at me, asking for more with her eyes.

"Of course I wanna done this. If a man can't look after his woman the way he's supposed to or can't or won't celebrate an anniversary with said woman then he doesn't deserve that woman!"

I giggled as Destiny deep-throated me with her tongue out. The tip of her spit-covered tongue graced the outline of my testicles and I stifled a chuckle.

"Yeah yeah, okay Noraya, make it into some Waiting To Exhale suttin if you want but you know the truth. This relationship was done from time ago, we just didn't cut things off. If you think we've been as happy as we've been in the past then fine. But I know that's bullshit. And so do you. But, hey, whatever."

Noraya screamed in my ear and I had to move the phone away because she can scream as loud as fuck sometimes. This was one of those times.

Destiny looked up at me and the phone as I imagined she heard her as well. He put a finger over the phone and bent down to her again.

"Who told you to fucking stop? I didn't."

With her faux pas expressed and understood by the 'sorry daddy' eyes she gave me, I grabbed a handful of hair and made sure my dick was consumed by her lips, throat and spit. The more spit the better.

The phone convo with Noraya was coming to an end judging by her last scream of frustration and my time with Destiny was just beginning to get moist and interesting.

"Is there someone else?" Noraya asked in a strange fit of calmness.

"What?" was all I had to throw back. The question took me by surprise and was better than the stuttering and pausing that I was going to give her.

"You know what... phew... it's okay, don't worry about it. I bet I already know the answer to that one."

Destiny was getting sloppy to the point where a pool of her saliva gathered on my floor between her feet. She was moaning in her throat which vibrated along the length of me and ended in my balls.

"Erm, first of all... I never cheated on you before while we were together," I lied. It was a semi-truth as I hadn't ever cheated on Noraya until now but, technically, we were over so this didn't count. That's not to say that there weren't moments where I could've but, those were the days when we were happy. And I was happy to give my dick to one and one only. The idea of cheating on her was a Marmite of an idea. That was a LONG time ago.

I felt eyes from below looking at me. With my dick in her mouth, Destiny hummed her disapproval at my lies and waved an index finger at me.

"So you mean to tell me in all the time we..."

"NEVER!" I said honestly and adamantly as Destiny gagged on my dick.

"What was that noise?" Noraya asked, immediately.

"It's Deebo... he's got a fur ball," I lied. I hadn't seen my cat since I got home, but the lie was quick into my mind as I gave Destiny a screw face of epic proportions. She replied with a smile and a series of kisses on the head of my dick.

"Oh... okay... well... anything else you wanna say?"

At that moment, I didn't have anything else to say. In the middle of Noraya's question, Destiny took one last deep suck of my dick while I was looking at my naughty reflection in my floor-length mirror. The reflection of my super slick erection made me feel so alive. One bastard of a relationship was ending and before the ink dried on my parting papers, I already had my knocker covered in someone else's slobber.

Hearing Noraya moving around in her background, I stole myself away from my porn star pose – with my arms supporting my back –

and decided to bring the convo to a close so I could finish what Destiny started.

"Nah babe," I said with a reflex. "Nothing else. You know what, I'm sorry it's ended like this. I wish..."

"NO YOU'RE NOT! You probably... probably wanted this to happen that's why you didn't arrange anything for tonight."

"Look Noraya..."

I paused as her thicker cousin stood up in front of me, breathing close enough that I could smell my dick on her breath and she could hear Noraya's voice. She grinned and, in one motion, pulled her t-shirt over her head, exposing a bright pink bra. With her eyes holding mine in a searching staring competition, her short shorts came down next and revealed a blue thong.

I couldn't help the frown lines forming on my forehead as I stared at Destiny's mismatching underwear. Holding the phone away from my ear, I mouthed, 'what the fuck, you cyan match yuh panty dem?'

There was no reply from Destiny as she turned to walk away, giving a full view of her cheeks, which were damn near curving over her thong. Then I remembered I started saying something into the phone.

"Oh... erm... look Noraya, I don't want things to end on a sour note. We're both adults here and I don't want this to be a... hello? Hello? HELLO?"

"I'm here," Noraya replied.?" It sounded like you were gone..." "Nope, still here. So what were you saying?" "I'm sorry it's gone this way... that's all I wanted to say." Just then, Destiny's pink bra came flying through the air, hitting me

on the forehead and draping over my face before it fell to the floor. Looking up, I saw Destiny holding up her thong and disappearing towards my bedroom

"NO you're... not. But anyway, no point saying shit like that... it's done now."

Honestly, I expected more of a reaction from her considering it was still our anniversary. Me? I'd already checked out so I would be indignant but she was as cool and calm as I was.

Maybe she knew the end was nigh. Either way with the shape that just walked off towards my bedroom, I'd be getting over the breakup quick, fast and in a hurry.

"Alright well, I... OH FUCK!" "Terrence? What's wrong?" Noraya asked.?I couldn't tell her that as I walked towards my room, chasing Destiny

as I went, she jumped out from behind a corner and went back to her knees in front of me, this time with slickly-covered hands. She took both hands and wrapped them around my dick and made me feel like I was within inches of an orgasm.

"I thought I saw a mouse," I lied.

"So I'm a mouse now am I?" Destiny said with her mouth full of my head.

I silenced her with wide eyes, forcing my dick into the back of her throat. She took the thrust and held me there, flexing her muscles against my dick with her tongue out giving me the best blowjob I'd ever had. Hands down.

"Okay... well... I'm... I'm... geeez... I'm gonna go now 'cuz I'm knackered."

"No problem," Noraya said with an air of levity in her voice. "Good luck in life Terrence, I really mean that."

"You too Nora...good luck in life! I hope you find someone who gives you exactly what you want."

"Oh don't worry about me. I've got more than enough options of men, women and couples, who'd like to scratch my itch."

"Whoa, women and couples?" I asked, more intrigued than before. She'd never told me she got down like that. Why didn't she tell me she got down like that? We might've made this work if she shared that information.

"Yessur... I was gonna ask if you wanted to do something tonight but, now I don't need to so it's all good."

By this point, disappointment was seeping in. Something inside was telling me I'd just made a massive mistake while Destiny was working me with two hands and a supremely wet mouth. I was leaned back against a door frame in my corridor fist pumping the air trying to hold back.

"Oh," was all I could say to that. Sounds like I could've had the dream in my lap; two women, one dick, lips on either side.

"Alright... well, I gotta go... the girls are coming..."

"How though?" I pondered while confused as Destiny knew I was on the merry road to Cum-shire. "If we were supposed to be going out tonight, how could you have planned..."

"You do not have the right to ask me shit anymore... and I didn't necessarily say the girls were coming round... I just said the girls are coming..."

Just at that moment, a loud female, orgasmic scream erupted in Noraya's background, adding to the moistness being dripped onto my floor from Destiny's mouth. I couldn't hold it in any longer and I began to fuck her mouth faster and faster. Looking down and giving her evil eyes and screwed lips, I could feel a streak of evil running through me as, in my head, I was shouting for her to 'take that dick deep bitch!'

Whether she heard me or not I don't know but she did as she was told and I felt the back of her throat slide against the head of my dick. I punched the air twice, held the back of Destiny's head and felt my balls twitch.

"So, what are you gonna do tonight then?" I threw in, feeling the end of the conversation and the end of my restraint.

"If you really wanna know Terrence, I'm gonna do some girls tonight. Gonna drink some drink, smoke some smoke and eat some pussy tonight."

"Oh," I said as calmly as possible as I slapped the wall, held Destiny's face in front of me, slipped out of her mouth and came.

Her lips took the first jerk that limped out. Each proceeding jerk shot further and further up her face and into her eyes and hair. I looked like an out of control fire hose the way I spurted on every inch of her face and she took the shots willingly. Licking my cream on her lips while still trying to suck me was a visual orgasm in itself and I kept going, sticking my final limping streams on her lips.

"Have a nice night and a nice life Terrence," Noraya said.

"Yeah yeah, you too," I replied, unclenching my body and failing to catch my breath. I don't remember putting my hand over my mouth but the teeth marks in my finger told me that I'd kept myself quiet, even though the pain didn't register.

The feeling of an orgasm and the depleted, taking off the beer goggles sensation that followed, made me look down at Destiny, covered in sperm from hairline to her chin with a curve of disgust in my lip. She was running her fingers through the white cream on her face and sucking it off in a Jada Fire motion. And I didn't really like Jada Fire... her braces used to scare me.

"'Night Terrence," Noraya said. "Goodnight Nor..."

She hung up before I could finish her name.

TALK TO ME AGAIN

Two minutes and counting.

In my head and my heart, I had a feeling Terrence would flop tonight, I just hoped he'd finally fix the fuck up. And our anniversary would've been the perfect scenario.

But that's hope for you. Sucks you in for an adventure then spits you out into a pile of shit.

That's why I've been home ALL day waiting for something. A card, some flowers, a text or tweet even. Maybe even a tagged picture on Instagram... but nothing. Toilet trips were quick and quiet just in case a delivery man came and I didn't hear the door. My phone was reset and reset again to make sure I was capable of receiving any message. Even my shower this morning was quick and speedy just in case.

But no delivery man from Interflora came. No singing telegram with a bunch of balloons and a box of chocolates. No mystery box containing a clue as to what we'd be doing tonight.

Absolutely Nathan. And it's out two year anniversary today.

And now he has one minute left to call me.

It's not like I didn't have shit to do today. I could've gone carnival with my girls from work and been on a float with some rum punch skanking my ass off and grinding on some dreadlock dude with wicked waist action. But no... here I fucking am, at home in my tracksuit bottoms, string vest, no bra and Adventure Time slippers listening to slow jams on the radio like a sad case.

I swear, he needs to make something happen in the next 43 seconds or he's gonna be single real quick. I mean it, this is the last straw.

I mean, what, am I not worth it? Am I not worth celebrating? Are WE not worth celebrating?

30 fucking seconds...

I'm not the type of person to be pessimistic but I just KNEW he'd fuck today up. All while I was cleaning, washing, doing something to keep those negative thoughts away, they just kept creeping in.

'He's not gonna turn up...'?'He hasn't planned anything.'?'I'm gonna be here all day and he says he loves me.' 'Might as well choose my toys from now.'

I switched from the bottle of pinot to vodka and cranberry 20 minutes ago because I knew this night was gonna be a flop. I wish I never wasted my time shaving for him. I almost didn't but it would've been worse if he did sort something for us and, by default, I'd have to give him some with my bushy mound.

Six seconds...

I turned off the Harry Potter film that was playing in the background and put my mobile phone next to my house phone, took a finishing sip of my drink, poured another and rested my face on my hand.

His time was up. According to what I said to myself, our relationship, right now, is over. Could still be saved though, depending on how long it takes for him to call.

One minute passed.?Another one followed.?Three more came after.?I poured the same drink, this time in a pint glass, as more minutes

passed and I could feel my stomach warming up. More anger than alcohol.

Five more minutes passed by the time I was halfway through my new drink and feeling content and woozy at the same time. The wavy filter on my vision was from the drink but the contententment was the feeling of coming to the conclusion that this – me and Terrence – was definitely over.

He knew as well as I did that tonight was ride or die for our relationship. Things had been souring between us steadily for months... I knew it, he knew it, we spent hours going over how things had changed between us instead of having sex.

GOD!?Don't even get me started on the sex.

I'd lost concentration on my phones, turned my TV back on and put on All Dat Azz 22 which I left in my DVD player from the night before. Pressing play, remembering the last time we had sex, I don't remember having an orgasm... I don't even remember enjoying it. I DO remember planning how I was going to redecorate my flat though. That was fun.

With another long, glass-finishing sip done, I had to take a breath. It was as if I'd forgotten what was in the glass. Living so deeply in a livid emotion but with such a calmness washing over me was making me fearful for the moment when he actually called. He might get me cool, calm and collected. He might get me irate, calculated and vengeful. Who knows. Depends on how much I drink between now and his phone call. Whenever that will be.

What a prick! Not even a text just to say 'happy anniversary babe, I've got a situation, I'll call you later.' Even if his battery died on his phone, he could still get a message to me.

It's moments like this that make me want to start up smoking weed again. That lovely feeling of relaxation that comes with a spliff would be perfect right now, instead of this tense, annoyed mood that has got me on edge and annoyed.

Bringing the bottle of vodka into the lounge and pouring cranberry straight into the bottle, I gave the litre bottle a shake and fell into the sofa and exhaled, scanning my Twitter timeline for a comment that mirrored how annoyed I felt. Unfortunately for me, everyone was still

out at carnival or on their way home to get ready for the night full of after parties. Another moment for me to feel like an absolute hobbit of a hermit in my home clothes. I was gonna check my Instagram timeline but I imagined pictures and videos of other people's fun would just piss me off even more.

With my lips pursed like I'd just sucked on a lemon, I opened the Textgram app and began to write. I felt like I needed to exhale exactly how I was feeling about this night and someone needed to read it. Someone needed to know just how shit of a boyfriend Terrence was and how shit it was for me right now.

Sitting at home on my anniversary having not heard from my man all day!

My fingers wrote and rewrote varying levels of anger in my post. Swear words were mixed and remixed, Patois was used then taken out, something about his home training was almost sent before I thought that was a bit rude considering me and his mum got on like a BBQ house on fire.

In the end, I went for sweet and to the point:

'If ya man can't or doesn't want to celebrate your two-year anniversary with you, then he doesn't deserve to be with you for another two years!'

Draped in a Tahoma font and a Valencia filter, I read what I wrote and took a swig from the bottle of vodka and cranberry before I sent it. Tagging it to my Twitter, Tumblr and my FaceBook so everyone and their mother can see it, I pressed send, watched it finish up and deliver to my timeline and felt pretty fucking good about myself.

"Fuck it," I mumbled to myself, picking up my phone and texting my weed-selling pal Cevin next door.

Okay, not exactly a pal, more like someone who is still waiting for the day I became single again so he could slip me some dick. But, a good person to have around when you want a spliff or two but don't wanna pay for it.

I'll tell you this though... staying in for the night and doing nothing is not on my plan sheet. I had enough after-party invites I put to the side in favour of Terrence and our anniversary but that's not happening any more so... why not?!

With Cevin replying that he'll drop a spliff by in a moment, and my phone now alive with open invites that were previously closed, I took another sip of my drink. Even though I was planning a new night, I was still fuming over what my night could've been.

"Fuck tonight and fuck you Terrence," I said to no one particular.

My eyes glanced at the time and it was slowly approaching 8pm, not that I cared any more. Terrence could've come to my house in a helicopter and taken me to Prince's house for dinner cooked by

Brad Pitt and served by Idris Elba in nothing but a spinning bow-tie, I still wouldn't give a fuck. All my fucks were long gone.

My drink was depleting in large gulps that were swallowed in one. I had to rest on the arm of the sofa to make it to my feet. I could feel that I'd gone too far drinking from the bottle but it was done now. The alcohol was in my system, my legs were shaky as hell and my vision was blurred righteously. I was well and nicely fucked. But this was where I wanted to be, especially as I was still angry over the wasted day. No, I was angry because the last two years felt like a complete waste of my time.

Time I would not be getting back.

A soft knock made me lean my head towards my front door and listen. I wasn't sure if it was in fact my door and I continued to listen, standing still but leaning.

The door knocked again, this time louder, and I jumped into more unbalance which made me fall back onto the sofa.

"Shit, fuck," I moaned to the door.

Pausing the porn, I took uneven steps to the door, running hands through my hair, trying to make myself as presentable as possible. But not too presentable, otherwise Cevin would see that as a sign to come in and chill and it wasn't that kind of evening.

"Who is it?" I asked, looking through my peephole that'd been shattered after one drunken argument with Terrence.

"Your weed," a thin voice replied.

Opening the door and thanking Cevin at the same time, I said, "You have no idea how much of a..."

But it wasn't Cevin at the door.?It wasn't someone who even looked like him or even worked for him. It wasn't even a dude.?It was a woman.?Four of 'em.?And one of 'em held out a bag of weed as an icebreaker considering I

had no idea who they were.?" Erm... ooooo, hello ladies," was all I could manage.?As one woman in front of the other three looked me up and down in

my house clothes, my phone rang. I wanted to pick it up in case it was Terrence. Not for excitement or celebration; that ship had sailed. This was to cuss him out and end the relationship. And really I didn't wanna have to call him back. He fucked up so he should call me.

"Noraya, is it?" said the tall, chocolate, slender one in the standing closest to me.

"Yeah, erm... what can I do for you?" I said, using my peripheral vision to notice that all four of the women at my front door were different variations of beautiful.

"We... erm... well... do you wanna go and answer your phone? Your face says its an important call."

"Yeah," I said looking back and forth from the women to my phone. "Hold on one second."

I skipped drunkenly skipped to my phone and picked it up, balancing on one leg. The display said it was Terrence and I instantly prepared my indignant voice and attitude disposition.

"Hello?" I said in my best sleepy voice. As if on cue, a yawn ripped through my face, follow through sound and all.

"Hello? Oh hi... I thought it'd go to voicemail," Terrence said. I could hear in his voice that he really hoped it'd go to voicemail so he wouldn't have to speak to me. One of his regular things to do.

"Why would it do that? I've been waiting for you to call me since how long and it's only now you call?" I was standing flat on my feet with one hand in the small of my back. I wished I never finished that bottle so quickly. "No apology, no information on what we're doing, no nothing... I bet we're not even doing anything."

"Hold on, I haven't even said hello to you and already you're on my case... no how was work, no happy anniversary, nothing!"

"Oh Terrence, if your gonna be stupid about this then come off my phone, 'cuz I'm already pissed off at you..."

From the way the conversation had begun, I knew he was going to have a whole load of reasons and excuses to explain why we were not going anywhere or even doing anything together on our anniversary. I had a feeling that the longer this conversation went, the quicker our relationship would be over.

"I HAD TO WORK ALRIGHT?!" he shouted at me. This was not the way this conversation was going to go.

"First of all," I started, letting him know that he was about to get it.

"I don't know who you think your talking to but stop it, 'cuz I'm not a child or a dog so don't talk to me like one. Secondly, it's all good you had to work but did you tell me you were working today? Did you let me know you'd be finishing work late today? Did you tell me anything?"

"My battery died so I couldn't call out and you know how the underground is. Up then down, up then down. Reception then no reception."

Just as I thought, excuse after excuse, no responsibility for his actions or lack of them. I slapped my forehead in frustration at how stupid and immature he sounded.

The underground is like your fucking life Terrence. Up then down then up then down. You've been down for a fucking minute though.

"He sounds like a right knob cheese," a voice said behind me. So close was the voice that me and my skeleton jumped one after the other. I spun in my slippers to see the last of the women sitting down on my sofa, all with their legs crossed in sync.

The frown on my face was automatic for a number of reasons: Who the fuck invited them into my yard,?Who the fuck were they and;?What kind of women cross their legs at the same time?

And why were they here now?!

So many questions and no time for answers as they all looked me with varying degrees of interest. There was something about them that made me feel comfortable with them sitting on my sofa like I invited them in and made them drinks. The one who had the bag of weed, which she now gave to me, was sitting closest. A very tall, athletic type with beautiful golden legs was sitting next to her and a petite lady with great smile sat next to a slightly bigger lady with a similar smile. And they were all looking at me and my starting to sweat self.

"So, what are we doing then?" I asked, looking into the eyes of the athletic one. "Fuck all the bullshit, are we doing anything tonight yes or no?"

"Well, it's late now, everywhere is closing or closed or not open because it's bank holiday and..."

A heavy, sarcastic, 'I fucking told you so' sigh tore through me. "So we're not going out to celebrate our anniversary then?"

"Why you saying it like that? It's not like we're weren't gonna do anything, it's just..."

Feeling like the eyes in my living room were now undressing me, I held the phone away from my mouth.

"Sorry, who are you ladies?"

They all looked at each other and smiled which broke into laughter, which turned into loud chuckling. I'm not one of those people who's a fan of people laughing in my presence without sharing the joke. At that point, I start to feel laughed at and I don't like that.

They must've felt my mood shifting as the apparent leader of the foursome stood up quite quickly. So fast was she on her feet with her arm out that I stumbled back a little.

In her outstretched arm was a card that I didn't notice at first. A brilliant shade of woozy was hazing me over quite nicely so everything wasn't as clear as it should've been.

The card in my hand felt smooth as silk and I read the only words on it. Angel The Devil.

What the fuck? Was that her name? What kinda name was Angel The Devil?

On cue, she pulled up to my other ear and whispered, "It's a name I've earned!"

Her breath in my ear, the touch of her arm on my shoulder, the air between us getting instantly...

"WHAT HUH? What the FUCK were we gonna do? What was your big, bad plan to take me out tonight?" I threw the energy back to the conversation I was supposed to be having.

"The plan WAS, actually, dinner at the Oxo Tower, then drinks at Smollensky's on The Strand and finish at The Jazz Cafe."

"Really?" I said, with a hint of shock and a dash of 'I don't believe a fucking word you're saying'. On paper it sounded great but, as a woulda, shoulda, coulda, it didn't mean shit.

"Oh whatever Terrence, that sounds like some perfect... bullshit! What, you think you can throw together all the things I like and say that's what we were gonna do? I'm not an idiot Terrence, you may like to treat me as one but I'm not. So, before we say anything else, are we going out tonight yes or no?"

"Like I said, it's too late to go anywhere now. The reservations I made have gone and there's just no..."

All I heard him say was no and that was enough for me to hang up on him.

Cancelled that bitch like Nino Brown, yes I did.

This guy is really and truly something else. And this was who I gave the last 730 days of my life to? Prick.

"So," I turned to the women in my living room who seemed content watching the demise of my relationship. "What can I do for you ladies?"

"Well Noraya, my name is Angel. Angel the Devil and these are my right hand ladies. Dee Deena The Teaser, Marquita The Teacher and Kandy Eat Me and we're here on behalf of The C.L.I.T.S..."

"I'm sorry you're here from the who?" My eyebrows were furrowed deep into my eyesight and my lips were saying 'C'mon Son'.

"The C.L.I.T.S sweetheart," said the athletic one with the curly hair pulled back. "I know it's a mouthful but that stands for Clever Ladies Investigating Terrible Situations – the C.L.I.T.S!"

The confusion on my face didn't go anywhere. In fact it got worse. Then I laughed.?" Yeah, we get that a lot," said the tiny lady with the golden smile. "I

still love the name though." "Yep and we're here to help you have a brilliant anniversary." More strangeness on top of more confusion on top of everything else

today and I didn't know what to think.?" Your whaaaaaat? Who are you? Who told you it was my

anniversary? Did Terrence send you? Okay, seriously, who are you and what are you doing here?"

The answer threw me off and suddenly made me quite conscious that I was alone and now there were four strange women in my space looking at me like I was the stranger.

"Well, here's how it is," the bigger lady with the bigger smile said. "YOU told us about your anniversary."

"Who did? I did? When did..."

"Your Instagram mi dear... watch a woman's insta long enough, you'll figure shit out."

"Figure what out? Look girls yeah, either tell me what the fuck is going on or I'll call the police and you can leave by force. Your choice."

Then my phone started ringing again. And I called it a vibrating fuck for doing so.

I looked down at it, torn between finishing the finishing conversation with Terrence or continue to find out who the fuck these clitoris women were.

First things first... Terrence.

"Hello?" he said.

I didn't want to hear his voice, I didn't want to hear him take a breath, I didn't want to even recognise he existed.

I crossed my arm across my body while looking at the strange women who thought it was okay to enter my space and get comfortable. My eyebrows raised and I looked at them saying, 'well, either speak up or get arrested bitches'.

"Hello?" Terrence said again.

"Hello? SAY SOMETHING FOR FUCK SAKE!" I shouted, making the four women in front of me jump. The thick lady with the pretty lips, who was apparently called Kandy Eat Me, stood up followed by Marquita The Teacher and, what was the last one... Deena Teaser or something like that, she stood up to while Angel The Devil stayed seated.

That Deena had a body on her. She works out... I need to look like that. Such a tight body felt quite intimidating to my slight pudge and what felt like the beginning of bingo wings.

"What'd you want me to say Nora?"

"That's your problem TERRENCE... you don't know what to say or do or anything. It's our fucking anniversary and you haven't even said 'happy anniversary'. No flowers, no card, no nothing from you. And this is from the guy who tells his friends that he's romantic and he does this and that for his girl blah blah FUCKING BLAH!"

Multi-tasking my way through what was going on and wondering why the strange women, who apparently follow me on Instagram, have turned up to my yard. Now three of 'em are standing and one is sitting down.

Whatever it was, my guard was up.

To my right, Kandy rolled her neck and closed her eyes before pulling her t-shirt over her head and laying it out on the table then sitting down with her leg crossed.

I wasn't sure I was staring at a topless woman on my sofa until she sat down and her C, possibly D, cups jiggled against her chest, as she smiled at me.

"Okay," Terrence said on the phone, pinching my attention. "Don't talk to me like that, yeah? WHAT do you care what I say to my friends about you? Huh? And really, like I said before, I didn't even wanna celebrate this anniversary. I think they're stupid but nooooo... you just kept on and on and on and on..."

"And on..." I felt like interrupting him. "But if I don't go on then nothing gets done."

"Oh yeah sure, okay Nora... if you say so. The same way nothing got done for our first anniversary but we still ended up in Vegas right?

That was all your planning wasn't it? Huh? All you? You booked it, you planned it, you arranged cover at work, you did it all didn't you?"

"Hello? HELLO? You're not even fucking listening to me are you? OH MY GOD!"

"OI OI OIIIII... don't shout at me!!! Yeah?! I get that your pissed off and I'm sorry I've messed up our anniversary but don't TALK TO ME like that!"

"Or what huh? What you gonna do? Fuck up the day even more? Promise to take me somewhere else then flop at the last minute? You're not even planning to come round and fuck me! God, you are well and truly shit!"

"Yeah well, if I'm shit, then you appreciate shit 'cuz you've been with me and JUST found out I'm shit!"

Just as I could feel my mind ready to really let him have it, with my eyes darting from Deena, Marquita, Kandy and Angel, another woman made a move.

Deena reached for her waistband and pulled her skin-tight leggings down to her ankles, drew them smoothly over her heels and laid them out on the table next to Kandy's t-shirt. She sat down and looked at me like she didn't just sit her very sexy, but asshole naked-self on my sofa. Like that was okay.

I don't even sit ass naked on my sofa. Itches my pum pum. But Deena looked like she was sitting comfortably, looking at me with a deep stare. Like her eyes were saying something to me but I couldn't understand the language.

Whatever they were saying, was not more attention-grabbing than the sudden movement from Marquita, who flashed a smile that lit up her whole face and made me smile in return, even though Terrence was still there.

"You know what Terrence, this is the last straw for me. I didn't want to say anything because I know how you get when you hear it but... I've fought off a lot of men to be with you. And I mean a LOT. I could be riding some Grade A chocolate dick on a private jet right now, but I chose to stay with your Oyster Card clart because I thought we were working to something..."

"Yeah uhh huh..."

Marquita reached for the nape of her neck and began to unbutton her full-length fur coat. With every button that popped, more creamy skin shone back at me. I bit my lips uncontrollably as she showed that she was good at what she was doing. She made each button pop slowly out of the material and there was me, holding my breath until the button popped loose then silently exhaling.

Was The Teacher naked underneath that coat??Terrence had to go.?" But, you don't wanna work to nothing do you?" I suddenly remembered. "You seem content driving your little trains and smoking weed and doing fuck all. That's why I know you didn't plan anything for tonight. You're just..."

Two more buttons popped at her navel and I was sucking air through my teeth, waiting for the buttons to reach just low enough to...

"Oh WHATEVER NORA... I'm always this and that and the other... if I'm all these fucking things then why are you even with me?"

"Because I fucking lo... you know what? I don't even know!"

For fuck sake! This guy was ruining what was turning out to be a pretty good, but slightly, well more than slightly, weird anniversary for me. Yay for me.

There were breasts on the right, an asshole naked model or dancer on my left and something getting real interesting right in front of me. No wonder my nipples were poking through the holes in my string vest.

My arm, which was still held across my body defensively, dropped and dangled beside me. I wanted to reach out and help her with the last few buttons, maybe use a helpful finger to see if she truly is naked under there.

"You know what Noraya, I'm tired of this. Always having something to say about me and my life and what I do. Always wanting to change me, always wanting to tell me how to do things better... LEAVE ME THE FUCK ALONE INNIT?!"

"Well then," I said as Marquita reached the penultimate button on her coat and stopped as it was about to pop. "Since you don't want my help making changes in your life that would benefit you that YOU... you said you wanted to make then fuck you! I'm tired of feeling like I'm dumbing myself down and not aspiring as high just to make you feel better. If you're happy playing this middle fucking ground and not climbing higher then by all means do that! But I'm not gonna be here to watch!"

I was gonna be here, watching that last fucking button about to pop... go on, go on... POP dammit.

"Uhh huh sure..." Terrence said, interrupting again. "You know what, lemme just say what needs to be said. Noraya... I don't wanna do this anymore."

"Yeah well, from the moment you didn't call me at 7:30pm, we were over, you just didn't know."

"Well whatever. Well let's done then 'cuz I can't be bothered to be going back and forth with you over all your shit and..."

"MY shit?" she replied. "How you mean my shit? What have I done to.."

"Look Noraya, let's not okay, 'cuz this could go on and on and on. I'm done arguing with you okay?"

The button was going slowly. My head was staring straight down and I could feel the eyes of the room on me.

"Pop it," Angel said.

Marquita popped the button and her fur coat fell open and draped down her shoulders and onto the table, covering Kandy's t-shirt and Deena's leggings.

She didn't move, she just stood in front of me, watching me watching her while Deena, Kandy and Angel were watching me.

"SO... that's two years down the fucking drain, just like that?" I asked Terrence, still trying to bring this drab conversation to a speedy end.

"Do YOU want to done this Noraya?" "FUCK YES!" "Huh?" "Of course I wanna done this. If a man can't look after his woman

the way he's supposed to or can't or won't celebrate an anniversary with said woman then he doesn't deserve that woman!"

The three women sitting down all clapped towards me and caught me with a massive grin. Marquita didn't move her arms at all, she was just looking at me. Still smiling, but her eyes made the smile something more than just 'hi how are you'.

"Yeah yeah, okay Noraya, make it into some Waiting To Exhale suttin if you want but you know the truth. This relationship was done from time ago, we just didn't cut things off. If you think we've been as happy as we've been in the past then fine. But I know that's bullshit. And so do you. But, hey, whatever."

Out of fucking nowhere, Marquita put her hand down the front of my tracksuit bottoms with another hand around my neck, found me curiously wet – like she knew it would be that easy – and slipped a slim but effective finger inside me. I screamed like a white woman in a horror movie.

It happened so quickly, I couldn't stop her and by the time I fully realised what she was doing, it felt too nice.

"Not yet Teacher, give her a moment to enjoy that..." Angel said in my comfy seat, pressing play on the DVD player. I even forgot that I'd left the porn paused.

Like I was thinking about that. My mind and my pussy were focussed on the finger inside me not moving but making me feel good all the same.

Wesley Pipes was the first voice I heard from the TV behind me and I could picture the exact scene as Marquita winked at me and slowly slid her finger out.

Watching her stare at her wet finger, with my own hand across my mouth, I played calm, hoping that Terrence would interpret my scream as frustration instead of what it really was.

It was really good is what it was. Teach on Teacher.

"Is there someone else?" I threw into the conversation. I didn't care about what the answer was, but there had to be someone else. Not really the thing to be asking considering a complete stranger just finger fucked me in my living room without my permission. Although I didn't NOT give her permission.

"What?" Terrence replied, his tone hiding the sound of a secret.

"You know what... phew..." A delicious exhale slipped out of me. "It's okay, don't worry about it. I bet I already know the answer."

"Erm, first of all... I never cheated on you while we were together," he lied.

"So you mean to tell me in all the time we..." "NEVER!"

Marquita, the small but imposing teacher, moved her wet finger from between us to inside her mouth and sucked long and hard, with her eyes never leaving my own.

"What was that noise?" Something in Terrence's background caught my aural attention even though my visual attention was held by two semi-naked women, one full naked woman and another one who was calling all the shots.

"It's Deebo... he's got a fur ball."

Angel, from my favourite seat, with the DVD remote in her hand, clicked her fingers and Marquita shuffled backwards and sat her naked self on my sofa. Another naked pussy on my sofa cushions.

"Oh... okay... well... anything else you wanna say?" I gave Terrence, with my attitude on full blast.

"Nah babe, nothing else. You know what, I'm sorry it's ended like this. I wish..."

This was exactly what I didn't want to hear. Crap. Claiming zero responsibility, egotistical, annoying crap. The shit Terrence was shovelling my way was pushing my irritation level past the maximum and into the final reserves. None of that was helped by the C.L.I.T.S – what a fucking name – that had taken over my living room watching me like the last piece of chicken at the Last Supper. Right now, they had more of my attention than Terrence did.

"NO YOU'RE NOT! You probably... probably wanted this to happen that's why you didn't arrange anything for tonight."

Terrence lost my attention when all four women stood up together and began to walk towards me. There was no sign from Angel for them to get up, it was like they knew when it was time to do so. And they did with their eyes fully focussed on me.

Marquita on my right and Deena on my left both held their hands out to me, while Angel was mouthing for me to put the phone on speaker. Doing as I was told, without thinking twice, but still confused as to who the flying fuck these C.L.I.T.S were, I put the my phone on speaker and laid it on the table at the foot of Marquita's fur coat.

"Look Noraya, I don't wanna things to end on a sour note. We're both adults here and I don't want this to be a... hello? Hello? HELLO?"

I slid my hands into the ones open to me and was led to the table and made to sit down, feeling the warm springiness of fur under me.

"Vest and tracksuit bottoms off," Angel said quietly.

"I'm here," I replied with a crack in my voice. What did she mean vest and tracksuit bottoms off?

"It sounded like you were gone..."

"Nope, still here. So what were you saying?" "I'm sorry it's gone this way... that's all I wanted to say." "NO you're... not. But anyway, no point saying shit like that... it's

done now." "Alright well, I... OH FUCK!" "Terrence? What's wrong?" I asked, allowing my vest to be taken

over my head while my tracksuit bottoms were softly rolled to my ankles.

"I thought I saw a mouse," Were you looking in a mirror?

"Okay... well... I'm... I'm... geeez... I'm gonna go now 'cuz I'm knackered."

"No problem!" This felt like the longest breakup in relationship history. "Good luck in life Terrence, I really mean that."

I didn't mean that at all. I was hoping one of his trains would get derailed and he'd suffer some long standing injury that would make him not be able to work again. Then he'd truly miss me and see that I was the best thing for him.

Having these thoughts while Marquita pulled my bottoms off my feet, Deena removing my vest and Kandy rubbed my neck and shoulders, was mind masturbating. If Terrence was capable of making me feel like this, who knows, there might've been a future for us.

"You too Nora... good luck in life. I hope you find someone who gives you exactly what you want."

"Oh don't worry about me. I've got more than enough options of men, women and couples, who'd like to scratch my itch."

Angel came and stood in front of me while Kandy was rubbing my shoulders, Marquita ran her hands up and down my legs and Deena played with my nipples.

"Whoa, women and couples?" Terrence asked, obviously excited.

"Yessur... I was gonna ask if you wanted to do something tonight but, now I don't need to so it's all good."

"Oh."

Me and Angel smiled at each other and Kandy winked as they watched me play with Terrence's mind, which was probably somewhere between a threesome and a two-headed blowjob. Either way, the fantasy was all he was going to get because this ship had officially sailed.

"Positions ladies," Angel said, standing above me. Kandy pulled my shoulders back and I felt myself tipping backwards while Deena and Marquita helped me flat onto my table. I could feel the frown lines form deep on my forehead as I tried to hold myself up but there was something in Angel's chocolate features that told me I wasn't going to come to any harm. It was a combination between the lips and the eyes.

My phone was handed to me so I could keep talking to Terrence who had no idea what was going on around his voice. If this was a video call, he would've cancelled the whole break up and been round here dig damn quickly.

But this was all for me. Whatever it was.

From the moment I saw them at the door, I hoped it would be what it was. Didn't think it would be 'cuz unbelievable shit like that never happened to me. This was something that happened to someone who'd come and tell me what happened. But never to me.

Laying down on my living room coffee table, on top of a fur coat, t-shirt and leggings, I felt a slender hand run between my thighs and slowly force them apart and my slow and steady breathing froze. All that could be heard over Pinky fucking Lethal Lipps with a strap-on was my heartbeat that felt like it was making my whole body throb.

My lips were moving to make sounds but nothing came out. Deena had my right nipple in between two wet fingers, Marquita had her full lips over my left nipple and Kandy was standing over me, giving me a view of her breasts from below. And all three of them were playing with themselves. Except for Angel. I couldn't see what she was doing but I could feel her touching me sporadically on my legs, making my skin feel like it was on fire.

A moan on my left drew my eyes away from Kandy, who had one hand rubbing the fullness of her breast while the other disappeared beneath her belt line.

This must've been a moment of understanding as the three women surrounding my upper half all began to moan in unison while Angel's hand made contact with my lower lips for the first time.

I jumped, I couldn't help it. Everything up to now had been ideas and possibilities and 'I wonder ifs' but now I was being touched, even though the question of who they were and what they were doing here was yet to be fully answered, I still didn't get how they found me. There was no link information to where I was on the Instagram post so how did they...

"Alright... well, I gotta go... the girls are coming..."

"How though?" Terrence said, again reminding me he was still there. "If we were supposed to be going out tonight, how could you have planned..."

"You do not have the right to ask me shit anymore... and I didn't necessarily say the girls were coming round... I just said the girls are coming..."

Angel appeared in my line of sight and gave me a solo round of applause before disappearing again. I found her when her fingers spread my lips and her tongue flicked my clit.

The phone dropped from my hand as my back arched, my eyes closed and three C.L.I.T.S masturbated around me. I'll tell you... this wasn't how I envisioned spending my anniversary but it would more than do.

I wasn't sure what Angel was doing but I could feel her fingers leaving wet trails and spots on my inner thighs. Mix that with the sound of three different women moaning and hip grinding around me and it didn't take a scientist of rockets to figure out why I was wet.

I did mention that every single one of these women was hot as a flying fuck.

"Give it to her Kandy," Angel said with a muffled mumble.

Looking up, I saw Kandy begin to squat down above me, bringing her wining waist lower down on top of my face. I didn't know what their plan was but I was close enough that I could see moisture on her lips. I didn't even realise she took off her trousers but she had. And there were thick thighs and an even thicker pussy looking down at me.

"Ready ladies?" Angel asked no one in particular. Then the women stopped.

My nipples were up standing and moist and my legs, which spread as wide as possible of their own accord, missed the feeling of Angel between them as she stood up.

"Ready," Kandy said.?" BEEN ready," Deena followed.?" Start the count ATD," Marquita said, hovering close to my nipple

like she missed it.?Angel looked at me and winked. I took the reprieve as a chance to

pick up the phone and see if Terrence was still there. He was unfortunately. I heard the tail end of a question as I put the phone to my ear.

"... are you gonna do tonight then?"

My anger was starting to rise as my horn took over and I wanted the ladies to get right back to where they were. "If you really wanna know Terrence, I'm gonna do some girls tonight. Gonna drink some drink, smoke some smoke and eat some pussy tonight."

"Oh,"

"One..." Angel started as she ran her hands up and down my thighs. "Two..." Kandy said, getting her wet fingers ready above my head. "Three..." Deena added, with a pleasurable grimace on her face. "GO!" Marquita finished.

At the same time, at different points on my body, motherfucking pleasure started. If you've never felt motherfucking pleasure then you won't know what I'm trying to say. My nipples were covered by Deena and Marquita's lips, while feeling the muscles in their arms moving below my line of sight. Kandy was displaying excellent thigh muscle strength by hovering close enough to my mouth that I could pout and taste her. And Angel... oh Angel... she was my favourite C.L.I.T so far. She had her lips clamped on my clit with her tongue poking. And she had two hands doing other things down there that I'd never felt before. Two fingers from one hand were sliding inside me – quite easily by the way – and one finger from her other hand was rubbing very quickly on my urethra, which was weird as fuck but felt GOOD!

Motherfucking pleasure ladies and gentlemen.

Timed to perfection, the three C.L.I.T.S continued to moan at the same time at different octaves as Angel literally fucked me with two hands and her mouth.

I was floating high on a cloud of 'what the fuuuuuck is going on in my life' that had me spread on my table like a platter of delectables. And everyone was enjoying a piece of me.

"NOW!" Angel mumbled.

Kandy was first to cum. I know this because her moan was the loudest as she began to leak across my forehead, making me look up and watch her pussy contracting and her thighs shaking. Deena sounded like she was going to be next as her lips tightened around my nipple and her arm tensed and froze. She didn't release her lips from my nipple as she came and the vibrations from her throat felt delicious on my chest. And she apparently set Marquita off, who was humping her fingers and flicking my nipple with her tongue at the same speed. Her mouth released my nipple and she looked at me again, this time with frown lines dancing across her forehead. She was squinting at me, biting her lips and swallowing hard but making no noise. Her neck was tense and her eyes became glassy and, with the other women still cumming, it was a silent orgasm that really held my attention.

Not for long though, because Angel – who watched and waited for Marquita to cum – sped up with her tongue and both her hands.

I tried to move but she held my thighs down and the C.L.I.T.S held my body so I couldn't move. I wanted to arch my back, feel myself, tap my foot, turn my head, do something. But I was restrained from my head to my arms to my thighs and I freaking loved it.

Angel got faster and faster and the C.L.I.T.S cheered her on as her fingers became a blur. All I could move was my hips, which I thrust against her mouth.

"Nyam dat," Kandy said quietly.?" She's going for the squirting move," Deena said breathlessly.?" I'm in there next," Marquita said.?" Have a nice night and a nice life Terrence," I added, failing to make

my voice sound normal.?Hold on, what squirting move? I don't squirt. "Yeah yeah, you too," he replied.

Angel then went poco loco between my thighs with her fingers and I lost it. My teeth were grinding together, I could feel my eyes rolling back in my head and my awareness of the room was drifting away on a sea of a delicious feeling that was tearing up my spine. Being held down multiplied the sensation and to look up at the orgasmic faces staring down at me in a realm of sufferance added a touch of sexual restraint to the proceedings.

My attention was drawn to the phone, where Terrence was holding a silence of his own. I was actually quite surprised he didn't hear any other voice but mine during the whole conversation. Then again, he wasn't very attentive.

And here I was. Flat back on my living room coffee table with three strangers holding me down and another stranger eating my pussy and about to make me cum.

My stomach tensed up, I began to thrash my head from side to side while Kandy ran her lips up and down my forehead.

In my head I was screaming every obscenity known to man, and in three different languages too. The orgasm I could feel growing inside me was deep and rode each breath, making each one heavier and

heavier. My thighs shook as my pussy throbbed three times then let out a sound I'd never heard it make before. I felt the orgasm before my pussy began to contract around Angel's fingers. The chocolate temptress between my thighs groaned with me as I stared at the back of my eyelids and squirted over onto the TV. I didn't realise I did this at the time but the video clip I was mysteriously sent a few days later told me so.

Angel made sucking noises and moaned while sucking her fingers with the other women following in succession. I was off with the fairies at this point. I had an instant headache, my eyes were squeezed shut, there was liquid creeping down the crack of my ass onto Marquita's fur coat and I was yet to release the muscles in my stomach.

"'Night Terrence." I managed to whisper.

"How 'bout a quick C.L.I.T.S train before we go ladies?" Angel said, now standing up. The other ladies stood behind her in front of my open thighs and super sensitive pussy that was still throbbing.

"Mind if I go first?" Marquita said. "I really want this one."
"Goodnight Nor..."

I hung the fuck up!

MYSTERY OF JILL

Epiphany

Flip side, stomach meets sheets? He plows inside as if he's making beats As if this year's harvest depended on it Bendin' on it

Jillian tapped Gerard on the shoulder repeatedly while he was pounding away at her and she was pumping into the air with his rhythm. She was trying to say something but it was lost in the air being pushed out of her as he wrapped his hands around her thighs. She pushed her chin over his shoulder and held onto his strong back, letting her fingers feel the muscles work. Mixed with the way he seemed to fit her so perfectly, Jillian held her mouth open waiting for a sound, anticipating it's sudden eruption but nothing came out.

A strong growl erupted from Gerard's chest, his waist digging deep and his hips making small circles.

"Foooooor fuck sakkkkeee..." she screamed while digging her fingers into his back. Her walls were clenching around him and he was still moving inside her, making her look like she was going to sneeze while Jill Scott's voice gave them instructions.

The orgasm came with her

Gerard slipped out of her without warning. The shock of his dick missing from her comfortable spot made her skin crawl suddenly and a cold breeze brushed across her nipples. She didn't have time to enjoy it as he grabbed her ankle and and spun her instantly onto her stomach.

"OoOoOoOooo..." she giggled.

Jillian didn't have time to laugh as Gerard parted her cheeks, smacked a hand on her lower back and dipped deep into her as the bass gave him a beat to pound to.

He wasted no time working up to a groove and got right back to his speedy drive. Her cheeks bounced back against his hand and he pushed them back into his thrust and all she could do was thrash from side-to-side and attempt to rip through the hotel pillow.

She buried her face in the soft white cotton and screamed as loud as she could, having three orgasms back-to-back while Gerard refused to let her stop and take a breather. He balled a fist and pounded the mattress with his other arm flexing next to her head.

In her mind, Jillian was thinking if death by pleasure was possible then her body was ready to be harvested for organs.

Gerard growled again with shallow hip movements, Jillian slapped the bed three times and raised her hips as another orgasm rippled across her back. Her legs kicked up and connected with his shoulder and sent him spinning off the bed.

Jillian was laying on her side, her face searching for an answer while biting a finger. Her legs were doing bicycle kicks and her other hand was clamped between her thighs. And she arched.

"Bending on it," she mumbled to herself.

Crown Royal On ice

Your hands on my hips pull me right back to you, I catch that thrust give it right back to you, You're in so deep I'm breathing for you,?You grab my braids arch my back high for you Your Diesel engine,I'm squirting mad oil on

"Get off me, I'm serving dinner!" Jillian chortled, holding a plate of rice and peas and BBQ chicken in one hand and a wooden spoon in the other.

"Put the plate down for a sec..." Gerard muttered, dipping behind his wife with his hands snaking around her hips. She giggled as his nose tickled her neck and the plate wobbled in her hand.

"Stop it babe, the food will get cold." "We have a microwave." Gerard slid the plate out of her hand and grabbed a cheek with his

other hand while humming the melody to Jill Scott's Crown Royal on Ice in her ear.

"Oh come on... not that song..." "Yep, that song," he uttered while working his hips against her. "Okay... dinner can wait." Gerard gripped onto her waist and walked her to the counter, the

lyrics being hummed between them both. His fingers danced down her thighs to the hem of her dress, lifting the material higher and higher. Jillian wanted to complain but the chiffon brushed against her skin something nice and she closed her eyes as he hummed into her neck.

With her palms flat on the counter next to her array of seasonings and her extra large glass of wine, Jillian stepped back into him as her dress climbed slowly over her naked behind.

"It's only now I'm finding out you have no panties on?" "... hands on my hips pull me right back to you..." she whispered. Doing as he was told, Gerard pulled her back to him while letting out

a breath so he could inhale her scent. He reached down to his tracksuit bottoms and pulled them down just below his testicles. His erection sprung against her cheeks repeatedly, making her legs separate and her heels clip clop on the kitchen floor.

"You didn't have any on either," Jillian hummed, looking over shoulder.

"...in so deep, I'm breathing for you..." he committed with his voice sounding almost breathless.

The sound of the door knocking broke their spell and made them fix their clothes properly as their parents arrived for dinner.

"Your diesel engine..." he said smacking her ass.?" ... I'm squirting mad oil on," she replied, licking her lips at him.

Love Rain

The rain was fallin' and slowly and sweetly and stinging my eyes And I could not see that he became my voodoo priest?And I was his faithful concubine?Wide open,wide, loose like bowels after collard greens

The mistake was made?Love slipped from my lips?Dripped down my chin and landed in his lap

Jillian lifted her thigh revealing Gerard's slippery face while trying to catch her breath from an orgasm that just left her and thrown a leg cramp in for good measure. She rested her head on her arm talking to herself.

"You gotta stop, you gotta... whoooooooooooo... I need a minute!" she huffed while grinding her hips on his forehead.

Gerard swallowed and wiped a fresh splash of something from his cheek, looking up at the panting Jillian with wonder in his eyes.

"Come on baby... let it go." "It's not easy you know. You have no idea how good it feels." "I want what I came for! Wide open wide..." he sang. "You know how

she said it. 'The rain was falling and slowly and sweetly'." "You gotta stop using Jill Scott against me. It's not fair!" "'And I was his faithful concubine...'" "Fine, okay... just shut up..." Jillian dropped her leg and covered his

face enjoying Love Rain as it pounded bass heavy in the bedroom. Holding onto the bed frame and balancing on the tips of her toes,

Jillian rode his face to the drums. Deep, deep, groove, skate, groooooove, deep grooooooooove, deep deep grooooooove.

Her face was a picture of concentration and struggle, trying to hold herself in place without running before he got what he asked for.

She dropped her body and spread her legs, working her hips back and forth, listening to his lips smacking with her liquid in between. The sound rattled in her ears over the creaking of the bed

"OoOoOoOooo... the mistake has been MADE..." she puffed in between short sharp breaths.

Gerard held onto her thighs and pulled her down, making her grind deeper and moan louder. A strong growl and muffle grew from his stomach and he said something that was lost between the rubbing of their lips. His tongue was dabbing at her and she could feel another, stronger orgasm beginning to make her toes curl.

Jillian was sure she came because she screamed. She didn't feel the rain leave her lips but she heard Gerard lapping and swallowing as her body went limp and she fell back onto a wet patch that stretched the length of their bodies.

I must... Remember... To thank him...

Later.

POWER OVER THE POWERFUL PART B

Whatever words were coming out of his mouth stopped. "Speechless huh? Yeah I got it like that." "I'm sorry," he muttered then cleared his throat. "I just... I haven't ever been offered something like that before." "Yeah, sure, let's call it an offer." Whatever that meant, Nathan frowned and looked back at his food, trying to finish as quickly as he could. As much as he was enjoying watching her walk and move and bend over, the offer seemed like too much too quickly.

What if fucking Godfrey's wife made him lose his job in some way? Off the top of his head, he couldn't see any way Godfrey could legally sack him but he knew men at the top could always find creative ways to make it stick.

He could feel Asitah's eyes burning through him waiting for a definitive answer. The pressure was rising in the room and Nathan began to sweat. With his last piece of chicken and vegetables swallowed, Nathan took a finishing swig of his drink and exhaled.

"Another drink? Alright."

She was up on her feet and had his glass and empty plate on the way to the breakfast bar.

"You know what? Honestly, I appreciate the... offer. But I don't wanna..."

"What? You don't want to WHAT?"

Asitah stopped making the drink and slammed the bottle of Wray and Nephews on the counter.

"I don't want to ruin what I've got. I've been looking for work for a long time and I know it's just..."

"Alright then," she said, going back to pouring the drink. "No problem. You don't have to, it was just an idea. GODFREY? He said no. Fuck, I owe that fat tub of shit £20."

"I don't want you to think that I don't find you attractive or..."

"The way you've been watching my ass, I know you'd fuck me. But I understand your reason."

Asitah gave him his drink and frowned as Godfrey came back in the room with a clean, food and gravy-less plate.

"You'll get your money later," she whispered as she past Godfrey, who was enjoying a chuckle to himself. "Dessert will be a moment."

Nathan could hear the defeat in her voice. Her imagined she was the type of woman who was used to getting what she wanted, when she wanted it. And if she got neither then the whole world suffered as a result.

He was wondering to himself why in the hell he actually said no. In his mind were all sorts of scenarios where the flirtatious housewife ended up bent over the table taking some good meat in her system. In his fantasy, he said fuck it to the food, cleared the table with one swipe of his arm. The commotion of plates breaking would make her look at him but it'd be too late because Nathan would be in her

personal space and ready to pull her by her hair to the table. Slam her down like he didn't give a fuck, lift her dress, pour wine down the crack of her ass – while Godfrey is sitting there – and absolutely abuse her pussy. Then he'd remove his hand because he'd want Godfrey to hear what was happening to his wife. Nathan would want him to hear the table scooting across the floor, knives and forks falling to the ground and the end of probably the best day of his sexual career.

But he said no. From the moment the offer was presented, he wasn't feeling it. Sure he was a freak and enjoyed the freaky things in life, but tonight, he was shown that he wasn't as freaky as he thought he was.

She picked up a bottle of Wray and Nephews, held her thumb over it and drizzled the clear liquid into the pan. A fierce flame jumped into the air but Nathan had his eyes locked on Asitah and the cool, calm way she shook the pan until the fire died.

She moved the pan off the fire and scooped slices of browned bananas on a side plate next to an individual soufflé.

"Tastiest thing on earth besides me, right chunky butt?"

"Yes babe," Godfrey replied deflated. He was staring straight ahead with his back straight and his hands on the table like he was under strict instruction.

Nathan took a sip of the stronger, slightly tangier drink, wincing for a second as the rum made its way down his throat and into his stomach. With his eyes clamped shut, he wriggled in his seat waiting for the burn to pass.

When he opened his eyes, a steaming white plate of sliced caramelised bananas were criss-crossed next to a ramekin of a steaming individual soufflé.

"I have to say Mrs... Lupalinda, your food is to die for!"

"Still not tasty enough for you to fuck me though right?" she muttered to herself.

"I, erm, what?" "I said I hope it's tasty enough for you." Asitah slid a plate in front of Godfrey and one for herself before

sitting down with a fresh drink.?" Oh, don't worry about my dry throat," Godfrey shouted, getting up

and making his own. "Just 'cuz you wanna fuck another of my staff, don't worry about what I want!"

With his face in his food, Nathan pretended he didn't hear what Godfrey just said but he was already doing the maths. Another colleague? Who was the first? Was this an old situation? Was it in McDonalds? Did the person still work there? So, if he wasn't the first, how many were there?

"Don't mind him, he's just mad 'cuz he doesn't go five minutes before bussing his chunky nut."

Nathan couldn't control the burst of hilarious energy that erupted from his lips. "Oh shiiii... sorry about that Godfrey, that was funny."

"Don't listen to her, that only happened like three times." "Exactly... three times too many."

"Out of like hundreds of times we've had sex, it's not bad."

"It's still three times. Nathan, can you count how many times you've popped too early?"

His mouth was busy enjoying the combination of rum and bananas until he looked up and realised he was asked a question.

"Erm, I've gotta be honest. And this isn't me just boasting but that's never happened to me before." Nathan lied.

Just because he wasn't going to have sex with her, didn't mean she had to think any less of him as a lover.

"See, there you go. Younger, fitter, more handsome and doesn't cum first? You wanna get married Nathan?"

Asitah finished with a raucous laughter that made both Nathan and her husband stare at each other before looking back to their plates.

That was the first moment Nathan noticed his lips clapping together like he could taste something but couldn't figure out what it was. He took another sip of his drink, swallowed and could taste the same thing again. Then the spoon fell from his hand.

Asitah put her spoon in her mouth and grinned while Godfrey looked at Nathan out of the corner of his eye but kept his face on his food.

"You okay Nathan? You don't look so well." "I feel... funny." "You don't look funny," she replied, lifting a banana slice over her

mouth, letting drops of rum fall between her lips down her chin.?His body began to feel numb washing from his neck all he way down

to his toes. He tried to lift his drink but his hand wasn't responding to the order sent from his brain.

"I can't..."

His head fell back against the chair, his hands fell to his side and his mouth fell open. He couldn't feel his food being digested or even his toes as he stared straight ahead at Asitah who was chuckling silently.

"You just don't like to be told no do you?" Godfrey said with a mouthful of banana.

"When was the last time you told me no?" Godfrey looked up.?" Exactly, you know better than that! Look at him. So handsome. You

know what, fuck this food." Asitah picked up her drink and knocked it back in one giant sip

before throwing her glass over her shoulder. Before it broke, she swiped her hand across the table sending dessert plates, glasses and cutlery sprawling to the floor. Godfrey must've seen it coming and lifted his plate off the table before her arm cleared everything.

"Good luck," Godfrey said to his food. He looked at Nathan sitting at the head of his table, knowing exactly what was going on.

Nathan wanted to turn and look at his manager and ask him what the hell he meant but his head didn't move. All he could do was turn his eyes to the man who was licking his dessert plate. Behind him, Asitah was moving quickly around his shoulders. She kicked off her shoes, hitched up one side of her dress and lifted a thigh onto the table.

"I don't get told no a lot Nathan. In fact, you're the first to ever tell me no. Can you imagine how that makes me feel?"

With each word, she climbed on the table and sat in front of him as he looked like he was sleeping with his eyes open. His bottom lip was dangling open as her leg lifted over his head and slid next to him.

"That makes me feel undesirable. And I'm not undesirable am I Nathan?"

She pushed his chair back with her feet then put them on his arm rests, pulling her dress up as she got comfortable. His eyes dropped to the space between her thighs, enjoying the flex of her thigh muscles.

He wanted to tell her no and slide a hand up her thigh at the same time but nothing from his shoulder, his arm, hand or fingers moved. His mind was screaming but his body language was cool, calm and collected.

"You eat pussy Nathan? You think he eats pussy babe?" "I don't think he eats pussy sweetheart." "Oh no, you don't eat pussy?" Nathan blinked.

"Was that a yes or a no blink? I dunno. I think it's best to find out."

Asitah didn't waste any time in reaching for her panties, which she pulled down her knees. Her legs came together and her French knickers flew over his head.

She wrapped her legs around the chair and pulled him between her open thighs. He tried to turn his head but, still, nothing moved as the scent of her pussy replaced the delicious food he'd just devoured.

"What did you use on him?" Godfrey asked, still looking at the wall in front of him.

"A little opium in his drink and a mix of Chlorprocaine and Epinephrine and in his food. Just enough."

"She must've really wanted you!" Godfrey mumbled. "I don't like to be told no!"

Nathan felt his head being turned. His eyes drifted up and saw Asitah's foot moving his head. He wanted to yell and curse her out for putting her foot on his head but he couldn't do anything but watch.

"You want some good advice? Next time a married woman offers you sex while her husband watches, just say yes. You never know when she might drug your food and fuck your face."

He couldn't stop the fact that his face was drawing nearer and nearer to her groin. Her legs, which were stronger than they appeared under the dress, flexed as she spread them further.

"Ready?" she asked Nathan

He blinked again. In his mind, he was screaming his head off, telling her to get the fuck off him and let him go.

"I'll take that as a yes!"

Her hand wrapped around his head and pulled him forward as her legs lifted to accommodate his face.

"Yummy," Asitah said as Nathan's face fell into her groin. She put her hands on the side of his head and held his skull as she laid back on the table and began to grind her hips.

"Now that is what I need. Why didn't you just say yes Nathan? Huh? Would've been a lot more fun if you could finger fuck me at the same time but hey..."

She lifted his face to look at him. His eyes were still looking forward but his face was devoid of emotion. She let go of his temples and let his face drop onto her clit while Godfrey was sighing heavily behind her back.

"Something to say back there bread loaf?" "No," he replied keeping his face straight.?" Less talking, more listening..." She was running his face up and down her pussy while laying on the

table. He could hear a lot of slurping and squelching but couldn't feel his tongue moving.

"Okay, let's get it... I'm gonna need to squirt on you now 'cuz... well you turned me down. You don't mind do? You don't think he minds do you baby?"

Asitah laid flat and turned her head to look back at her husband. "I think that ship has sailed baby boo." "Okay," she said.?Her legs wrapped around his head and locked in place while her

waist was grinding on the table. She laid back and put her arms on the table, loving the view of his face humping up and down and her fingers reaching towards Godfrey's plate.

"Oh fuck, I think he DOES eat pussy... shiiit me uppppp..." she moaned while banging her hand on the table. She ran a hand over her breasts and thrashed from side-to-side as she forced Nathan's head into her groin so hard, she could feel the bones in his cheeks.

"OH!" Asitah said once, using the fingers from one hand to slide inside with Nathan's face. "Taste that!"

"I don't think the table's gonna make it." Godfrey said with a smile.

"It better make it otherwise you're the one that's gonna fix it after I'm done."

Her ankles tightened around his head while her hips sped up and her finger was slipping from his mouth to between her lips and over her clitoris. With her husband's heavy breathing behind her, Asitah felt her body beginning to tense up.

"Okay... ooookay... well fucking plaaaaaaaaayed!" "Come on his face baby!" "OoOoOookay baby... I'm gonna cum... I'm gonna cum... right on his

motherfuuuu..." Asitah came. The table collapsed while she was holding onto his face

and she pulled him forwards with her in an almighty crash of pleasured screams and broken wood.

"Told you!" Godfrey mumbled.?Asitah looked between her thighs at Nathan's dripping face.

"Well look at you!? Make sure you keep him around chunky butt."

CHAN'GLO THE GLOVED ASSASSIN – C.L.I.T.S

"Well you made it this far... well done to you. You wouldn't believe how many men actually don't physically make it this far."

Lamar woke up again, trying to figure out when he exactly went to sleep. His head was pounding, he had chains back on his wrists and he was surrounded by darkness. Again.

"What's with all the fucking darkness? What is this the league of shadows?"

"Something like that," a voice replied. "All this time and you still don't know who we are?"

"Clits or pussies or something like that."

"Don't let Pandora hear you say that, she'll trim your ball sack hair with a straight razor. And make you watch."

A spotlight appeared over a woman sitting at a vanity desk with light bulbs around a large mirror. She had her back to Lamar, looking at him in her reflection and was wearing a long evening gown with a slit from her ankle to her hips. One of her legs was exposed and she was admiring her gloves which extended to her elbows.

"Do you know how amazing women are Lamar?" "I can't stand you lot right now to be honest." "Really? But you know you can't live without us right?" "So I guess your the good cop then? The other fucking nutters I've

met tonight all have violent and potentially psychotic tenancies." "You're not wrong there." "So what are you supposed to 'teach' me?" The light over her went out and Lamar was plunged into darkness

again. His eyes tried to focus on where he was just staring when the woman who was sitting down spoke again. This time from behind him.

"My name's Chan'Glo The Gloved Assassin. Thus the gloves."

Lamar turned around as her gloved hands ran down his neck. He jumped nervously and tried to use his hands, which strained against the chains.

"What the fuuuc..." "See? How can a woman do that? Amazing, right?" "This is some juju business," Lamar groaned trying to move his neck

from her fingers. "I'm coming back for all of you!" "Coming back where? Do you even know where you are?" Lamar fell silent as the hands slipped away from his neck and

disappeared into the darkness.?" Just LET ME..." "Shush..." Chan'Glo's gloved finger appeared on his lips and he recoiled against

the chair as she hovered above him.?He looked at her once, then twice, then a third time to make sure he

was actually seeing a woman in full-length gown floating above him. He couldn't control the pie-shape of his eyes and the full circle of his mouth as he looked up at her in shock.

"Women, Lamar, make the world go round. We start wars, cause car accidents and societies and civilizations were built on images of us. We

make you smile on good days and rub your backs on bad days. You are miserable without us yet constantly try and replace us with another version of us. I mean without us, where would you put your dick besides a sock? A vaseline palm just isn't the same is it?"

"How the fuck are you doing this?" Lamar had to ask.?" I'm a woman. We can all do this," she laughed then disappeared. Lamar tried to follow the sound of her moving but he couldn't hear

anything. His head was turning all around, trying to find where she would appear next.

"This ain't teaching me shit. I've figured out that none of you slags are the man around here so where's he at? I'm tired of all these fucking games."

Chan'Glo appeared through the darkness on his right and he turned to watch her walk towards him. Her leg was walking strong as it cut between the material and he watched her muscles contract with every step she took. She reached him and swung a leg over his lap and sat down. He tried not to act scared as she had just disappeared and reappeared and apparently levitated as well. Now she was touching him, running a hand up and down his naked chest, feeling his heartbeat.

"Women make you nervous, confident, powerful, amazing. We can make a man feel like he can climb the highest mountain or swim to the lowest point in the ocean. Think of all the times Keisha has got behind you with something. Like that time you wanted to work for that company in King's Cross and she got behind you and bigged you up and, what happened? You got it."

Lamar looked up at her, completely confused.?" How the fuck do you lot know this shit? Did Keisha tell you all this?" "Nope, we are a clever bunch of ladies you know, hence the name. I

thought you would've at least clicked onto that by now." Chan'GLo wrapped her legs around the chair and began to grind her

hips on her seat. Lamar couldn't help the erection that started to stretch out.

"I don't know what you lot want but..."

"We want you to appreciate the woman you have and the things she does for you. That's what we're all about. You could be single or you can realise you have an amazing woman on your team who wants the sun to shine on you and the ground to throw up money wherever you go."

Lamar felt a gloved hand sliding down his chest as he looked her in her beautiful eyes. The hand continued down his stomach and was about to stroke the base of his length when that voice from the darkness broke his concentration.

"Erm... excuse me Chan'Glo... that's not what we do here? Geez... what is with you women today? All fingers and tongues tonight... right, could you send him to me please?"

Chan'Glo sighed. "Awww mayne, come on. This woman is such a pervy watching perv."

"I heard that!" the voice replied. "No need for sleep, just wheel him through."

Lamar felt her hand freeze as she climbed off him with a hefty huff and a puff, mumbling something under her breath about not being able to have any fun.

"Come on then. The boss will see you now." "Who?" "The woman that makes sure we don't get too touchy feely or want

us to have ANY FUN!" He heard her walk behind him then he began to slide through the

darkness until something at his feet hit a set of double doors and pushed them open. His eyes adjusted to the low tube lights that lit up a hallway ahead of him. Doors ran off in different directions on either side and he tried to get a picture of where he could possibly be.

"Come on you," Chan'Glo said, walking ahead of him. The chair suddenly started moving as she curled her index finger towards him.

"Lamar is going to see the Chef... say bye ladies."

While the chair was rolling of it's own accord Chan'GLo, who was swishing her hips with catwalk flair, knocked on doors as she passed them.

Heads began to pop out of doorways and Lamar recoiled as each one greeted him on his way.

"Good luck Lamar," Becky Becky Two Times said, peeking out of a door and disappearing again.

"He survived the Nurse? Gwan Lamar," Roro The Lady shouted from a door he was yet to pass.

"Stay out of here Lamar, if you know what I mean," Dee Deena The Teaser shouted in his ear as he passed her door.

"£10 says he'll be back! Men are stupid creatures, just watch!" screamed Zeah The Ball Crusher.

Lamar wasn't sure where he was but it had to be one hell of a facility considering he'd been taken into some weird looking rooms and some of them were massive in size. His mind was trying to calculate where in London he could possibly be.

"Shave and a haircut," Nurse Grimy Core mumbled as she peeked through her door playing with a scalpel.

Lamar looked forward as Chan'Glo walked through a set of double doors into more darkness and his rolling chair followed.

"Oh for fuck sake," Lamar moaned.

INSIDE A MASTURBATOR'S MIND

Where's the vaseline?

I spend so much fucking time looking through shit than I do masturbating.

Roxy Reyno... no, I don't like the way she sounds. Pinky... hmmm... nah, she's too professional. Skyy... she gives good head. Maybe a random Black clip. That'll do.

Oh shit, look at that... let me get comfortable. I am tired as fuck but I need a nut.

I feel like I've seen every video on this freaking site. And this one. And this one. Page 11, 12, 13... 26, 27, 28, 29... look at my dick... how can I have been looking at this crap site for 38 minutes and I'm nowhere near cumming?

How about something different tonight? Let's see what categories they got... I've seen enough amateur... mostly ugly white girls caught on camera. Asian, anal, no, no... big boobs, not tonight, cuckold, hmmm... not in the mood to be fucking someone else's wife tonight... Cumshots... I need something longer... for fuck sake.

Tissue...

Where is that video of the chunky woman who gives those really sloppy blowjobs? And she was sloppy with it too. She made that video when she had the Wendy's cup and she put the dick in the cup... And she has those ridiculously massive titties. And the one where she had the orange wig. That's not the one I'm looking for. I want the one where she had the jeans jacket on.

Shiiiiiiiit... oh fuck, it hit me in the mouth again...

Oh it's a big booty night tonight. Cherokee first, then Pinky... nah... I don't know what it is about Pinky that just doesn't get me hard. She's not natural enough.

I wonder what that woman sitting across from me would do if I pulled my dick out on this train and started wanking while looking at her? Could I get her to spit on my dick and really fuck her throat? She looks like she'd choke on it? Maybe she'd like it.

Oh shit look at those eyes... I'd jerk out a wicked nut on her face and make her look at me. Hmmm... where's my phone? I need to take a sneaky picture of this one. GOTCHA!

Let's have an old school night tonight. Oh yeah, Janet Jacme, followed by some Kitten and Vanessa Blue. I swear those two are in a bisexual cult because they have the same tattoo on their arms. Imagine a bisexual cult that worshipped my dick? Hmmm...

Who gives better head: Jada Fire, Ayana Angel or Lethal Lipps?

What was the fucking point? I feel like that was a waste of time.

Whoooo... not yet... not yet... I wanna long one tonight. Reaaal long.

How many times am I gonna watch this same old clip of this same woman? Every time. But she makes the cum feel so good.

Why are there chunks in my cum?

Oh dear God... Italia Blue, the things I would do to you. I would really fuck you over and mess you up something nicely. You have no idea...

what happened to her? I haven't seen anything new from her for ages. I've seen all these... the Christmas outfit, on the exercise machine, the one on BangBros... I sure do miss Italia Blue.

Ohh MY GOD... I haven't cum like that in a long time. That shit went past my face... shiiiiit, if I didn't move, that would've hit me in the eye...

Easy... easy... eassssssy... no, not yet, you're not gonna make me cum yet... oh no, I'm gonna make you work for this one.

It doesn't taste bad at all! Women making noise about nothing. Tastes like iron. Like I know what iron tastes like. But it doesn't taste bad. Not really.

Thank you Lethal Lipps... you can suck my dick anytime...

Okay, let's get comfortable. Tissue, check, full screen, checks. Hmmm... here we fucking go. Roc and Shay. Okay, open that ass up and... oh yeaaaah, get in there... she could try and ride me like that... I'd handle that... he does well though. Oh fuuuuck, I would've cum by now... that looks like it feels too good. Yeaaaaaah baby, get it, get it... get it! Oh fuck baby... here I cum
.

Geez, I've masturbated damn near every... nope... it's every day this week. Hold on, it was twice on Wednesday.
Pornhub, xvideos or... awww fuck it... I'm going to bed.

LEAVE A DONATION

"One more road and I'm good to go/ one more road and I'm good to go/ one more road and I'm good to go/ then I'm out this bitch and I don't have to do it no more!" Jerome sang to himself as he walked down the path of a house where the lights were on but no one came to the door as he knocked.

Catching the curtains twitching out of the corner of his eye, he left the path with a loud swing of the gate and some loud under the breath cursing.

"Stay in ya yard if you want but I got one more road to go," Jerome continued, turning the corner and making his way to Rabbit lane. "One more road to go..."

It had been a long last day for the warm chocolatey, suited and booted black man who could visualise reaching the office, handing in his I.D. Card and skipping all the way to the train station where he would never have to see those end of the train line stations ever again. Working for way too long as a charity worker, he was used to travelling to Chorleywood on the Metropolitian line, Hatch End on the Overground and Totteridge and Whetstone on the Northern line then have to train it all the way back to his studio flat in Brockley.

As a cool Chingford breeze washed over him, Jerome turned onto Rabbit lane and felt like he could see a light at the far end of the road. Usually, he'd be working with a partner who would take the even number side of the road while he worked the odds. But today, he was on his own and was only working the odds. In his mind, he had checked out of the job when he gave his one month's notice. Long walking hours, disrespect from everyday people in the form of slamming doors in his face, being told no in numerous foul ways. So sticking to the rules of the job was an option he felt he no longer had to take. What were they going to do, sack him?

He stopped at the top of the road and tried to count how many houses he had to visit, selling his direct debit account discount offer for numerous third world charities who wanted to help those less fortunate. For his last week, Jerome's line manager put him on the worst account the company held which was for P.I.N.S (Paraplegics In Need of Sex). The name alone sent chills down his spine as he anticipated the looks he would receive from people who were thinking the same thing as him, 'who the fuck made a charity giving money to people to spend on prostitutes?'

Jerome understood that disabled people had needs too but to start a charity to pay for prostitutes?

"Fuck it, one more road to go..." Jerome said to himself as he scanned the road one more time before walking up the first path.

He inhaled deeply, taking note of the meticulous flower arrangement in the front garden and sighed heavily as he ran through the script in his head.

"Hello, my name is Jerome and I'd like to borrow just a few minutes of your time to talk about disabled people. More importantly, disabled soldiers. Did you know that 80% of soldiers of war who come back are disabled? Well, we here at P.I.N.S would like to make a life for them where they are comfortable, relaxed and at peace with their disabilities. That's why we secure prestige visitors to check on them and make sure they are okay."

That last line of the script was the part that made the first six houses slam the door in his face before he even pulled any literature out. He expected his demeanour and professionalism to dwindle at the first door but, each door he knocked on, was greeted with his biggest smile and most enthusiastic sounding voice he could muster. Even the Jamaican man who laughed and closed the door in his face was ignored as Jerome was immediately on to the next one.

Looking up the road, seeing he was almost half way done, Jerome checked out and went home in his mind. He opened his front door, kicked his shoes off, opened a beer with his teeth and exhaled while falling on his sofa bed. Wiggling his toes and undoing his shirt buttons, Jerome was home and no longer a door-to-door salesman.

In reality, he had seven more houses to go before his daydream was his real life movement.

October was throwing colder winds at him the further he travelled down the road, kicking crispy leaves at his feet.

"Five more houses to go," Jerome sang with more funk, noting the lights on house six were out.

The next house made him hopeful of a quick turn around as only the hallway light was on. Jerome was thinking of not knocking and hopping the fence to the next house, bringing himself closer to a more relaxing reality.

"Cha..." Jerome said, pressing the doorbell with his leg shaking. He was hoping there would be no movement behind the glass door and counted to five before spinning on his heels and back down the path he went. In between licks of wind, Jerome thought he heard something that sounded like a door flap creaking open. He turned and caught the flap closing and a hand disappearing behind the glass.

"Was that child or adult?"

Whatever it was, his attention was drawn to it and took him back to the front door.

He knocked again.

The same silence greeted him. Instead of walking away, Jerome waited at the door, hoping the flap would open and confirm that he wasn't going crazy and he did in fact see a red hand.

On cue, the flap opened and closed quicker than before and Jerome smiled. "Hello?"

"Hi," a voice replied back.?" Is your mummy or daddy home?"

"I'm mummy," the voice said through the door flap.?" Oh, okay... well, could you open the door so we can..." "Wu Tang Clan!" "Excuse me?" Jerome said, taken aback.?" Wu. Tang. Clan!" The woman repeated it slowly and it still made less sense to Jerome,

who was shaking his head at the door.?" Erm, I'm here from P.I.N.S and..." "Last time," the voice said. "Wu. Tang. Clan?!" "Ain't nuttin' to fuck with..." Jerome said, thinking and laughing to

412

himself. "Geez, I haven't heard that song for ages." Inside he was screaming WTF??He knew the name of the hip-hop group well. He grew up on their

music, bought all of their albums and was familiar with everything about them from their individual raps to the science behind their name,

Never in his door-to-door career had anyone thrown a classic hip- hop group at him instead of opening the door. He played along, remembering the next line in the song and nodding his head.

He knocked again and this time silence replied. Craning his neck to look through the glass doors and through the door flap, there was no sign of life where he just heard a female voice. He stood there a moment, thinking, 'I swear I was just talking to someone'.

The door creaked opened and his mouth and his eyes dropped as he stared at a five-foot six-shaped figure in a head-to-toe Deadpool outfit. Covering the shape's face was a mask with large white orbs for eyes and kitchen utensils around attached to a utility around her waist. Spatulas on the hips, spices attached to a utility belt across the front and long wooden spoons criss-crossed across the back. The shape looked Jerome up and down and turned its head to the side while breathing heavily.

"Wu Tang Clan?" the shape said again.

Jerome was stuck with his mouth and eyes locked open. With the door open, a fresh scent of incense past him on his way into the atmosphere, catching his nostrils while he was stuck on stupid.

The outfit shaped around the person brilliantly, hugging her nicely in the crotch with a defined triangle imprint that had Jerome licking dirty thoughts in his mind.

"Ain't nuttin' to fuck with," Jerome said again, still shocked, but also throwing up the Wu Tang symbol with his hands.

"Good... I was hoping so," Deadpool said before grabbing a handful of Jerome's shirt and tie and pulling him into the doorway.

Unprepared for the speed of movement, Jerome flinched as the door closed behind him and he was pushed up against it. One red hand ran up and down his chest while the other ran along his jawline.

"Are you SURE?" Deadpool asked.

"Am I sure what? I'm not sure of anything since Deadpool opened the front door."

"Are you sure Wu Tang Clan ain't nuttin' to fuck with?"

Jerome didn't need to think about his answer. "The Wu is the way, the Tang is the slang..."

Deadpool held a finger over his mouth and stopped him from talking. In the moment of silence, Jerome's eyes took in the hallway décor, looking for a picture of who the mystery Marvel comic book character could really be. Lots of erotica decorated the walls and stood on side tables in figurines of adventurous positions.

"I don't think..." Jerome started but was cut off.

"You'll definitely do," Deadpool said, reaching for her mask. She slid it over her face and a caffe latte face with hair pulled back in a ponytail stared at him.

"Damn, Deadpool is sexy as fuck," Jerome said with no care.?" Thank you... now we don't have much time so..." Jerome kept eye contact with the beautiful woman with the ravishing

eyes who rocked a half smirk while lowering herself down his body. Watching her move, his mind sent the words and his lips began to move but the stare in her eyes kept him silent. Her eyes looked away from his momentarily to look at his belt as she slid to his waist before she locked them back on him.

Jerome could only watch her open his belt methodically without taking her eyes off him. She let both ends of the belt fall free and reached straight for his button in a fumble of fingers and excitement. Jerome could hear her growling under her breath and moaning as she got closer to what she was reaching for.

His zip came down but she struggled with his button. She tried to unhook it but no luck. She tried to be calm and slip it out one side at a time with no luck and she tried to flip it out with no luck.

Growling loudly, she pulled at both sides of his trousers and his button ripped off his trousers and danced across her wooden floors.

"Fucking button... just come the fuck off, what the fuck..." Deadpool said to Jerome's trousers.

The furore of her frustration was evident for Jerome to see and her hunger to get to his dick was making him harder.

"Come OFF!" Deadpool shouted and yanked his trousers and boxer shorts to the ground.

"Shiiiiiiit," Jerome moaned, feeling his feet slide forward before catching his balance. "Look, erm... I don't think..."

"Good," she said, looking up at him with his dick getting harder in her hand. "Don't think!"

Her mouth enveloped the entire length of him and she slowly withdrew her lips back to his tip in one smooth movement. Any complaints or truths Jerome was about to reveal sucked back into his mind while his eyes locked with hers.

His hands curled into fists then he opened his palms and slapped the door before bringing his fists to his head, thrashing from side to side.

Back down at his waist, Deadpool, also known as Tamala, was collecting spit in her mouth which she pushed down his shaft with her lips. With her hands reaching round to hold his cheeks, she slowly worked her way down on the meat in her mouth, gagging as she went. The Deadpool outfit hugged her perfectly and made the moment her nipples rise a neck-to-ankle experience. The red material pulled up all around her, especially in the crotch, which was getting wetter. Spots of saliva were dripping on her top, leaving spots of dark material across her chest.

Jerome was in two worlds. His mind was away with the fairies, pixies and unicorns but his eyes were glistening in the beauty of a pretty lady who knew how to work her mouth in subtle ways that had the necessary effect on his knees, which began to buckle. The P.I.N.S leaflets in his pocket fell to the floor, but he couldn't see anything except the head moving in his lap, slurping and spitting a trail that ran down his trouser leg.

He threw his head back and banged it against the door, making him suck in air through his teeth. One because of the pain he felt in the back of his head and two because Tamala was pushing his dick to the limits of her throat.

Her eyes were slits of seductiveness and her tongue worked in vicious circles in between dips in and out of her mouth.

"Shiiiiit... Erm... Deadpool..." Jerome said, looking down, feeling conscience of the fact that he had no idea what her name was.

"Just call me T," Tamla said. "T is good enough." "No... this MOUTH is good enough... what the..." "Shhh... less talking... there's not a lot of time left..." "Not a lot of wha..."

Jerome was lost in the way she was spitting on her hands and circling his dick, listening to globs of saliva slapping the floor. His hands unlocked from the fists they were in and slid up her arms, squelching and throat moaning erupting from her throat followed by a hungry growl.

His hands slid slowly and cautiously up her arms, across her shoulders and up the back of her neck, waiting for a disapproving movement from her which said 'keep ya hands still' but she just kept on sucking.

"What a daaaaaay, what a daaaaay," Jerome said, his hands wrapping round the back of her neck.

A single look from her twinkling eyes told him he was all signs go to fuck her face. He squinted back, asking with his eyes, 'you sure?'

Tamala opened her mouth wide and stopped moving, with her eyes locked on him. Mascara-coloured tears stained her cheeks and her face was a glow with mouth water and pre-cum which she rubbed around her face.

Jerome leaned off the front door and locked his fingers behind her head. Watching Tamala shuffle on her knees, moving into a taller position, Jerome grinned. There was no way in heaven or hell that his last street would provide such an unexpected bonus. There were a few budding wannabe pimps in the office who puffed up their chests with stories of nipples popping out or managing to catch women as they've come out of the shower. But this was the stuff of office legends and Jerome knew he was going to leave that office the king of kings.

With his fingers firmly locked behind her head, a steady stance and a mischievous grin creeping across his lips, Jerome thrust his hips once and Tamala gagged instantly. Her chest heaved, veins grew either side of her neck and strains of liquid continued to stain her outfit. Tears danced on her eyelids and filled her Disney eyes before streaming down her face. All while she looked straight up at Jerome asking, 'is that it?'

Widening his stance, Jerome thrust again with an extra stroke on top, this time deeper than before. Tamala gagged again, coughing spit onto his dick and stomach and moaning approvingly. She held her arms behind her back and continued to look up, daring him to do it again.

Three short thrusts and one deep thrust which he held for a few seconds and Tamala looked away from him for the first time, making Jerome giggle to himself. He was thinking that she'd taken a good length of him but she still had work to do in order to get the rest in. But she looked like a trier and God blesses the triers, he thought to himself.

Pushing his dick to the side of her mouth, Tamala mumbled, "Clock is ticking sir..."

Jerome took his dick from her mouth and reinserted straight into her throat, sliding his hands over her slicked back hair, making her head tilt backwards. He could feel himself getting harder in her mouth.

He used his thumb to wipe away her black tears while holding her jaw open and standing on his tip toes, taking a moment to really enjoy what was going on.

The red material with black piping stretching gloriously across her bent legs, the random pattern of darkness splattered across her chest, black smudges across her cheeks, the silence of her home amplifying the sounds of her mouth, the doorknob pressing against his lower back, loose strands of hair tickling his fingers, the groans of pressure erupting from her throat, his boxers and trousers bunched at his ankles, the erotic figures looking at him from over her shoulder, the jingle jangle of kitchen utensils, the depth of her throat and the amount of saliva puddling on the floor between his legs.

In between each glance at his surroundings, Jerome looked down at Tamala with eyes of disbelief as she felt his eyes on her. The watched feeling made her mouth performance become more porn with sloppy, moan-filled kisses on his head, long licks along his length, face slaps on

her cheeks with his dick and mumbled indecipherable words in between.

He had one hand on the top of her head and one under her chin, guiding her to the best feeling position.

"Hurry up," Tamala mumbled, forcing his dick to the furthest depths of her throat.

Jerome squatted slightly and held her face tightly, feeling anger at the rush she was putting on him. He wanted to take his sweet time with her skills. Switch from fast and violent to soft and smooth, have her hold her tongue out and watch the spit extend from her tongue to his dick, lay her on the floor and T-bag her, find out if she had the skills to take his dick and testicles at the same time. But this was a random moment he didn't expect so beggars weren't going to be choosers.

That's when the warm feeling of eruption started in his balls. His dick hardened in Tamala's wetness and she was forced to adjust her mouth. His moans became sporadic and words found their way out of his mouth.

"Fuck me four ways from Sunday, that's good head," he moaned deliciously, palming the back of her head and making her dip with his fingers. The walls of her mouth were tight against him and sent muscle jerks up his stomach.

Down below, Tamala was sweating profusely. The skin-tight material coupled with the constant neck movement and the heating being on made beads of perspiration slide down her neck and between her shoulder blades.

The way he was forcing his dick deep, making her gag, said that he was closer than close. His toes began to curl in his Clarks, a tingle travelled up his legs and he found the right amount of pressure in her mouth to coast him to a face-painting orgasm. All she had to do was hold her face exactly where it was.

"Shiiiiiiiiiiiiiiiiiiiit," Jerome stretched out looking to the ceiling as Tamala adjusted her mouth and opened her throat to him. "That's what I'm talking about... riiiiiiiiiiiiiiight there..."

The feeling of his orgasm rising had become a whole body experience and his entire being started to shake. Tamala's face was held in place as Jerome let out a loud howl, letting her know he was about to come.

"On my face, like we agreed..." Tamala mumbled.

On the other side of the front door that Jerome was using as leverage, a man in a suit walked up the path. He walked proudly and full of confidence as he got to the door and was about to knock but he stopped. The sounds coming from the other side of the door were enough to make him put his ear to the door in confusion.

"Huh?" he said to himself and pulled his phone out of his pocket.

Jerome was in a world body-buzzing bliss so he didn't hear the gate close or the footsteps leading to the front door. He was focussed on keeping the sensitivity at the tip of his dick. If he could do that then he'd be cumming and be able to look down at Tamala's white-streaked face with the sheepish grin of, 'what do I do now?'

His legs squatted deeper and his grip on her face stronger as Jerome heard the sound of a phone vibrating. He could feel it under his shoes and followed the sound to an end table where her phone was ringing. Curiosity, while concentrating on her mouth, made him look at the name on her phone, which said a 'Friend' was calling.

The fact that she didn't even move towards the phone made Jerome more ravenous to come on her face than ever. She was only on one thing and one thing only... his dick and that was the only goal she could see before her.

That was until she heard a voice on the other side of the door. She looked up at Jerome and could see that he was also listening to the voice.

Jerome kept fucking her face, while listening as two male voices spoke on the other side of the door.

"Who the FUCK are you?" one voice said." I'm... erm..." replied the other, more Cockney voice.?" Okay, I'm gonna ask you one more time and then I'm gonna start

fucking someone up." "Listen mate... I dunno 'ooo you are but..." "I fucking live here so, I'll ask again, who the FUCK are you?!"

Jerome was starting to sweat while thinking to himself, 'who the fuck is that?'

His nervous eyes dipped to Tamala, her chin coated with saliva, as she made her mouth into the perfect shape for his dick, seemingly oblivious to the discussion outside her front door. He knew between six and nine good strokes and he was golden. But the hullabaloo outside the door was distracting him.

He reached for focus on the task at hand by running his hand across her dripping wet chin, enjoying the cool feeling of the sticky liquid on his fingers and making his dick rise back to its full-standing glory.

"I'm a friend of Tamala's...she invited me round."

"Why would my wife invite round some pencil-neck white boy to our house?"

"YOU'RE MARRIED?!" Jerome shouted, making everyone pause. The men on the other side of the door stopped talking on the doorstep while Tamala stopped with his dick held in her throat.

He couldn't see a wedding ring due to the fact that her Deadpool outfit covered her hands and there were no pictures of a happy or unhappy couple anywhere he could see.

Her eyes looked up at him with no remorse as she flexed her throat muscles, making his body spasm uncontrollably. She held the stare and the corners of her mouth rose in a smile.

"If my friend is outside the door then who are you?" she asked, flicking her tongue over the head of his dick.

Jerome held her the back of her head and let her flex as a key slipped into the lock next to his hips. His face swung to the lock and he pressed his feet into the floor, waiting for the door to open against his back. But nothing moved as they key entered but didn't open the door.

The first series of bangs on the door were less police raid and more Jehovah's Witness.

"TAMALA OPEN THE FUCKING DOOR!"

"Not yet honey... kinda busy at the moment." Tamala said, taking the dick out of her throat and holding it away from her face.

"I'VE GOT YOUR 'FRIEND' OUT HERE SAYS YOU INVITED HIM ROUND!"

Tamala looked up with her eyebrows raised, waiting for the answer herself. Jerome looked down at her with confusion across his face. He wasn't sure what answer they were expecting. He stared at her differently, now that he knew her name. It seemed to fit as Tamala, her husband and her friend were all hung on silence as Jerome looked around for an answer.

"I'm... Jerome from P.I.N.S." he said tentatively, with his hands still holding Tamala's face.

"WHO THE FUCK IS JEROME... NAAH... YOU'RE NOT GOING ANYWHERE," the husband said, holding onto the stranger standing on his doorstep. "SO ONE ISN'T ENOUGH, YOU HAD TO INVITE TWO DICKS ROUND?"

"Well, if you and your brother aren't enough for me then I'm gonna have to find pleasure elsewhere," she said turning her head to the door while flicking short stabs at Jerome's dick.

"MY BROTHER AS WELL?! ALRIGHT THEN... WATCH WHAT HAPPENS WHEN I GET IN THIS HOUSE... OPEN THE FUUUUUUUCKING DOOR!"

Tamala looked up, "You're DEFINITELY under the clock. He'll go for the back door in a minute, which isn't locked so... either come or go..."

"OPEN THE DOOR YOU FUCKING SLAG BITCH..." the husband shouted, pounding on the door with a fist while holding onto the other visitor at her door who was trying to escape the grip that had his shirt twisted around his hand.

Jerome could feel fear beginning to run through him. Beads of sweat were forming on his itchy forehead and the corridor seemed warmer than it was when he arrived. The feeing of arrival he'd worked up to had dissipated and his erection was all but limp in her grip. He wasn't sure how big her husband was but from the vibrations of the door pounding behind his back, Jerome could sense a strong hand and foot behind it.

"Open your mouth and stick your tongue out," Jerome said, taking his dick from her grip.

He ran it against her wet, dripping tongue until he began to rise, listening to an angry inaudible conversation on the doorstep. Jerome thought he heard a punch land as someone moaned in pain behind him.

"YOU THINK YOU CAN GET RID OF ME THAT EASILY? I TOLD YOU I'M NOT FUCKING GOING ANYWHERE..."

Jerome returned to his stroke, one hand under her chin and the other on her forehead. Dipping slightly, he aimed straight for her throat with a slow stroke that tickled the underside of his penis but felt good at the same time.

Watching her eyes, Jerome could see she was looking towards the side of her house. They both heard the creak of a metal gate.

"Come on for fuck sake," Jerome said, feeling under pressure. Watching mouth water leak onto the floor was the porn Jerome needed and he felt his balls tighten.

It was then that he looked up, down the corridor and into the kitchen where a tall figure filled the back door window. A large angry face stared back at him as he continued to fuck Deadpool in the face. She raised her arm to wave at her husband, who was desperate to get in the house.

The handle on the door began to rattle but Jerome kept his eyes on the prize on her knees in front of him. He was closer than before and he didn't want to lose the feeling.

At the back door, the large figure was pointing at him and flicking quickly through keys.

"I'd hurry if I were you... he sounds pissed off," Tamala said, keeping her mouth open.

Jerome was dipping his hips to get to the back of her throat.

The man at the back door had a key in the lock but it wasn't the right one.

Jerome lost focus temporarily when he heard the key in the backdoor, watching to make sure it didn't open.

The man switched to another key and screamed out in frustration.

Jerome looked down and knew he was a second from painting all over her. In his mind he was planning past his orgasm; had his trousers up and was off running down the path, not stopping until he reached the train station.

The man threw the keys down and began to punch the glass. Having to watch an angry man punching a glass window just get to him made Jerome aroused in a different way and he began to smile at him. Then he winked and that really pissed him off.

The man disappeared from the door, leaving Jerome with nothing but face fucking to focus on. His stroke slowed further and every thrust made Tamala heave, but hold in her gag reflex.

"Alllllllmost there," he said under his breath, wanting to drift away and let his head fall back. But a quarter of his attention was on the back door.

"OH DON'T FUCKING WORRY HONEY... I'LL LET MYSELF IN..."

Those words sounded ominous coming from the back door where no one could be seen. With the sound of squelching and and splattering making him tense up, feeling the good feeling of an orgasm arriving, Jerome froze for a moment, hovering peacefully in the limbo of almost ALMOST there and nowhere near.

"Oh yeah, oh yeah, oh yea, oh ye..." Jerome trailed off, making a fist with his hand. He banged it against the front door.

He reached down, slid his wet dick out of her Tamala's mouth and moaned as her eager, anticipating face tilted back with her mouth open. Jerome's moan was loud and unashamed and his first stream of semen went over Tamala's waiting face and onto what looked like a very expensive rug leading towards the kitchen and the back door.

Jerome's hands and body were concentrating on the orgasm which had arrived and was now splashing on Tamala's excited face. But his eyes were the size of saucers as he watched an extra large ficus come flying through the back door.

Below, Tamala was licking her lips, using her gloved hands to scoop loose trails back into her mouth while moaning extra loudly.

"FUCKING COME DID YA?! COME ON MY FUCKING WIFE!?" the husband said, reaching for the lock through the glass-less door.

Tamala had his dick in her hand and was sucking every last soldier out of Jerome while he tried to reach down for his trousers, watching the back door lock click and the door fly open.

"Shiiiiiiiiiiiiiiiiiiit," Jerome said, pushing Tamala onto her ass and fumbling with the front door lock. Holding his trousers up, he fiddled with the fancy lock, hearing a kitchen draw open.

"I'M GONNA FUCKING KILL YOU!"

Sweat marked his armpits and Jerome could feel semen tricking down his thighs, running a cold shiver down his spine along with fear.

"Come on, come on, come on... FUCK!"

"Turn it left, then right Jerome from P.I.N.S," said Tamala, sucking her fingers and sitting on the floor, with her truck-sized husband coming up quickly behind her with a meat cleaver.

The weight of his footsteps told Jerome how close he was and if he didn't get the door open and slip out of it soon, he was going to be cut in half.

He turned the lock to the left and heard it click before turning it to the right for a deeper click and the front door opened.

"ON MY FUCKING RUG?!" the husband shouted.

Jerome swung the door open, still holding his trousers and took one huge leap out of the door. He wasn't sure if he felt the wind from the blade brush past his head but he didn't wait to find out. Taking three steps at a time, he landed on both feet and didn't stop. He jumped over the unconscious man in the suit at the foot of the steps and ran while doing up his belt and trousers at the same time.

He didn't look back until he was a good seven to eight houses away, and he could no longer hear the heavy breathing of a man with a meat clever behind him.

A healthy distance had been made between Jerome and the cleaver wielder and he began to jog as he was about to turn onto the main road.
"I'M GONNA FIND YOU AND WHEN I DO..."
"YEAH... WHEN YOU CATCH ME, THANK ME FOR MY DONATION..." Jerome shouted, giving the middle finger as he took off around a corner, merging into a massive group of commuters who'd just come out of the train station.
"The boys in the office won't believe this one."

FETISH OF THE FULL-FIGURED

Cheryl drank two bottles of Pinot Grigio, four glasses of vodka and Red Bull, three and a half shots of Tequila, two brandy jelly shots and was wobbling towards her bed, kicking off her heels.

"You have no idea how funny you look right now!" Byron laughed, stumbling into the bed side table.

"Awww... whatever fucking... what..." Cheryl fell back on her bed and watched the ceiling spin.

"Just 'cuz it's your birthday, doesn't mean you can't get alcohol poisoning."

Cheryl's thick figure rolled from her back to her stomach as Byron walked around the bed.

"Take my skirt off please. I'm feeling..." Cheryl sighed and closed her eyes, breathing heavily.

"Oi oiii... don't fall asleep on me. We've got birthday sex on the menu."

Byron had half his clothes off by the time he looked at Cheryl, who was out like a light. Laying on her side with her skirt down to her knees and a deep bassy snore erupting from her throat.

"Awww babe, don't fall asleep."

Byron stumbled to the bed and tried to wake his sleeping girlfriend. She separated her thighs and itched the black patches on her inner thighs before passing gas and clapping her lips together.

"Fat fucker!" Byron mumbled as he slapped Cheryl's hips and sat on the bed while checking his phone. "You know how fucking horny I am?"

Cheryl was overweight and happy to work it and that's what Byron liked about her. She didn't act like her weight was a hindrance on her life or could stop her from doing anything and it was that bubbly, life- affirming personality that drew Byron to her side for the past four years.

"Bitch!"

He tried to stand up but he fell back on the bed. His stomach started to rumble and gripe, which paused him. He covered his mouth and before he could make another attempt to get up, chunks of chicken and sweetcorn began to pump through his fingers.

Leaning forward, he aimed his mouth away from the bed and Cheryl's sleeping body and threw up on the floor.

"Eww for the love of fuck..." Byron said, spitting in the puddle of brown and yellow mush on the floor. He got up from his hands and knees, sipping water from the side table.

He unbuckled his trousers, making sure they missed the vomit puddle by his feet.

"I swear I didn't drink that much!"

His body dropped back and he exhaled, trying to ignore the feeling of a second wave of vomit rising up. He finished the water and dropped back next to Cheryl who was snoring contently.

Behind him, Cheryl burped and farted at the same time while moaning pleasurably.

Byron's stomach calmed down as Cheryl's gas passed his nose. He wrinkled his nose and turned to look at her.

"What the fuck was that baby?"

Cheryl was laying on her side with her shirt open, exposing her fully rounded stomach which rested on the bed next to her. She scratched her stomach while Byron was watching with a growing erection in his boxers. He could feel his nipples rising and his stomach calming as her bra rose and fell.

"Fuck this!" Byron said taking a deep breath.

Ignoring the rising smell of chicken and sweetcorn, Byron took his dick out from the flap of his boxers and got on his knees on the bed, shuffling next to Cheryl.

Uncovering her stomach and folding her shirt behind her back, Byron opened his thighs and scooted right up to Cheryl. He ran a hand over the rolls of her stomach and watched his erection stand tall.

"Hmmm..."

Byron reached into his shirt pocket and pulled out a small tub of Vaseline. He dabbed two fingers in and smeared the cream in a valley of her stomach, grinning as he anticipated the feeling. He dabbed again and rubbed it on on his dick.

"Oh yeah," he said.

Cheryl began coughing in her sleep and Byron moved quickly, dropping his dick in a groove of her stomach. Keeping his balance steady, he stayed still hoping she wouldn't wake up.

"Lupalinda," Cheryl muttered before falling back into her slumber.

With hands on the meat of her stomach, Byron stroked her skin against his dick and shuddered while looking at the ceiling.

"Fuuuuuuck... this feels fucking good."

Watching his dick slide between the rolls of her stomach, Byron began to grind harder. He wanted to moan and slap her skin but her snoring kept him silent. The fact she was asleep made him pump slowly while moulding her skin around him.

"Oh yeah... that's the shit I'm talking about... come on... yeah..."

As he was fucking her stomach, making her rock back and forth, he could feel goodness sneaking down his spine. The Vaseline in her crevice was mixing with his pre-cum and creating a white cream that was foaming around his dick.

"Oh fuccccck," Byron moaned gripping her stomach tight. "Come on you big bitch! Make me nut!"

Byron swallowed hard, making sure any feelings of throwing up were contained and pushed to the back of his mind. He pulled her skirt down and separated her thighs so he could get a wet finger inside her.

"Oh yeaaaaaaaah," he shouted.

Cheryl woke up suddenly, looking around the room as Byron's dick slid out of her stomach groove. He held himself and started to masturbate quickly. He came hard and shot over her body where it splattered into his vomit mush on the floor. The following thick streams sprayed over her clothes, the bed and in her afro puffs.

"What... did... huh?" she mumbled.

"Ohhhh..." he moaned and whistled while working the rest of his seed out. "Oh baby, I love you!"

Cheryl looked down at her stomach and sighed, dropping her head back on the bed. "Did you just fuck..."

"Your stomach yes. I told you not to fall asleep."

"You are... fucking sick!" Cheryl mumbled then covered her mouth and jumped off the bed, getting ready to vomit.

As her feet hit the ground, her toes slipped in Byron's sperm and vomit and she slipped, grabbing for anything that would break her fall.

"Oh shit baby, I erm..."

Byron couldn't see where Cheryl fell but he could hear her as she screamed and was throwing up at the same time.

"WHAT THE FUUUUUUUUCK?" Cheryl shrieked.

PANDORA THE COOK – C.L.I.T.S

Lamar blinked. Once, then again. A third time to be sure and a fourth followed with a smile.

He could smell the scent of eucalyptus bedsheets and an annoyingly loud ticking clock.

He was in his bed.

His eyes closed then opened again widely as he rolled his wrists, no chains or restraints of any kind. He moved his feet, no chains or restraints. He rolled onto his back and sighed as he stared at his ceiling, enjoying the sounds of random traffic passing by his window.

"Lamborghini mercy... what kind of fucked UP dream was THAT?" "I love the way every single man we've visited thinks it's a dream." Lamar frowned and shot up straight as he heard a voice that wasn't

Keisha's.?At the foot of his bed stood 19 women in dark robes with hoods up

and the letters C.L.I.T.S across the front in pink letters.?" Morning Lamar," said a voice to his left.?He turned to see a woman sitting in her robe with her hood down

around her shoulders, rolling an unbelievably long spliff.?" I don't remember you," Lamar said, looking her up and down.?" So it wasn't a dream then? You weren't supposed to meet me, not

until the end." "Where the fuck is..." "Shhhhh... Keisha's sleeping." The woman sitting in his favourite smoking chair pointed with her

face for Lamar to look behind himself. He turned slowly to see Keisha's shoulder rising and falling with sleep.

He turned back to the women standing at the foot of his bed looking in his direction and the one woman sitting next to him.

430

"Pandora The Cook. Nice to meet you," she said. "I would offer to shake your hand but I'm kind of in the middle of something at the moment."

"You do what's you're doing," he said quietly.

"So, Lamar," she whispered as she sprinkled crushed weed over a layer of tobacco. "How do you feel?"

"Confused as fuck!"

"Aren't they all?" a voice said from the cluster of women and they all giggled.

"Ladies... thank you. Now, it's okay to feel confused. I would be. It's not like any of this is normal. I'm here to basically answer the hundreds of questions you've had for my girls."

"WHAT THE..." "Shhh..." He whispered. "What the fuck are you doing in my house? How the

fuck did you..."

"Okay, I'm gonna answer the questions that matter. We are the C.L.I.T.S – that stands for Clever Ladies Investigating Terrible Situations and we are a group of intelligent and very sexy women who... know stuff."

"What, breaking and entering? Kidnapping? Torture?" "Who tortured you?" "I might have a little bit," a hooded voice mumbled. "Yeah, me too."

"I wanted to fuck his face a little."

"Okay ladies, bring it back home. What we do isn't torture. What we do is mainly entertainment for ourselves. But we entertain ourselves and try to help men like you. Did you know Keisha is a day or two away from breaking up with you?"

"How the fuck could you know that? What, one of you bitches psychic or suttin'?"

A collective groan rose from the women.

"You know what a bitch is Lamar? A bitch is a beauty in tremendously cute heels. I heard that somewhere and I like it. So, please be more creative with your put downs. Number two, after all the the things my ladies have shown you, do you still think we don't know how to find shit out? We're women Lamar, we know when we've reached or are about to reach the end of our tether with a man. And you sir are skating on slush at the moment."

"You lot think after all this, I'm staying with Keisha? She got you lot to do this to me."

Pandora rolled a small piece of card into a tube and slid it on the right side of his super duper spliff.

"Keisha didn't ask us to do this to you. Keisha doesn't even know who we are. Well she does now 'cuz we left her a little note to let her know we were gonna borrow you for a minute but none of this is up to her. We've been watching you."

"What the fuck for?" Lamar began to swing his legs out of the bed and he heard something click clack from the direction of the women. He slowly put his feet back under the duvet.

"Didn't I just say you're skating on slush? That means thin ice is no more... you've past the last nerve, pissed off is where she is and all it takes is one more argument, one more complaint, one more look of disgust in your direction and it's bye bye Lamar. One more disappointment in the journey of your relationship career."

Lamar frowned. "You don't know my life." Licking the sticky part of the paper, Pandora started to roll. "Erm, Tisha – three months. Yvette – two months. Eva – a week.

Madeline – four weeks, Rashida, Elaine and Janine – one session. Stacey, Francis..."

He was looking at Pandora like she reached into his loins and ran down his conquests and failures like they were names on a spreadsheet.

"...the Creole lady, what was her name? Janet... that didn't last long at all did it? Briana, Verina, Ursula, Trentina, Dionne, those sisters. I mean come on Lamar, you can trust that we KNOW you!"

"Who the FUCK are you lot?" Lamar asked with disgust and confusion on his face.

"We told you. Clever ladies investigating terrible situations. It may seem like we just wanted to have fun with you by tying you up and making you our bitch in many different ways, but as it always is with women, there's a method to our madness. We've been trying to remind you of the many ways to love and appreciate the one that loves you. Trust me, we've seen Keisha knock back some real absolute PDTO's so she must REALLY love you."

"What are PDTO's?"

"Those men that make your panties drop and your thighs open. For a man, it's that woman with a nice ass and a nice tits that makes you fantasise about opening her pussy and fucking like it's the last nut on earth. For us, there are men out there who walk past us and it's like we have to fight to keep our panties on."

"Hold on, when was she talking to..."

"Focus Lamar, this isn't about when has she been talking to other men, this is about you fixing up yourself so you never have to worry about her talking to other men. For the record, she's knocked quite a few back."

"Look at it this way," said a voice he recognised from the group.

"She's knocked back enough potential PDTO dick, there'd be enough for us if we took 'em."

"Exactly. You've got a beautiful girlfriend there Lamar. Remind her of that everyday. From now on, every orgasm you give her will be heaven sent, every meal will be restaurant quality, you'll pay attention like it's money out of your pocket and Keisha will be bragging to her friends about how absolutely amazing you are. And you know why Lamar?"

He was listening intently as she spoke. "No, why?" Pandora rolled her spliff, which was as long as a coat hanger. "Because if we hear otherwise, we're gonna have to come back here

and borrow you again for our intensive weekend experience. And there's more C.L.I.T.S there. And you don't wanna meet the rest of us. So, do we have a deal?"

For the first time, Lamar didn't know what to say. For most of the night, he had been pissed off and irritated that he had been subjected to all of this beyond his will. He was going to contact some of his 'friends' who knew people to find these women and make them pay. But, with the women standing at the end of his bed, and one of them lighting a spliff next to him, Lamar felt fear.

All of this for Keisha? He thought.

"Yeah, we have a deal!" he said, actually believing the words he was speaking.

It wasn't like he didn't love Keisha. She wasn't perfect but she was perfect for him. Everything about her curved exactly to him, they laughed like maniacs, enjoyed a drink or two and even supported the same football team.

Lamar started to think about his treatment of Keisha over the years and he could see where he started to fall off. He loved her but he didn't show her as much as he used to.

An image of the multiple camera shots of his poor love making popped into his head and he looked up into the corners of his room, making three women laugh in the group.

"Deal?" Pandora asked again, lighting a match and taking a long inhale.

"Yeah, we got a deal." Lamar replied.?" Thought so. Yay... none of them ever say no, I love it." The women gave each other high-fives at once and Lamar jumped. "So, now what?" "Now, you go to sleep and enjoy the rest of the time you have left

with your lady. Night night." Pandora The Cook took three tokes of the long spliff, inhaled three

times then blew the smoke in Lamar's face. He blinked repeatedly, enjoying the smell of beautiful high grade before he closed his eyes.

That was the last thing Lamar saw or heard.

His eyes opened and he was laying on his side, facing the wall. He blinked a few times before looking around, sitting up and scanning his empty bedroom. The sun was rising through the window, dancing over the edge of the bed. He could hear Keisha breathing behind him, looking over his shoulder at her. She was peaceful and breathing quietly, unaware of the madness he went through while she probably laid out, enjoying the bed without him.

Sliding quietly out of the bed, Lamar shuffled into his slippers and crept out of the bedroom. He was following his nose which took him to the kitchen and his eyes lit up and he rubbed his hands together excitedly.

On the breakfast bar was a spread of so much food, Lamar didn't know where to look. Steaming scrambled eggs, bacon, pancakes, potato hash, fried tomatoes, French toast, waffles, fruit salad, slices of ham and cheese and a bowl of Croissants and muffins.

"Oh HELL YEAH!"

Approaching the feast, Lamar's eyes drew to a small card in front of the food.

He read to himself.?" Let's start with breakfast." Keisha slid her arms round his waist and looked around his arm. "Start what? OoOoOooo yum... breakfast."

"Let's start with breakfast," he repeated.

Lamar turned the card over and ran his finger over the embossed letters.

C.L.I.T.S

THE HEAL OF HEELS

Tatiana Blue I am.?And in case you don't know, I'm the sexiest bitch in this book! Let's just get that out of the way.?It's a big truth, hard for some to take and there is no one that can

tell me any different. Not even Mr Oh.?This isn't his story, this is MY story. You already know most of it,

thanks to him and his tales of Tatiana, but this one is my story. I'm telling it from start to finish and I'm gonna fill you in on all you wanna know.

So let's rewind for a second and flashback to the last time you saw me. That was Russell's place after leaving him tied naked to a chair after having given him some good, sweet extra loving.

Well, first things first, yes I was pregnant, I wasn't joking about that. Yes I know it wasn't the best way to do it, but I'm not your every day, normal type of woman now am I?

I'm normal now though.?Normal ish.?I'm the proud mother of Charlotte Florence Blue, the most beautiful,

amazing, tiniest, most chocolatey little girl I've ever seen.?Hell yes I'm biased and I don't give a fuck. Ain't no baby prettier than my little Cha'Cha.

So you've been wondering where I've been and what I've been doing. Well I had a baby. But before that, I was a busy little bitch (that's beauty in tremendously cute heels).

After I left Russell's that day, I went on what people on road would call a 'madness'. I had to get busy, I had nine months to get as many shoes as possible before I couldn't see my own feet any more.

I was dangling from factory ceilings while trying not to vomit on security guards below, cramping while trying to climb out of a fourth floor window, experiencing false labour while being chased along a rooftop, back pain while holding Chloroform over a designer's face. I was picking Gianvito Rossi leather mesh pumps and

Givenchy floral print leather from Selfridges and Zanotti snake stiletto sandal and Charlotte Olympia what's the scoop satin pumps from Harvey Nichols while my stomach got bigger and bigger.

I say nine months, it was more like seven before I well and truly gave up and couldn't lift my own body weight. I had my girl Maya help me when I got too heavy.

Oh, I've been training her. She's a good little thief now too. Real quick, nimble, very clever, but she's part time though. I don't think

she's ready for a full-time lover of stealing shoes but she's a great help.

By the time I had what I needed, which was enough shoes to keep and enough shoes to sell, I figured, steal some for myself, steal a few more in different sizes and colours I don't like and sell 'em on eBay.

And guess what? I'm doing alright. Well more than alright. I've got eBay on lock right now. I got shoes flying out the door from like five or six different eBay accounts and I'm making money foot over ankle. I think it's six accounts... no, seven. Actually... wait... is it eight? Oh, I dunno.

Either way, I'm their highest seller at the moment. And if your wondering how you can sell stolen shoes on eBay and not get arrested, well, why the fuck would I tell you that? Get your own hustle. Let's just say, I don't need to go back to a regular nine-to-five any time soon.

Yeah, I'm THAT good right now.

Well, at this current moment, I'm actually not doing too well but we'll get to that in a minute.

So, after I stopped stealing and took Maya's advice and just relaxed and sat at home watching my stomach grow and dealing with the morning sickness, stretch marks, loss of appetite and badly swollen feet, my Charlotte was born a month and a half early at Whipps Cross hospital in Leytonstone.

Little madam came into the world peaceful and pristine as you'd like and she's been that way ever since. This was ideal considering where we live now but, again, I'll come back to that in a minute.

To be honest, I'm a shoe thief on hiatus at the moment.

I'm elbow deep in nappies from a child that shits more than she eats, my place has become a mountain peak of vests, baby towels, bottles and formula tubs and my days of fabulous, free travelling, intricate heel lifting manoeuvres are a memory to me.

I can't tell you the last time I went to one of my stash houses and just sat and looked at my shoes. I can tell you the last time I got shit on my hand changing a nappy though.

If I'm honest, I miss my babies like a man misses pussy in prison. All of 'em. My Aquazzura Beverley Hills sandals, my Sophia Webster butterfly pumps, my Giuseppe Zanotti biker boots. I miss the smell of my Alexander McQueen cage sandals, the way the heel looks on my Alexandre Birman python sandals, the ruffles on my Nicholas Kirkwood ruffled pumps, the colour on my Casadei monochrome leather. My

Valentino Rockstud heels, my Zanotti snakeskin boots, my Saint Laurent Tribute sandals. I miss them all.

Do you know how many new pairs of Louboutins there are that I don't have? It's like sacrilege. I managed to hit the Louboutin store on Motcomb street before Charlotte but the day I went to the Mount street store in Mayfair, a stomach cramp kicked in and that was the last time I went out to 'work'.

You know who I really miss? Maybe even more than my shoes? I miss Russell... that man has been the sugar in my dreams ever since I last saw him. Ever since the arrival of our baby, yes OUR baby. Of course I put Russell on the birth certificate. He IS her father whether he knows it or not.

But that's a chapter that is going to be opened and maintained today.

Today is nine months to the day that Charlott.e was conceived and I'm actually nervous.

Me. Tatiana Blue. NERVOUS. Ha!

I haven't been this nervous since Harrods and that was years ago. Well there was this one time in Italy when I saw an

Interpol car as I left a warehouse but this feeling is definitely worse. It's the feeling of knowing you're in trouble and you still have to go home and face the music.

I told Russell I'd be back in nine months and I plan to keep my word. Of course he doesn't know that I'm already here and have been living above him since but hey, if a policeman can't find you and you live on the floor above him, maybe he should find another job.

We moved in, well we were moved in, about a month and a half ago. Due to the fact that my princess came early, I decided I wanted to be able to keep an eye on Russell and make sure he stayed ready for me, well us, to come back into his life.

I got the 'still very secretive about what he does' Quincy to help move our stuff in with the help of some of his 'friends' Real quiet men who didn't say much but looked like they'd possibly killed once or thrice before.

I would've moved myself but Quincy pointed out that there was more chance of me running into Russell that way so he and his boys moved us right in. Feng sui'ed the place and everything.

Two spacious bedrooms, open plan kitchen, balcony with an excellent view of the Olympic park and literally across Great Eastern road from my old flat. Always tickles me to think that if Russell moved here a few years earlier, he would've found me without even realising he was looking for me.

So here I am. One floor above Russell Reed, the policeman with a fetish for illegal upskirt film making, the father of my child and the sexiest piece of chocolate this side of the Thames. And he has no idea I can see him.

Another bonus to having Quincy move me in was that he noticed the security cameras in the building which had been tampered with. A small but noticeable black box had been fitted to each camera and blinked a green light next to the camera's solid red light. If you didn't know what you were looking at then you wouldn't think anything of it. But Quincy, as I've said, does some very strange, clandestine work and he noticed it straight away.

The little black box gave someone direct access to the camera feeds, allowing them to watch the comings and goings of every resident in the art deco tower block called the Stratford Eye.

Could've only been Russell. He WAS thinking about me after all. He knew I'd come and he wanted to watch me when I arrived. So sweet. You know you're on a man's mind when he alters every security camera in the building to make sure you arrive safely.

When Quincy called me at Maya's, where I was staying, and told me, I thought it was so romantic. He went to all that trouble for little old me!?

I got Quincy to put a scrambler on his cameras so every time I came or went, the feed scrambled. Was a bit more trouble to get that fitted. Quincy had to actually break into Russell's flat to get that in place but he did it. Even slid in a multi-view camera behind his wall clock so I could watch him in his apartment from wherever I wanted.

With soundproof covering on the wooden floors, me and Charlotte slipped in at night and woke up the next morning watching Russell sleeping next to his camera feeds, looking for me when I was already here.

And here we are! Charlotte is sleeping, Russell is home from work early and about to have a shower and Maya is on her way to...

My front door knocked, taking me away from one of my many many eBAy accounts, which were all just anagrams of my name: Labia Tauten, A Butane Tail, Anal Tuba Tie, Bail Ate Tuna, A Beat Untila, Labia Tea Nut, Bait Ale Aunt, to name a few.

With Charlotte taking a nap, I shuffled to the door, tying up my dreadlocks, which were down to my lower back and took a long stretch, giggling to myself that it could've been Russell at my front door.

Peeking, just to make sure it wasn't him, I opened the door and yawned in Maya's face.

"Ewww... dragon breath," Maya said with a hearty chuckle. "You ready to do the do?"

"Of course not, I'm shitting myself. I'm usually all Slick Rick about this, but I've never done THIS before. Did you get my text?"

Maya slid past me grabbing Aretha, my left breast, while my arms were behind my head wrapping my hair.

" No, my phone is doing some madness at the moment. Where's my lil' Blue thang?"

"Shuuuuush with your loud self, she's sleeping..."

I paused. I had to because my eyes and ears were now drawn to Maya's feet. More to the Charlotte Olympia suede boots that she was about to clop on my floor.

"Ermmm... hello?" I said, pointing at her feet.?" Oh yeah, the 'rules'." "They're not rules, it's one rule," I replied kicking the door closed.

"No heels on the floor." Maya unzipped her boots and I tried to remember the last pair of

boots I stole and, for the life of me, I couldn't even picture them in my head. I couldn't even remember the door number of one of my stash houses, let alone all four of them.

My fingers slowly caressed the suede of her left boot and jealousy washed over me from my head to my toes. I wanted them. I wanted the satisfaction of picking them up from a secure place without anyone knowing I was there.

"You like?" "These are very yummy scrummy. Where'd you get 'em from?" "Brit Awards. Hilton Hotel. Katy Perry. She had a pair in red too

which I got for you." "Thanks and say no more," I laughed at the 'road' colloquialism,

trying to suck the green-eyed fever into the pit of my stomach. "Nervous are we?" Maya whispered, walking on her tip-toes towards

Charlotte's room.?" I am a little, I'm not gonna lie but it feels like this is gonna be the

end of a big storm that's been raining over my head." "Yeah, yeah, yeah... fuck all that philosophical shit, this ain't

Instagram. How are you feeling about seeing him again?" "Who, Russell Reed, the father of my child, the policeman who has been working for years trying to arrest me, the upskirt fiend who became a father against his will? Yeah, I'm feeling upbeat, chipper and Kool and the gang."

Maya poked her head in Charlotte's room before sliding on her socks across my floor and into the kitchen.

"For such an event, we need libation," Maya said, finding a bottle of white rum in my cupboard.

"Fuck yeah," I added, glad that my girl was here to help me numb the nerves that were making my hands shake.

The reason I was so nervous about seeing Russell again is, well, since the day I closed his door, I felt guilty. I didn't exactly give him a chance to do or say, well, anything. I didn't give him a chance to get to know me or find out anything about me. Then again, his nine-to- five consisted of trying to find and arrest me so the guilt wasn't pure. I felt kind of justified-ish.

I could've just taken him home, found out what he had on me and kept it moving. I didn't need to fuck him, technically rape him, and let him get me up the duff. I didn't need to take all those pictures and leave them in the envelope, even though that was fun. To be honest, I'm not as radical a thinker as I used to be.

Fiddling with my fingers, and flexing my toes on my hardwood floor, I didn't see Maya standing in front of me holding a glass of grey liquid and a rolled up spliff.

"To the balcony," I chanted.

The sun was going down in the distance bathing the skyline in orange and purple while traffic provided the soundtrack to a perfect London evening. No breeze, nicely warm t-shirt weather, perfect.

"So, talk to me buttercup... you're about to see the love of your life for the first time in nine months, how're you feeling?"

"Less questions, more lighting."

I waited for her to light the spliff before snatching it out of her hand. The shock on her face and the playful kick she gave me said she knew she got caught slipping.

"So what're you gonna say to him?"

"I'll start with hello and freestyle from there I guess. To be honest I've just been watching the days tick away without thinking about what I would actually say to him."

This was my first spliff in a long time. After I got pregnant, I quit smoking altogether and I told Maya not to bring any weed around me until the the day I planned to see Russell.

I'd only taken three tokes and I wished I didn't wait so long between spliffs because I could feel my entire body throbbing on a cloud of hazy goodness. The skyline fogged over right before my eyes and I had to rest my head on the balcony railing for a moment.

"What is this?" I asked, handing the roll up to Maya. "Don't ask, don't tell." "Yeah, but I am asking, so do tell."

"That's what it's called, don't ask, don't tell." "For fuck sake!" I laughed.?Numbness was throbbing through my lips and I sat down with my

back against the glass railing.?" What time you going down there?" "As soon as this drink is finished. Best to just do it and get it out of

the way." "Yeah, I agree," Maya said blowing smoke rings into the air. "Just

have it done and done. I know your probably thinking about what his reaction will be... do you think he'll have you arrested?"

"I wasn't thinking that, but I am now. Thanks dipshit."

Maya couldn't stop laughing. "I am sooo sorry, I thought you would've realised that he could be SO pissed off that he actually arrests you. Imagine if he did. He'd arrest you for not only the shoes... and if they have a file on you as big as you say then that's a LOT of shoes, right?"

"Oh yeah..." "Then there's the kidnapping, the torture, the..." "Wait, I didn't torture him. I just drugged him and tied him up.

That's not torture," I reasoned while exhaling thick smoke above my head slowly.

"Well it's not a spa treatment. You know how the law works. They'll call it torture. So that's theft, no that's multiple theft, burglary, kidnapping, torture, assault, rape..."

"Is it REALLY rape? I mean he never once told me to stop. That's my defence. The whole time, from the moment I slipped him in to the time he came, he never once told me to stop. Alright, yeah he told me to untie him but he never said stop."

"That's your defence?" Maya laughed.?" And I'm sticking to it." We shared a high-five and a chuckle as the marijuana mixed with

the rum/ginger beer in my glass and I felt good all over. I was starting to feel less nervous about seeing Russell and worrying less about being arrested. To me, that was a long shot. He'd have a lot to do if that was his plan and I don't think he'd do that. He better not.

Fuck that, Russell loves me. He wouldn't do that.

"So you really think he's gonna be like 'oh hey, there you are, I've been looking for you'? And that's it?!"

The picture of such a simple reintroduction in my head made me laugh out loud while inhaling and I started coughing heavily. Maya slapped and rubbed my back while laughing at me with drool around the corners of my lips.

I caught my breath. "You trying to fucking kill me?"

"I'm just tryna prepare you for every eventuality that could happen. This isn't just you coming home after a long day at work... he could actually punch you in the face."

"He's a fiend for an upskirt but he's not stupid. Punch who and live where?"

This was what I needed. My home slice, ride or die, been there since day one friend in my corner making sure I've got my shit right before going down there and expecting happy families. Not that I hadn't thought about it myself. That Russell might not be so happy to see me and wanna do something stupid like take me in. I've taken steps for that eventuality, just FYI.

If you know my story, then you know Maya's been there from day one. She's become the voice in reason when I get ideas of grandeur like stealing from a Sultan with security in every room of his house or some shit like that. That one was definitely a challenge by the way.

I took the last puffs of the spliff and threw the burning end over the balcony, backed my drink and jumped to my feet.

"Starting to hear that Rocky music in your head huh?" Maya asked, slowly making it to her feet.

"Yep... the drink sweet me, the weed sweet me, I'm sweet and ready to go."

She rubbed my shoulders like a trainer motivating a heavyweight before a prize fight. I let my dreads loose and swung them free, ready to close a chapter and possibly open a new one. I suddenly felt immensely conscious of myself and my body and the way it had changed during the pregnancy.

Quincy and Maya said that I looked exactly the same but I felt different. I felt heavier in the thighs, my six-pack wasn't as visible as before and Lauryn and Aretha, my breasts, had gone up two cup sizes.

"Let's go get 'em champ..."

We marched back into the flat humming Eye of The Tiger. Maya spun me by my shoulders and gave me a once over from my hair to my face – pulling random fluff from my cheeks – to my clothes, which were tracksuit bottom comfortable.

"No I'm not gonna change Maya!" "Whaaaaaat? I didn't even say anything." "You didn't have to... I could see you were about to say suttin'." "You know maybe a dress or some tight trousers, show him what is

truly standing at his front door." "I'm not going there to fuck him am I?"

"But if he offered you some dick, you wouldn't take it? God knows he hasn't had any in a while, no thanks to you."

"First of all," I said pointing at Maya with a full comedic attitude. "He doesn't know I've been sneaky enough to cock-block every piece of pussy he's tried to get since I left. Secondly, if Russell Reed offered me some dick, you best believe that dick is accepted, signed for and delivered on time, yessur!"

Our combined cackle must've sounded awful to my neighbours but the way my given fucks were set up, I just didn't care. Let 'em hear. Let him hear.

"Okay, well, on with the footwear and get yourself gone."
I froze.

This was it. The moment I'd been building up to for the last nine months. I was about to be face-to-face with Russell Reed, the man I wanted. The man I knew was the man for me who was also my complete opposite. Him being a law man and me being an unlawful woman. I was so lost in my own thoughts that I didn't notice Maya sat me down and was putting my Adidas basketball boots on my feet.

"You can do this... look at it this way. Get this done and we can start giving Charlotte to Russell while we 'work'."

"Always a silver lining with you ain't it Maya?" "Hey, the sun has to shine on a dog's ass some day." This woman was so stupidly funny and it was little lines like that one

that made me glad I had her as a friend. Pretty much my only friend. As a shoe thief, you meet a lot of people, run from a lot more people

and get close to very few. I met and kept in contact with a few mums I met during my pregnancy but I don't keep in touch as much as I used to. Sucks but its the life you choose right?

My arm was pulled and I jumped to my feet and was shuffled in front of a full length mirror next to my front door.

"You ready?" Maya asked, with her head peeking around my hair. "I'm ready." I wrapped a stretch of material around my dreads. "You ready to go get your man?" Maya put my jacket on my

shoulders.?" He's already my man, I just need to tell him that!" "Damn right!" "Okay, let's g... hold on where's my phone?" I spun on the balls of my feet, trying to remember where I was when

I last saw my phone.?I called Maya to make sure she was still coming and sat... it's on the

sofa.?As if on cue, my phone started to ring.

"Thanks babe, I know where it is." I mumbled to Maya.?" That's not me calling you." "Oh, well then who the hell..." Finding my phone nestled between the cushions, I checked the

display and saw that Quincy was calling me.?" What it is Mr Secretive? Off somewhere being secretive?" "I found him!" "You what love? You found who?" "Him. I found him!" "No! No you fucking didn't!? Not now! Awwwww for fuck sake!" I started to lose it. I was about to throw my phone against my front door when Maya slid in and took it from me, sensing the rising anger in me.

"Who is this? Oh hey Quincy, wassup?"

He obviously told her because she turned to me with her mouth open and a hand on her chest. I stood in front of her with my hands on my hips not sure what the fuck to do.

"Ask him if he's sure. This isn't something to get wrong. Ask him." "Q-Ball, are you SURE it's him?" I watched Maya intently. I knew whatever her facial reaction or response, the truth was, Marcus had been found.?She looked at me with her hand still on her chest and nodded with her eyes closed.?This was not what I needed. I had just mentally prepared myself for a new beginning with a man who I'd already drugged and kidnapped and here comes that wank faced cunt hole of the past who was definitely owed a drugging and a kidnapping. And a beating. And a castrating. And a water-boarding. And a Jack Bauer style interrogation and torture session.

Oh yeah, I was pissed!?Do you even know who Marcus is?! Lemme refresh your memory...

Marcus. Mr Marcus.?M and M. Motherfucking Marcus.?Marcus is the reason why I am the way I am. Technically.?Marcus is the bastard I hate.?GOD... you have no idea how much I absolutely detest that man. I mean deep down loathing.?Every woman, and I mean every woman, has a man who has come through their life who they will hate FOREVER. Marcus is mine.

Years ago, me and Marcus used to go out. I was a working, earning, shoe addicted woman doing my thing. Working in insurance for high end boutiques and shoe stores. Things weren't great but we were together. Wasn't love yet but that's not to say it may not have happened one day. Anyway, I took a picture of myself in a pair of shoes and a skirt. Nothing sexy really, just wanted to see how my latest purchases looked with a skirt I'd just bought. Ladies, you've been there right? Well, he thought I took such a picture to send to someone else so he decided to burn my shoes. Not just some of my shoes, ALL of my shoes. Every single last pair of shoes I owned. Oh wait, no, he didn't just burn them, he poured bleach on them first and then he burned them. In my own car.

Just N*Sync. Gone.

And that is why I hate Marcus with the passion of the Christ. I'm not gonna go on about how much I loathe him and how much I really really loved my shoes but when you pay for shoes and something happens to 'em, you get upset. One, 'cuz they're your shoes and two 'cuz you paid for 'em. Then I was mad depressed for a while, then I met Maya and Quincy, Harrods happened and the rest is history.

By this point, I had to sit down because I could feel myself shaking. Moments ago, I was shaking because the thought of seeing Russell again made me physically nervous. Now, it was Marcus making me shake because I was getting more and more angry. I must've looked pissed because Maya hung up the phone and was sitting by my side with her arms around my shoulders telling me to calm down. She'd seen me pissed over the years when I heard his name or something reminded me of him. I don't even watch porn with Mr Marcus any more because of him.

And Mr Marcus could've definitely been granted five minutes with Lauryn and Aretha back in the day.

"So what's the plan Stan? I know there's no point trying to even to talk you out of doing what I know your gonna do," Maya said with her head resting against mine. It was like the physical connection of our skulls allowed our thoughts to travel into each other's mind. She knows me better than anyone. She knows when she can offer me reason and I'd accept it and when she should just shut the fuck up and make sure I know all the angles before I go and do something stupid.

I know I hadn't been Tatiana Blue the elegant and calculating shoe thief in a while but boy did it turn on. My first thought was heels. Which shoes was I going to disgrace this fucker with and which stash house were they in.

I've got four places set up in London. One in Dalston, one in Finsbury Park, another in Hammersmith and a studio in Peckham. Two in Los Angeles, one in Greece, a two bedroom in Dubai and three in Japan.

What, you think all those shoes just sit up under my bed? Come on now. I've got THAT many shoes that I need THAT many places to put 'em. I've got people living in some of my stash houses – a la Men in Black – but most of them are closed off and inconspicuous.

Oh... and Maya got me another one in Mauritius as well.

Anyway, I wasn't thinking of flying out to get a pair of shoes, although my mind did seriously contemplate it for a minute.

"Where is he?" I asked, brushing my dreads out of my face.

"Huh?" Maya played stupid. Trying to delay the inevitable. As my friend, I appreciated the fact that she at least tried, but she knew I didn't wanna hear anything else except for where I could find Marcus so I could calculate how long it would take to get there from my place.

I found my phone and called Quincy back. He answered first time. "Where is he?" My voice was cold.? " Shepherd's Bush. Seems like he's celebrating a birthday." "His birthday isn't until..."

Quincy cut me off. "It's not his birthday." "Oh reaaaaaally?" Then I started to laugh. God knows why but if I knew Marcus, he

was probably dishing out some elaborate evening of this and that and ending in some dick, like it's an appropriate birthday present. Like 'hey, happy birthday, I got you some dick. The same dick I give you throughout the year. And many happy returns.'

I hate men that do that shit. At least get me some heels and some dick.

My mind got back into business mode. Shepherd's Bush. From Stratford, that's clean across London. With night dropping, that might be a bit of traffic. I was cutting through London in my head, seeing myself passing London Bridge, up Embankment and on to...

And that's when I knew that I was a shoe thief for life, not just for Christmas. You know what I remembered is also up in that side of London?

Mount Street. The last Christian Louboutin store on my list of shoe shops I was yet to steal from.

"Yeah, you see that smile there? I don't want no part of what thought is behind that evil grin," Maya said, jumping up from the sofa. "You know," I couldn't even pretend. "Mama's going to get her some

REAL nice shoes before she goes to see that prick."
"OOOOHHH THE BITCH IS BACK!" Maya shouted.
"Shuuuuuuuuuuuuush, if you wake her, I swear..."

Maya covered her mouth. "Sorry. Come on say it with me, it's been a long time since we've done it..."

"Okay, come we go..."

I got to my feet and stood in front of Maya and we turned our backs to each other. She grabbed my bum to let me know she was going first. We began to two-step away from each other while humming a random beat.

"Bitches ain't dogs or holes for men to feel..." she started. "Bitches are beauties in tremendously cute heels!" I finished.?We walked five steps away from each other and turned on the fifth

step, striking a pose so fierce, both Mr and Miss Jay would've been proud.

Maya giggled before me and admitted defeat in the stare down before reaching for her drink.

"So, what was that smile all about?" "Mount street." Maya rolled her eyes. "Ah, the last on your list." "I didn't tell you about the time I went down there when I was

pregnant, like seven months. And I walked in to just look at the shoes. It was weird to be window shopping and know that I wasn't going to be back in the shop after closing taking what I wanted. But I just wanted to be in the presence of brand new Loubous, you know my fetish has never left."

"You and those damn shoes. They're not even all that..."

I cut her off. "Let's not do this again, alright? Leave my shoes alone."

"So anyway..."

"Yeah, I went down there and as soon as I walked in, the woman in the shop looked at me like I was about to give birth on the floor. She was trying not to touch me and basically trying to usher me out. Properly gave me the 'oh you can't afford to shop here honey' look."

"And Lord knows you hate that!" "Yessur I do..."

Even though I was planning a new caper and enjoying the excitement of the science of stealing, breaking it down as an idea on the fly, a thought of Russell tickled my spine. Marcus never left my mind. To me, this last assignment was like killing two birds with one stone. Hit my last store and hit my last memory in one night.

The sweet sweet feeling of before had me thinking clearly as I looked down at my phone.

"Oh shit, Quincy, are you still there?"

"You finished your little lesbifriends session? Or do you wanna know where he is?"

"Gimme."

"I've already sent you the address. He's with a woman named Roz. It's her birthday and I've also sent the link to the feed for your viewing pleasure."

I sighed. "Thanks dude. I owe you one. I'll get Maya to suck your dick the next time she sees you."

"Erm... how do you know I haven't already sucked his dick?" Maya jumped in.

"HAS she already sucked your dick Quincy?"

He groaned. "Oh whatever you two. I'll get a shoe box ready, just call me when you need it, alright? Good luck... and have fun."

"Will do."

I hung up the phone, handing Maya my glass. She walked to the kitchen and I shuffled to Charlotte's room thinking of the perfect multi- functional outfit for the evening's festivities. As a shoe thief turned mother, all my spandex outfits and Lycra suits were replaced with comfortable tracksuit bottoms and comfy Air Max 180s.

But I always kept a black long sleeve top and leggings. I wanted to wear it for Russell. I imagined him wrestling it off me, bending me over a counter and fingering me. In the all-black outfit that would've been purely sublime.

That was when I remembered just how much work I suddenly had to do. Mount street. Marcus, then home to deal with Russell.

Yeah I could've just said fuck it and left Marcus and Mount street alone and just dealt with Russell but that wouldn't be very Blue of me now would it?

Opening my alternative wardrobe after checking on Charlotte, who was out like a light, I had to dig under blankets, bibs, unopened packs of vests and duvets before I found my old work bag.

"Well hello you," I said to my tool bag carry case.

Containing everything a shoe thief needs. I won't go into what I had in there, you'll find out in a few.

I got changed so quickly, I walked out and caught Maya by surprise. I checked my phone for the address and calculated a route from Mount street to Roz's place in my head.

"Know where you're going?" "Yep," My mind was racing through London.?" Are you sure you wanna do this tonight, I mean..." I brushed my finger over Maya's lips while she was talking making

her words end with a 'lubber' at the end.?" You know there's no point, so don't even," I said.

"Alright, well take my car. We'll be okay here, just go do what you have to do, come home, get ya man and by the morning you should have some police dick in your mouth."

I frowned. "Er, yeah thanks Maya."

Then I thought about it. Didn't seem like a bad way to start the morning.

Bag on my shoulder, with my phone in my bra and Maya's keys in my hand, I gave her a high five and a nipple flick and took the stairs, feeling alive all over again.

That same nervousness that I felt back in Harrods all those years ago was running through me. Marcus was on my mind that night too but the pain of his shit was fresh back then. I'm older now. Don't care as much. But he still has to recognise just how much he fucked up.

I lifted the hood on my top and ran straight into the car park, straight to Maya's car and slid in with one swift movement. Maya's convertible Audi TT smelled like Black Love incense as I hooked up her GPS and put in my route.

Reverse, spin round and I was quickly dodging cars on the Bow flyover on my way to Aldgate. I'll admit, I wasn't driving safely at all but I didn't care. I was a confident, risk taking driver, didn't try audacious shit, but I could pull off a ninja move or two.

The HMS Belfast flew past me on the left and I was turning right on Embankment in what seemed like under 10 minutes. From Stratford, that's at least 20 minutes on a good day but that's how fast I was driving.

All the while, Marcus was on my mind. As angry as I was, I hadn't thought about how I'd feel about seeing him again after so long. I mean, I am forever angry at that man and what he did, over fucking nothing. Okay, lets say I HAD taken that picture of myself to send to another guy, did the punishment fit the crime?

FUCK arse no!

And if you agree then you might as well fuck off now 'cuz this story ain't for you boo boo.

Another five minutes and I was passing Green Park and driving slowly past Mount street, looking for somewhere to park.

I forgot how opulent the shops were in this part of town as I past Marc Jacobs and found a spot 150 yards away from the Louboutin store. Not ideal I know but I drove around for ages looking for somewhere to park and this was the best I could kind. Considering I was basically freestyling this job, I didn't have time to plant my getaway vehicle properly so this would have to do.

My phone vibrated against my nipple and made my shoulders shimmy. I laughed to myself as I slid the car into the spot in one whip to the left and one whip to the right.

I told you, I'm a gangster driver.

The engine died and I sat there for a minute. I didn't anticipate I'd be there so quickly so I wanted to take stock of what I was about to do.

I'd already done the homework on this place before Charlotte was born so I knew the layout and how I'd get in. I just wanted to watch the silence of the area. Didn't want some random pacing policeman to walk past and catch me hanging through a skylight.

My fingers caressed my bag on the passenger seat and I could feel my tools, ready to be used.

Excited was an understatement. I was hype. Like a missile just waiting to be let off so I could fuck some shit up.

As I said before, it'd been a long time since I'd been all up in the shit again so I had to take a second to just, you know, savour the moment.

Air sucked in through my nose and out through my lips. I slipped my ear piece into my ear, just in case Quincy had something to say. Grabbing the bag, I got out of the car and moved swiftly but nonchalantly to the side of the building, hugging the wall with my back.

First things first. Security cameras at the back.

I rifled through the side pockets of my bag and found my EMP disabler which was disguised as a blusher compact. One press of the button on top and electronics in a 100-foot radius go night night.

The red light on top of the camera disappeared and I left the wall and looked straight to the roof, which was my way in.

"Gloves," I said to myself. Back in the bag and I found my contact gloves, which I always loved using.

Ever since I played Call of Duty: Black Ops 2 and they used those gloves which stick to surfaces, I was extremely giddy when Quincy hooked me up with a pair for free. Strong enough to hold my weight and even work in the rain, I put them on slowly, savouring more of the moment.

"OoOoOoOooo... this is gonna be so fun." My nipples rose against my bra as I approached the wall, guestimating that it was about two storeys straight up.

"Let's see if you still got it... of course I still got it, who the fuck do you think I am..."

And there it was. My other voice. The one that pops out and talks back to me when I'm out working. She was as funny as me, always made me question everything and saved my ass a lot too.

"Let's go then... after you..." I said to myself as I touched my first glove hand on the wall. The back of the fingers lit up with a green light on each finger as I came into the contact with the wall. My other hand did the same and I could feel my hands sticking. Rolling one hand up the wall and sticking again, I left the ground and began to climb the wall.

Spiderman makes it look a lot easier because, as a spider he has sticky shit on his feet. I was literally lifting myself up by my hands so it was a struggle to get half way.

My arms were burning because I hadn't kept up my gym routine and my legs were scrambling against the wall trying to give extra rise.

Honestly, I was sweating like Django. Trying to catch my breath but not wanting to stop either. Nothing like stopping halfway then looking up and realising you still got half to go.

"Thought you said you still had it... oh fuck off..."

Hand by shaky hand, I kept going until I could see the top of the roof. My hand was close enough to reach it as I grabbed the ledge and held on, knowing I was a hand and a hoist away from being up the bloody wall.

I was seriously tired and out of shape. Maya would be giggling her ass off if she could see me now. Out of breath just from scaling a wall. Luckily she wasn't there to see me struggle.

When my heartbeat slowed to a normal pace, I inhaled deeply and lifted myself over the ledge with a 'hurumph' and a 'come the fuck on' to motivate me.

My dreads were longer than they were on my last assignment so I had to carry extra weight and, honestly, I was already knackered. But I had a long night ahead of me and I had no time to waste.

I scooted low across the roof to the skylight that looked right down onto the shop floor of the Louboutin store. The moon above was peering straight through giving me a clear view of oh so many of my babies, just waiting to come home with me. My bottom lip was low and I was probably drooling at that moment.

A quick rifle through my bag and I found my trusty old lock picker. The same one I used in Harrods. Doing what I do, you go through a lot of tools but this one had sentimental value. I became attached to it and it's been with me ever since.

I felt around the circular dome for a lock and felt it move under my fingers.

"OoOoOo..." I said to myself as I tried to lift the dome and watched it rise. "Well ain't that something?!"

As I slowly lifted the glass, I looked around the inside of the dome lid for any silent contact alarms I might've tripped by mistake. None. I

looked down for any cameras in the vicinity but the EMP would've taken them out. I used another one just to be sure.

A short electrical fizz as the EMP hit the ground and I was good to go.

Back to the bag for my belt, which I wrapped around my waist and hooked onto the wire that I secured to the base of the skylight.

"Always love this bit," I said to myself as I calculated the drop, adjusted the rope and stood over the open skylight.

I jumped into the air and fell feet first into the shop, hearing nothing but wind and wire running in my ears for a second. I was obviously still good at what I do because my feet stopped so close to the floor I felt my toes poke the ground.

"Rico suave," I giggled as I looked around, taking a mini torch from my pocket and putting it in my mouth. I spun around the wire for a second before unhooking myself and crouching next to a plinth of shoes. The glimmer of shiny red bottoms next to my corner eye instantly distracted me. My lips couldn't stop from rising into a dirty great big smile.

It felt good to be back doing the thing I loved more than anything in the world. Well, after Charlotte. It wasn't like a transformation into becoming who I am, more like a realisation. You know when you watch kung fu films all your life and somehow think you can do kung fu, it's kind of like that. Because I used to work with shoes back in the day, I just really thought if I ever stole a pair, I'd get away with it. So I did. Well, I do.

Scanning the room and turning my gloves off, my eyes were catching shoes, more shoes, the counter, more shoes, stockroom, more shoes...

BINGO... stockroom.

I moved low past so many shoes from my Louboutins mental list that I kept stopping to stare.

"Ooo, the Armurabottas... OH shit the Mado boots... Fuck me, my walls are gonna love those Azimut boots, come to mama..."

And this is where I fucked up.?I touched a shoe.?Ever since having Charlotte, though I haven't been stealing shoes,

I've still been making a list of shoes I want. Maya has been helping with some but there are some I've wanted to get for myself. Just to feel the pleasure of taking them for my very own. There were 10 pairs of Louboutin shoes and boots I wanted and each and every single one of them was catching my eye.

My list consisted of the Lady Spiked platform pump in Leopard print, Taclou spiked heel leather knee high boots, the Python peep toe, the

Armurabotta Pointy Thigh High boot, Snakeskin Daffodile pump, Spike wars women's ankle bootie, Mado lace up leather over the knee boot, Azimut leather caged boot, Monicarina leather thigh high boots and and and... the best of them all, the Sexy Strass peep toe heels – four inch pump with peep toe heel, covered in crystals.

Oh those were coming home with me in multiple sizes.

And that's the shoe I touched. I had to. Reached out and picked it up from the display. The second I did it, something felt wrong but then I didn't hear anything and there wasn't any sticker or badge to indicate a secret alarm.

"You've tripped a silent alarm," Quincy said in my ear suddenly. I thought he was God the way he spoke so out of the blue. That used to happen all the time back when I first started and Quincy would be in my ear, silent until the last minute. And because his voice is deep, it sounds like God. Or at least James Earl Jones.

"Shiiiiiit... you had to fucking touch didn't you... erm, it was a Sexy Strass, of course I had to touch..."

"Oiiii, could you two pull it together for a minute and focus, thanks," Quincy yelled at me. At us.

"Stockroom. There's a door out of the building in the stockroom, if I remember correctly." I was talking and moving at the same time. Past the counter, I didn't have time to be sneaky about it and kicked the stockroom door open first time. The door burst open as I heard a siren in the distance.

"Fuck, fuck, fuck, fuck," I kept saying to myself. I mean what were the odds of my first day back in the game and I trip a silent alarm. What a piss take.

I took the torch out of my mouth and shone it in the stockroom of boxes of shoes in multiple sizes. I slung the bag off my shoulder and pulled a larger bag out, whipping it to life before laying it on the floor.

Then I got to work.

The first shoe I found was the Python peep toe in my perfect five and a half. I took a six for eBay purposes. I did the same with the Taclou, Mado and Azimut boots but I took three sizes of the Armurabotta, the Monicarina and the Lady spiked platform pump because Aretha's nipple told me to. I couldn't find a five a half in the Snakeskin Daffodil or the Spike Wars ankle boot so I took a five and six while the single siren got closer in the distance.

The last shoe on my list, the one that started all this quickness – the Sexy Strass – needed three five and a half sizes, two sixes and two fives. Just to cover my bases.

With my boxes stacked, I pulled up the sides of the bag and zipped it up. Covered and ready to go, I squatted low, swung the arm of the bag over my shoulder and lifted from my knees.

Another reminder I was out of shape as my legs and ankles cracked.

Considering I was carrying 28 pairs of shoes, I was able to move quite freely on my feet, even as the weight of the bag pulled me back off balance.

I got to the door of the stockroom and realised that the siren I previously heard in the distance stopped. Dropping the bag silently, I peeked around the stockroom door and I saw two plain clothes officers cupping their hands on the store windows.

There was something familiar about them but I couldn't quite place them until one of them with a classical Nigerian face reminded me.

Femi and Jamal. Russell's police friends.?I couldn't fucking believe it. Of all the police in the world!?The dudes I let into Russell's flat after I... well you know.?I could hear them arguing about whether or not to break into the

shop to investigate.?" I can see a wire hanging from the skylight. I HAVE to break in,"

Jamal, the bigger one of the pair said.?" You just wanna smash suttin' don't you? Been a while since you've,

you know, smashed huh?" Femi said, looking in my direction through the window.

Thank God the darkness covered me. "Shit..." "You know they're coming in don't you?" Quincy said out of nowhere. "Yeah I know... Well, long as I've got my trusty taser, I'll be alright." "I hope you kept up some training 'cuz here they come." Quincy went silent as the front door of the Louboutin store flew open

in a crescendo of glass and metal.?" If anyone asks what happens, you did this yeah? I'm already on my

second warning, I don't need the paperwork." Femi said as Jamal moved slowly through the open door with a big ass torch shining from left to right.

I ducked down so the counter separated us and moved back into the stockroom, almost tripping over my bag of shoes.

"Don't fuck about," I whispered to myself.

"Wire through a skylight, who else could it be?" Jamal said, treading carefully.

"No way! You really think the legend would trip a silent alarm?"

"She's been quiet for how long now... maybe she's been out of the loop and she's a little rusty?"

"Who the fuck is rusty?" I asked myself. "Oh I'ma make sure I fuck HIM up, about rusty!?"

"You take the stockroom, I'll look for the master switch."

"Why is it always me who gets sent into the dark places where people with knives can hide? Your the one with no neck, why don't you go into the darkness for once?"

"Are we really gonna do this now?" Jamal said, shining his torch towards the stockroom. The beam of light shone over my head and onto empty spaces where boxes were missing. "Grow a pair and check the stockroom."

"Don't worry about my pair," Femi said, shining his torch towards the stockroom. "Your mum grows 'em for me."

"JUST... go!"

I was still crouched by the door with my taser in my hand wondering to myself, would I have been caught by the silent alarm in my prime? It was a slick little thing. No sticker on the shoe or the surface. To be honest, I couldn't even see it.

That was a thought to save for later. Meanwhile, Femi had his light on the door which I'd beautifully kicked open.

"Door's been kicked open," he said.?" She's slipping," Jamal shouted back.?" I swear, that guy and his fucking mouth." I wanted to make sure I

got my taser on that Jamal. He apparently didn't rate me at all.?I could see the beam from Femi's torch getting closer to the door

and I got primed on the balls of my feet. Ready for him to appear around the corner and out of Jamal's line of sight. I sunk back deeper into the stockroom, sliding the bag with me as I moved.

"You wanna add assaulting a police officer to your already massive list of shit?" Quincy said in my ear.

"STOP doing that," I muffled. "And it wouldn't be the first time."

Femi appeared in the doorway of the stockroom with his torch in front of him, wielding it like a light-sabre. I'd tucked behind a wooden crate of shoes so the light missed me as he moved forward, right into a dark spot.

With the dark floor coming to light, getting closer to the crate, I held the taser by my foot and prepared myself.

I could hear him breathing heavily, his feet moving nervously towards me. As the light fell on the tip of my Nike, I flashed the taser once. By the time he swung the light towards me, I was already in his personal space, pushing the taser into his neck and holding it there. I covered his mouth as he tipped backwards and I held him on his way to the ground. As he lay down, his body convulsing, I replaced my hand with my crotch as I sat on his face. Kinda pointless really but useful in the sense that I was able to keep him quiet with my hands free and ready, just in case the Deebo-looking one followed behind.

"Shush," I said looking down at Femi, whose eyes were staring straight up.

If you investigate me properly, you'll find out in police reports I have an affinity for shocking people with a taser in the neck for a long time. I don't know what it is about electrocuting people like that but... hey what can I say? It makes my toes curl.

As I was looking towards the stockroom door, Femi's leg kicked out and knocked over a stack of shoes boxes next to him. The noise freaked me out and I instinctively put the taser to his neck again and shocked him until his eyes closed and he started snoring.

"FEM? FEM... you alright in there? For fuck sake, and they still don't wanna give policeman guns," Jamal mumbled to himself. He then got on his radio and sent a request for back-up, possible officer injury and the gun cops as well.

"This is turning from bad to worse," Quincy said all God-like.?" Who you telling?" I replied looking around for something, anything. I was already at a disadvantage because I couldn't see where Jamal

was in the store and I had no way to incapacitate him from where I was. The back door in the stockroom was blocked by a large stack of shoes boxes and I was running out of options.

With Femi snoring against my crotch, tickling my clit, I leaned forward against the door frame and peeked around to see Jamal looking in my general direction.

"I know its you Blue. Seems like your slipping in your old age."

"Who's old?" I grumbled. My ego made me respond. "It's like riding a bike. Speaking of bikes, how is my baby Russell?"

"Pissed and looking to arrest your clart as soon as he sees you."

I banged my head against the door frame. "Awww, I bet you a pair of shoes he doesn't."

"Keep talking bitch, you ain't going anywhere right now so just sekkle yu'self. Your lift is on the way!"

"Snowball him," Quincy said in my ear.

"Really Q-Ball? A snowball is all you have to offer as a way out of this?"

"Trust me, it's your only shot right now. Make it a good one." "Yeah thanks," I gave him my full sarcasm.

To the uninitiated, the snowball is the oldest trick in the book and kids still play it today. The snowball is the classic trick to use against an opponent who may have you pinned down in a snowball fight. You need two snowballs for this distraction technique where you throw one snowball into the air in order to distract your victim. The higher you

throw it, the better the distraction, then hit 'em with the face smasher as they're still looking up.

Less snowballs, more shoes.

I ducked to the floor and found a Lady spike platform pump and an Azimut boot in odd sizes and I got back to my crouching position against the frame of the door.

"More police in six minutes, if your gonna do it, do it now!" "Okay, geeez, don't rush me." Peering around the frame, I saw Jamal had abandoned his search for

the main light switch and was slowly backing out of the store.?It was that classic now or never moment.?I mumbled to myself, "Bitches ain't dogs or holes for men to feel,

bitches are beauties in tremendously cute heels!" Armed with the Lady spike in my left hand, I threw it with a hook

462

and watched it toss high into the air, over the counter and towards Jamal who saw it too late. He raised his arms up to protect his face and was hit in the hand by one of the spikes. By the time he winced and began to check his hand, I had already thrown the Azimut boot, reached for a Mado boot close at hand and threw that too. He looked up in time to see both boots coming at him, square in the face one after the other. He tumbled backwards, tripped over the frame of the broken front door and began to fall.

I heard his head hit the ground and wasn't surprised to see him not moving from behind the counter. I sprung from the stockroom and ran up on him with the taser and sat on his chest. His body vibrated as I shocked him twice but he didn't move. I checked his pulse which was pumping strongly, which meant he'd just knocked himself out. Big for nothing.

I put the taser to his groin and shocked him for five seconds, counting with full Mississippi in-between.

"Who's old and slipping? Bet your dick's gonna feel old when you wake up you Spongebob-shaped dipshit!"

"MOVE!" Quincy shouted in my ear.

I was back in the stockroom, hoisting the bag over my shoulder and wriggling through the stockroom door. I looked around at Femi who was still snoring and wobbled through the store, stepping over Jamal's carcass.

"When you hear shit pop off, go in the opposite direction," Quincy said in my ear.

"Huh?"

"Just get to your car, and when you hear shit, drive in the opposite direction and quickly."

I jumped into my first step the air and took off running, pointing Maya's key at the car as I approached. The lid of the boot popped open and I slung the shoes in, slammed it shut and got in as sirens seemed to erupt from all angles. I started the engine as Floetry's In Your Eyes began to play.

My heart was beating so quickly I could hear it.

The sudden car crash that took place in my rear view mirror made me jump as my peripheral vision caught it. I turned around to look because it sounded like such a violent accident.

"Go, now!" Quincy said in my ear. "Have a good night. Let me know when you want the shoe box."

"Thanks Q-Ball," I said, putting the car in first gear and tearing off down South Audley street, taking back roads until I was up near Knightsbridge, checking my mirrors as I swerved slow cars and jumped yellow-into-red traffic lights while looking over my shoulder.

With a road of moderate traffic ahead of me, I slowed down and exhaled heavily, sliding my earpiece out and resting my head back. This was always the moment I liked to think about just what shoes I had picked up and how sexy they were going to look on my feet. Then the daydreams of my walls contracting began and my nipples hardened. Lauryn first, then Aretha.

The further away I got from the scene of the crime the better. Not like I wasn't on my way to commit another crime but that's neither here nor there to be honest.

By the time I got up to the Olympia, I was nodding my head along to Jill Scott's Can't Explain like I was on a night-time drive. I knew the best thing for me to do was own my anger and not let it own me. If my anger took over, I knew I'd possibly kill Marcus and, for my list of crimes, I'd never killed anyone. Okay, I've assaulted, kidnapped, caused actual and grievous bodily harm, put someone in a coma once – that wasn't my fault – but I've never killed.

Erykah Badu came through Maya's speakers with Master Teacher part two as I turned into Aynhoe road, giggling that Marcus was currently with a woman who lived on a road called Aynhoe. I couldn't help but see the words 'any hoe'. But my beef wasn't with her, if anything I was probably saving her from some shit.

I turned the engine off while the car was rolling down the street and steered it into a large space across the road from the address Quincy had given me.

In the dead silence of night, I sat with my neck craned, staring at a five-floor house with basement and attic.

464

My blood began to boil because I knew Marcus was in there somewhere and I didn't like the fact that I couldn't watch his body
vibrating due to severe electric shocks to the face, spine and groin. Not yet anyway.

Scanning all floors, trying to gain a clue as to where he could be, I looked at the third floor window and saw him stand with his hands on the curtains. He grinned into the night before drawing them closed.

I actually punched a fist into my palm as I reached into my bag, pulled out my multi-shot stun gun, two tasers, my lock picker and some lipstick flashbangs.

I was going in there ready for some shit to pop off. Getting out of the car and closing the door with a bump from my hips, I slipped my tools between my the waistline of my leggings and looked at the house.

I hadn't done any rock climbing in a long time but it was like dick, something you never forget. My earlier wall-climbing exploits proved I was out of shape but I still had the skills. Hand here, foot there, hand hold there, foot hold there. Bish bash bosh.

"Oh wait, let's do this properly."

I unlocked the boot and looked at my haul for a pair of Sexy Strass heels and hooked them into the heel-holders I had on the back of my leggings. Both heels latched in and rode against the small of my back as I stretched, looked left and right and crossed the road, feeling my anger build.

The thought that kept running through my mind was that this wasn't what my life was about any more. I was over Marcus but I wasn't over what he did to me. I wasn't doing this for me, I was doing it for my shoes. The ones that never were. The ones that I never got to wear. The collectibles. The beautiful ones that always smashed the picture. Always every time.

I looked up one more time and took one look around before hopping up six steps. I jumped over a railing and onto a window frame, reached up for the ledge of a window box on the third floor and hung there for a moment. I had to wait to see if the ledge would hold my weight if I lifted myself up. Nothing like falling half way because the ledge gives way.

I grunted silently, feeling the added weight of my hair as I pulled myself onto the window ledge of the last place I saw Marcus. Thanks to a large tree in front of the house, I was shielded from nosy neighbours who may have been wondering about the dread-locked woman all in black climbing a window ledge in the dead of night.

With my feet pressed up against the wall, I held myself against the window securely.

Why I didn't use my gloves, I don't know.

After a moment of stillness, just to make sure I was steady, I tried to look through the closed curtains.

I could see Marcus sitting on a bed with his clothes on, but it was the naked woman tied to the bed that was more distracting. Her face looked confused as she said something to Marcus and he replied back calmly. I couldn't make out what they were saying.

Then a naked man stood in the doorway of the bedroom drying his hands. The woman on the bed, who I imagined was Roz, looked as confused as I did.

Marcus stood up and started to take his clothes off as the naked man walked closer to the bed. The woman began to struggle against her cuffed wrists and that was when I'd seen enough.

I had my lock picker working on the window, watching for any signs that I was being too loud. The one thing I could trust is that none of them would think that it was a shoe thief hitched against the window trying to pick the lock. Which was what was actually happening.

The lock was an easy one – early 90s, single glazed window – and I had to catch the window as it started to swing open. I held it before the hinges started to creak, listening for a sign that anyone in the room might've heard. The sounds of the room came to life and I could hear Marcus goading with his begging voice while Roz was demanding to be untied.

A lipstick flash bang rolled off my fingers as I found a gap in the curtains. Pressing the top of the lipstick and watching it roll towards the bed, I counted to three and shielded my eyes with the curtains as it went off and a scream and two shouts went up.

The flash of light caught them all as I pushed the window open and moved low across the floor, making sure my feet made no sound. Cutting through the veil of smoke, I was crouching behind the naked man who was rubbing his eyes vigorously. I put out a taser in each hand and swung one up to his neck and one between his ass cheeks and shocked the shit out of him.

I've shocked a lot of people in my time but this was the first naked guy I'd lit up.

And between the cheeks too.

Trust me, to watch him jump into the air, his legs go all spaghetti- like and his arms die at his side before he hit the ground was hilarious. He started foaming at the mouth and everything. Meanwhile, Marcus was rubbing his eyes, while Roz continued screaming, unable to rub her eyes.

"What the fuck was that?" Marcus said with an arm across his eyes. "I can't see shit!"

"That's how I want you," I said to him.

My first words to Marcus in over 11 years.

I stopped tasing him in his neck and but continued up in his ass. I reached for my multi-shot stun gun and fired at Marcus' torso. Eight pincers attached to wires shot out of the gun as he squinted in the yelling gentleman's direction and attached to his skin, making him fall on the bed across the naked woman who was lightly wheezing.

"FUCK meeeeeeeeeee..." Marcus said on the bed as I pressed the trigger then stopped. Pressed then stopped. Pressed and held then stopped.

The pleasure I received from watching his body do the white people dance across the bed was priceless. I wanted to keep shocking him but I didn't want to take all the pleasure away from making him suffer.

"MARCUS WHAT THE FUCK IS GOING ON?!" Roz shouted with her eyes firmly shut.

"Trust me sugar, he has no idea what's going on. Nice boobs by the way," I replied, reaching for her restraints and untying her.

Roz's arms fell over her face and body as she rolled off the bed, pulling the sheet with her and squinting. I approached her with a dressing gown I found on the back of a chair.

"Here, put this on." "Please, don't hurt me..." "As cute as you is, its not you I'm here for, is it Mr Marcus?" I looked back at him, laying on the bed. Roz put the dressing gown

on as I walked to the bed and began to tie his arms to the same restraints.

"There we go! Nice and tight. Now we can talk!"

For five minutes, I paced the room, up and down, left and right. I was wrestling with what I wanted to say to Marcus when he woke up because he went to sleep. There was so much going through my mind at that moment. I wanted this for so long and it seems to have run up on me without being ready for it.

Not like I hadn't just assaulted two police officers and robbed one of the most high end shoe shops in London so I was allowed to be a little distracted and unprepared.

Whatever I was going to say, I needed to say it now. I paced past the bed where Marcus was frowning in his slumber. With his naked buddy still face down with a taser between his cheeks, I played with the trigger of the stun gun I was still holding with the pincers stretched across in Marcus' chest. Roz had moved from the floor to a chair in the corner of the room and was given explicit instructions not to try anything stupid or she'd dance like they did. That was all the threat I needed.

Marcus was greeted with two hefty slaps, back and forth across his face. He woke up instantly with his eyes as wide as moon pies. He took a second to focus before his eyes turned to me lording above him.

"Tatiana?! What the fuck are you doing here?" "Hello Marcus," I replied, calmly.?If you know me then you know the best time to be worried about me or what I'm going to do is when I get very calm. It's like the more stressed and angry I get, the calmer I become. And that's when I start thinking. And God help you if I start thinking.

"What the FUCK?" he shouted at me.

I couldn't help the wide grin across my lips. "What the fuck indeed? I bet you didn't think your evening would end in seeing me again, did you?"

"What the fuck are you doing here, how did you find me?"

"Oh, so you were hiding from me then!?" I turned to Roz. "See he WAS hiding from me."

She had no idea what I was talking about but just the fact a strange woman in all black made the room go white then take out two full grown men with tasers and stun guns made her agreeable.

"Hiding from you for what?" Roz said quietly with her knees pressed against her chest.

"Yeah Marcus, why don't you tell Roz why you were hiding from me?"

Marcus winced as he looked at the floor and saw the still, but breathing body of his friend.

"What the fuck did you do to Ohren? Is he dead?" "Does he look dead? I don't think he is anyway," I played with him. "Bitch, what the fuck are you doing here?" "Do you know what a true bitch is Marcus? I've renamed it. A nice

little slogan for what a bitch is, you wanna hear it?" Marcus struggled against the restraints on his wrist and threw his

body all over the bed, grunting and groaning. He didn't realise I went all scouts on the knots around his wrists so he wasn't going anywhere. "A bitch to me is a beauty in tremendously cute heels. You like that?

I do... I honestly felt really clever when I came up with that. What do you think Roz?"

"It's funny." "What are you doing here Tatiana?" "Ah the ultimate question. What am I doing here!? What AM I doing

here Marcus? Don't you think I might be here for the same reason you're hiding from me?"

"Why ARE you hiding from her Marcus?"

"Don't worry baby, I'll get us out of this."

I got down on my hands and knees and crawled up to Marcus on the bed; his body laying off the side but his hands still tied up.

"Erm..." I said quietly. "How EXACTLY are you gonna get 'us' out of this? You're looking pretty fucked up right now."

"I swear to you Blue, I'm gonna..."

I slapped him with a swift and decisive backhand. "You're gonna do what? Honestly, Marcus, what exactly could you do? You can't hit me 'cuz your hands are properly hooked up. Those pincers in your chest can conduct up to 3,000 volts of electricity so you don't dance until I tell you to."

"Are you out of your fucking mind? Slap me again and see what happens to you."

So I did. I slapped him a few times. Forehands, backhands, I slapped him up and down his face, I gave him slaps like The Three Stooges.

I really slapped the shit out of him.

It was beautiful to watch him turn his face from side to side without being able to do a damn thing about it.

"Marcus? MARCUS? Look at me!" His drooopy eyes opened and met my cold stare.?" Good. This IS happening, there's nothing you can do about it so

you're just gonna have to suck it up, okay? OKAY? Good, so get yourself up and let's do this like adults."

"You've tied me to a bed and you wanna talk like adults?"

"Erm, didn't you just have our Roz here tied to a bed? Was our boy Marcus about to offer you some birthday dick Roz? Hey, is that short for Rosalyn?" I got up and walked to where she was perched.

She lifted her head from her knees. "Yeah it is."

"Thought so. Love that name. Was he about to offer you some birthday dick?"

"Yeah, erm... I was blindfolded and then we had sex or at least I thought WE had sex and..."

She stopped as she realised she was about to tell a stranger about her birthday night.

"Yeah, I can figure out the rest. I was watching. Marcus pulled the old 'two dick trick' did he? Naughty boy... he asked me if I wanted to try that and I told him to fuck himself."

"Really?" Roz said, looking towards Marcus.

"Yep... introduced me to the guy and everything. He looked like... hold on..."

I walked over to the sleeping black man on the floor with the taser between his cheeks.

I no longer own that taser by the way.

Crouching to his face, I recognised him as the same man Marcus introduced me to way back when.

"Well I'll be... same guy!"

I was having fun now. I had control of the room; Marcus was under massive control and was shifting back onto the bed, Ohren was still out cold and Roz looked like she'd seen a ghost.

One swift hop and I was sitting on the edge of the metal bed frame with my feet on the bed while facing Marcus.

"Hey Marcus, nice to see you. Actually that's a lie, it's not nice to see you. It's nice to have you in front of me so I can say some things."

"Say whatever you want, I don't give a fuck. I'm gonna find you and your done, you hear me? You're dead."

"Sorry to shrink your dick Marcus but you're not the first person to threaten to kill me. You're maybe the third man tonight who wants me dead though."

Marcus tried to kick out at me but his foot didn't reach. We shared an awkward moment where he looked at me, trying to think of some other way to get to me.

"Say what you want and run, ya get me?" Marcus sneered.

"Alright 'blood', but, before I finish here and go HOME, I just have a few things I need to get off my chest."

As I spoke, I unlatched the heels from the back of my waist and began to put them on while turning to Roz.

"Sorry for having my feet on your bed. I won't be long I promise."

Out of the corner of my eye, I could see Ohren shivering in his sleep. It was fun to see Marcus watch his friend trembling on the floor then down at his chest.

"Don't worry about him, he's out. I've never tasered a guy in his ass before. In his cheeks, yeah, but never in his ass. Apparently it knocks you the fuck out. Maybe the neck helped too, anyway... I'm not here to talk about your slimy friend. You know why I'm here Marcus."

"You come all this way about your fucking car? After all this time?!"

"My car? I don't even remember what car it was. I'm here about my shoes Marcus."

"Your shoes? Them worthless suttins?"

"And, see, this is why I..." My finger was quick on the trigger and I shocked the shit out of him. His hands clenched, body tensed and his toes curled as I watched the wires dance all the way to his chest with an electrical snap.

"Fuck you Tatiana..." "I would if I could but I can't so I won't!" "I swear..."

"Stop swearing and shut your mouth. Roz, lemme' tell you what Marcus did..."

I sat there on the edge of her bed in the most bedazzling shoes and told Roz everything. From the relationship to the picture to the bleach to the whole burning bullshit. I left no stone unturned and made sure she knew exactly how it happened. She watched me talk with my hands and describe, very calmly, how Marcus killed my life and everything in it. I went into the depression, the time off work, the alienation, my absolute not giving a fuck about anything, only stopping when the story got to Harrods.

"What do you think about all that Roz? Does that seem fair to you?"

She winced. "Nah, not really. That's a really fucked up thing to do. You set her car on fire?"

Marcus looked towards Ohren.

"Why does everyone keep talking about the car?" I asked no one in particular. "He destroyed my shoes. All of 'em."

"Why are you sending pictures to a next..."

I cut him off. "If you even think about saying that ghetto shit to me, I'm gonna slap you then I'm gonna shock you. For a long time."

He stayed silent.

"I told you back then I only took that picture... you know what, I don't care about that any more. I'm just here to tell you... thank you."

"Thank your mum, you bitch."

"I am a bitch right now aren't I?" My feet kicked out towards him with a smile. "I say thank you Marcus because, right now, I have more shoes than I know what to do with. I have so many shoes, I can't keep 'em in one place. And ultimately, I have you to thank for that. Without you, shit wouldn't have happened the way it was supposed to. So thank you Marcus. You're a wank faced cunt hole but you made me so happy in the process."

I shocked him as I continued talking.

"But don't get it twisted, you destroyed my shit. Like, actually ruined my shoes. My life. You poured bleach on 'em. And you whistled that bullshit song you know I hate. And for WHAT? Huh?"

Marcus looked like he was transforming while receiving the Holy Ghost at the same time as doing the Funky Chicken. It was immensely fun to watch, just to watch the spit fly out of his mouth.

The tip of my finger was turning white because I was holding the trigger with power and venom. I felt calm and collected as I slowly let go, watching the pincers rest in the middle of raised bumps of red skin on his chest.

I sighed heavily and let my head fall backwards. I turned my head to the left and caught Ohren twitching. To the right and Roz was still frowning towards Marcus.

"Right, my work here is done I think."

Slipping back into my 180s and reattaching my Strasses to my shoe holders, I hoped off the bed.

"So now what?" Marcus groaned. "You think you're just gonna walk away and disappear?"

"No, not really," I said, handing Roz the handle of the stun gun. "I'm going home to be with my family. I've got bigger fish to fry than you right now Mr Marcus. Bigger dick shall I say."

I pulled out my phone and called Quincy.?He answered on the third ring. "Can I have my shoe box please?" "Sure," he said. "Shoe box delivered." "Thanks hone." I hung up with an incredibly wicked smile. I know it was wicked

smile because both Marcus and Roz looked at me with different levels of fear in their eyes as I moved towards the window.

"Right, Marcus. As a leaving present, I got you something special. Something you're REALLY gonna love."

It was super duper fun to watch Marcus prepare himself by trying to sit up, giving as much attitude as he could. Roz was holding the stun gun like it was about to explode.

"I got you a shoe box. It's not literal, it's metaphorical. You see, in this shoe box Marcus is a whole load of fuck up. Fuck up that won't necessarily hit right now but it's still a load of fuck up."

I opened the window and hopped onto the frame.

"In this shoe box is the destruction of your credit score, the cancellation of your tenancy agreement, a fraud report sent to the Tax department about irregularities in your name, 12 points added to your driving licence, in effect cancelling your driving licence. Your bank accounts have been closed, your car is being impounded as we speak and I wouldn't try and fly anywhere any time soon. You're on a watch list or three or twelve."

With each consequence I ran off, Marcus' mouth fell lower and lower. He looked shocked, then surprised, then confused. His last facial expression was the realisation that I was talking some kind of truth.

"Whatever bitch," were the last words he threw at me.

"Ya mama's a bitch! Now is that the female dog or my sexy version? Have a nice night you guys. Roz, sorry about ruining your birthday. But hey, have some fun of your own. Oh, and close your eyes."

She didn't say anything back. I didn't wait to hear her speak as I was out of the window and scaling down the wall while throwing another lipstick flash bang into the room.

Marcus screamed as Roz must've jumped from the sudden bang and squeezed the trigger of the stun gun at the same time.

Just the sound of his screams made me chuckle as I hopped down onto the steps and took them all at once. The feeling of 'over' I was searching for coursed through me all at once.

Maya's car 'zoop zooped' as I pressed the alarm and I got in, sitting in silence for a moment. My eyes drifted towards the window, just in case they came to look but that last flash bang would've kept them occupied.

I sucked in an amazingly large breath of air into my lungs and exhaled ever so slowly.

I'd finally found and dealt with Marcus. I could go on and feel like that wanker's cloud won't hang over me any more. You see the thing with Marcus was that I didn't hate him. We were good together back in the day. He was a good guy, I was happy. We weren't about to break up, put it that way. So the way things ended, I was kinda upset about it. For a second. The death of my shoes whitewashed that completely. I hadn't even thought of Marcus in that kinda light since this whole thing happened. But, how was I feeling at that moment? Like I was done. I mean I didn't steal shoes just to get back at Marcus but I wanted to be stronger because of him. And I was. I am.

By the end of the breath, I started the engine and enjoyed the purr on my thighs which mirrored the noise I was making in my chest. I pulled off the longest wheel spin and was out there, making sure everyone heard me as I left.

At this point, I felt good. Wicked, brilliant in fact. I felt like going home to deal with Russell was going to be a clean slate. A fresh break. Maybe a nice little family set up. I always wanted one of those, remember? Maybe this was about to be my chance to set that up.

As I stopped at a set of traffic lights, I remembered that I hadn't checked my phone since it vibrated against my nipple earlier. I felt my boobs and found it nestled against Lauryn on the left.

Keeping one eye on the lights, I saw a number of missed calls and messages from Maya that made me sit up in my seat. I only felt one vibration yet I had all these missed calls and messages.

Opening the first message while putting the car in first gear, my eyes widened in fear:

That was it.

'Come home now!'

Nothing else, just come home now.

Any parent knows how scared I got at that moment. When the person you leave your child with sends you that kinda message over and over and over again, you shit yourself.

My hype over Mount street and Marcus disappeared and panic mood set in. I tried to call Maya back and her number just rang out.

I looked at the red light. Looked left, then right, slipped the car out of first and back in, then tore across the empty intersection with a million visions running through my head. I graced into second gear, revved then slipped into third burning through Knightsbridge, down Pall Mall in a blur and jumping a serious red with a handbrake turn at Embankment to fly past London Bridge.

You can imagine what I was thinking. I was the most worried that something happened to Charlotte. Maybe the police had become slick over night and found out where I live. Of course I was thinking it could've been Russell finding me too. With all the set up and the sneaking around and the breaking into his place and the no heels in the flat rule, it would piss me off if he simply came upstairs and found me.

I was doubting my decision to move so close to Russell as I pulled a slick move past a taxi at a changing light at Aldgate. I'd always been a fan of the rule 'hiding in plain sight'. I use it avidly and you wouldn't believe how easy it is to steal a pair of shoes by just doing it in front of someone. In my head, the one place Russell wouldn't look for me was directly above him. Maybe he thought I'd pop by for a visit but not that I'd move in and live above him while watching his every movement.

Then I had a random thought and wondered if Marcus was as slick as he threatened. Maybe he'd found my yard and done something to Maya.

I tried her number again. Nothing.

It was the vagueness of the message that worried me the most. And then why would you send the same message over and over again. No voice mail either.

My eyes caught the rear end of a turning police car as I pulled out past a bus at a red light and burned through, not checking the crossing for pedestrians. Fear and adrenaline took me through, but when I realised there was no one on the crossing, I exhaled and sped up. Mile End station flew past me in a heartbeat as I leaned forward, pushing the car faster and faster, the engine being the only music I needed.

I started rocking in my chair getting more and more angry. The not knowing was what was killing the most. Maya was my good good

friend so if something was really wrong, she'd find a way to let me know. But I didn't get anything except come home now.

I literally flew over the Bow flyover, swerving to compensate for the moment of flight. I was sweating, doing 70 and holding the wheel with my thighs while tying my hair up.

Whatever was going on, I was going to be prepared.

"I swear if anyone has touched you Cha'Cha, then their gonna see a really angry Blue... and they don't want that... calm the fuck down... I will not calm down..."

I took my foot off the pedal for the first time since Green park as I curled around Great Eastern, looking at the large block of luxury flats I lived in. I slowed down to take the first left and slowed down further as I approached the second left that took me into the car park.

I didn't take any time to scope the place out or figure a way in that would give me an advantage. I buzzed my way into the building while sprinting and trying to call Maya back but she still wasn't answering.

Breezing past the lifts, I took the stairs climbing them three at a time. I was bouncing off the walls trying to get extra leverage that would carry me quicker to my place.

My hair was wildly bouncing behind me as I reached for banisters to help pull me up the stairs while I kept trying Maya's phone. Her number was ringing but she still didn't answer.

"Mayaaaaaaa..."

I climbed to my floor and slammed the door open, turning down the corridor and almost slipping. One hand on the ground and I was back on my feet and flying the down corridor. I took four heavy steps to stop outside my front door because I was running so fast with my taser in my hand. I slid a few inches on my toes before reaching for my keyhole.

"Shit! Where's my keys?" I felt my body for the keys, not sure where I last saw them.

One hand slapped the door while the other was feeling Lauryn and Aretha to see if they were holding my keys.

"You left 'em in your fucking bag... shiiiit... I couldn't have... I bet you did..."

By the time I ran my hands over my lock, I was frantic. I couldn't hear the TV or anything from inside. With my ear pressed to the door, I slapped it lightly, hoping Maya would hear the soft rhythm and open the door.?In my head, there were about six men standing in different places around my flat. Military types: crew cuts and no neck watching the perimeter, awaiting my mystical magical appearance.

My fantasy was broken as the door swung open while I was still feeling myself for my keys. Maya looked at me with stoic eyes holding her arm across the door blocking my way in.

She didn't say anything, just looked at me, which freaked me out even more.

"Where's Charlotte? Is she okay?"

I didn't wait for an answer and pushed past her, feeling my dreads slap her in the face. In my head I thought I'd apologise later but I needed to see that Charlotte was okay. Plus the fact she still wasn't saying anything made my stomach churn. As I raced through the living room, seeing everything still in place and no soldiers, I damn near tumbled through the door of Charlotte's room looking straight at her crib.

Empty.?" MAYA, WHERE THE HELL IS..." "Stop shouting before you wake our daughter." I heard that deep sexy voice and I knew what was so wrong.?" Ain't you just a slick rick..." was the last thing I said before a man's

handkerchief came from over my head and smothered my mouth and nose. I tried not to breathe in as I wrestled the hand from my face. But whatever was on that handkerchief must've been odourless because I felt my legs go out from under me. My body began to drop as a strong arm hooked around my waist.

I lost consciousness as my body flopped on the bed and a figure walked past me holding Charlotte in his arms.

And this is where I've woken up.

My whole evening. Everything up 'til now and I get caught slipping with the old handkerchief trick. And so easily too.

I was offended.?My mouth was itchy, my nose was burning and my feet hurt.?Then my panic mode kicked in. I couldn't hear Charlotte or Maya or

the TV or music. Just silence.?I stared at a spot on the ceiling and moved each of my limbs, feeling

for any drowsy movement, just in case I had to hop out of the room on some gangster shit.

My stomach muscles contracted and I slowly rose, keeping my ears peeled for any sound.

The last moments before I lost consciousness waved through my mind in a haze and I could see bits and pieces. The one thing I remember hearing was the voice.

Russell's voice.

My legs slunk off the bed and I squatted to my alternative wardrobe while keeping an eye on the door. One hand rifled around until I found my cattle prod nestled under an industrial-sized pack of nappies. My hand wrapped around it and I instantly felt more positive.

Staying low, I slid to the door and turned the handle slowly, wincing at every creak. I peeked around the door and could see a low light coming from the lounge.

"Quincy, you there? What the FUCK is..." I felt my ear but my earpiece wasn't there. Didn't even realise it was gone. OR did I take it out after I left Mount street? Wasn't sure, didn't care.

With the cattle prod trailing behind my back, I started to move out of the bedroom and into the dark corridor.

"Could we, for once, just do things normally?" Russell said.

I didn't expect to hear his voice and I looked up. My head spun around wondering how the hell I could be seen when I was moving so ninja-like.

"Normal? Us? Nah!" I shouted back as I rose to my feet. I snapped the elastic from my hair and shook my head like Bob Marley feeling the rhythm.

I focussed on the light at the end of the corridor and walked slowly. Charlotte gurgled quietly and I was able to exhale a sigh of relief.

"You hungry honey?" I joked.?" Don't you fucking dare! This is not a joke!" "OoOoOo serious Russell... I like this already."

By the time I got the end of the corridor and turned into the living room, my heart was all over the place. Butterflies in my stomach were fluttering like a fresh spring but my legs felt like they were on rum and Red Bull.

Lauryn and Aretha felt like they were perking up and I ran my hand through my hair and, as my living room came into view, I could see the back of Russell's head. He was sat on my sofa with his legs up and Charlotte nestled in a blanket in front of him. She was wide awake with her hands wrapped around his index fingers gurgling on one of her random freestyles.

I wanted to stroke his neck with one hand and shock him with the other. Over his shoulder I could see him playing with Charlotte and making faces at her. But I didn't want to see his face. Not yet.

"Where's Maya?" I asked with a strong grip on my cattle prod.

"I sent her home. No point her being here as well. And if I do need to find her, at least I'll know where."

"Find her?" My mind was racing.?" What, you don't think I know the set-up? Tut tut tut... silly Blue."

There was something about the way Russell was acting. Very cool, calm and collected. Kind of like the way I was behaving when I last had Russell in my presence. Tied naked to a computer chair with plastic sheeting under him, just for effect.

He was behaving like he knew something I didn't, which made me feel uncomfortable in my own space.

"Okay," I started. "So, what now?" "We wait two minutes. And then we talk." My eyebrows burrowed down across my eyes. I was sitting in a state

of confusion because I expected the next time I saw Russell, he wouldn't be as calm as he was. He was staring at Charlotte, who was mesmerised by the outline of his face.

"Why two minutes?" I asked, hating the feeling of not knowing what was gong on.

"Don't worry about that yet. Let's just say, one way or another this is gonna be done."

I could feel Russell smiling to himself as I inhaled heavily and slowly walked around the sofa. Every part of him that came into view excited me with each step I took. By the time I reached the side of his face, I looked out of the corner of my eye. His face was exactly as I remember it.

Chocolate isn't the word.

Though both my parents are black, I've been blessed with a rather caramel-ish hue but Russell was the definition of chocolate. Like India.arie chocolate.

Bald head and chin strap beard, Russell had his feet up on my coffee table with Charlotte in his lap and they were staring at each other.

The first time Russell lifted his eyes to look at me, I didn't know what to say. I was running through my mental roladex for a quick retort or something that would break the ice but nothing was coming to mind.

"Hey," was all I could think of.?Geez, I forget how handsome he was in the flesh.?" What's up?" he replied.?This jovial interaction irritating me because he played along. He was

riding the fact that he knew something that I didn't.?Tapping the cattle prod against my thigh, I balanced my weight on

one leg and folded my arms.?" So, how have you been?" The buzzer to my door down went off and we both looked at my

intercom system. I looked first because I wasn't expecting anyone, especially at this time of the morning. Russell slowly got up, whistling

Pharrell's Happy as he walked to the door bouncing Charlotte in his arm.

I watched him like 'what the...'?He answered the intercom and told someone to come straight up. Charlotte spit up and Russell wiped her mouth with a wet wipe he

had in his hand then looked at me. The smirk on his face was one I couldn't place. Was it anger? Hilarity? Was it the smile of a plan coming together?

My grip tightened on the cattle prod and I ran my finger over the power button, reminding myself where it was just in case I had to use it quickly.

We looked at each other for about 40 seconds. His eyes were all over me in my black outfit and my eyes were already under his clothes, running a mental hand under the waistband of his underwear. He was inhaling the scent of my neck and running his hands up and down my backside. My fingernails ran down his bald head and it hurt but he liked it. Then we kissed.

That's what happened in my head but in reality we were just standing across the room from each other saying nothing but thinking everything.

A strong hand knocked the door and broke our stare-a-thon. My hand gripped tighter as he turned around and opened the door, not far enough for me to see who was there.

He mumbled to the person behind the door, took an envelope, thanked them and closed it again.

My mind was planning shit. Hop over the sofa, two steps and I'm on him. Take Charlotte from him while shocking him in the ribs, find out what the hell is in that envelope and gain control of the situation again.

Russell walked back to the sofa, in my direction.

It was a lot to watch him come towards me but not knowing what to do about it. He had Charlotte nestled comfortably in his arms so I didn't want to do anything that would endanger her. The way he held her told me he knew that too.

He sat on the sofa, put Charlotte back in his lap and began to open the envelope.

"What's that?" I asked, curiosity getting the better of me. I knew he was waiting for me to ask and I held off for as long as I could.

"An envelope. You know what they are DON'T you?"

The first shot. It had to come somehow and Russell sent the first barb referring to the envelope. He was obviously still upset about that.

"Yessur I do. But I don't know what's in that one... cha, I need a drink."

All this tension was killing me. I had no idea what was going on around me and for someone who's used to having so much control, this feeling was rancid. I had to try and gain some equilibrium as the cattle prod didn't seem as useful as it did before.

As it stood, Russell had the upper hand and he was holding onto it. He found out where I was, apparently introduced himself to our daughter and had his feet on my furniture like he'd breezed past guest status and was allowed to do so.

I tossed the cattle prod on the solo chair and shuffled to the kitchen, exhaling and taking my trainers off. Exhaustion was beginning to seep into my muscles. My thighs had been busy all night and were contracting of their own accord, my arms felt like jelly and I rubbed my eyes for what felt like the hundredth time.

"Drink?" I asked him.?" Not while I'm on duty, but thanks." The words 'on duty' made me pause on my way to the kitchen. My corner eye went directly to my cattle prod, wishing I didn't put it down. Seemed like I may have a third policeman about to be put to sleep.

Slowly and more cautiously, I opened the cupboard and pulled out a pint glass, filled a quarter of it with white rum and the rest with cranberry juice.

I needed a strong drink.?" So, what'd you think is in this envelope Tatiana?" "Oh, so you wanna play that game do ya? Not tonight Russell, I'm

tired." He looked at me, raising his eyebrows. "Really? Like the last nine

months have been a jog in the park for me as well right? What do you think is in this envelope?" He asked again, more sternly.

I flopped into the seat with my cattle prod bouncing between my cheeks. "Don't know, don't care. If it ain't the coordinates to my bed then I don't care."

I really did care. It might've been an arrest warrant, pictures, could've been a bomb. Well, would've been a very sophisticated bomb if it was but my mind was all over the shop.

Russell, in his black Adidas tracksuit, reached into his pocket and pulled out Charlotte's bottle. He held her under his arm, slipped off the lid and poured some on his wrist before putting it in her mouth.

She took it without any fuss. Something I hadn't been able to do since she was born.

"You know what? I knew you were here. This whole time." "Liar," I threw back.?" You think you can move in directly above me and I wouldn't know?"

"Yes and I think your actually kicking yourself that you probably had your boys in blue looking for me all over the place but you didn't send them to the floor above yours. I KNOW you didn't know shit."

"And how do you know that?" Russell said, pulling a piece of paper from the envelope.

"You're not the only one who can watch people on cameras ya know?!"

He chuckled. "I thought something was wrong with the cameras. When did you do that?"

I winked at him from behind my glass as I felt control swerving back in my direction. I had him lying to me already which means there was control up for grabs.

"Alright, one nil to you. This'll make it one all."

He looked at the paper while I took a long sip, closing my eyes as the rum woke a fire in my belly.

"So she IS my baby?" I raised an eyebrow and gave him my best 'C'mon Son' face.?" Is that what that is? Paternity test? Really Russell? Do I look like

one of your side dishes?" "After everything you've done to me, you want me to answer that

question?" "Your safety may depend on it if you don't," I fired back, feeling

strength return to my body. It was definitely Dutch Courage but I rode it.

He chuckled again as Charlotte dozed off in his arms.?" I had to be sure. It's not like we did this conventionally." "Yeah... erm, about that, I'm sorry." I didn't hear the words until they came out of my mouth. I'd never,

for once, taken the time out to think about what my games had to done Russell and his normal life. To me, it was all about me and what I wanted. Maybe he didn't want this in his life. Maybe he wanted to stay a swinging single bachelor law man who doubled as a documentary maker. If you can call filming upskirts documentary making. Settling down was something I always saw as a dream for other people. I mean, criminals in general, never seem to make it to the end of the movie with their ill-gotten gains, a white picket fence around them and a family to love. I never saw myself as one of those people. I just liked shoes and felt like they were owed to me. I wasn't trying to get away from anything, I just wanted my shoes. But children and a man to come home to? That was a fairytale. Happiness like that was something that stopped when hoes, side pieces and Olivia Pope became more acceptable than a stable relationship or marriage. I saw it as something I wanted but could never have. And as someone who always finds a way to get what she wants, that always burned me.

And then Russell came into my life. Well, perved into my life. "What are you sorry for?" "Everything. Drugging you, the 'borrowing'..." "You mean the kidnapping?"

"Yeah, that too."

"The envelope, the slapping, Harodds, the tying me up, all of that too yeah?" Russell's voice was getting angry.

"Look, I'm apologising alright? Don't push it."

"YOUR DAMN..." He looked down at Charlotte and whispered. "...damn right you should apologise. Not like it'll help but it's duly noted."

"Oh yeah, the envelope..." I couldn't hold my laughter.?" What POSSESSED you to do that?" I knew this was coming. The age old questions he had since our last

encounter at his place nine months ago.?" Alright look," I sat up straight with fire burning throughout my

entire body. "I'm gonna do this once and once only so pay attention, alright?"

"Go 'head."

One heavy sigh and I went in. "Those pictures weren't about you. There were just insurance. You know what, in fact, let's go right back. Harrods. That WAS you wasn't it? That was you chasing me, wasn't it?"

"So you do remember?"

"Only when you just said Harrods. YOU were the guy in the control room? Man, I remember the way you came around the corner and..."

"Yeah, you hit me in the chest with a taser and left me there!" I bent forward in laughter. "What a small world!" "Ain't it just?" He replied unimpressed. "That shit hurt you know!?" "Another thing I'm sorry for. Anyway, the pictures. I had to take

'em. What if you woke up and decided you wanted to arrest me? What if you found me? I'd have nothing."

"Of course you'd have nothing. Don't you realise that stealing is an actual crime? That you're a criminal? Wanted on five continents?"

"Yeah but who am I hurting? Do you know how much these shoe designing sons of bitches get paid in insurance payouts? They make more back if the shoes are stolen than the actual price of the shoes. No one loses out, I win every time. Done and done."

"But..."

"Look, I'm trying to apologise here. Could you shut up for one minute? For fuck sake."

Russell squinted at me. "Go on." "So... I'm just sorry." "Do you know how hard it was to explain those pictures?" "Didn't you hide it?" "No time, thanks to Femi and Jamal. They found it under the sofa

and had it open before I could untie myself." "Those two... yeah," I trailed off, wondering if they were still lying in

the Louboutin store unconscious.?" I was suspended, I had to move, I changed stations, all because of

you and your 'insurance'." "How did they feel about you being the father of my child?" "You think I told them that? I'm not stupid. That would've been a

bigger investigation, more time off without pay. I didn't need the headache. I already had enough headache worrying about if you were telling the truth or if you were even pregnant."

"Well surprise motherfucker!" I raised my glass and knocked the rest of my drink back and slunk into the chair flexing my toes and simmering on annoyance.

"So what now Russell? Your sitting there like you have all the answers and you know what's what, what now?"

"Oh we're not done talking yet." "But I'm tired and..." "Busy night? Looks like the clothes of someone who didn't wanna be

seen." "Look," I started as I stood up with my cattle prod. "I'm beat up

right now. If you're gonna arrest me or call for back up, please call Maya first so she can take Charlotte. Otherwise, close the door on your way out and let your head get small in the distance. Alright? Peace."

The way I walked off, it was like I ripped my last rhymes of the evening, dropped the microphone and left the stage. It was perfect as I could feel his eyes watching me saunter off.

Yeah I sauntered.

I didn't walk quickly, just slow enough that he could watch my cheeks bounce away in my leggings.

I wasn't sure what the fuck he was going to do but I knew that I'd given myself the power back by walking away from him. The instant he didn't call after me or threaten me with arrest, I knew he wasn't here for that.

Watching him with Charlotte, the way he smiled at her and watched every nuance of her face, said that he was here for his chance to be a father.

As much as I didn't know whether or not Russell wanted this for himself, I was answered when I watched him feed her. He had the

correct amount measured in her bottle and was feeding her without any drama. Whenever it was me with Lauryn or the bottle, I was always greeted with the lips closed and then the wailing.

"Night," I said as I disappeared into the corridor.?" We're not done Blue." "Then come finish me off then!" I slammed my bedroom door and took a running jump onto my bed.

I wasn't lying about being tired. I was absolutely bushwhacker knackered. It wasn't just a normal day of baby sitting and selling shoes. I was back in the swing and apparently I had some training to do to get my body back in shape and research to do because that silent alarm thing must be new.

The sigh I sighed when my head hit the pillow was like an orgasm after an orgasm. I flopped around on my cold duvet for a few moments until I warmed up then wrapped myself up, listening for any sounds from the corridor.

Russell's heavy stomp could be heard as he walked up the corridor, deviating right to go into Charlotte's room.

I knew he was coming in here to fuck me.

First of all, I'm sexy as fuck and dressed all in black. I've got an ass like Trina in her early days, my dreads come like Nerissa Irving and my legs are Tina Turner in her prime. Unless Russell became gay and I missed it then he was coming in here to fuck me.

To be honest, after the night I had, I needed it.?Believe it or not, Russell was the last time I had sex.?Yeah I know, THAT long ago. I've been CLOSE a few times like, don't

get it twisted, I've done some stuff but no one has, ya know, 'been up in the club' since Russell. Before him, I was scratching my itches regularly. I had pieces all over the place. Not like, north, south, east London. Like southern California, Dubai, Genoa, two in Mali and some others scattered around. And as I said before, it scratched an itch but wasn't the healing cream I needed.

That turned out to be Russell.

I don't know what it is about that man that attracts me so much but I just wanna lay my head on his chest and watch random shit on TV. He makes me wanna live that life, even though I'm still partially buzzing at all the shoes in the boot of Maya's car just waiting for me to touch 'em.

I want to live both lives to be honest and if I can't then one will have to go but when I want something, chances are I'm gonna get it. Nine times out of ten , I get it. Or I destroy it so no one else can have it.

Yeah, issues I know.

My bedroom door creaked open and Russell turned the light on and stood in the doorway.

"Come on, let's finish this," he said.

"Russell, look. Here's the skinny right now 'cuz this isn't as fun any more." I unwrapped myself from the duvet, sat up and put my hands in my lap with my back straight.

He looked uninterested.

"I am tired. I've had a long fucking day and an even longer night and I just want to lie down. That's all. Your here now and you know the truth. You know everything..."

"I don't know where you were tonight."

"Are you my man to be asking me that question?" I threw back at him, running my fingers through my dreads which cascaded over my shoulder. "Or you asking me as a boy in blue?"

"Where were you tonight?"

"Are you asking me as Russell the policeman or Russell the potential love of my life?"

Damn Dutch Courage.?" Where were you tonight?" I sighed. "I went to see an old friend. I owed him something." "And what was that?" "A goodbye." "You went to see a friend just to tell him goodbye!?" "It was a different type of goodbye." My nose wrinkled and I grinned to myself as I watched Russell throw

a veil over his emotions as he listened. My vagueness in my answer balanced between a goodbye between friends and a goodbye from between the sheets.

"And where does this friend live?"

"Now you're starting to sound like a policeman and, if I remember correctly, you gained entry to my abode without my permission . So if you're not arresting me then I don't have shit to say."

"Have you been with anyone else since you left?"

"Ah haaa, now THAT sounds like Russell the potential life partner talking. And the answer is no."

"Why not?" he asked, moving to the end of my bed. He sat down with a glass of something in his hand and he took a long sip.

"You just want me to boost your ego don't you? Okay, fine. I haven't been with anyone else, mainly because I was pregnant. And that's gross. If I can't have the father of my child dancing in my club then I don't want no random ravers in there. For me sex is a stab wound on a plaster of a relationship and I was tired of stab wounds."

He frowned. "What club?"

"Oh, okay. When I say up in my club, that's what I mean when I talk about sex. You know, UP in the club?"

"For God sake Tatiana, you really are fucking nuts." "Why thank you." "Just because I'm being cool and calm with you right now, don't think I'm not still pissed with you for everything you did to me. I mean, seriously, who do you think you are?"

From running my fingers through to re-twisting my dreads, I looked at Russell with a confused face.

"Erm, I'm Tatiana Blue, the baddest bitch of them all! You know who I am Russell, that's why you fell in love with me. You see, I know why you're here. Stop me if I'm wrong."

"Okay."

Kicking my feet out of the bed, patting the mattress next to me for him to come and sit, I took his drink from him and knocked it back. "So, you found me, right? Now as a policeman, that puts you in a pretty precarious situation. Because if you know where I am then it is your duty as an officer to report my whereabouts and detain me until I can be taken in, right?"

He nodded.

"If I could guess, from the first missed call I had from Maya, you've been here for most of the night. I see no signs of you detaining me or back up being called. Which means you haven't reported my whereabouts have you?"

He nodded again.

"Alrighty, but that's still bothering you right? But at the same time, on the other side, there's Charlotte. You've met her, you can see how absolutely amazing she is and you want to see more of her don't you? Maybe more of me too?"

He didn't nod but instead looked at my bottom lip. Told you he was going to fuck me.

"And now you don't know what to do. Call me in or live a life with one of the most hunted criminals in your office. Decisions decisions."

I was weighing up my hands when, quick as a flash, Russell brought his hands up and latched one side of a pair of handcuffs on my wrist. By the time I knew what was going on, he was pulling me to the foot of my bed and latching the other side of the handcuff on my wrist, which he'd looped quickly through a railing.

"Whoa whoa whoa..." was all I could say. In trying to pull my cuffed wrists out, a metal railing stopped me, in effect, detaining me on my own bed.

"Looks like someone's been practising. That was quick."

"I've always been that fast, you just never got to find out 'cuz you tied me up the last time you met me. Not so nice now is it?"

I shook my head. "It's alright. All depends on what you plan to do with me in this position though."

"You think this is all a joke don't you? You think walking into someone's life and rearranging it for your own pleasure or for whatever you want is okay? Like you're THAT important. You can't just do what you want or take what you want in life. There's consequences."

I was tipsy now as whatever he was drinking slammed against my senses.

"OoOoOo... that sounds promising."

I watched him walk around and felt him kneel on the bed next to me as I laid down on my stomach.

"This isn't a joke Tatiana." "You know you say my name in such a sexy way?" Then I heard a sound. I heard it before because I had a flick knife

too so I knew the sound when the blade drew out. The excitement of a possible dicking disappeared and I started to fiddle with the handcuffs. I'd gotten myself out of tighter situations so I wasn't worried. With my legs free, I could bump him off the bed with my hips, onto my knees and, once the 'cuffs were off, whoop his ass.

Then fuck him.

There was no way this story is going to end without him being up in my club.

Before I could shunt him with my hips, he climbed on top of me and things suddenly seemed more promising, although the policeman with the flick knife did worry me a bit.

He brushed my hair out of the way, grabbed the hem of my top and cut slowly from the base of my spine, letting the knife glide through the material up to my neck.

"Tell me about the first pair of shoes you ever stole."

"Is this foreplay?" I asked, turning my head to take attention away from the fiddling I was doing on the 'cuffs.

"Tell me," he said with an airy tone. The wings of my top fell aside and I could feel his eyes on my back. His fingers ran down my spine where I could feel him staring at the 68 tattoos of shoes that ran from the nape of my neck to the crease of my buttocks.

With space for one more.?The Strass would make a beautiful addition.?" It was way back when I used to work for Fierce Security Insurance.

We used to have big clients like Harrods on our books, Harvey Nichols,

Selfridges, the big boys. Anyway, something... happened to me and I had to take some time off."

"What happened?" His hand reached around my neck.

"Is this gonna be used against me in a court of law? 'Cuz I'd at least like to have a solicitor present during foreplay?"

"Information collected during foreplay doesn't count. It'd be inadmissible. Just tell me."

"It's a VERY long story which ended tonight so, for now, let's just call it the 'unfortunate incident."

Russell undid my bra and ran his fingers along the muscles in my back.

"One day, while I was off, I found I had the keys to one of the stores we were working with. I went to return them one day and I saw this woman trying to steal a pair of shoes. Proper rookie job. Standing in front of the security guard AND the camera. Pretty little thing. I didn't want to see her get arrested so I stopped her and told her to leave. Took her business card and she was gone.

"I went out for a cocktail or six and came back to the shop but it was closed. So I took the keys I had and let myself in. I'd probably knocked back like every deadly cocktail on the menu because I was falling all over the place. The alarms weren't on because they were going through a refit of the entire store so I just walked in and sat there for a while. On the floor, just looking around at all the shoes. And I saw the pair that the woman tried to steal earlier and I literally said fuck it. I went in the back, got two pairs and was gone. That simple."

"Is that why you are the way you are now?" "How am I?" I asked turning around slightly.?" All fucked up and shit?" Russell opened a door to me being offended then he slid my leggings

down to my ankles in one swift movement. The shock of the air touching my skin made me instantly raise my hips and he smacked me on my left cheek.

"First of all, yum but OW! Secondly, I'm not fucked up. Do you think it's easy doing what I do and staying one step ahead of you plonkers? Remember, you're not the only plonkers in the world looking for me. Someone as 'fucked up' as me couldn't run as many stash houses as I have, never been arrested and be the best shoe thief in the world could they?"

I could feel myself getting angrier.

"FUCKED UP?! Did this sunnuva... just call me fucked up? Listen sweetheart, you're lucky I'm not some hood, investigating all your social networks lab rat who's addicted to benefits and only wants to

fleece you. Baby, I've got more money than you. I make more money in a day than you do in two weeks."

"Not anymore you don't." I lost it.?" Look Russell, I see what you're trying to do. Revenge for what I did

to you. Revenge for the pictures I took. Revenge for the kidnapping. All of it. I get it. And you're going for dramatic with flick knife and the handcuffs but..."

My fingers undid the last latch and I quietly slid one side of the handcuffs off my wrist but kept my hands in place.

"Tatiana Blue, I am arresting you for..."

He didn't finish because I spun around, slamming my arms into his side and knocking him off the bed.

I'd had enough.

This fucking or arresting game had worn on my last nerve and I was out of fucks to give. My legs were out of my leggings and I discarded the shred of my top, tied my hair in itself and went to work.

I wasn't sure where he was going with all of this but I wasn't going to let him finish. I hopped off the bed, stepping on his knife hand at the same time. I slid that away, squatted next to him as he began to get up and put him in a headlock.

"Oh, what we gonna fight now?" he mumbled as I tightened my grip around his face.

He pushed against my arm as we both got to our feet. I tried to lean back to put more pressure on the lock and he stopped halfway to a vertical base.

"I'm feeling froggy so I jumped."

Out of nowhere, his arms grabbed my waist and before I knew it, I felt myself being tossed over his head, back onto the bed and clean off the other side.

Landing straight on my naked ass, I gathered my senses and got straight to my feet. Russell had done the same on the other side of the bed.

We were both huffing and puffing at each other, fighting for control of the situation with the bed in-between us. I watched him look up and down at me as my whole body throbbed with excitement and adrenaline. He looked at Lauryn then a long hard look at Aretha with my hair all over the place.

"You need to take more clothes off if we're gonna do this."
"I'm taking you in," he said breathing heavily.?" Listen to you, sounding like you're about to have an asthma attack.

Trust me, you're not!"

That must've been Russell's go sign because he scrambled across the bed at me. He planted his hands and hopped across just as I shuffled forward, grabbing his head in a reverse headlock and dropping my weight on his back. His body dropped on the bed and I squeezed his neck as tight as I could, spun around on top of him and got my arm back around his neck with my legs wrapped around his waist.

With his face in the mattress, I couldn't hear what he was saying but they were strong words as he grunted once and made it to his hands and knees with me attached to his back like a dreadlocked, Velcro thick bar of caramel. Slowly, he backed off the bed and I pulled my other arm around his neck for better leverage and to hopefully bring him down again but Russell was grunting like a man on a mission. He turned around and pressed himself against the wall then pushed back, making us fall onto the bed.

I hit first and the air knocked straight out of me. I tried to hold on to him but he was already turning around on me before I could get my grip back. A flash from my childhood kicked in and I grabbed his t- shirt from the bottom and pulled it over his head.

"Oh, come on Russell, not the old school ones," I said, trying to shuffle out from under him. My knees managed to work up to his chest then my feet and I pushed him off the bed. He looked like he was airborne for a moment before he hit the wall while still tangled in his t- shirt.

That stopped him as his back slammed against the wall and he sat on the floor, sliding onto his side with his arms still up.

He huffed.?I puffed.?His t-shirt came off and I could see on his face that he was done. His

left eye was squinting while his right eye was wide open and his mouth was sucking in air like it was his last.

Erm, of course I felt proud. Not like I fight men regularly but I always felt like if it ever came down to it, I could take Russell in a one- on-one fight. I always keep myself fit but doing what I do requires an extra level of fitness that includes yoga, Pilates, spin classes, intensive swimming, I trained with an MMA fighter and I run, like, everywhere. I ran from Greenwich park to the Olympic park in about 45 minutes. I don't think I have it like that any more but I'm still sprightly. I may not be Ali in his prime but I'll Mayweather your ass.

If only Jamal could see me now, about slipping.

"Are you gonna eat my pussy now or you still going on with this arrest talk 'cuz I wanna get some sleep." I found the flick knife on the floor and began to play with it.

"What do you want from me Tatiana?"

I leaned forward on my knees. "To have you say my name like that ALL the time. Do you really think I would go to all this trouble just for some up in the club time?"

"What do you want? Huh? Do you want us to be together?"

"For God sake Russell, you're a policeman and you still can't figure it out. You've been chosen."

"For what?" he asked, leaning against the wall to slide to his feet. "To love me." "Is there a list?" "Nope. Just you."

"You know this is gonna be really difficult to maintain. The top brass at work REALLY want you. They seem to think you've gone underground and hope to catch you letting your guard down."

"Well good luck to 'em. That's a bonus of being with you. You know what they'll do or say before they do."

"We can't just be together," Russell moaned. He tried to make it to his feet as he ooohed and aaahed to his knees and dropped his head on her bed.

"Why the fuck not? If you can tell me you don't want me in any way shape or form, I'll disappear. And you know me Russell. You know I can disappear like a fart in the the wind."

I had to put it all out there. From his mysterious entrance to his chit- chat and the handcuffs and the fight, I wasn't sure what Russell wanted to do. It seems like he was fighting the conflict of keeping it professional and being 'the man' who brought in the legend that is Tatiana Blue or keeping it emotional and building a life with the legend that is Tatiana Blue.

I don't just say I'm a legend by the way, that's what they actually call me. If the shoe fits, you know I'm wearing it.

Russell climbed up my legs and looked like he was praying to me as I flicked the knife between my fingers.

"Look Tatiana, since you left me, there hasn't been anyone else in my life. It's been one disaster after the next. Like someone decided I had to save myself for you."

"Oh, yeah, sorry about that." "So its like... whoa whoa, why are you sorry?" He looked up. "Don't worry about that, that's for later." "It feels weird to say that I missed you when you left but I did. My

relationship with Tara felt apart after you left. She didn't believe that you drugged me in those pictures of us fucking. Can you believe it? Chief of police didn't believe evidence that was right in front of her? How did you do that by the way?"

I scoffed. "If you know how to make a woman think then you know how to make a man lay when he's unconscious to make a woman think."

"Geezz, you're no joke are you?"

"Seems like you're only starting to figure that out. Are we any closer to fucking yet?"

"You know if we have sex, that means it's gonna be me, you and Charlotte. Where did you get that name from? I like it."

I scooted across until Russell was kneeling between my thighs and playing with my hair.

"The first pair of shoes I took from the shop when I was drunk. They were Charlotte Olympia. Gorgeous things."

"You couldn't name our child after a pair of shoes you bought? No... she had to steal 'em."

"Yep. You're lucky I don't steal drinks otherwise she would've been called Baileys." I said, passing the point of impatience and opening my thighs slightly. "So, erm... how 'bout erm..."

I whistled and pointed between my thighs and Russell chuckled. "What makes you think I do that?" "If you don't then we're you're gonna get cheated on a LOT in this

relationship.?" Touché," he said as I ran my hands over the top of his bald head

and led him to my lips, which were squelching between my thighs. The game was over!?I got my man!

It sure did take a hot minute and a scuffle but all that just made me want him that little bit more. It takes a strong man to deal with me so the fact that Russell even tried is tick in his box. I was hot and sweaty, my dreads had fallen out of the knot I put them in and were tossed back as Russell's tongue parted my lips and found my clit.

The way I had to cover my mouth as an electric feeling rippled up the shoes on my spine. With my head towards the ceiling, my eyes rolled back in my head and as Russell beginning to slurp with my fingers rolling across his scalp, I sighed pleasurably. He rubbed my thighs while my hips were pushing to meet his mouth as if the more I gave him to eat, the hungrier he became.

My hips had a groove all their own as he put an arm around my back and pulled me deeper into his face. I arched my back and let him pull

me in, looking down to watch the splendour of a man, no MY MAN, getting my club all ready for his entrance.

Dreads dropped around us and created a private room where all I could hear was the sound of his lips against mine and the smell of my sex rising from his face.

"Are you sure you're ready to be Mr Blue? It won't be easy, especially being the law man that you are."

Russell didn't respond. He stayed where he was, using his tongue in slow circular motions around my clit. I wanted him to enjoy me, especially as it was the first time he got to have me while conscious.

My thighs hoisted into the air and Russell made me lay back as he stood up with my thighs in his strong hands. He looked Neanderthal in the face as he pushed my thighs back. I took them from him and watched him drop to his knees again and rub his face up and down my pussy, looking at me for approval.

My lips turned up. "Hmmm, not bad. Not bad at all. I think we'll keep and train this one."

Lifting his head every now and then to look at his wet mouth, I felt like a queen taking advantage. I was holding his face still and making my pussy glide into his face by flexing my hips. He'd hum and stop then hum and stop every time my thighs blocked his mouth.

He started fucking my pussy with his tongue and I had to let go of his head before I squirted all over. It was our first official time together and I didn't wanna subject him to that just yet.

Unless he made me that is.

I slid my hands under his chin and pulled his face from my crotch and lifted him up for a very wet and tasty kiss.

Our lips slid against each other and we both hummed and fought to get the rest of his clothes off.

Whatever indecision Russell was suffering with before, he wasn't any more as he ran his hands all over me, making my body tingle. There was something about Marcus... I mean Russell's fingers... eeeek... that's embarrassing.

God forbid I ever make that mistake to his face. Don't tell him I said that please?

I tasted exquisite from Russell's face and it made my kiss more hungry in his mouth. He stood up and I made sure my lips were stuck to his. My hands wrapped around the back of his head and held on as Russell dropped his tracksuit bottoms and his erection sprung up against my stomach.

We both looked down at his dick and, for the life of me, I couldn't remember Russell packing such a mammoth of a package before.

Lengthy and girthy enough to be just right, he was. And with a bit of a curve at the end just to set it all off and seek out those hard to reach places. I ran a hand over it and did a double take, as if Russell had grown over the last nine months.

"You sure this is what you want?" Russell asked me with my thighs in the air.

"THEE worst question to ask at THEE worst possible moment. What if I didn't want it? You would've talked yourself out of some pum pum right there."

"I'm just checking."

I grabbed his dick and, with our heads touching, we both watched me lead it between the lips of my low faded pussy, which slurped at his arrival. His head glazed through my lips and found my opening before I could adjust myself to receive him.

My fingers dug into his shoulders and he cringed at the pleasure and the pain coursing through him. His back arched as I dragged my fingers from his shoulders to the middle of his back.

"Shiiiiiiiiiiiiiiiiiiiiiiiiiiiiiiiiiiiiiiiiit," Russell trailed off into silence as he withdrew his hips and gave me an almighty first stroke.

I knew such a stroke was coming but I still wasn't ready for it as I lay back and just took it, allowing the pain to strike first before diluting with pleasure.

Beneath my pelvis was a world of good feelings, eruptions and new beginnings as I instantly had an orgasm. I didn't see it coming, especially as I knew my cum number so I knew how may of those strokes it would take to get me off.

One? I definitely didn't see that coming. Lol, see what I did there?! (Didn't see the cum coming? Wow, tough room.)

My fingers dug into his scalp and my legs kicked into the air in celebration. I wanted to scream my fucking head off but so was the quickness of the orgasm that it got stuck in my throat. All I could do was open my mouth and stare at the ceiling as Russell froze to let me cum then continued stroking.

I let out one good, "OH MY FUCKING GOD!"

My brain told me not to blaspheme but Russell's dick told me something completely different and I listened to the latter.

Russell planted my feet on his chest. There was no pause in the stroke and he was back at it and inside me, swirling his hips in different directions.

I could feel his helmet dip and withdraw to the left against my walls and the feeling made me flash through the shoes I currently owned in Maya's boot. Each and every single one made my nipples more erect and Russell's stroke that little bit more electric. He had a hand

reaching down to cup my buttocks, which lifted me closer to him. The way his dick slipped into the hilt of me made my legs extend and kick him off me as I felt another orgasm rippling from my scalp to my toes.

"What's wrong?"

I didn't speak to him as my knees rolled into my chest and I draped my hair over my face so he couldn't see me cumming. Not that he needed to see my face to know. There was nothing I could do to stop the eruption and I didn't care how I looked, I was stuck.

I must've gone from Sayian to Super Sayian to Super Sayian three in the space of 11 seconds.

Russell hooked my hair out of my face and looked down at me, screwing my face like I downed a cocktail of lemon, lime and baking soda. I was pulling my knees in tighter, trying to stop the goodness but I seemed to make it worse.

"For fuck... oh God... oh God oh God... ohGodohGodohGod!"

He was obviously not ready for me or what I was capable of as I squirted very hard and suddenly. I heard the sound of something slapping Russell's skin as I arched my back off the bed. Squinting while squirting, I saw Russell hadn't moved and was running his hands through the liquid that dripped from his neck downwards.

My hips, waist and shoulders were vibrating on different rhythms and I went from my back to my front and onto my side, trying to get it to stop.

Suddenly, my body was spun onto my stomach, my cheeks were spanked and Russell slid inside me with no ceremony.

Just how I liked it.

"Oh no you don't. You trying to write me off?" I asked him, trying to wrestle out of the position.

"Yes I am," he replied, laying his weight on top of me and refusing to let up.

I collapsed flat as he began a slow stroke which grew into a speedy, deep, slamming pulse that had our skin clapping like a standing ovation. I had nowhere else to go but to take the slaying that was being dished out.

Like I cared.

It was some of the best dick I'd had... ever! And I'd only felt two positions so far.

I was grabbing all about the bed, trying to slap or scratch him but he wrapped an arm around my neck and rode me deep.

"Allllwaaaays... my... diiiiiick," I shook out of my mouth as I tried to pull myself across the bed.

With the way Russell was giving me the concentrated, repetitive stroke from behind, I kept cumming and cumming and wanting and

wanting. On one hand I wanted a moment to stop and enjoy the flurry of orgasms that were hitting me but on the other hand, I wanted more.

I wanted dick for each and every one of my shoes. I wanted dick for the exit I pulled to get out of Mount street, dick for the fact that Marcus was somewhere in London trying to pull stun gun pincers out of his skin. I wanted dick just because I hadn't had dick in so long. I wanted dick for each of stash houses. I wanted dick for my sexy dreadlocks. I wanted dick just for dick's sake.

"I should've fucked you when you were awake a long time ago," I mumbled, squeezing my walls against him.

"You should've. You could've been cumming on me for ages." Russell replied then twisted me on my side, curled my top leg and slid in from the side.

Scissors style.?" Oh... you fucking fucker you..." No more words after that. As much as I had slept with Russell

before, in a manner of speaking, I didn't remember him being so... much. From the side, he came in my club so quick and deep, I actually tried to get away. Like, I was trying to crawl my way off the bed.

I wasn't rookie enough to fall in love just because of a good dicking, but this was making me fall in love with every stroke. I was imagining our future together, maybe one day showing Russell my shoes, running in the park as a famiily, Timberlands for me , Russell and Charlotte. Summers in Victoria Park, outings to the Science Museum, dinner for two at Smollenskys on the Strand, hotel getaways to the Hilton, complaining about clothes being left on the floor, weekly shopping trips, greeting Russell with 'hey honey, welcome home' after he finishes work.

With my arm hooked under my bent leg, helping him reach deeper in my club, I was pulling my own hair.

Flashes of my future stabbed into my mind with each of Russell's thrusts. "You know I'm keeping the fuck out of you don't you and this dick?"

I was breathing fast but the strokes were getting faster. I didn't have anywhere to turn or anywhere to go and Russell had the meat of one of my cheeks in his hand and was lifting it to get in further.

"You fucking Versace Olympia open toed pumps you!"

Russell's dick had me talking about shoes that didn't exist while he's was breathing normally like this type of sex was an easy walk in the park.

I'd never been so unfocussed in my life.

"You gonna cum on your dick?" he asked, turning my head and making me look in his eyes.

I tell you, I didn't know what to fucking say to that. I mean I was seriously on cloud 18 'cuz I passed cloud nine like six orgasms ago with the last three sliding through on the back of others. I'd never had a dick before. Sure, I'd monopolised a few of 'em in my time but I never had one that I felt was mine all mine. Like a dick I could call and say, 'Mama Blue needs to be seen to' and know that the dick is pleasure guaranteed. The idea of my own dick made my walls tighten around him as he was pumping me on the maximum speed setting. Drips of sweat fell onto my body and I reached back to slow him down but he batted my hand away.

"If this is your dick, then THIS is my pussy!" Russell said.?" Erm... dunno 'bout that. We'll see on that one." And then something ridiculously amazing happened and I well and

truly realised fucking Russell was the one for me. An orgasm crept over me.

Not like any of the others he'd given me, this one was ten times more powerful. My walls stopped throbbing and stayed gripped on his dick. I tried to tell him to stop moving but he wasn't listening.

"Oh God babe... wait... wai... just one minute so I... whoooa..."

My arms and legs punched and kicked until Russell slid out of me and that's when I truly began to enjoy the orgasm. With Russell leaving my walls to do their thing, my clitoris hummed and the feeling travelled from my groin all the way up to my mind. The headache was instant, everything went silent, I arched myself in the Crab position and stayed there for about 20 seconds. My feet were sliding on the bed but whatever was attacking me had my mid-section in a state of shock.

And the feeling wouldn't stop.

Have you ever had one of those types of orgasms ladies? Those corrupt your soul orgasms? Find you a man who can do that because GOOD GOD!!!

By the time my body came down from whatever lightning bolt it was riding, I was sweating like I spent a week in a hot box. My headache had graduated to full on migraine, every muscle in my body felt like it had been exercised extensively and I couldn't feel Russell's presence as I rolled from side-to-side.

He was sat at the head of the bed, watching me with a smug grin plastered across his face.

"Now who else can make Tatiana Blue come like that?" He said.

"You like saying my name don't you?" I replied. I noticed that he always said my name like it wasn't real. And with a real element of surprise in his voice.

"So? It's a sexy name."

And that was the first moment I saw Russell letting his guard down and no longer dancing on the line between policeman and potential lover.

It took everything in me to push up off my stomach and make it to his chest. He opened his arms out to me and I snuggled in his personal space, enjoying his heartbeat pounding against my head.

"So is this us now Russell? No more trying to arrest me and all that shit?"

"I guess this is us."

"You guess?" I tried to act offended but my insides were still tensing so my attempt must've seemed quite feeble, considering what I'm capable of.

He looked down at me. "This is us. Me, you and Charlotte. No more stealing though, you hear me?"

I couldn't help the volume of the laugh that climbed out of me. I slapped his thigh with an open palm. "You're funny Russell."

"You can't just do whatever you want. You've got a family now."

"My daughter is my family. You? Well we have to see if you're worthy."

"I haven't once mentioned the fact that I haven't cum yet. That should count for something, especially as you just caught the Holy Ghost."

"Okay," I concurred. "That's point scoring on a massive scale but, as far as family, we'll see."

"Do you love me Tatiana?"

Who the fuck said anything about love? I looked at him asking that same question with my screwed up face. There had never been any man who had been lucky enough to say he had Tatiana Blue's love. There was never anyone who had the correct mix of normal and abnormal that I required. Handsome with a touch of uncouth. Immaculate but a little messy. Honest but has the ability to toe the line when he needs to. Would allow me to get away with shit but then knows when and, more importantly, how to keep me in line.

Yeah, you can see why I never found anyone. I'm picky as fuck. "I...I don't wanna taser you right now, does that count as love?" "No. I want a straight answer." I sighed as he curled my hair around his finger, making my toes

tingle. "I want you around me all the time. If that's love then yes I love you."

In my head I was screaming, WHAT THE FUCK DID YOU SAY THAT FOR?

"Would you give up your shoes for me?" I scoffed. "You REALLY are a silly rabbit aren't you Russell Reed?" Charlotte's ear-piercing scream broke the sensual moment and we

both jumped off the bed on opposite sides, looked at each other naked, then smiled.

"You go ahead," I said, sitting back on the bed. "Daddy." "I like the way you said that." "You perv. Go and check on your daughter." "No more stealing!"

Russell put his bottoms back on, went to the bathroom to wash his hands and face and went to check on Charlotte as I laid back on my bed and exhaled. My lower half had stopped throbbing but my stomach muscles would tense sporadically to remind me of what took place.

I could hear Russell talking to Charlotte and I couldn't help but smile. Was I really gonna become a housewife with two point four children and a network of mother friends and birthday parties and dinner on the table and supermarket shopping and all that normal shit? Why not?

Okay, well, maybe not exactly like that. Maybe the odd foray into the mix of stolen heels, just to keep a taste in my mouth and some shoes on my feet. Mother by day, shoe thief by night.

Another orgasm rumbled in my stomach as I tensed my entire body into the foetal position and the last thing I remember hearing was Charlotte gurgle and Russell breaking down her brand new family tree.

I don't know what a perfect life is but I fell asleep feeling like I finally had it.

Shoes, my man and my baby!

Hold on, you didn't think I'd actually give up stealing by the end of all this did you? Well aren't you a silly rabbit?!

BLUE VIEWS

Tatiana wielded her Hitatchi wand massager like Conan The Barbarian over Russell's bald as she laid back, letting air out of her lungs at the same time as Flying Lotus' Tea Leaf Dancers played on Solar radio.

"What the fuck is that? Looks like a shower head!" Russell said, kneeling between Tatiana's open thighs. He adjusted the pillow under her lower back with sweat and her juice dripping down his forehead.

"Just like a man to not know about the most important sex toy since the vibrator. This is the... you know what, there's no point. Just keep doing what you were doing."

"Yes Miss Blue."

Tatiana purred. "Keep saying my name like that and you'll have to call me Mrs Blue."

Russell didn't respond. He grabbed the base of his slippery eight and three quarter inches and slid his head inside her. She smiled as he inserted more and stopped.

"Lemme try something," Russell said.

As hard as he could get, he squeezed his dick at the base to make sure he was at his maximum girth and he circled his hand. He could feel the head of his dick making circles inside her and so could she.

Tatiana's eyes rolled in the back of her head before she closed her eyes and let out a large puff of air.

"Well that's different!"

The more circles he made, the more she slid her back side-to-side across the bed. Her moans were lighter than the ones she had before their little break but more of those circles and she knew she'd be growling again real soon.

She brought the wand down to her clit as Russell leaned upright with the moonlight catching his body perfectly. Tatiana ran a hand up and down his chest before turning her massager on and softly dabbing it on her clit.

The first touch was sinful and her back arched off the bed. Russell took that time to fully slide inside her and she opened her mouth to scream but his hand covered her mouth.

"Shush your fucking mouth!" he said sternly while working his lower half. He could feel every muscle in his back moving as the vibration travelled through her clit and onto his dick.

"Geret off," Tatiana mumbled as she fought his hand away with her eyes crossed. "You have NO idea how great this is!"

"Thanks." Russell replied. "Not you, the wand!"

After those words came out of her mouth, Tatiana closed her lips tight and screwed up her face with her dreadlocks loose and all over the place.

"Keep doing exaaaaactly that..." she trailed into silence as she ground the wand hard into her pussy.

Russell had two hands on her waist and was bringing her into him, which intensified the stroke as her walls tightened around him.

He was looking to the ceiling, riding the good wave with Tatiana's extremely toned thighs parting wider before him and her hips grinding.

Their skin was slapping, their rhythm was matching, her pussy was leaking and his dicking was reaching. Tatiana slapped the pillows next to her and threw them off the bed but she kept the wand in place on her clit.

"O... okay..."

Tatiana's stomach muscles clenched, her thighs tensed, her body froze and everything went silent as Russell continued his solid and smooth stroke. She moved the wand from the left of her clit to the right and that was it for her.

"OH YOU SWEET DICK FUCKER YOU!"

The pressure of the orgasm made her walls squeeze so hard that she forced Russell out mid-stroke. As he slipped out, she bucked her hips and began to squirt. The first stream hit the pillow but the more she moaned, the higher the cascades of liquid flew past Russell's shoulder.

He counted 12 individual squirts and smiled, extremely proud of himself. He'd made women squirt before but never on such a grand scale.

By the 13th dribble, the wand rolled out of her hand and lay next to her on the bed as she throbbed with a hand between her thighs.

"Oh yeah, I'm done. I. Am. Done!" "Are you okay?" "I... see... it's stu... stupid quess... oh fuck me..." Something rippled through her and she straightened her back and

stayed motionless for a number of seconds before exhaling and taking a series of short breaths.

"Yeah, you're okay. I'm thirsty. You want a drink?"

Tatiana tried to reply but she could feel the shivers of the ripple coming back and she didn't want to move for fear of bringing it on again. She lifted an arm in the air and waved it like she just didn't care as the ripple started again.

"Oh sweeeeeeeet Strasss heelss..."

Tatiana froze again while gritting her teeth. She rolled onto her stomach but that did nothing to stop the orgasm that was incapacitating her as she heard Russell feet slap on her floor towards the kitchen.

She pounded the bed and laughed while still trying to catch her breath. "So this is the sex I'm getting? Yay me!"

On the night stand, where she reached over and turned down her Bose system, her phone vibrated.

A message from Quincy told her to check her e-mail.

As quick as her shaky fingers could swipe, Tatiana read the one sentence message.

'A little something for your viewing pleasure.' Quincy

She scrolled down and saw a video attachment, clicking instantly.

Her app loaded the video and she sat up against her remaining pillows, brushing her hair behind her head.

The video came to life in an explosion of colours. The film maker was was using a hand held camera in a crowd of very loud women. The camera was pointed to the stage where a male stripper was dancing for a woman with a very manly jaw.

The camera person zoomed in on the stripper and Tatiana recoiled with a hand over her mouth.

"Marcus?"

The stripper went into his routine and the video stopped and an arrow pointed to the bride-to-be and said next to it, 'man'. The camera changed from the hand-held view to a shot of the same room but from a security camera above the stage. The arrow pointed again and pointed to every person in the room and the word flashed again on the screen.

MAN.

"Oh Marcus... that hungry for money are we?" Tatiana said, laughing and snapping her fingers. "Go 'head Marcus, shake what ya mama gave ya!"

Just then, Russell walked into the doorway of the bedroom with Charlotte in one arm, two cans of ginger beer and his phone held between his shoulder and his ear.

"Yeah, okay, hold on one second. In fact let me call you back." He hung up.

"Babe, you need to see this video. It's hilarious!"

"Erm, honey," Russell said sarcastically. "Did you taser Jamal and Femi this evening?"

Tatiana was looking at her phone and stayed looked at her phone, trying to hide the smile that was growing on her face. She didn't mean to laugh but the memory of how she managed to get out of the Louboutin store and past Femi and Jamal the police officers tickled her.

"Wait a minute," she jumped up on her knees. "I didn't hit Jamal with the taser. He knocked himself out. Well actually, I did taser him but after, but he deserved it. D'you know what he said to me?"

"Is this our life now? You go out and do your shit and I have to pretend like I'm not a policeman?"

Tatiana's phone rang. "Oh, look, my phone's ringing. Hold that thought and I'll be right with you."

Russell scoffed as Charlotte gurgled in his arms and the sun came up over Westfield in the distance.

"Hello, Maya? Gurl..." "So you ARE okay then? Thanks for letting me know." "Oh shit, sorry. Yeah, I should've called you soon as. We're all okay.

As you can imagine we had a lot to talk about." "Oh did WE?" Maya said.?" I think it's we. We talked about it a little and I think we might be

we." "How exactly is that gonna run?" "Exactly how I say it runs. Don't you know who I am? I'm Tatiana

Blue, the baddest bitch in heels. Miss 'take your shoes without you even knowing'. That's me."

"Look. We've got a problem. Well, YOU have a problem."

Tatiana put her phone on speaker and began to tie her hair up as Russell threw her a can of ginger beer and walked off mumbling to Charlotte. She caught the drink just before it reached her face.

"What problem? From where I'm sitting, everything is Bisto." "Tatt, listen..." "I got my man, my baby, some wicked dick..." "Tatt, your..."

"I got..." She looked for Russell before whispering. "I got a shit load of new shoes and I didn't pay for one of 'em... And Marcus is mad at me... AND I'm naked. What could possibly be a problem?"

"Tatt... two of your stash houses have been robbed." "I'm living la... WHAT? WHAT THE FUCK DID YOU SAY?" "Quincy wanted to tell you but he thought I should..." Tatiana stood up on her bed. "ARE YOU FUCKING SERIOUS? WHICH

ONES? HOW MANY SHOES?" "Your studio flat in Greece and one of your L.A spots." "DON'T FUCK ABOUT MAYA! HOW MANY SHOES?!" "All of 'em!" "WHAAAAAAAAAT?!?!"

54098107R00281

Made in the USA
Charleston, SC
26 March 2016